KNEES UP
MOTHER EARTH

KNEES UP
MOTHER EARTH

ROBERT RANKIN

Copyright © Robert Rankin 2004
All rights reserved

The right of Robert Rankin to be identified as the
author of this work has been asserted by him in accordance
with the Copyright, Designs and Patents Act 1988.

First published in Great Britain in 2004 by
Gollancz
An imprint of the Orion Publishing Group
Orion House, 5 Upper St Martin's Lane, London WC2H 9EA

This edition published in Great Britain in 2005 by
Gollancz

1 3 5 7 9 10 8 6 4 2

A CIP catalogue record for this book is
available from the British Library

ISBN 0 575 07649 6

Typeset at The Spartan Press Ltd,
Lymington, Hants

Printed in Great Britain by
Clays Ltd, St Ives plc

For Jo Fletcher
With love and laughs

1

It was only yesterday and the weather, it seemed, was good.

Mahatma Campbell put his best foot forward.

This foot, the left, was bandaged somewhat about the second toe and encased within an argyle sock, darned at the heel by the mother who loved him. Foot and bandage, sock and what-have-you lurked within a boot of the seven-league persuasion.

On his right foot the Campbell wore a slipper.

The knees of the Campbell were naked, as indeed were his arms. The loins, trunk and chest of him were clothed respectively in a kilt with ample sporran and a vest with room for improvement. The face of the Campbell was redly bearded, the head of him heavily turbaned.

Had he not been so unevenly shod, the Campbell would most certainly have strode, but given the inequilibrium of his footwear, this was an impossibility. And so Mahatma Campbell limped. And as he limped, he sang a song of lochs and byres and bonny banks and braes. And when his memory failed him, he whistled the refrain.

Mahatma Campbell limped the streets of Brentford.

The time was six-fifteen of the early morning clock, the day was a Wednesday, bright and sunny, but with that ever-present fear of precipitation the Campbell had come to live with.

The month was that nippy one known as November.

Mahatma Campbell limped along Moby Dick Terrace, Victorian artisans' cottages sheltering beneath slate roofs to the left and to the right of him, a post box to his rear, a pub rejoicing in the name The Four Horsemen in the near distance before him. Clipped box hedges confined fussy front gardens, hanging baskets of Babylon hung and a tomcat snored on a windowsill. And the Campbell, in song and in whistle, limped on.

As he reached the Ealing Road the Campbell turned left and limped past Bob the Bookie's and Peg's Paper Shop.

Norman Hartnel[*], husband of the abundant Peg, numbered the daily papers, a sprightly whistle issuing between his lips. He viewed the Campbell's passing through the shop's front window, which was sorely in need of a clean. Norman momentarily ceased his whistling and crossed himself at the Campbell's passing, for Norman feared the Campbell as surely as the Campbell feared precipitation, but Norman had not yet come to live with *his* fear. Upon this particular November morning, Norman wore a shirt that was in need of an iron, a shop coat that was in need of throwing away, trousers that were in need of a crease and a pair of black brogues that were *never* in need of a polish. Because Norman had once been in the Navy, and those who have once been in the Navy *always* polish their shoes.

When the Campbell's passing had passed Norman by, Norman took once more to his sprightly whistling, and once more to the numbering of papers – although now incorrectly, and in a less steady hand.

'Norman,' came the voice of Peg, bounding from the kitchenette and striking the shopkeeper in palpable waves that travelled through his wig and rattled the back of his head. 'Norman, have you finished yet?'

'No, my dear, not yet.' Norman chewed upon his bottom lip. She hated him, that woman, Norman knew that she did. But Norman didn't hate her in return. He still loved his Peg, his little Peg, his pretty little Peg. But she was no longer the Peg of old, with whom he'd shared kisses and more down beside the canal. She was no longer little, and nor was she pretty. But her Norman still loved her. In his way.

[*] Not to be confused with the other Norman Hartnel.

'Get a move-on, you lazy sod.' Further sound waves struck the shopkeeper and Norman got a move-on.

Norman always enjoyed the numbering-up of the papers. He enjoyed being the first in the borough to read the news of the day. He enjoyed the responsibility of sending Zorro the paperboy forth into the borough, bag upon his shoulder and bicycle saddle beneath his bum, to spread the daily news.

Most of all, Norman enjoyed the numbers of the numbering-up. Norman had a preoccupation with numbers. Numbers were Norman's current obsession.

'Everything,' Norman had told Neville, the part-time barman of The Flying Swan, during a recent lunchtime session when Norman should have been at the cash-and-carry purchasing bulls' eyes, mint imperials and party packs of Fisherman's Friends, 'everything is dependent upon numbers. Everything can be explained numerically. Everything can be reduced to a numerical equivalent.'

'Everything?' Neville cast Norman a quizzical glance with his good eye and continued his polishing of an already dazzling pint glass. 'Surely not every single thing?'

'You name it,' said the numerate shopkeeper, 'and there will be a number to its rear somewhere about.'

'Cheese,' said Neville, as he so often did when stuck for something sensible to say (which wasn't so often as it might have been, as Neville was noted for the wisdom of his words).

'That's too easy,' Norman said. 'The entire cheese-making process, indeed the very protocols of cheese-making – formulated, if my memory fails me not, by the Elders of Zion way back in the year known as dot – depend upon numbers. It's all weights and measures and time-spans, not to mention the number of holes.'

Neville chose, upon this occasion, to heed Norman's words and not mention the number of holes.

'Chickens, then,' said Jim Pooley, who had once owned a chicken, having been tricked into purchasing it by a gypsy who had assured him that it was a goose. And one that laid golden eggs. Sporadically.

3

'Chickens, eh?' said Norman, who knew the gypsy in question and had briefly considered running away to join the Romanys for a life of romance and rheumatism. 'Chickens are a prime example.'

'Steak is a *prime* example,' said Old Pete, whose half-terrier Chips was rumoured to have once been an accountant named Trevor before he had been transformed into a dog by a gypsy curse. 'Prime rump steak. You'll never get a decent steak out of a chicken.'

'Doesn't matter what,' said Norman, 'feathered fowl or four-legged friend. The numbers are there in the DNA. It's all been worked out by mathematicians on computers. The entire universe is one big mathematical equation.'

'How big?' Pooley asked.

'Very,' said Norman. 'Same again, Neville.'

'So, what is the point?' Pooley now asked.

'It's a kind of mathematical full stop,' said Norman, informatively. 'Its technical term is the *decimal point*.'

'That's not what I mean.' Pooley made to sup ale but found his glass empty. 'Same again for me, Neville,' he said. 'Norman's in the chair. His number just came up.'

'It didn't,' said Norman.

'It did,' said Jim. 'I've been counting. But what I'm asking you is this: what is the point of trying to reduce the universe to a mathematical equation?'

'For the thrill of it,' said Norman, and he meant what he said.

'You can see that he means what he says,' said Old Pete.

'I do,' said Norman.

'Then tell me this,' said Old Pete, 'can you reduce to a mathematical equation the beauty of a young girl's eyes filled with the first light of love?'

'Well—' said Norman.

'Or a baby's smile?' continued Old Pete. 'Or the scent of a rose with spring dew upon it? Or—'

'Stop,' said Norman, 'you're giving me a crinkly mouth.' And he dabbed a tear from his eye.

As did Jim Pooley. 'Golly, Pete,' said Jim, 'I never knew you had such feelings in you.'

'I don't,' said the oldster, amidst immoderate chucklings. 'I'm just winding up this buffoon.'

'Thanks a lot,' said Norman. 'But numbers *are* everything and I firmly believe that *everything* can be reduced to mathematics. Everything.'

'Life, the universe, and everything?' said Jim. 'The number you're looking for is forty-two, is it not?'

'Don't you start,' said Norman. 'But I repeat: I sincerely believe that there is a mathematical formula behind *everything*. And whoever discovers this BIG FIGURE would not only *know* everything, he'd be able to *do* everything also and I'll prove it to you one day.'

'How?' Jim asked.

'From small beginnings come great things,' said Norman, who favoured a proverb. 'But the lion never roars until he's eaten.'

'I'll drink to that,' said Jim.

Norman got a round in. 'I will succeed,' he told the assembled company of doubters and he raised his glass in toast. 'As surely as one and one make two for most of the time, I will.'

And indeed Norman would – well, he almost would – and with the most alarming consequences.

But Norman's quest would not be an easy one. Mathematics had moved beyond the blackboard and the abacus. These were the days of the computer. And Norman did not possess a computer. He had considered purchasing one, but even the cheap ones were, in his opinion, expensive . . . which was why he had decided to construct his own.

Norman was no stranger to the do-it-yourself kit. He had purchased more than a few in the past, before it had dawned upon him that it was hardly 'do-it-yourself' if all the pieces had been pre-constructed by someone else. Real do-it-yourselfing was *really* doing-it-yourself, from the ground up.

You needed certain components, of course; you couldn't be expected to mill every piece of metal and hand-carve every screw . . . which was why God had granted man the ability to create the Meccano set. And with the Meccano set Norman had proved, time and time again, that all things – well, *nearly* all things – were possible.

And if you happened to pick up a few other little bits and bobs from here and there along the way, well, that wasn't *really* cheating.

So, upon this bright and early morning, Norman continued with his incorrect numberings of the daily papers and, once done, he sighed a certain sigh and took to leafing through the uppermost *Brentford Mercury* on the pile.

A pre-leaf perusal of the front page found Norman viewing the day's banner headline: COUNCIL TO VOTE ON CLUB'S FUTURE. Norman knew the tale behind this well enough – the sad and sorry saga of Brentford's football club. From its golden years in the 1920s, when Brentford had twice won the FA Cup, and Jack Lane, the now-octogenarian landlord of The Four Horsemen, had captained the glory boys and hammered home the winning goals on both occasions. Through the many years of hurt, with the team slipping down and down the divisions, until this very day.

With the team having so far failed to win a single match this season, the club in debt to the tune of millions and property developers circling like horrid sharks seeking to snap up the ground, tear down the stands, rip up the sacred turf and build executive homes upon the site.

Norman shuddered. It was a tragedy. A piece of the borough's precious history would be wiped from the map. It made Norman sick at heart.

'It is an outrage,' cried Norman, with fire in his voice. 'An outrage and an abomination.'

'What was that?' Another sonic shockwave struck the shopkeeper's head, this time nearly dislodging his wig.

'Nothing, dear,' said Norman. 'And I'm almost done with the numbering.'

The numbering.

Norman viewed the figure upon the front page of the *Brentford Mercury*. The figure of the debt. The millions owed by Brentford United Football Club — surely such a sum could be raised if everyone in Brentford dug into their pockets. They'd only need to fork out . . . Norman's Biro moved about upon the blank area of newssheet where the theatre review would have been had the *Mercury's* inebriate critic, 'Badger' Beaumont, got around to filing his report. Norman's Biro moved and many figures were written (many, too, were crossed out and rewritten). Many more were also crossed out. Norman, for all his love of numbers, wasn't much of a hand at sums. He really *did* need a computer. Norman flung the now defunct Biro aside.

And Norman took to leafing again.

Page two had little to offer Norman, other than an advert announcing the arrival of Count Otto Black's *Circus Fantastique*, presently pitching its big top upon nearby Ealing Common. This at least had Norman doing so-so movements with his head, for he harboured some fondness for the circus.

There was also an article penned by local guru and self-styled Perfect Master Hugo Rune, extolling the virtues of Runesthetics, a spiritual exercise programme of his own conception that promised, for a fee, to enlarge that certain part of the male anatomy which teenage boys generally sought to enlarge through methods of their own, sometimes with the aid of tapes rented from the video section of Peg's Paper Shop.

Norman raised an eyebrow to Runesthetics and then lowered it again. He had once invented a system of his own to further that particular end. It had involved Meccano. And, later, several jars of Savlon.

Norman leafed on. It was, as ever it was, and ever it most probably ever would be, the same old, tired old news for the most part. And for the most part Norman took as ever he had, and probably ever would take, a certain pleasure and comfort in its same old, tired old sameness. Flower shows, fêtes, functions and funerals. And car-boot sales.

And Norman leafed on until he came to the page before last. And there for a while he dwelt, amidst the small ads.

And there Norman's right forefinger, its nail sorely in need of a nailbrush, travelled down column after column . . .

Until . . .

It stopped.

And the shopkeeper took from the top pocket of his brown shop coat, a pocket that was in need of some stitching, a pencil which was, as it happened, *not* in need of a sharpening. (Norman's spell in the Navy had taught him, in addition to the importance of a well-polished shoe, to keep his matches dry, his underwear clean and his pencil sharp, for obvious reasons.)

And Norman took up his pre-sharpened pencil and encircled an advert with it:

I HAVE A LARGE COLLECTION OF UNWANTED COMPUTER PARTS AVAILABLE FOR DISPOSAL. FREE TO FIRST APPLICANT. TELEPHONE THIS NUMBER FOR DETAILS.

Norman read the telephone number to himself and his hand moved in the direction of the telephone upon the shop counter.

'Norman, come!' bawled the voice of Peg from the kitchenette.

And all of Norman moved in the direction of this bawling.

Mahatma Campbell's limping, which had carried him past Bob the Bookie's and Peg's Paper Shop, carried him further up the Ealing Road, past The Star of Bengal curry house and The Flying Swan.

Neville, ever an early riser since that morning when he'd

once risen late and felt certain that he'd missed *something*, viewed the passing Campbell as a shadowy form through the etched glass of The Swan's saloon bar window panes.

Neville, a practising pagan, demurred the crossing of himself, but said *blessed be* and ventured to the whisky optic for a measure of golden breakfast.

Of the looks of Neville, what might be said? In the favour of him, much. He was tall and lean and scholar-stooped, with a slim and noble head, the hair of him a-brillianteened and the good eye all a-glitter. Dapperly decked was he in the habit of the professional barlord: white shirt, black trews, black weskit and clip-on dicky bow, plus a very dashing pair of cufflinks whose enamelled entablatures spoke of a Masonic connection. Classic 'Oxford' footwear was well buffed, though through personal fastidiousness rather than naval training. A certain spring was normally to be found in his step.

And Neville was the part-time barman of The Flying Swan.

True, there were none who had ever known him to miss a session, or take a holiday, or even a day off. And Neville lived in, above the bar, in the humble but adequate accommodation. But *part-time barman* was his job description; it was the job he had applied for and the job he had been given. And it was the job he did, and the job he did well.

And the job he loved.

Yes, loved. For Neville loved Brentford. The borough, and its people, and this pub. *His* pub. Not that it really was *his* pub, it wasn't; it was the brewery's pub, and every so often the brewery let Neville know it, in manners that lacked for subtlety and finesse. They organised things for Neville to do. Theme nights. Promotions. Pub quizzes. Neville weathered these storms. He pressed on, and persevered. He knew how things should be, and how things should be done. Things *should be* as ever they had been, and things *should be done* to keep things that way.

Neville tended the beers: eight hand-drawn ales upon

draught, the finest in Brentford. And the finest of the finest being Large.

Neville tended the bar, an elegant Victorian bar with a knackered dartboard and disabled jukebox, a row of Britannia pub tables, a mismatched variety of comfy seating and stools at the polished counter for regular stalwarts. There were Spanish souvenirs behind the bar. Ancient pictures of indeterminate things upon walls of faded paperings. A carpet that had known better days, but appreciated those of the present, which weren't too bad at all.

And the whole and the all and the everything that made a real pub a real pub caused a pause in the step of those who entered The Flying Swan for the very first time, who breathed in its air, soaked up its ambience and said, as many before had said and many yet to come would do:

'*This* is a pub.'

Neville tossed back his golden breakfast and shrugged away the shudder that the Campbell's daily passing always brought him. Today was a new day, another day; hopefully, it would be much as the old day that it had replaced had been, a pleasant and samey prelude to the one that lay beyond.

And so on and so forth, so to speak.

Although it did have to be said that today *was* going to be slightly different for Neville the part-time barman.

Hence the shoes.

Hence the shoes? one might ask. What meanith this?

What meanith this is this: the shoes were an anomaly. Bright and shiny, yes, as was the norm for these shoes, but not at this time of the day. At this time of the day, Neville was normally a carpet-slipper man. Monogrammed were Neville's carpet slippers, his own initials woven in cloth-of-gold upon a brown felt surround, with soft India rubber soles. The pair a present from the mother who loved him. But he was not wearing these today. Today Neville wore the classic Oxfords, those brogues that, in their unassuming, understated way, had helped to forge the British Empire.

The creation of Lord Oxford, who is now remembered solely for his shoes.[*]

Not that Neville was wearing the *actual* pair that had helped to forge the British Empire. But his *were* of a similar design.

And they *were* upon his feet at this time of the morning.

So, why?

Because Neville had an appointment this morning. One that he did not wish to keep, but one he knew that he must keep. It was an *official* appointment. Not one of brewery business, but of *other* business. It was a matter of duty that Neville keep this appointment. And Neville was a man of duty.

The classic brogues pinched Neville's toes; the certain spring that was normally to be found in his step had today deserted him. Neville limped from the saloon bar of The Flying Swan and returned to his humble yet adequate accommodation above.

Mahatma Campbell limped on. And on he limped until he reached the football ground, Griffin Park. And here he ceased to limp, for here he stopped and, bending low, removed his seven-league boot and shook from it a stone. And then he replaced the boot upon his best-foot-forward.

And then he reached into his ample sporran and withdrew a ring of keys. Selecting one of these, he presented it to the padlock that secured the gates of the football ground, unlocked same and swung open these gates.

And then, a-singing and a-whistling the portions of the song that he could not remember, Mahatma Campbell entered Brentford Football Ground.

And the sun rose higher in the heavens. And the birdies sang and the folk of Brentford slowly stirred from their beds and, as is very often the way, things began to happen.

[*] And his dictionary, of course. And his bags, although not so much nowadays. As they've gone out of fashion.

2

James Arbuthnot Pooley, Jim to his friends and all else besides, awoke from his bed to a day where things were already beginning to happen.

Jim's awakenings, for indeed these were in the plural, had about them a deliberate quality, a certain restraint, a cautiousness, a subtlety. These were not the sudden springings into consciousness of those dragged into the world of work by the clarion call of the alarm clock. Jim had long ago discarded his. These were more the gentle easings into wakefulness associated chiefly with the idle rich. Although it must be said that the idle rich are generally introduced to the new day by the butler drawing the curtains, or by a young woman skilled in those arts which amuse men doing pleasant things to them beneath the silken sheets.

Jim was *not* one of the idle rich.

Jim was one of the idle poor.

Although to Jim's credit, he was rarely ever idle. Jim was of that order known collectively and depreciatingly as 'the ranks of the unemployed', which is to say that he did not hold any regular employment. Jim was not, however, a 'dole-queue scrounger'. Queueing for anything was not in Jim's nature and the local labour exchange had long ago given up on Jim and withdrawn his dole cheque accordingly.

Jim would, if asked, have described himself as an entrepreneur. Which was a good word and covered, as many other good words do, a multitude of sins. Not that Jim would ever have considered himself a sinner. For he had so very few vices.

He was basically honest, loyal to his friends and lies

sprang but rarely to his lips. He was a 'chancer' and a 'bit of a lad' and a 'rough diamond' and many other things besides, but he was *not* a bad man. Jim was a *good* man.

A good unemployed man and one with a stinking hangover.

Jim did plaintive mewings and some groanings, too, for good measure. Sunlight of the day where things were already beginning to happen elbowed its way with difficulty into Jim's bedroom, negotiating the unwashed windows, the unwashed nets and the whoever-washes-them-anyway bedroom curtains. The light that triumphed over these difficult negotiations fell in a wan pool upon the face of Jim Pooley.

A good face, a basically honest face, a young and, some might say, a handsome face. A face with clear blue eyes, an aquiline nose, a merry mouth loaded with fine white teeth, a decent pair of cheekbones and a chin that, if it lacked for a certain determination, amply made up for it with an abundance of pre-shave stubble. The hair of Jim was dark and brown, and his limbs were long and lean.

The eyes of Jim did squintings and focusings and takings in of the new day and then the mouth of Jim did smilings. Another day, another challenge, another chance to succeed. The hangover would soon depart with the coming of breakfast and Pooley, unfailingly cheerful, would get stuck into the day.

Of Jim's rooms, what might be said? Well, mostly they were dry. They were sparsely furnished in a manner not to Jim's taste, but as these were rented rooms of the furnished persuasion, there was little he could do about it. These rooms were not so clean as they might have been, which is to say as clean as they might have been, if Jim had chosen to clean them. These were unkempt rooms, small and unkempt rooms: a bedroom, a kitchenette and something that loosely resembled a bathroom, if you didn't look too closely at it.

They were certainly not the rooms of the idle rich, although rumour did hold in the borough that the eccentric millionaire Howard Hughes had once occupied them. But then local rumour also held that Pocahontas had once roomed at The Flying Swan and that Karl Marx had regularly taken tea at The Plume Café around the corner.

And as rumour is generally based upon fact, and facts are undeniably true, there seems no reason to doubt these rumours.

Jim did not enjoy living the way he did. His unfailing cheerfulness belied this fact, but fact indeed it was. However, Jim held to the philosophy that there can be no beauty without ugliness, no enjoyment of pleasure without the experience of pain and no appreciation of the joys that wealth can bring without having first suffered the miseries of poverty.

And as it was Jim's intention – indeed, the very key that wound the very clockwork motor that powered his very being (verily) – that he should shortly become rich, the squalor of his rooms afforded him a certain cerebral satisfaction.

And how would it be that Jim might achieve his ambition? Why, through the science of betting, of course. For James Arbuthnot Pooley was a dedicated Man of the Turf. What pennies Jim managed to acquire, he invested, day upon day upon day, in his quest for wealth through the medium of the Six-Horse Super-Yankee Accumulator Bet.

The Punter's Dream.

This particular dream had only once, as betting history records, been brought to waking reality. And to a Brentford man it had been, one Steven Montague Dean, son of Cyrus Garstang Dean, supplier of winged heels to the classically inspired gentry. The year was 1928, coincidentally the year that Brentford United had won the FA Cup for the second time. And whilst Jack Lane was being carried shoulder high through the flower-bedecked streets of the borough, Steven Montague Dean had stolen silently away with his winnings, leaving the family firm to flounder. And was never seen again.

Local rumour held that Mr Dean had spent his winnings

purchasing a kingdom somewhere in Afghanistan, where he installed himself in a palace of ivory and spent the rest of his life in the company of concubines.

Jim Pooley had a similar future all mapped out for himself.

Upon Jim's bedroom mantelpiece there stood a lone, framed photograph. It was of Steven Montague Dean, clipped from a 1920s copy of the *Brentford Mercury* that Jim had come across in the Memorial Library.

A single candle oft-times burned before this photograph.

Pooley had by now arisen from his bed. He had shaved and bathed, abluted, suited and booted, and now he set off for the day in search of his fortune. His rooms were in Moby Dick Terrace and, following the course taken by Mahatma Campbell two hours previously, Jim marched purposefully up the terrace, turning left at the Ealing Road and passing Bob the Bookie's.

Jim would presently return to Bob the Bookie's.

Jim now entered Peg's Paper Shop.

'Watchamate, Norman,' said Jim, a-greeting the shopkeeper.

'Watchamate, Jim,' Norman replied.

'Spring cleaning?' Jim asked.

Norman sighed. Deeply. 'Tell me, what do you see?' he asked.

'A gingham pinafore about your shoulders and a feather duster in your hand.'

'Yes,' said Norman and he sighed once again. 'Your eyes do not deceive you. Where there's muck, there's brass, they say, and a penny saved is a penny earned.'

'Right,' said Jim, giving the shop a visual once-over. It was as ever it had been (and in the Brentford shape of things, as it ever should be) wretched. The sweetie jars lining its sagging shelves were the same jars that Jim had gazed longingly at as a child. Several actually contained the selfsame sweets. The faded adverts for tobaccos and snuffs – products that were now little more than memory – still patched over the Edwardian wallpaper. The cracked glass-fronted counter presented a fearsome, if dusty, display of out-of-date fireworks. The video section was velvet with dust. The lino was yellow and so was the ceiling. Colour co-ordinated. Just so.

'It's all just so,' said Jim. 'Why would you wish to dust it?' And here a tremulous tone entered Pooley's voice. 'You haven't won the Pools, have you?'

'The Pools?' Norman scratched at his brow with the non-feathered end of his duster. 'Have you become bereft of your senses?'

'It's a personal philosophy thing,' Jim explained, inadequately. 'So you're just having a little dust?'

'Peg,' said Norman, which explained things more than adequately.

'A *Sporting Life* and five Woodbines please,' said Jim. 'And I have the right money and everything.'

Norman placed his feather duster upon the counter and sought out the Woodbines. They were to be found where they were always to be found. Except today they were not to be found, because Norman had run out of Woodbines and forgotten to order any more.

'I'm out,' said Norman.

'That is a statement easily proved erroneous,' said Jim, turning a copy of the *Brentford Mercury* in his direction and perusing the front page, but failing to take in the dire headline regarding the terrible fate that most probably lay in store for Brentford's football ground. 'You are not out, but clearly here. Body and soul. Mind and spirit. Duster and pinnie and all.'

'Out of Woodbines,' said the shopkeeper.

'Out of Woodbines?' It was Jim's turn to scratch at his head and in deference to Norman, he, too, did so with the feather duster. 'You're never out of Woodbines.'

'Am today.' Norman plucked the feather duster from Jim's hand, a hand which now grasped it rather too firmly. Brightly coloured feathers fluttered towards the linoleum. 'Look what you've done to my duster.'

'Out of Woodbines?' Jim now shook his hungover head and attempted to digest this unthinkable intelligence. 'I don't know what to say.'

'You could say, "I'd like a packet of Senior Service instead and here's an extra two and sixpence for a new duster."'

'I could,' said Jim, 'but I think it most unlikely that I would.'

'How about five Capstan Full Strength and two bob for the duster, then?'

'I think I'll just take the *Sporting Life*. There might be a packet of Woodbines left in Neville's machine at The Swan.'

'Ah, no.' Norman dithered. He was a businessman, was Norman. He also considered himself an entrepreneur. It was more than his soul could stand to lose a sale. 'Just hold on,' said the entrepreneurial shopkeeper, 'I have something here that I think might interest you.'

'Is it one of the Hydra's teeth?' asked Jim. 'I've always been interested in seeing what those lads look like.'

'New fags,' said Norman. 'A salesman brought them in yesterday – they're on a promotional offer. They are most inexpensive. In fact, you'll get ten for the price of five Woodbines.'

'Ten for the price of five?' Jim considered the unlikelihood of such an offer. It was surely the stuff of fantasy. 'Let me have a look at these fags,' he said.

Norman hastened to oblige his potential customer. He delved amongst boxes behind the counter and presently brought to light a garish-looking package.

Jim cast a doubtful eye over it. 'It's rather bright,' he observed.

'Bright and breezy,' said Norman. 'A little like your good self, if you'll pardon me saying so.'

Jim now made a doubtful face. Norman broke open the garish-looking package to expose a dozen similarly garish-looking packets of cigarettes. He held one up before Pooley's face.

'Dadarillos,' said Norman, and then read aloud from the packet, ' "Dadarillo Super-Dooper Kings are an all-new smoking taste sensation, a blend of the finest long-grain tobaccos and an extra-special secret ingredient that—" '

'I don't like the sound of them,' said Jim.

'But look at the length of the blighters.'

Jim took the packet from the shopkeeper's hand and weighed it in one of his own. 'Ten for the price of five,' he said, digging coinage from his pocket. 'I do believe that this is going to be my lucky day.'

And so Jim left Peg's Paper Shop, a packet of Dadarillos in his top pocket and a *Sporting Life* tucked beneath his right arm, and pressed on about his daily business. His next port of call was The Plume Café, once patronised by Karl Marx, who had by chance penned his later-to-be-discarded script for *Manifesto: The Musical* at the very window table at which Jim now chose to take his breakfast.

The Plume Café is worthy of description and will receive it in due course.[*]

Jim downed eggs, bacon rashers, Brentford bangers and the inevitable fried slice and, having concluded his repast, dabbed a paper napkin of the gorgeous gingham persuasion about his lips, bade his farewells to The Plume and his hangover and took himself to his very special place.

The bench before the Memorial Library.

It was here, when the weather held to fair, that Jim sat daily to peruse the pages of *The Sporting Life* and compose the ever-elusive winning Six-Horse Super-Yankee.

Jim took from his pocket the pack of Dadarillo Super-Dooper Kings. For one composing the Super Yankee, one who would be King, the synchronicity was not lost upon Jim.

'I feel certain,' said Jim to himself, 'that this really *is* going to be my lucky day.'

Jim opened the pack, took from it a cigarette of con-

---

[*] In fact, in Chapter Four.

siderable length and placed it in his mouth. He pulled his ancient Zippo lighter from the pocket of his ancient waistcoat and brought forth fire from it. And puffed upon his cigarette.

'A mellow smoke,' said the connoisseur. 'Perhaps lacking the coquettish charm of the Wild Woodbine or the aromatic allure of the Capstan Full Strength, but nevertheless . . .'

He took a deeper draw and collapsed into a fit of coughing. 'First of the day,' he managed between convulsions. 'Always a goodie, but a killer.'

And then Jim applied himself to the task at hand.

They were here, he knew it. And they were: those six horses that, if correctly deduced to be the winners, could transport the deducer of same from poverty to riches in a few short hours. It all seemed oh-so-simple.

But would that it were so.

Jim puffed some more upon his fag and cast a professional eye down the columns of horses. There were many here that he knew, many that had let him down and thwarted his plans, many others that had sprung from nowhere to aid in the thwarting. But the winners *were* here. And he should be able to find them – a man of his calibre, a man of his dedication. Jim focused his eyes upon the page and did deep concentratings. Fiercely deep these concentratings were, fiercely deep and intent.

'Vagabond.'

Jim blinked his eyes. Vagabond? Was this the voice of divine inspiration? Which race was Vagabond in?

'Vagabond!'

Jim glanced up. A fellow was peering in his direction – a painfully pale but smartly dressed fellow peering from the open window of a very smart-looking car. A smart-looking car that Jim had not heard pull up at the kerbside in front of him.

'Vagabond!' this fellow persisted.

'I am no vagabond,' said Jim. 'I'm an entrepreneur.'

'Entrepreneur, then,' said the fellow. 'You're a local bod, are you not?'

'Born and bred and proud of these facts,' said Jim, adding, 'Please go away now, I'm busy.'

'Need directions, local bod, entrepreneur, or whatever.'

Jim peered back at the fellow peering at him. 'Why do you peer so?' Pooley asked.

The fellow's head withdrew through the open window of the smart-looking car and then re-emerged in the company of a stylish pair of mirrored sunspecs. 'Light's a bit bright,' said the fellow. 'Better now.'

'I'm so glad,' said Jim. 'But please go away.'

'Need directions to the town hall.'

'Why?' Jim enquired.

'Because I don't know the way.'

'I mean, why do you want to go to the town hall?'

'None of your damned business, nosy vagabond layabout lout!' said the fellow in the mirrored shades.

'Please yourself, then,' said Jim, returning to his concentrations.

'So which way is it?' the fellow demanded. 'Speak up, moron: the town hall.'

'Right at the top and then third on your left,' said Jim, smiling sweetly.

'Fine.' The head withdrew. And then the head re-appeared. 'Is that a Dadarillo Super-Dooper King you're smoking?' the mouth in this head enquired.

'Actually, it is,' said Jim, smiling even more sweetly than before.

'Splendid,' said the fellow. 'Recommend them to your friends. If you have any friends, you loser.'

'*What*?' exclaimed Jim.

But the window closed with an expensive swish and the car departed soundlessly.

Jim Pooley returned once more to his concentrations. The rude man's words might normally have upset the sensitive Jim, but not, it seemed, upon this day.

Upon this day, and at this particular moment, Jim felt mighty fine. He generally felt *pretty* fine, but then he *was* unfailingly cheerful. But upon this particular day and at this particular moment he felt *more* than pretty fine. He actually felt *exceedingly* fine.

Jim took from its packet another Dadarillo Super-Dooper King and lit it from the failing butt of the first.

'I really, truly, truly feel,' said Jim, drawing on this cigarette and speaking through the smoke, 'that this really, truly, truly *is* going to be my lucky day.'

3

Neville the part-time barman sat with his arms firmly folded and his knees and heels together. He was not, however, sitting where he would have preferred to have been sitting – to whit, at his favourite corner table in the saloon bar of The Flying Swan.

Rather, Neville sat, most uncomfortably, for the seat was hard and his smart shoes greatly pained his feet, in a chair of the utility persuasion in the council chamber of Brentford town hall.

Because Neville the part-time barman was also Neville the part-time councillor.

The lads who frequented the saloon bar of The Swan had put Neville's name forward (for a bit of jolly) at the last local council elections, and so great was Neville's reputation for being 'a good man' that he had been voted into one of the two seats on the council which had recently become available due to unforeseen circumstances. Whatever those may have been.

Neville now occupied one of these two seats. Most uncomfortably.

Neville's knowledge of local politics extended little further than a summation of opinions postulated within the confines of The Swan's saloon bar, generally after what is known as 'the Ten O'Clock Watershed' – that time after which men have sunk sufficiently in their cups to spout all manner of opinionated toot with complete and utter conviction. And make many promises that they will never keep. And no one blames them for it in the morning.

Because it's a tradition, or an old charter, or something.

Neville had accepted his post because of his sense of duty to the borough that he loved in the genuine hope that he *might* be able to make a difference. He didn't trust any of the other councillors. They were all up to some kind of no-good, Neville just knew it. He couldn't prove it, but he knew it all the same. Local councillors were *always* up to some kind of no-good, always had been, always would be. It was also a tradition, or an old charter, or something. And it went on in *every* local council up and down the land.

Neville sat and glowered and whistled under his breath. A low and ominous tune, it was, and one that suited the scene.

To Neville's right sat councillor Vic 'Vanilla' Topping, business partner of Leo Felix, the Rastafarian automotive dealer who ran Jah Cars, the previously-owned-car emporium down beside the canal. Vic was in his forties, about as broad as he was long and dodgy as a day that had no ending.

To Neville's left sat Mr Gwynplaine Dhark. Mr Gwynplaine Dhark managed Brentford's one and only theme bar, which had but recently opened within the chapel that had up until a few months before been Brentford's one and only Spiritualist church. This had come as something of a surprise to the congregation, who could not for the many lives of them understand how it had been granted planning permission.

The name of this theme bar was The Beelzepub. It was a satanic theme bar.

The Beelzepub catered thus far to a somewhat limited clientele, mostly callow acne-faced youths with a penchant for black T-shirts and a bit of Death Metal. And elderly spinsters who had nowhere to go on a Tuesday night now that the Spiritualist church had closed down.

Exactly who had voted Mr Gwynplaine Dhark on to the local council baffled Neville, but he felt certain that the Powers of Darkness must have had some hand in it.

Neville, whom most who knew him would have sworn did not possess an ounce of malice in him, hated Mr Gwynplaine Dhark.

And Mr Gwynplaine Dhark hated Neville.

But Mr Gwynplaine Dhark was democratic.

He hated everyone.

Across the council table sat a further prial of councillors. There was Councillor Doris Whimple, a woman of considerable tweediness who bore an uncanny resemblance to the now legendary Margaret Rutherford; Councillor Arthur Doveston, octogenarian beekeeper and enthusiastic pamphleteer; and Councillor David Berkshire, local librarian and a man of so slight a presence that, should he enter a room, that room would still for the most part appear to be empty.

Neville didn't notice him for a minute or two, but when he did he nodded a greeting, which was returned by a vague and wistful nod of the councillor's head.

And that was that for the Brentford councillors: two publicans, a used-car dealer, a lady of the Shires, one ancient and one all-but-invisible librarian.

And all of them, with the exception of Neville, in Neville's opinion, were up to some kind of no-good.

At the head of the council table stood a grand mahogany chair. It was a heavily carved chair and heavily crested, too, with the badge of the borough – two griffins rampant flanking a pint glass of Large. It was the Mayoral Chair.

The Mayoral Chair was unoccupied.

The Mayoral Chair was always unoccupied.

The Mayor of Brentford did not attend council meetings. He did not attend any meetings at all. The Mayor of Brentford was an ornamental hermit who lived in an oak tree in Gunnersbury Park.

Neville unfolded his slender arms, gave them a stretching, placed his hands upon the table before him and began gently to drum his fingers to the beat of his beneath-breath whistlings. Doris Whimple raised a powdered eyebrow and did *tut-tut-tuttings* with her pinkly painted mouth.

Neville ceased his drummings. 'Should we begin the meeting?' he enquired.

'No can do, old sport,' said Vic Vanilla. 'Have to wait for the arrival of his nibs.'

'The Mayor?' said Neville.

David Berkshire tittered, although none of them heard him do it.

Doris Whimple shook her head, releasing lavender fragrance into the morbid air. 'The Mayor will not be attending,' she said.

'But surely,' said Neville, 'this is a most important meeting.'

'The Mayor will *not* be attending,' Doris Whimple repeated sternly.

'Oh,' said Neville.

'You know, his nibs,' said Vic, elbowing Neville gently in the rib cage, 'the bloke with the bunce.'

'From the Consortium,' said Mr Gwynplaine Dhark.

Neville glanced in the direction of the rival publican and received a gust of his brimstoned breath.

'The Consortium,' said Neville and lowered his gaze. He knew well enough about the Consortium, the Consortium that intended to purchase the football ground, tear up the turf and rip down the stands and build their damnable executive homes on it.

Neville took his pocket watch from his waistcoat and flipped open its cover. 'It's now ten-fifteen,' he observed. 'This fellow is a quarter of an hour late. Perhaps we can start the meeting without him. Perhaps we can settle this with a show of hands now. I'm certain that none of us *really* wants to see the football ground go – it is, after all, the very heart of the community.'

'The Church of St Joan is the heart of the community,' said Doris Whimple. Mr Gwynplaine Dhark sniggered. Vic Vanilla shrugged. Neville, who had always considered the saloon bar of The Flying Swan to be the true heart of Brentford, kept his own counsel.

The outer door of the council chamber opened, flooding sunlight into the room. A figure stood, dramatically framed, in the brilliant opening. 'Greetings one and all,' said this fellow, striding forward into the chamber.

'Close the door behind you,' called Doris Whimple,

which raised a wan smile from Neville. The figure returned to the door, slammed it shut, strode forward once more and came to a halt behind the Mayoral Chair. He carried a slim, black executive case and his face was painfully pale. He glanced from face to face of councillors all, though his glancings were guarded behind his mirrored sunspecs.

Shifty, thought Neville. *Very shifty*.

'Shufty,' said the fellow. 'Gavin Shufty, representative of the Consortium. So sorry I'm late. I asked directions from a local bod sitting on a bench in front of the Memorial Library and the buffoon misdirected me to the council dump.'

Neville managed a bit of a grin in response to this intelligence.

'But no matter.' Gavin Shufty pulled back the Mayoral Chair and seated himself thereupon.

A gasp went up from Doris Whimple, and one would most certainly have also gone up from the aged Councillor Doveston had he not been fast asleep and dreaming of bees.

'Oh, excuse me,' said Gavin Shufty, making as if to rise, 'have I committed a social gaffe? Is this someone's chair?'

'It's the Mayor's chair,' said Doris, tinkering with the brooch on her breast, a brooch in the shape of a foxhound savaging a peasant.

'And where is his worship, the Mayor?' enquired Shufty.

'He is not attending this meeting.'

'So, no damage done, then.' Gavin Shufty hoisted his executive case on to the council table and opened it. 'Down to business, then. I've drawn up the contracts — I'm sure you'll find them most favourable, if you know what I mean, and I'm sure that you do.' And he tapped at his nose as he said this.

'Contracts?' said Neville. 'What contracts are these?'

'For the purchase of the football ground by the Consortium.'

'Oh no,' said Neville. 'No, no, no. This meeting is to debate the matter of selling the football ground. It is not a forgone conclusion.'

'Really?' said Shufty. 'Then I must have got my figures

26

wrong. Let's see.' And he drew from his case a pocket calculator of advanced design, which was very possibly powered by the transperambulation of pseudo-cosmic anti-matter.

Or possibly not.

And tapped at it with his forefinger.

'No, I am correct,' he continued. 'The club, which is to say the council, that owns the Griffin Park ground is in debt to the bank to the tune of £1,650,320.'

'No,' said Neville. 'Surely not.'

'Oh no.' Gavin Shufty struck his forehead. 'My mistake.'

'Phew,' said Neville.

'It's £1,650,689 – I forgot to take today's interest on the debt into account.'

Neville groaned dismally.

'Only joking,' said Shufty.

Neville brightened.

'You don't really owe all that money to the bank.'

'Blessed be,' said Neville.

'You owe it to the Consortium – which, in an act of supreme public spiritedness paid off the loan to the bank and took it on for you. So, to business, the contracts.'

'No, no, no,' said Neville and he shook his head once more.

'Does anybody else have anything to say?' asked Shufty. 'I find this vagabond frankly annoying.'

'What?' went Neville.

'I have something to say,' said Gwynplaine Dhark.

'And that is?' said Shufty.

'Where would you like us to sign?'

'Now you're talking my kind of language.'

'No,' said Neville. 'This isn't right. This isn't how it should be.'

'No,' said David Berkshire. 'I agree. It isn't right.'

'Seems you're all on your own, then,' said Shufty to Neville.

'No,' said David Berkshire. 'I said no, too.'

'And *I* heard him,' said Neville.

'So,' said Gavin Shufty, 'two dissenters. How about you, madam?' He addressed Doris Whimple. 'Surely a beautiful and intelligent woman such as yourself does not wish the council to go into further endless debts to save a football team that has not won a single match so far this season and shows no hope of ever winning one. Not when the handsome sum the Consortium is prepared to pay could be spent on numerous community projects.'

'Well,' said Doris Whimple, 'I did hear some talk of a community centre.'

'I have the plans here with me in my case. Your name is, madam?'

'Doris Whimple,' said Doris Whimple.

'What a pretty name. The new community centre lacks for one, perhaps you would care to honour it with your own?'

'Now, see here,' said Neville.

'Desist in your puerile protestations,' said Gwynplaine Dhark. 'The cause is a lost one. Bow to progress.'

'Quite so.' Gavin Shufty beamed upon Gwynplaine Dhark. 'And your name is, sir?'

'Dhark,' said Dhark, 'Gwynplaine Dhark.'

'A noble name, and one that I feel should grace one of the roads of the new estate of executive homes. Dhark Crescent perhaps, or Dhark Street.'

'Dhark Alley more like,' said Neville.

'So, who else? You, sir?' Gavin Shufty addressed Vic Vanilla.

'Vanilla Way will do fine for me,' said Vic Vanilla. 'That and all the other little matters we spoke about on the phone.' And Vic Vanilla tapped at his bulbous nose.

'Quite so,' said Gavin Shufty. 'It's all in the contracts.'

'No,' protested Neville once more. 'It's quite clear to me what's going on here.'

'You're the barman from The Flying Swan, aren't you?' said Gavin Shufty. 'I was warned about you.'

'This is disgraceful,' said Neville, rising from his seat. 'This is bribery and corruption. I will have no part of this.'

'Sit down, Neville.' Vic Vanilla gave Neville's jacket a tugging. 'You'll do all right out of this. You'll make enough to buy The Flying Swan from the brewery, if you want.'

Neville looked down at Vic Vanilla. 'What did you say?' he asked.

Vic gave his nose another tapping. 'Shares,' said he. 'We, as signatories on behalf of the council, are each to be awarded one thousand shares in the building project.'

'It's all legal and above board,' said Gavin Shufty. 'One thousand shares each, the same agreement that we have reached with all the other councils we've dealt with. The shares are without value until the new executive estate is built, at which point, when the new homes go on sale, they rocket to at least one hundred pounds a share. Perhaps more. You can sell them, should you so wish.'

'One hundred thousand smackers,' said Vic, now rubbing his greasy palms together. 'That would buy you The Swan, wouldn't it?'

'It would,' Neville whispered.

'And all strictly legal. Owner of your own pub. Ain't that every part-time barman's dream?'

Neville nodded thoughtfully. 'It is,' he said in a wistfully whispery voice.

'Then go for it,' said Vic. 'The team's a dead'n. The Brentford Bees have had their glory days, way back in the nineteen-twenties. The ground's never even a quarter full on Saturday afternoons. No one really cares any more. I'll bet you've never even been to a game.'

'I'm always working.' Neville sighed.

'You could hire in some bar staff and support another side, buy a season ticket,' said Vic.

'We have executive boxes available at most stands,' said Gavin Shufty. 'You'd be welcome at any, at no charge, of course. Shareholders are always welcome. All you have to do is hold on to one share in order to qualify.'

'Cheese,' said Neville and he stared into space. It was one of those thousand-yard stares, which are always into some kind of space. A thousand yards away, most likely.

'So,' said Gavin Shufty, 'are we all done? How goes the vote?'

'You have mine,' said Mr Gwynplaine Dhark.

'And mine, too.' Vic Vanilla raised a thumb.

'And mine also, I suppose,' said Doris Whimple.

'You, sir?' Gavin Shufty turned his mirrored gaze upon David Berkshire.

'I don't know,' said that man.

'Did he speak?' Shufty asked Gwynplaine Dhark.

'He said yes,' said Mr Dhark.

'No, I never did.'

Gwynplaine Dhark stared hard at David Berkshire. It was a penetrating stare. A *very* penetrating stare.

'Yes, all right, I suppose,' said David Berkshire.

'That would be four out of six,' declared Gavin Shufty. 'Motion carried, I believe. I'll just hand out these contracts, then,' and he proceeded to do so.

Neville slowly sat himself down. He still had a good old stare on him, of the thousand-yard variety rather than the penetrating. A contract was duly thrust before him.

Doris Whimple awoke Councillor Doveston. 'There's something for you to sign,' said she.

'Is it about bees?' asked the old duffer.

'In a manner of speaking, yes.'

'Then I'll sign it.'

'That makes five out of six, then.' Gavin Shufty returned to the Mayoral Chair. 'Democracy at work. Always a joy to behold.'

Pens were taken from breast pockets, tops were pulled from these pens, signatures were signed.

'You, sir, please,' Gavin Shufty said to Neville. 'You appear to be in some sort of trance. Could someone give him a bit of a dig?'

Vic gave Neville a bit of a dig. 'Bung on your moniker,' he said.

Neville took *his* pen from *his* breast pocket. It was a Parker. Neville unscrewed the cap.

'There's a good boy,' said Mr Shufty in a patronising tone.

Neville turned his head and stared at Mr Shufty.

'No,' said Neville. 'I won't do it. It's wrong. All wrong. I may never have seen Brentford play, but I support the club. You can't just wipe it away with a stroke of a pen. It's part of Brentford's glorious heritage, part of the stuff of which Brentford is made.'

'You're outvoted,' said Mr Shufty. 'It doesn't really matter whether you sign or not.'

'It's wrong.' Neville turned towards his fellow councillors. Scanned their faces. Saw the greed.

'You *don't* care, do you?' he said. 'You were voted on to the council to care, but you don't. You just think of yourselves.'

'That's not entirely true.' Gavin Shufty had a smug face on. 'They just know a lost cause when they see one. Brentford football club is finished. It's history.'

'Glorious history,' said Neville.

'But history none the less for it. History that will not repeat itself.'

'It might,' said Neville. 'There's no telling.'

Gavin Shufty laughed. 'Brentford *might* win the FA Cup again, is that what you're saying?'

'It might,' said Neville once more.

'Don't be absurd.'

'But what if it did?'

'If it did?' Gavin Shufty laughed. 'If that bunch of losers were to win the FA Cup, then I'd tear up these contracts.'

'Would you?' Neville asked.

'Absolutely.' Gavin Shufty had a very smug face on now. It was beyond smug. There was indeed no word to describe such a face.

'And what about the money?' Neville asked.

Gain Shufty burst into a fit of laughter. 'Tell you what,' he said, between guffawings, 'the Consortium will write off the debt, how about that?' And then he laughed some more.

Neville was definitely *not* laughing.

31

'Write it on, then,' said he.

'Do what?' Shufty asked.

'Write it on to the contracts. What you just said – that if Brentford were to win the FA Cup, you'll write off the debt.'

'That's absurd,' said Gavin Shufty.

Neville nodded sombrely. 'I know,' said he. 'It's totally absurd. So what harm can it do?'

Gavin Shufty wiped tears of laughter from his eyes and slowly shook his head. 'Are you serious?' he asked.

'Yes,' said Neville, 'I am. As you say, I can do nothing to stop this. I'm outvoted. I could abstain and not put my signature to this contract, but I am only a human being and I would dearly love to own my own pub. But I am not only a human being, I am a Brentonian. And Brentonians will rise to the challenge when called upon to protect what they care about.'

Gavin Shufty laughed once more. 'I'm afraid that this is one challenge that Brentonians will *not* be able to rise to,' said he.

'Then humour me,' said Neville. 'What do you have to lose?'

Gavin Shufty gave a shrug. 'Absolutely nothing,' he replied.

4

John Vincent Omally, bestest friend of James Arbuthnot Pooley, crested the canal bridge from the Isleworth side and soared down into Brentford. Omally soared upon Marchant, his elderly sit-up-and-beg bike. There were times when John and his bike did not see eye to eye. As it were. Times when John cursed Marchant and Marchant returned John's curses with what is known in military circles as 'dumb insolence'. Troubled times were these for the both of them.

But not on this particular morn.

Upon this particular morn, boy and bike were as one, in cosmic synthesis, in a harmony that bordered on the divine. Marchant declined to snag John's turn-up in his chain wheel and John felt not the need to chastise Marchant for his bad behaviour. The sun shone down and God was in his Heaven and to Omally all seemed more than just all right with the world.

That John, a curly-haired son of Eire, Dublin born and Brentford bred, should be approaching the borough at this time of the morning rather than stirring from his cosy bed in Mafeking Avenue, just to the rear of Peg's Paper Shop, would have surprised none who knew John well. John was a bit of a ladies' man. And as the now-legendary Spike once put it, 'One bit in particular.' And upon this particular morn, John was returning from a night of passion with an Isleworth lass whose husband worked the night shift at the windscreen-wiper factory.

John did whistlings as he rode along, and singings, too, and sometimes reckless chucklings. That one day he would be made to pay for his transgressions, brought to book and no doubt soundly thrashed by some cuckolded hubby, perhaps played a part in these whistlings and singings and reckless chucklings as well. For it was the risk that did it for John – the risk, the thrill and of course the joy he brought to the women that he pleasured.

Not that John was a bad man.

No. Like unto Pooley, his bestest friend, and unto Neville and unto Norman, John Omally was a good man. John was as Jim, which is to say basically honest. Indeed, he was the partner of Jim, a fellow entrepreneur. Together they toiled hard evading what is so laughingly described as 'honest work'. Together they lived by their wits. Together they drifted through life.

And happily.

Down the High Street came John, sometimes on the road and sometimes on the pavement, oblivious to hooting horns and startled shoppers. Onward, ever onward. 'Til he stopped. Before The Plume Café.

Omally dismounted, leaned Marchant against the café window to enjoy the late-season sunshine and entered The Plume Café.

The Plume Café had seen better days, and had probably even enjoyed them. These better days had been during the post-war years, those years known as the nineteen-fifties. Rock'n'rollin' years these had been, of Teddy Boys with Brylcreemed heads and long drape coats and fat-soled brothel-creepers. When Elvis was King and fags were three pence a packet. And you could buy a dog for a shilling that was big enough for all the family to ride on. And whose name was Jack.

The Plume retained features of this glorious decade, including an espresso coffee machine that still made impressive noises. Whilst concealed behind its bulk, Lil, The Plume's proprietress, would furtively ladle a spoonful of Maxwell House into a stranger's mug and shake it about a bit. It also boasted a jukebox of the Rockola persuasion, now sadly scarified with the rust but still with its original selections: 'Wild Gas On Saturn' by The Rock Gods;

'Standing in the Slipstream of the Jets' by The Flying Starfish From Uranus; the 'Two-By-One Song' by Little Tich and The Big Foot Band; 'God's Only Daughter' by The Sally Girls; and selections from *Armageddon: The Musical* sung by the original cast. There were 'contemporary' chairs and Formica-topped tables and even those plastic tomatoes that dispense ketchup when squeezed. And those chrome-topped glass sugar dispensers, which rarely dispense anything, even when shaken with surpassing fierceness. The Plume remained as those who had always known it knew it, and those who knew it, knew it well. And loved it also.

And so also loved they Lil.

The sign above the door proclaimed in faded italics that The Plume was the property of one Mrs Veronica Smith, but whether this was Lil, none asked, nor even thought to.

Lil was Lil, or Lily Marlene to a stranger, a Junoesque beauty now in the middle fullness of her years. A suicide blonde*, all pouting lips of rubeous hue and mammaries to set a young lad's loins a leaping, with skirt that little bit too short, heels a tad too high and those parts that were clothed pressed into garments of a size that didn't 'fit all'.

It was popularly believed by the good men of Brentford that they did not make women like Lil any more, and so she was adored by them. Yet they feared her in equal measure, for Lil was fierce.

Omally, who had known many women of the borough and indeed the surrounding territories, did not number Lil amongst his conquests. Although he flirted with her mirthfully, and she with him, such a liaison – interesting though it might have been for the both of them – would have been, in Omally's opinion, and no doubt Lil's, inappropriate. A friendship existed between them, a deep friendship that would not have been strengthened by sexual congress; rather it would have been severed.

Omally entered The Plume Café and breathed in of its ambience: the fragrance of frying, the bouquet of bacon, the

*Dyed by her own hand (humour).

heady scent of the sausage. Of customers there were but several: a tall youth named Cornelius Murphy munched upon bacon sandwiches in a window seat and discoursed with his dwarflike comrade Tuppe; a salesman, travelling in tobaccos and ready-rolled cigarettes, downed cornflakes alone in a corner; and a native of the Andaman Islands took tea with an elderly sea captain.

Omally nodded good mornings to each and to all and for the most part these were returned to him. The Irishman approached the counter; the eyes of Lil, framed by their painted lashes, fell upon him.

'Well,' said Lil, a-pushing out her bosoms, 'if it isn't my own dear John.'

'Indeed if it isn't,' said himself. 'Hail, Lily, full of grace. Blessed art thou amongst women.'

'The usual?' said Lily.

'The usual would be sublime.'

Lil set to the frying of John's usual. And John watched her at it and smiled as he did so.

'That idiot grin becomes you,' said Lil, cracking three eggs simultaneously into the cacky pan. 'It is surely the grin of one who has recently enjoyed the illicit favours of another's wife.'

'Perish the thought,' said Omally. 'My heart belongs to you.'

'Your heart, then, should perhaps inform your penis of this truth.'

'Perhaps so.'

Lil heaped several pre-cooked-and-ready-for-a-warm-up bangers into the cacky pan and shook the pan around upon the gas hob.

'Do you never think about settling down, John?' she asked through the smoke.

'All the time,' said himself, 'which is why I always keep on the move.'

'You could do little better than to find yourself a good woman.'

'There are many to be found.' John turned towards

36

himself a copy of the *Brentford Mercury* (numbered by Norman for a house in a nearby street and wrongly delivered by Zorro the paperboy who cared nought for Norman's numberings) which lay upon the counter and viewed its front page. 'Many, many, many,' he continued in a wistful tone.

'You are a scoundrel.' Lil popped two doorsteps into the toaster and rammed down the starter with a thumbnail painted Rose du Barry.

'Poo,' said Omally. 'This sits most uneasily.'

'You have some complaint to make about my seating?' A fierceness arose in the voice of Lil.

'Not a bit of it, fair lady. I allude to the headline news upon the day's broadsheet. Inasmuch that the council are, as we engage in pleasant social intercourse, sealing the fate of the football ground.'

'I didn't have you down as a supporter, John. A small bird whispered into my ear that when a match is on, you are generally to be found in the arms of the goalkeeper's wife.'

'A damnable lie,' quoth Omally, for indeed it was, it being the centre-forward's wife that John was prone to visit. 'But this is an outrage. I shall write to my MP.'

'Your MP?' Lil laughed. 'You've never even voted in your life.'

'Voting for the lesser of two evils holds no appeal for me.'

'Let's face it, John.' Two charred doorsteps leapt suddenly from the toaster to be deftly caught by Lil. 'The club is finished. Everyone knows that it's finished. It was just a matter of time before some big business concern bought up the land and built housing on it.'

'Outrage,' declared John. 'Iconoclasm.'

'I'll bet you've never even been to a match.' Lil scooped up the contents of the cacky pan, which now included mushrooms, bacon, black pudding and a beetle named Derek, and delivered this eclectic cuisine to a dinner plate that had once boasted a willow pattern. This, in turn, in the company of the burned toast (now buttered) she delivered unto John Omally.

'And a mug of tea,' said himself. 'In my usual mug.'

'I'll bring it over,' said Lil. 'Enjoy.'

Omally bore his breakfast to the nearest table, which although not his favourite was not entirely without favour and set to tucking in. Pull down the football club, he thought as he ate. Appalling, diabolical – why, that would mean pulling down The Stripes Bar beneath the south stand, where ale at below-average price could be enjoyed at hours that were outside those of normal licensing. And, of course, it might well leave the Bee's centre forward with nothing to do on a Saturday afternoon. And of course there was the matter of Brentford's glorious heritage. And such like.

Omally pressed on with his repast. They'd sell the ground, he knew that they would. Those town councillors, they were all up to some kind of no-good, everyone knew that. All up to no good, with the exception of Neville.

Omally, as a regular in the saloon bar of The Flying Swan, held Neville in high esteem. In fact, it had been Omally's idea to put the part-time barman up as a candidate for one of the vacant seats on the town council – out of public spiritedness, of course. That and the fact that Omally had been told that council meetings often ran late into the night, which meant that Neville would have to leave the bar in the hands of Croughton the pot-bellied pot man, an inebriate buffoon who could always be inveigled into serving after hours.

A practice that Neville frowned deeply upon.

But you couldn't just pull down the football club, plough up the ground. You couldn't. You just couldn't.

Sadly, John knew all too well that you could. You just could. It happened all too regularly nowadays. In fact, it was something of a current fashion.

Lil brought over Omally's tea and stared down between her bosoms at the thoughtful Irishman.

'There's no stopping what can't be stopped,' she said, which rang a bell somewhere. 'Don't let it play on your mind, John.'

Omally sipped his tea and burned his mouth. 'It just doesn't seem right,' said he.

At length, John finished his breakfast and patted his belly. The morning sun shone in upon him and the Irishman's spirits, so recently lowered, were lifted again. Today was, after all, another day and a day that it was his duty to enjoy to the full, being the sort of fellow that he was – to whit, one who truly revelled in life. There were pennies that must be earned and then spent, things to do and people to see.

'Excuse me, sir.'

Omally looked up.

A fellow looked down at him, a fellow in a drab grey suit, with a painfully thin face and matching hair. A drab and pale grey fellow, all at odds with the day.

'How might I help you?' Omally enquired with politeness.

'It's how I might help you,' said the fellow. Which set certain alarm bells ringing.

'Oh yes?' said Omally, in the voice of undisguised suspicion.

'Oh, don't get me wrong. Might I sit?' The fellow did so without waiting for a reply. 'It's just that I'm in a bit of a dilemma and I think we might be able to help each other out.'

'I suspect that at least half of that statement might hold some degree of truth,' said Omally.

'Do you smoke?' asked the fellow.

'Ah,' said John. 'Duty-frees, is it?'

'Not as such. Allow me to explain. I'm a salesman, travelling in tobaccos and ready-rolled cigarettes.'

'I know,' said Omally. 'I saw you when I came in.'

The fellow shook his head. 'I sell these.' He hoisted a bulging suitcase on to the table, all but upsetting Omally's mug, tugged it open and withdrew a packet of Dadarillos. 'I'm covering this area. I've got a caseful, but the local shops don't seem very keen to purchase.'

'They wouldn't be,' said John. 'This is a very con-servative neighbourhood.'

'But they're half the price of normal cigarettes and nearly twice the length.'

'Half the price?' said Omally.

'And twice the length. And with the deal I'm giving to the shops, they'll still make more profit per packet than on normally priced cigarettes.'

Omally nodded sagely. 'Which prompts the question that will not be answered,' said he.

'Which is?' asked the fellow.

'What's the catch?' asked Omally.

'There is no catch – it's a promotional offer. The com-pany are literally giving these cigarettes away. They are convinced that once smokers try them, they will like them so much that they will switch from their regular brands.'

'And then the price will go up.'

'Naturally. Such is the way with business.'

Omally cogitated. And then he smiled. Although it was true that the local tobacconists would not care to take on new products, what with their clientele being so set in their ways and all, there were few folk who, when offered a good deal – under-the-counter, as it were, or off-the-back-of-a-lorry – would turn up their noses. And so where the shopkeepers of Brentford might fail to find custom, Omally, with his winning ways and the gift of the gab, which God had personally granted to Irish manhood to make up for the fact that their staple diet would be the potato, would, with the wind behind him and all things being equal and those that weren't falling in his favour due to his own exertions, SUCCEED.

'Two questions,' said Omally.

'Go on,' said the fellow.

'Firstly, how many packets of these cigarettes do you have?'

'Five hundred,' said the fellow. 'Yours for twenty-five quid.'

Omally nodded once again.

'And secondly?' the fellow asked.

'Secondly, why did you approach me, a perfect stranger, with this offer?'

'Ah,' said the fellow. 'Your name is John Omally, is it not?'

Further alarm bells rang in the head of John Omally. 'It might be,' he said with caution.

'Lily Marlene there recommended you. She said you'd be popping in.'

'Right,' said John, and he grinned his grin and put out his hand for a shake.

And John left The Plume Café somewhat heavier than he had entered it. Heavy of belly was John Omally and heavy of suitcase, too.

And John strapped this suitcase to the rear rack of Marchant. Mounted up and pleased with his good fortune and business acumen, for he had beaten the salesman down to twenty quid, he cycled away with a smile on his lips and a whistle between them.

And Marchant, appalled by the extra weight of the suitcase, snagged up Omally's right trouser cuff in its chain wheel and locked its front brake.

Which pitched Omally onto the kerb and wiped the smile off his face.

5

Neville the part-time barman stood once more within the sanctuary of The Swan's saloon bar. Behind the counter. In his carpet slippers. Neville pressed a shot glass beneath the whisky optic and drew off a measure of comfort. For Neville was sorely discomforted. Neville was a part-time barman racked with anguish and guilt, deeply shaken by the events that had so recently befallen him.

That he should have had to have been there, in that Godless, soulless council chamber, to witness the selling out of the borough's heritage. Not only that, but to have had to have signed – Neville's brain sought words appropriate – that pact with Satan.

And that he should actually prosper from the football club's destruction.

'I shall give every penny to charity,' said Neville, downing Scotch. But his words echoed hollowly in the otherwise deserted bar. He would *not* give it all to charity. He knew that he would not. For all of the goodness that Neville had in him, and there was much, it would take a gooderer man than he to give up all that money, to give up the dream of a lifetime: to own The Flying Swan.

Neville hung his noble head. He had done a very bad thing. But what else could he have done? Refused to sign his contract? That would have pleased the Consortium no end. One less batch of shares to hand out. There really had been nothing else he could have done. He had been helpless.

And this sense of helplessness added greatly to the part-time barman's despair. It was a terrible sensation.

Neville sighed a deep and heartfelt sigh and swallowed further Scotch. What else could he have done? Surely everything that could have been done to save the club had been done. There had been petitions and fund-raising nights and benefits and raffles and auctions and fun-runs and car-boot sales and pub events and—

Neville sighed once again. There had been none of these things. No one in Brentford had done anything. Folk had simply shrugged their shoulders and said 'it will never happen' and 'it can't happen here'. But it could and it would. And as the months had passed and it had become more and more apparent that it could and would happen, folk had said, 'It is an outrage, someone should have done something.'

But nobody had.

And now, it seemed, it was all too late.

Neville sighed some more and sipped some more of his liquor. And when he downed the last of his liquor he drew himself another.

A brisk rapping upon the saloon bar door stirred Neville from his dismal reverie. The part-time barman swung aloft the counter flap, padded across the carpet upon his carpet-slippered feet and drew aside the bolts. The door swung open to the day's first patron and this patron was Old Pete.

An ancient geezer was Old Pete,
Of rheumy eye and grizzled chin.
From his Wellingtoned feet to his flat cap of tweed,
He was ragged and dog-eared and going to seed.
He had served at the Somme for his country and king,
And his strides were secured by a circlet of string.
He had canker and gout and Health Service hips,
A stick that was stout and a spaniel called Chips.[*]

'Thirty seconds late in opening,' the oldster observed,

[*] Which was actually more of a half-terrier.

pocketing his retirement watch and hobbling past Neville. 'The world is ending and there's a fact for you.'

'My apologies, Old Pete,' said Neville.

'Worth a freeman's on the house, I would have thought.' Old Pete hoisted himself with difficulty on to his favourite barstool.

'Not in a month that is composed of Sundays all,' replied Neville, returning himself to his place behind the counter and lowering the flap. 'What will it be today, Old Pete? Large dark rum, as ever?'

'Large dark rum it is.' Old Pete secured Chips' lead to a stanchion on his stool that had been especially fitted for the purpose and observed Neville as he went about his business.

'You look the glum Charlie today,' said Old Pete. 'Is something troubling you, Neville?'

'Nothing that I would wish to trouble you with.'

'Thank the Lord of the lawnseed for that. I only asked out of politeness.' Old Pete accepted his large dark rum and paid for it with the exact small change. 'You need a pick-me-up,' said he, raising his glass of rum and giving it a tasting.

Neville sighed once more, but this time in company. 'I need something,' he said.

'*Mandragora officinarum*,' said Old Pete.

'Pardon me?' said Neville.

'*Mandragora officinarum*,' said Old Pete once more. 'It's a powerful aphrodisiac. It used to be known as the "gallows plant" because it was believed to take seed from the seminal effluvia that dripped from hanged criminals. I am currently cultivating a crop of it on my allotment patch. It's said to have magical powers – prolongs active life, increases virility, puts a spring into your step and lead in your pencil, so to speak.'

'I'm sure it does,' said Neville wearily.

'It does too,' said Old Pete. 'Do you doubt my words?'

'Oh no.' Neville gave his head further shakings. Old Pete was hailed hereabouts as a veritable fount of knowledge regarding all matters horticultural. What he didn't know about allotment cultivation, he didn't know because it didn't exist.

'Well, think on,' said Old Pete.

And Neville thought on. And this thinking on further depressed him.

James Arbuthnot Pooley entered The Flying Swan.

'Watchamate, Pete, Neville,' said Jim in a cheery fashion.

Old Pete grunted and Neville nodded.

'Oh dear,' said Jim, crossing to the bar and ascending the stool next to Old Pete. 'Do I sense an atmosphere of gloom upon this glorious morning?'

'It's Neville,' said Pete. 'His pecker's playing him up and his legs are giving out. Needs a dose of Mandragora. I told him.'

'There's nothing wrong with my pecker,' said Neville. 'Pint of Large would it be, Jim?'

'It would,' said Pooley, extracting the exact change from his trouser pocket and counting it on to the counter.

Neville drew the perfect pint and presented same to his patron.

Pooley perused the perfect pint, presented same to his laughing gear, took a taste and said, 'Ahhh.'

Neville managed a sort of smile. At least the ale was, as ever, superb. He rang up 'no sale' on the aged cash register and deposited Pooley's coinage therein.

Pooley placed his perfect pint upon the bar counter, took out his packet of Dadarillos, removed from it an overlong ciggie and lit up.

'God's garden-claw,' gasped Old Pete, sniffing at the plume of smoke that wafted in his direction. 'Smell's like a tart's laundry basket. What are you smoking there, Pooley?'

'Dadarillos,' said the lad. 'An all-new smoking taste sensation. A blend of the finest long-grain tobaccos and an extra special secret ingredient that . . .'

'Well blow it somewhere else, you craven buffoon.'

'Quite so,' said Jim, blowing it somewhere else.

'Not at me,' said Neville, fanning the air.

'I'm sorry.'

'So,' said Old Pete as Jim blew smoke down the front of his open-necked shirt, 'given your regular morning's contribution to Bob the Bookie's retirement fund, have you, Pooley?'

'I feel lucky today,' said Jim.

'Put your money into the soil,' saged the ancient. 'Great oaks from little acorns grow and the sprout is the father to the cabbage.'

'I'll stick with my system, thank you. It's just a matter of time.'

Old Pete sniggered. 'You craven buffoon,' said he once more.

And, 'God save all here,' came the voice of John Omally as this man now entered The Flying Swan. 'Morning, each.'

Jim waggled his fag-toting hand, Old Pete mumbled and Neville said, 'Hello.'

John placed his bum on the bar stool next to Jim and his elbows upon the counter. 'Pint of Large, please, Neville,' said he. 'Jim's in the chair.'

'I certainly am not,' said Jim.

'You will be,' said John, 'for I have a lucrative business proposition to put your way.'

'Not in my bar,' said Neville. 'Whatever it is.'

'It's all above board,' said Omally, accepting his perfect pint.

'On my tab,' said Jim.

'You have no tab,' said Neville, rolling his good eye.

Jim fished into another pocket and brought from it further coinage. Neville tossed it into the knackered cash register and rang up 'no sale' once again.

Omally tasted the ale and found favour with this tasting. 'We will speak shortly,' he said to Jim, 'but firstly we must talk of other matters. Let's be having you, Neville.'

'Pardon me?' said Neville.

'The meeting,' said John, 'that you have so recently returned from. At the town hall. Concerning the future of the football club.'

All eyes other than Neville's turned towards Neville.

'Aha,' said Old Pete.

'Was the meeting today?' Jim asked. 'Is the club saved?'

Neville chewed upon his bottom lip. His normally bar-tanned complexion was a whiter shade of pale.

'I like not the aspect of our barlord,' said Old Pete. 'It bespeaketh perfidy and tergiversation.'

Neville gave his lip a further chewing. 'I have to change a barrel in the cellar,' said he.

'No you don't,' said Omally. 'You have to tell us what went on.'

'I don't,' said Neville. 'I really don't.'

'Well then,' said Old Pete, 'I'm off to The Beelzepub. I'm sure that nice Mr Dhark will be pleased to offer his version of events. Coming with me, lads?'

Jim looked at John.

And John looked at Jim.

'Fair enough,' said Pooley.

'No,' said Neville, 'don't do that. Please don't do that.'

'Then speak to us, Neville,' said John.

And Neville spake unto John and unto Jim and unto Old Pete also. And the words that Neville spake brought no gladness to those ears that received them.

Quite the reverse, in fact.

'You did *what*?' quoth Old Pete. 'You signed away the club?'

'I was outvoted,' said Neville. 'I was powerless to stop it.'

'Judas,' said Old Pete. 'You have sold the borough's birthright for a mess of porridge.'

'It's pottage,' said Omally, who knew his scripture. 'But this isn't good, Neville.'

'Oh, come on,' said Pooley. 'It wasn't Neville's fault. What else could he have done? It's not as if he's going to benefit financially from this, is it?'

Neville shook his head vigorously. He had 'carelessly' neglected to mention the matter of the shares.

'You shouldn't have signed, though, Neville,' said Jim. 'If it were to come out in the local papers, there's no telling what people might do.'

'What?' said Neville. 'What do you mean?'

'I know what he means,' said Old Pete, miming the throwing of a rope over a beam.

'No,' said Neville, fingering his throat.

'It will be bye-bye to all this,' Old Pete continued. 'You'll be a social pariah, Neville. You'll be driven out of this pub. Tarred and feathered, I shouldn't wonder.'

'No.' The face of Neville was now a whiter shade of even whiter pale. His hands began to tremble and his knees to knock.

'Stop it,' said Jim to Old Pete. 'Can't you see that you're frightening him? They won't tar and feather you, Neville.'

'No?' said Neville. 'Are you sure?'

'Of course I'm sure.'

'Phew.'

'They'll probably just knock you about a bit. Break your legs or something.'

'Stop!' howled Neville.

Old Pete scratched at his grizzly chin. 'Horrible business, broken legs,' he said. 'The bones never knit together properly; I've been limping since I had my right kneecap blown away at Paschendale. I've a spare walking stick I could let you have cheap.'

Neville buried his face in his hands and began to weep. 'What am I going to do?' he blubbered between weepings.

'Well.' Old Pete glanced towards Jim and John and it was almost as if telepathic thoughts moved between them. 'There might be some way of keeping this from the public.'

'There must,' blubbered Neville. 'But what could it be?'

'Well,' said Old Pete thoughtfully, 'John, Jim and I might be persuaded to keep our mouths shut.'

Neville peeped through his fingers. 'What did you say?' he asked.

Old Pete wore a breezy grin upon his wrinkled face. 'Neville,' said he, 'you are a good man; everybody hereabouts knows that you are a good man. But you are also a foolish man. You don't really think that any of your fellow councillors will be owning up to their dirty deeds, do you?

They'll be keeping their heads down behind the sandbags. But you, however, told *us*.'

'But,' said Neville, 'but you're my friends. Surely I can trust my friends.'

'Indeed you can,' said Jim. 'We won't give you away.'

Old Pete cast Jim a disparaging glance.

'Well *I* won't,' said Jim. 'Neville's all right. *I* won't give him away.'

'Nor me,' said Omally.

'That's very fair of you both,' said Old Pete, 'and I applaud such loyalty. But then the two of you have your youth and your entrepreneurial enterprises. I, however, must drag myself painfully through my twilight years upon the pittance of a pension that the state but grudgingly doles out to me.'

'Ah,' said Neville. 'Another large rum, would it be? On the house.'

'Why thank you, Neville,' said Old Pete. 'That is most unexpected.'

'And you two?'

'Well,' said Jim, 'as you're buying.'

Neville went about his sorry business.

'It's such a shame, though,' said Jim, 'to lose the football ground.'

'I'll bet you've never even been to a match,' said Old Pete.

'No, but that doesn't mean that I don't support the team. In spirit, anyway.'

'Do you fancy their chances this season?' Neville asked as he pulled the pints.

Jim shook his head. 'Why would *you* ask a question like that?' he enquired.

Neville sighed another sigh. 'It was just something,' he said, 'something that came up at the meeting.'

'Go on,' said Omally.

'It was that swine Gavin Shufty,' said Neville. 'He was so full of himself that when I made the suggestion I made, he had everyone write it into their contracts. To mock me.'

'Go on,' said Omally once again.

'It's just this,' said Neville, 'and I know it's absurd, which is why he let it be written into the contracts. He agreed that if Brentford United won the FA Cup this season, then he'd write off the debt and tear up the contracts.'

'Win the FA Cup?' Old Pete began to laugh. Immoderately.

'Brentford?' said Omally.

'*Our* Brentford?' said Jim.

And then they, too, began to laugh.

'That's it,' said Neville, 'rub salt into my wounds. Rub my face into the dirt. Rub me down with creosote and sell me on to the circus.'

'I'm sorry,' said Jim, between guffawings, 'but come on, Neville. Brentford United win the FA Cup?'

'They do have until the end of the season. Shufty agreed that the Consortium would allow the team to play the entire season before the ground was torn down. I had him write that on, too.'

'You were certainly on a roll.' Omally clutched at his stomach and did rollings about of his own.

'Stop it,' cried Neville. 'It isn't funny.'

'No.' Jim fought with hilarity. 'It isn't funny, Neville. You really did do your best. But Brentford win the FA Cup?' And Jim fell once more into mirth.

'You rotten lot,' said Neville, turning away to seek more Scotch. 'I won't bother to ask you now.'

Jim raised a head from his chucklings. 'Ask what?' he asked.

'Whether you knew of anyone. I was going to, but I shan't now.'

'What are you on about, Neville?' said John.

'The manager's job.'

'What, for *here*? Are you going to quit and run before the tarring and feathering starts?'

'Not for here. And *I'm* not the manager here, as you know full well. Not that I've ever actually met the manager. I meant for the club. The manager of Brentford United quit

50

last week. He absconded with the takings from the club's bar.'

'I never knew that,' said John.

'Well, I did and Gavin Shufty did. And Shufty, who was laughing just like you are, even said that *I* could appoint a new manager for the team's final season. I was going to ask whether any of you might know of someone who—'

'Could take on the job and take the club on to win the FA Cup?' Old Pete all but wet himself with further laughter.

'But I won't now,' said Neville, tossing back more Scotch than was strictly good for him.

'Hold on there,' said Omally. 'Let us all slow down and think here for a moment.'

'Forget it,' said Neville. 'I'm not offering the job to you.'

'Not me.' John shook his curly-haired head. 'But possibly someone. Surely I've read of eccentric millionaire pop star types who buy up failing football clubs and lead the teams to glory. Wasn't there that fat pianist who wears the improbable wigs?'

'Ben Elton,' said Jim.

'Not Ben Elton, you buffoon,' said Old Pete. 'He was the bloke with the beard on the Treasure Island.'

'That was Ben Gunn,' said Omally.

'So which club did he buy?' Old Pete scratched at his flat cap.

'He didn't buy any club, Pete, he just rolled his eyes about. Had a great deal of hair, if I recall correctly.'

'I thought you said he wore a wig.'

'Bing Crosby wore a wig,' said Jim, 'but I don't think he ever played the piano.'

'Liberace played the piano,' said Old Pete, 'and I'm pretty sure that he wore a wig. He was a poof, of course – do you think it's the same fellow?'

'Bound to be,' said Jim. 'How many wig-wearing poofs do you know who can play the piano and buy football clubs?'

Old Pete counted on his fingers. 'Three,' said he. 'So, do we call in this Liberace to save Brentford or what?'

Neville made groaning sounds and buried his face in his hands once more.

Omally took to grinning. 'You know what,' he said, 'there might be a way.'

'To save the club?' said Neville. 'I've had quite enough for one day. Enough for one lifetime, in fact.'

'It might just be possible,' said John.

'Do you know the Liberace chap, then, John?' Jim asked.

'No,' said John, 'I don't. Forget about Liberace. Strike Liberace from your mind.'

Jim did so. 'That's a relief,' he said.

'What I'm saying,' said John, 'is that it might be possible to save the club. It might actually be possible for Brentford, under the right management, to win the FA Cup.'

'And you know how?' Neville asked.

'No,' said Omally, 'but I know of a man who will.'

6

Professor Slocombe dwelt in a large and stately Georgian house upon Brentford's historic Butts Estate. The Estate proper consisted of a broad tree-lined thoroughfare bordered by proud habitations of the Regency persuasion, which led to The Butts itself, a square acre of land once reserved for the statutory Sunday afternoon longbow practice in those long-ago days known as 'yore'. Here stood The Seaman's Mission, a hostel run by that charitable foundation to provide temporary accommodation for seafaring types who were down upon their luck. And many more splendid houses.

The wealthy burghers of Brentford who had ordered the construction of these wonderful buildings had attained their golden guineas through seaborne commerce: the import of spices and tea and opium and slaves. During these times, Brentford had been a prosperous community and upon May Monday The Butts had played host to the Bull Fair.[*]

Prosperity had left Brentford behind and the old rich had long departed. Rich folk still lived in The Butts, mainly outborough business types who earned their wealth in manners unfathomable to the plain people of Brentford, to whom they remained a great unknown.

There was much of the great unknown about Professor Slocombe. His origins were mysterious and it was somehow assumed that, like the mighty Thames which cradled

---

[*] It was at the Bull Fair in the year of 1760 that Dr Johnson viewed a live griffin in a showman's booth. See Boswell's biography, Vol. 14 Chap. 3.

Brentford in a loving elbow, he had always been there. Certainly Old Pete, one of the borough's most notable elders, swore blind and with vigour that he had known the professor since he, Old Pete, had been a small child, at which time this enigmatic fellow was already a very old man.

What *was* known about Professor Slocombe was that he was a scholar of many esoteric schools, possessed of knowledge and wisdom to equal degree. That he inspired a *frisson* of fear was not at all surprising, but he was a kindly man and those who sought his advice or counsel were never refused or turned away.

The professor was attended by a decrepit retainer named Gammon, a fellow who rarely left the professor's house and who dressed in the servant's livery of a time two hundred years before.

On this particular morning, Professor Slocombe sat in his study doing what ancient scholars so often do – poring over equally ancient tomes. His old, bowed back was towards the open French windows, through which drifted the heady fragrances of the gorgeous orchids that bloomed all year round in his garden, in seeming defiance of the accepted laws of nature. The perfumes of verbena and cymbidium and Yggdrasil entered the room, blending with the fusty, musty odours of the countless leather-bound volumes overflowing from the ancient bookcases that hid the walls. And other odours, too, odours subtle and without name, issued from the many stuffed beasts, some of which were certainly mythical, and the multifarious curiosa that loaded every horizontal surface in the room. Treasures glittered within glass domes – centuries-old weaponry and da Vinciesque models, meteorites and gemstones, fossilised fairies and withered Hands of Glory; elaborate preparations wrought by Frederik Ruysch, composed of foetal skeletons arranged in allegorical tableaux; beard clippings from the Magi, Caspar, Melchior and Balthazar; a pickled homunculus; and a complete set of *The Beano*.

The professor was slim and slight with wild white hair and pale-blue eyes that veritably twinkled behind his golden pince-nez. He was sprightly and vital and should an actor have been chosen to play him, that actor would surely have been Peter Cushing.

Professor Slocombe turned one vellum page and then another and then he closed his tome and sat back in his padded leather chair and spoke.

'Are you two going to skulk about out there for the duration of the morning?' he enquired. 'Or would you care to come inside and enjoy a glass of sherry?'

John Omally looked at Jim.

And Jim looked back at John.

'I never know just how he does that,' said Jim, 'but it never fails to put the wind up me.'

'Good morning to you, Professor,' said Omally, entering the old man's study in the manner in which he would enter a church: with a certain reverence.

'Morning, sir,' said Jim, a-following on.

'Good morning to you both.' Professor Slocombe swung his swivelling chair around and viewed his visitors. He stretched out his slender legs, placed his bony elbows on his bony knees and pressed his palms together. 'Come in, sit down,' said he.

Jim and John crossed the professor's study floor, stepping carefully to avoid contact with some priceless artefact that stood perilously upon a carved ivory column or a Turkish coffee table. John eased himself into a fireside chair. Jim eased himself into another opposite it. The fire in the hearth that burned throughout every season burned on, although it appeared to cast no heat whatever into the drowsy room.

'Somewhat early in the day for you two,' said the professor. 'I have become used to you visiting me of an evening, when The Flying Swan has cast you from its warm embrace and you still have points of dispute between you that I am called upon to settle.'

'Your wisdom is the stuff of local legend,' said Omally.

'And my sherry finds your favour, of this I am certain.'

Professor Slocombe rang a small brass bell that rested at his elbow on his desk and almost as it rang the study's inner door opened to admit the professor's wrinkled retainer, Gammon. This wraithlike being, clad in his antique livery of green velvet frock coat with slashed sleeves and emerald buttons, red silk stockings and black, buckled shoes, bore in his crinkly hands a silver galleried tray upon which rested three Atlantean crystal glasses of sherry.

'And how he does that also has me baffled,' said Jim, as Gammon inclined his fragile frame and Jim accepted the proffered drink with a courteous *thank you*.

'There's probably some trickery involved,' said Professor Slocombe. 'The quickness of the mind deceives the hand, I shouldn't wonder.'

John accepted a glass of sherry and so, too, did the professor. Gammon bowed his way backwards from the room, closing the door behind him. The three men sipped and sighed and sipped some more.

'Researching anything exciting?' John asked in the way of polite conversation.

Professor Slocombe smiled. 'Land charters,' said he. 'Not, perhaps, your mug of ale?'

'Interesting to yourself, though,' said himself.

'Pre-eminently. As you know, I am compiling a book: *The Complete and Absolute History of Brentford*. You would be surprised by the many interesting facts that I have turned up regarding the borough.'

'No we wouldn't,' said Jim, taking out his pack of cigarettes. 'There can be few places on Earth more interesting than Brentford.'

'You've never travelled widely, have you, Jim?' asked the professor.

'Jim gets a nosebleed if he goes on the top deck of a bus,' said John.

'I've been around,' protested Pooley. 'I've been as far south as Brighton. Once.'

'They brought you home in an ambulance,' said Omally.

'I fell off the pier,' said Jim. 'That water was deep.'

56

'There are more interesting places on Earth than Brentford,' said Professor Slocombe, 'though not many. Lhasa in Tibet, perhaps, the Valley of the Kings. Gandara – they say it was in India, you know. And Penge, which I'm told is a very nice place, although I've never actually been there myself.'

Jim took a cigarette from his pack. Omally spied Jim's pack for the first time and smiled to himself.

Professor Slocombe said, 'Please don't smoke in here, Jim, nicotine damages the books.'

'Sorry, Professor.' Jim looked longingly at his cigarette, then pushed it back into the pack and the pack into his pocket.

'You were saying,' said John, 'about Brentford and the interesting facts concerning local charters.'

'Must we go through this rigmarole?' asked the professor, sipping further sherry. 'You have come here with a definite purpose, I presume.'

Omally grinned and nodded.

'I will tell you this,' said Professor Slocombe, 'whether it will be of any interest to you or not. There is a mystery surrounding the ownership of the lands that comprise the borough of Brentford. Once, these lands were the property of the crown, but during the Crusades they were given in parcel as a gift to a knight by the name of Sir Edgar Rune, who had saved the life of King Richard. Certain titles went with this land that made Brentford a separate principality. I am presently researching into where these land titles eventually went. Who actually owns what? It is fascinating stuff. And it might well prove that Brentford is a separate state – indeed, a separate country.'

Omally stifled a yawn. And did so with considerable skill.

'If it turns out that I own the rooms I'm renting,' said Jim, 'then please put me down for a copy of your book when it's published.'

'Oh, I don't ever expect it to be published.' Professor Slocombe finished his sherry. 'This is more a labour of love. My love is for knowledge. All knowledge.'

'Do you know anything about football?' Omally asked.

'Aha, at last.' Professor Slocombe grinned from ear to ear. And his ears, as befitting an elderly gentleman, were large for the size of his head. For men's ears keep on growing, as those who know these things know well.

'Football.' Professor Slocombe tugged upon the over-large lobe of his fine left ear. 'Now what do I know about football?'

'I don't know,' said Omally. 'What?'

'Well,' said Professor Slocombe, 'I know that the game began right here in Brentford.'

'It did *what*?' The voice of surprise belonged to Jim Pooley.

'My researches disclose that the game began in the year AD thirty-nine, when Julius Caesar kicked the skull of a Briton across the ford of the river Brent and a plucky Brentonian booted it right back. The skull struck Caesar in the head, unseating him from his horse.'

'One-nil to Brentford,' cried Jim, beginning a Mexican wave.

'Something of an own goal, I'm afraid,' said the professor. 'Caesar had his troops lay waste to Brentford. His troops then played an impromptu game of soccer with the plucky Brentonian's head on the very area that is now Griffin Park.'

'Significant,' said Omally.

'That an Italian took the first kick? Possibly so; football is considered Italy's second religion.'

'Griffin Park,' said John. 'The football ground. That's what we've come here to talk to you about.'

'It was John's idea, sir,' said Jim. 'I've been telling him not to waste your time.'

'My time is *never* wasted.' Professor Slocombe raised a fragile hand. 'Word has already reached me regarding the decision of the local council to sell off the ground. I regret that I never stood for one of the vacant seats. I could probably have stopped it. I certainly would have put my name forward, had not Neville done so.'

Omally chewed upon his upper lip. 'It's a sad business,'

said he, 'a part of Brentford's glorious history being ripped like a bleeding heart from the prone body of the borough.'

'Most colourfully put, John. I did not know that you were a football fanatic.'

'It's "fan",' said John, 'and I'm not really. But this isn't right. You of all people, with all your knowledge and love of the borough, know it's not right.'

Professor Slocombe shook his old white head. 'It's not right,' he said. 'But I do not possess the financial where-withal to pay off the club's debts, if that is what you were thinking to ask me.'

'Well . . .' said Omally.

'You *weren't*!' said Jim. 'That's not what you were think-ing?'

'It was a thought,' said John. 'A thought, no more.'

'And that's why we came here?'

Omally shook his head. 'There's more,' he explained. 'The club can be saved – in theory. Neville got it written into the contracts. A company known as the Consortium has taken over the club's debts, but if Brentford can win the FA Cup this season, then the debts will be cancelled and the club saved.'

'Brentford win the FA Cup?'

Omally nodded.

There was a brief moment of silence and then Profes-sor Slocombe exploded into laughter. His frangible frame rocked and great tears welled in his dew-blue eyes. He clasped the desk with his delicate fingers and laughed and laughed and laughed.

Jim Pooley shivered. 'Now I know how Neville felt,' he said. 'It's horrible when you see someone else do it.'

Omally crossed himself. 'Holy Mary, mother of God, have mercy upon us,' he prayed.

At length, Professor Slocombe ceased his frantic hilarity. He sucked draughts of air into his narrow chest, mopped his eyes with an oversized red gingham handkerchief and repositioned his pince-nez on to his nose. 'You will indeed be the death of me,' he gasped.

'But it is possible,' said Omally.

'John,' said Professor Slocombe, 'many things are *possible* – but just because something is *possible* does not imply that it *can* or *will* be.'

'But it *is* possible,' Omally protested. 'Brentford could *in theory* win the FA Cup.'

'Could it?' Jim asked.

'Certainly,' said John, 'and in as little as eight games. Don't you know anything about football, Jim?'

'I remember Stanley Matthews,' said Pooley. 'Didn't he marry one of the Beverley Sisters?'

'That was Billy Fury,' said John.

'Wright,' said Professor Slocombe. 'Billy Wright.'

'They were brothers,' said Jim. 'They invented the jet plane.'

'Whittle,' said John.

Jim whistled.

'Not whistle, Whittle, Frank Whittle.'

'What team did he play for?' Jim asked.

'He didn't play for any team and he didn't marry one of the Beverley Sisters,' said John.

'Then you've got the wrong fellow,' said Jim, 'which goes to show how much you know.'

Professor Slocombe raised his hand once more. 'Stop it now,' he said, 'or I might be forced to give you both a smack.'

'I don't know much about football,' said Jim, 'but I know what I like.'

'Which is?' said John.

'Half-time,' said Jim. 'They give you an orange to suck, or is it a lime?'

'Limes are the navy,' said John. 'To stave off scurvy.'

'Scurvy?' Jim asked. 'Which team does he play for?'

'Enough,' said the professor. And he meant it.

'What I'm saying,' said John, 'is that it is *possible* for Brentford to win the FA Cup. And in eight games. It doesn't matter that they've lost every game they've played so far this season. Those weren't FA Cup qualifying games.

Those are the only ones they need to win. It works out at eight games, if they get eight straight wins.'

'Well,' said Jim, 'that seems relatively simple. How come the team's never thought of doing that?'

John almost gave Jim a smack, but he restrained himself. 'I'm quite sure the team *have* thought of it. Many times. At the beginning of every season. The problem is that the team is not a particularly talented team. It is a team that lacks for the vital spark which—'

'What John is trying to say,' said Professor Slocombe, 'is that Brentford United are, I believe the word is, *crap*.'

'Ah,' said Jim, and he tapped at his nose. 'I see.'

John Omally rolled his eyes.

Professor Slocombe shook his head. 'Exactly what do you want from me, John?' he enquired. 'Since financial support is out of the question, what is it that I can offer you?'

'Ah.' John Omally now tapped at *his* nose. 'Well, here's the thing. The Consortium have granted Neville the opportunity to appoint a new manager for the club.'

'Ah, I see.' Professor Slocombe now tapped at *his* nose.

'There's an awful lot of nose-tapping going on,' said Jim. 'Is it a Masonic thing?'

'I understand you,' said the professor to John. 'You are thinking that I might use my connections to secure a new manager for the club, one who might take them on to glory.'

Omally nodded enthusiastically.

Professor Slocombe tugged open a desk drawer. 'I'll have a look in my address book,' said he. 'I think I have Sven Goran Erickson's telephone number.'

'You do?' said John.

Professor Slocombe raised an eyebrow and slammed his desk drawer shut. 'No,' said he, 'of course I don't.'

'Oh,' said John.

'Should I laugh at that?' asked Jim. 'It was quite funny.'

'Do so and I strike you,' said Omally.

'Sorry,' said the professor.

John shrugged. 'It isn't what I was going to ask you

anyway. What I was going to ask you was this. It *is* possible for a team with little talent to beat a team with a lot of talent if the team with the little talent is led by a manager skilled in the art of tactics. Tactics win games. Life is all about tactics, in my humble opinion.'

'Your life certainly is,' said Jim. 'Especially when these tactics are being employed to win the affections of married women.'

'Sssh,' said John. 'Such indiscreet remarks are not worthy of you. What I'm asking you, Professor, is could you formulate a set of tactics whereby Brentford might once, for this season alone, actually *win*?'

Professor Slocombe stroked his chin. 'Hm,' went he. 'An interesting challenge. And one, I have to say, not without a certain charm. I agree with you that although improbable, it is certainly *possible* for Brentford to win through. But my days are full; I would not have the time in them to manage a football team.'

'I'm not suggesting that *you* manage the team,' said John.

'I felt that you were about to.'

'Yes, well, perhaps I was. Certainly your presence alone on the pitch would inspire the team. But surely you, a man of such erudite learning and with such a love for the borough—'

'John,' said the professor, 'with the possible exception of certain members of the town council, you would be hard-pressed to find a Brentonian who does *not* love the borough.'

'*Touché*,' said John. 'But if *you* could formulate the tactics, it wouldn't really matter who the manager was. His job would simply be to pass on these tactics to the team.'

'In principle,' said the professor, 'but you mentioned the word "inspire". A football manager must be able to inspire. He must have charisma.'

Omally threw up his hands. 'It was worth a try,' said he. 'The salary Brentford United can afford to pay a manager is now but a pittance. No professional manager would ever take over the position anyway. The team is doomed, the ground is doomed.' Omally rose to take his leave. 'I'm sorry,' said he, 'but Jim was right, I *have* wasted your time.'

Professor Slocombe nodded his head from side to side. 'Not so fast, John,' he said. 'And allow it to be said that I admire *your* tactics here. You know full well that if I could do anything to save the club, I would. And I agree with you that it *is* possible. And I would certainly be prepared to put my mind to the matter of tactics. In fact, to employ, shall we say, certain methods of my own to aid the team's advancement—'

Jim looked at John.

And John looked at Jim.

Then both of them looked back towards the professor.

'Tactics,' said Professor Slocombe. 'Tactics, certain other methods and a charismatic manager.' His head bobbed once more from side to side. 'That would be the winning formula.'

'It would,' Omally agreed.

Professor Slocombe gazed thoughtfully upon his uninvited guests. 'It is always a pleasure to engage the two of you in conversation,' he said. 'The two of you are, how shall I put this, *alive*. Yes, that's the word. You *live*. On your wits the two of you live and not entirely to the dictates of the establishment. But you are most certainly alive.' The professor noted well the twin expressions of bewilderment that had now appeared upon the faces of his guests.

'I think,' he continued, 'that together we might well succeed with what many would consider to be an impossible quest. To whit, to take Brentford to the very top this season, and to win the FA Cup.'

'Right,' said John. 'I'll drink to that.'

'Me, too,' said Jim, 'but my glass is now empty.'

'Mine, too,' said John, 'but I'll drink to it in principle.'

'Champagne,' said Professor Slocombe, ringing his little brass bell once more. 'This calls for champagne.'

'It does?' said Jim.

'If the professor says it does, it does,' said John, laying

aside his depleted sherry glass and rubbing his hands together. 'It does.'

'We must have a toast,' said Professor Slocombe, 'in champagne, of course, to the future success of Brentford United. And to its new manager.'

'You know the man?' John asked.

'The man sits here before you,' said Professor Slocombe.

'Then you *are* going to take the job?'

'Not me,' said the professor, 'but Jim Pooley.'

7

Jim Pooley was returned to consciousness through the medium of Professor Slocombe's soda siphon, applied towards his laughing gear through the medium of John Omally's hand control.

'Oh,' went Jim. And, 'Get off there,' and, 'Oh no,' and, 'Oh no,' again.

'Oh yes,' said the professor, nodding enthusiastically.

'Oh no,' said Jim once more, spitting soda as he did so.

'You are indeed the man for the job.' Professor Slocombe nodded decisively.

'I'm not,' flustered Jim. 'Believe me, I'm not.'

'Oh yes you are.'

'Oh no I'm not.'

'Are,' said the professor.

'Not,' said Jim. 'Not times squared, to infinity.'

'I'll take the job,' said John, 'if you're offering it.'

'I'm not offering it,' said the professor, 'Neville is.'

'He won't offer it to Jim.'

'No,' said Jim, 'he won't.'

'I'm sure he will if I put in a word for you.'

'Hm,' went Jim, wiping soda from his face. 'This is indeed true. But I don't want the job, Professor. I know nothing about football.'

'So much the better still, the team will not know you.'

'But many of the borough will. I'm not unknown in this area.'

'Then so much the better even stiller. You will be applauded as a local hero, a fearless fellow taking on what most would consider an impossible, indeed, a preposterous task.'

'I number myself amongst these considerers,' said Jim.

'Champagne?' Omally asked. 'Gammon brought in a bottle.'

'I can't do this.' Jim was on his feet now and preparing for the taking of his leave.

'You can.' Professor Slocombe poured champagne. 'And you will. I will guide your every step. I will, how shall I put it, invest you with a certain charisma. Under my guidance you will lead the team to victory.'

'Truly?' Jim asked, with more doubt in his voice than there are zeros in a googol, or coughs to get it right if you're unsure.

'Absolutely,' said Professor Slocombe.

'No,' said Jim, a-vigorously shaking of his head. 'I can't do it. I'm a nobody. It wasn't my idea to come here, it was John's. I don't want to be involved in this.'

'You'd rather just stay as you are, then?' Professor Slocombe fixed Jim with a stare.

'I'm happy as I am,' Jim said.

Professor Slocombe shrugged. 'Yes,' he said, 'I suppose that you are.'

'I know I don't amount to much.' Jim accepted the glass of champagne John offered to him. 'But I have my dreams. One day I'll win through. One day my ship will come into port.'

'This ship being of the variety that runs upon four hooves at Ascot?'

'Amongst other places.' Jim slurped champagne. 'I have tactics of my own. And winning formulas, in theory at least.'

'I'm offering you a chance to really succeed.' Professor Slocombe raised his glass to Jim. 'To do something really special that would benefit you as well as the borough as a whole. What do you have to lose in taking on this challenge?'

Jim Pooley shrugged, slowly and thoughtfully. 'Nothing specific. Although—'

'Although what?' the professor asked.

'My freedom?' Jim suggested. 'Football management is a full-time job and full-time employment has never sat altogether easily down to dine with me. In fact, it's generally departed prior to the pudding course and without paying the bill.'

Professor Slocombe nodded once more. 'But imagine what might happen if you saw this job through to its successful conclusion. How much did you lay out upon bets with Bob the Bookie this morning, Jim?'

'The usual,' said Pooley. 'A fiver. And if the horses come in, then that five pounds will multiply itself to nearly half a million more pounds of a similar nature.'

'I'll tell you what.' Professor Slocombe put his glass aside. 'I'll buy your betting slip from you now for – what shall we say? – one hundred pounds.'

'One hundred pounds?' said Jim.

'One hundred.'

'No.' Jim shook his head. 'This slip could be worth half a million.'

'I'll bet you one hundred pounds that it isn't.'

'You're getting me all confused,' said Jim, finishing his champagne.

'Me too,' Omally agreed. 'Where's this leading?'

'It is leading this-a-ways,' the professor said. 'Jim has the courage of his convictions. He believes in what he does, even though others – specifically, in Jim's case, Bob the Bookie – do not. Jim presses on, day upon day, certain that eventually he will succeed.'

'I will,' said Jim. 'Please do not deny me my dreams, Professor.'

'I would do no such thing. That would be unthinkable and it would be cruel and callous. What I am saying, Jim, is that you are a man of conviction. You persevere. You stick to your guns and to what you believe.'

'Indeed so,' Jim agreed. 'I do that.'

'So you will bet again tomorrow, should you fail today.'

'I will,' Jim agreed also.

'Then why not bet upon a sure thing?'

'I fail to understand you, Professor.'

'What odds do you think Bob would give you against Brentford winning the FA Cup?'

Jim shrugged and grinned and laughed a little also. 'I've no idea. One hundred thousand to one, at the very least.'

Professor Slocombe raised a snowy eyebrow.

'Oh,' said Jim. 'Then you really think . . .'

'I'm sure of it.' Professor Slocombe now raised a thumb to go with his eyebrow. 'In fact, the more I think about it, the more certain I become. The two of you have added a certain piquancy, a certain spice to a day otherwise bland. I am prepared to apply myself to this project. I cannot force you to take up this challenge. I can, however, ask whether you have faith in my judgement.'

'Absolute faith,' said Jim, because he did.

'Then let us drink to success.'

Jim shrugged. 'To success,' he said.

'Brentford for the cup,' said John Omally.

And they drank.

And later they walked, away from the professor's house and back along the tree-lined drive to the everyday sprawl that was present-day Brentford.

Jim had his head down as he walked. His unfailing cheerfulness was definitely failing him. John Omally was sprightly enough.

'There are many pennies to be made out of this,' he told the cheerless Jim. 'I can see the two of us prospering greatly from this fortunate appointment of yours.'

Jim ceased his walking and glared pointy knives at his bestest friend. 'You have got me into some messes in the past,' he said, 'but nothing on the scale of this.'

'You'll be fine.' Omally made a bright and breezy face. 'With the professor behind you and me at your side, what can go wrong?'

Jim dug into his pockets and sought out his fags.

'And that reminds me,' said John Omally.

★

At length, they reached The Flying Swan. It was at a greater length than the usual walking distance from The Butts because the journey had taken in the Brentford allotments, where John had displayed to Jim the fruits of his morning's business. To whit, the five hundred packets of Dadarillos he had acquired that morning from the fellow in The Plume Café.

'Wallah,' went Omally, whipping back the potato sack to reveal the hoard.

'Oh, splendid,' said Jim. 'As if things couldn't get any worse, you have secreted a hoard of stolen cigarettes in my allotment shed, along with your horrible bike. Perfect. How can I ever thank you?'

'They are not stolen,' John explained. 'And as *I* purchased them with our shared entrepreneurial business funds, you are entitled to half of the profits, as soon as *you* have sold them all.'

'Oh lucky man me,' said Jim Pooley.

The at-length to The Flying Swan was also increased by Jim Pooley making his second visit of the day to the business premises of Bob the Bookie.

At least Jim had a smile back on his face when he left these business premises. As evidently did Bob, whose loud and joyous laughter followed Jim on his way.

'It is going to be such a pleasure to take his money,' Jim told John as they proceeded on their journey.

John patted Jim upon the back and at that greatened length they reached The Flying Swan.

It was lunchtime now and The Swan was going great guns in the trade department. Young pale-faced business types, who toiled away in the nearby Mowlems building at jobs which probably involved computers, spoke noisily over their halves of cider and Lighterman's lunches.[*] John and Jim elbowed their way towards the bar counter.

[*] As Brentford *is* upon Thames, Neville eschewed the hackneyed Ploughman's in favour of a waterborne alternative. At least as far as the title went.

'Two pints of Large, please, Neville,' said John. 'Jim is in the chair.'

'I'm penniless,' said Jim, 'so I am not.'

Neville looked his patrons up and down, then up and down once more.

John and Jim looked back at Neville.

'Would you both just mind turning full circle?' Neville asked.

'Excuse me?' said Jim.

'Humour me,' said Neville. 'A little twirl, but slowly, if you'll be so kind.'

'All right then.' Jim shrugged and did a little twirl, but slowly.

John shrugged also and joined him in this curious perambulation.

'Happy now?' Jim asked.

'Absolutely,' said Neville. 'I just wanted to get a really good look at you both, from all angles, as it were.'

'I see,' said Jim. 'But why?'

'Because it is the last look at the both of you that I will ever be taking. *You're both barred for life!*'

'What?' Jim's jaw fell, to land with a palpable clunk upon his chest. 'Barred?'

'Barred!' quoth Neville. 'Now kindly get out of my pub.'

'Hold on there, Neville.' John made a cheesy grin. 'That is not at all funny. Look at poor Jim, the colour's gone right out of his chops.'

'Barred,' said Neville and he bared his teeth. 'Traitorous, devious dogs. Out of my pub now or I'll take my knob-kerrie to the both of you.'

'Five more halves of cider over here,' called a pale-faced business type.

'Be with you in a moment, sir,' said Neville. 'As soon as I have evicted these two undesirable elements from the establishment.'

'Neville,' said John, 'have you become bereft of your senses? It's *us* – John and Jim, your favourite patrons.'

'Curs and rapscallions,' cried Neville, reaching below the counter for his knobkerrie.

'Neville, please.' John raised calming palms. 'Whatever is going on? What is all this about?'

'You know full well. You put him up to it, I know you did.' Neville glared at Jim with his good eye.

'What did I do?' Jim Pooley clutched at his heart.

'I've just had a phone call from Professor Slocombe,' said Neville.

'Ah,' said John.

'"*Ah?*" Is that all you have to say, "*Ah?*"' Neville now raised his knobkerrie.

'I think I'll be heading back to the office,' said the pale-faced business type.

'It's not my fault,' wailed Jim. 'I didn't volunteer for the job. It was all Professor Slocombe's idea.'

'I trusted you.' Neville waggled his knobkerrie in Jim's direction. 'And I trusted this Irish ne'er-do-well. And what do you do? Stab me in the back, that's what you do.'

Jim Pooley shook his head. 'Never,' he said. 'We never did. We never would.'

'Manager!' Neville had a good old shake on now. His good eye bulged from its socket. 'You couldn't manage a knees-up in a whore house.'

'Neville, calm yourself.' John leaned forward across the bar counter. 'This could really work to your benefit. Allow me to explain. You see—'

But John Omally said no more, as at that moment Neville swung his knobkerrie and bopped him on the head. John's eyes crossed and then they closed and John sank slowly to the carpet.

Jim looked down in horror. Words tried to form in his mouth, but could not. He raised a bitter gaze towards Neville and prepared to leap across the counter and exact a bloody revenge.

But Neville swung his club once more.

And Pooley hit the deck.

71

8

Norman pressed home the bolts on the shop door and turned the 'open' sign to 'closed'. Norman always loved his Wednesday afternoons, when at one he could shut up shop and engage in his own activities. With Peg, his over-sized other half, off at her weekly meeting with the Chiswick Townswomen's Guild, Norman's time was his own. Certainly he was supposed to remove himself to the wholesalers to stock up on Pontefract cakes and liquorice sticks and jujubes and sherbet lemons. But as folk never bought those sweeties any more, and the jars that lined the dusty shelves always remained full, it didn't really matter anyway.

Norman divested himself of his brown shopkeeper's coat and hung it behind the door of the kitchenette, taking unto himself the patched jacket of green Boleskine tweed that had been his father's before him and slipping it on as if it were a loving glove. Norman let himself out through the back door, locking it behind him, and sauntered off to his lock-up in Abaddon Street.

Now, a lock-up garage is a wonderful thing, almost as wonderful in its way as an allotment shed. It is a 'man's' place, full of a man's accoutrements: tools and spare parts and things that no longer work because they need a few spare parts to set them going, and boxes of old magazines that must not be thrown away because there are interesting articles in them that might one day be interesting to read. And as with an allotment shed, or indeed a garden shed, there is always a half-bag of gone-solid cement that you always fall over when you come in. Which is there, as we all know, because it is a tradition, or an old charter, or something.

Norman unlocked and swung up-and-over the up-and-over garage door, stood in the entranceway and breathed in the ambience of his lock-up. It smelt good. It smelt of a man's accoutrements, of tools and spare parts and things that no longer worked because . . . and so on and so forth and such like.

Norman smiled the smile of inward satisfaction, stepped forward into his garage and fell over a half-bag of gone-solid cement. Righting himself, Norman smiled some more and sought out his car keys. Because Norman owned a car. Well, not a car as such – it was more of a van. In fact, it *was* a van. An Austin A40 van that Norman was restoring. And not only restoring, but improving, enginewise.

Norman had certain theories regarding the internal combustion engine, mostly of the nature that it was a most inefficient means of powering an automobile. Norman was working on an alternative drive system for the A40 van, a revolutionary new method of automotive propulsion. It was near to completion and only needed a few spare parts to keep it going as smoothly as he would have liked.

It was not your everyday revolutionary new method of automotive propulsion. This was something quite different.

Norman had modestly named it the Hartnel Grumpiness Hyper-Drive. It would, in Norman's humble opinion, bring joy to millions and millions of drivers who drove old and unreliable automobiles. Folk such as himself, for instance.

The genesis of this particular invention had come about when Norman had purchased a book called *The Power of Positive Thought*, written by some American woman with big hair and a lot of letters after her name that didn't seem to spell out anything sensible. Norman had read this book from cover to cover and then tossed it into the fire, where it burned most warmly, which was about the most positive thing it had done since Norman had purchased it.

The book was a load of old New Age toot, but it had set

Norman to thinking. What if you could harness the power of *negative* thought? There was surely a great deal of *that* in the world just going begging. If you could tune into *that* you'd surely have a source of almost infinite power. Because everyone, it seemed to Norman, was almost always in a bad mood about something.

Norman had been mulling this concept over in his mind whilst he drove along in his old Austin A40 van. In fact, he'd been mulling it over when the van did as it so often did – stuttered from life and rattled to a halt in the middle of busy traffic. Norman swore wildly at his van, bashing at its steering wheel with his fists. He got into a very bad temper. There was a lot of negative energy buzzing about in that van.

And so was born the Hartnel Grumpiness Hyper-Drive. Fuelled, if you like, upon road rage.

Norman had pushed the van back to the lock-up and broken out the Meccano set.

So far things had not been going quite as the scientific shopkeeper might have hoped with the Hartnel Grumpiness Hyper-Drive. But then, thought Norman, that was the problem. He shouldn't be *hopeful* about this project. Hope was positive. He should be gloomy, taciturn, without hope, he should begrudge every moment that he spent on the project. He should hate every moment, build up so much negative energy that the van would run for fifty years without requiring further shouting at.

Norman climbed into the driving seat and placed upon his head a helmet constructed from Meccano and Christmas-tree lights. Many wires ran out of the helmet and away to vanish beneath the dashboard where many complicated (and, many cynics might claim, ludicrous) electronic doodads of Norman's design and construction were linked to the mechanical gubbins that were the Austin's engine parts.

Norman keyed the ignition.

Nothing whatever happened.

Norman keyed the ignition again.

The result was identical.

'Start, you swine!' cried Norman. 'You useless, stupid van! Start, will you!'

The engine caught and *brmm brmm brmmed*.

'Brilliant,' said Norman. 'Good boy.'

The engine died.

'No,' shouted Norman. 'I didn't mean brilliant. I meant start, you pathetic . . .'

'*Brmm brmm brmm*,' went the engine. Norman swore and scowled and backed the van out of the lock-up garage.

In the past, if Norman had been going anywhere by van he would have taken great pains to plot his course in advance upon a London A–Z. Not so now. Now, if Norman had a destination in mind, he purposely drove in the wrong direction with the intention of losing himself. Losing himself made Norman angry, and the van ran so much better when he was angry.

As Norman drove up the Ealing Road he was quite surprised to see an ambulance parked before The Flying Swan and a bit of a crowd gathered about it. Norman took a right into the area where the blocks of flats stood because it was a really tricky place to drive through. You could get quite upset by all the speed ramps and one-way systems.

Norman's van *brmmed* away.

Norman growled at the speed ramps and the Christmas-tree lights on his Meccano helmet glowed brightly.

Norman was late for his appointment.

'Bloody van!' he explained upon his arrival.

The fellow with whom Norman had this appointment did rollings of the eyes, which Norman found most alarming.

'Do you want these computer parts, or what?' the fellow asked.

'I certainly do,' said Norman. 'Where are they?'

Norman and the fellow stood beneath the shadow of railway arches. These railway arches were on the border of Chiswick, which Norman also found most alarming as they were relatively near to where his wide-loaded wife would be having her weekly meeting.

'They're in here.' The fellow, a small, squat fellow with an over-large head and curious smell, fumbled a key into an antique padlock. 'I've just inherited these premises and all this old gear is stored inside. I just want it all cleared out. You can take as much as you want – all of it, if you want, I won't charge you.'

'That's most generous,' said Norman.

'It's not,' said the fellow, 'because it's all junk.'

'One man's junk is another man's treasure,' said Norman.

'Not in this case.' The fellow forced open the door, which creaked and groaned upon its hinges.

Norman peered into the all-but-darkness. 'Who did this place belong to?' he asked.

'My granddad,' said the fellow. 'The stuff belonged to him, I suppose.'

'Computer parts?'

'They're *very old* computer parts.'

Norman's eyes were becoming accustomed to the dark. He peered into the gloom. Inside there were many crates, many Victorian-looking crates. Many of these Victorian-looking crates had been prised open. They all appeared to contain—

'Computer parts?' said Norman once more. 'These look more like old wireless parts. They're all valves and—' Norman took a couple of steps into the gloom of the archway and lifted up bits and bobs for perusal. 'Mostly valves.'

'It says "computer parts" on the crates,' said the fellow. 'See.' He pointed through the gloom. There, on the side: *Computer Components. Babbage Nineteen-Hundred Series.*'

'Babbage,' said Norman, thoughtfully. 'The only Babbage I've ever heard of who has a connection with computers is Charles Babbage. He invented the Difference Engine in 1832. It was considered to be the world's first computer.'

'There you go, then,' said the fellow. 'They're all museum pieces, aren't they?'

'I don't think they're exactly what I was looking for,' said Norman. 'I was hoping for something a little more "state of the art".'

'For free?'

'Well, there's no harm in hoping. Hope springs eternal and the language of truth is simplicity.'

'And my dog's arse smells of margarine,' said the fellow. 'Do you want this gear or not? Because if you don't, I'll get a skip down here tomorrow and bin the lot.'

'No,' said Norman. 'I'll take it. I'll take it all.' He peered all around and about. There were *a lot* of crates. 'It will take a few journeys, though. I will get very angry if my van doesn't work properly.'

It was seven o'clock in the evening before Norman had the last of the crates installed in his lock-up. There was now no room for his van.

'Damn it!' swore Norman.

His van *brmmed* its engine.

'Not now,' Norman told it. 'Nice van, be quiet now.'

The van switched off its engine.

Norman locked up the garage, locked up the van and took himself off for a pint of Large at The Flying Swan.

He entered the saloon bar to find Neville engaged in conversation with two young policemen from the local constabulary. Norman recognised these two to be none other than Constables Russell Meek and Arthur Mild, regular botherers of Norman.

'It's not what you think,' Neville was heard to say. 'And I won't be pressing charges.'

'Pressing charges?' Constables Meek and Mild did *ho-ho-ho-ings* in the manner of the now legendary Laughing Policeman.

'It's hardly a matter of *you* pressing charges, now is it, sir?' said Constable Meek.

'I'm the injured party,' Neville protested.

'Not quite so injured as your two victims, who even

now lie recovering from concussion in the Cottage Hospital.'

'They're not badly hurt, are they?' Neville was heard to ask.

'They'll survive. Thick skulls, the both of them. And the both of them *known faces*, as it were.'

'I've been under a lot of strain,' said Neville. 'They drove me to it.'

'You'll be pleading diminished responsibility, then,' said Constable Mild, 'at your trial.'

'Trial?' Neville's good eye rolled.

Norman found this most alarming. What *was* with all this eye-rolling today? 'Evening, Neville,' said Norman. 'Pint of Large, please.'

'Ah,' said Constable Meek, 'it's Brentford's Porn King.'

Norman ground his dentures. 'I'm *not* Brentford's Porn King,' he protested. 'Those magazines arrived by mistake. They weren't what I ordered.'

'You had them in your rack,' said Constable Meek. 'What were they, now? *Cissies On Parade*, the "periodical for businessmen who like to dress as babies". And *Banged Up and Gun-Totin'*, "naked pregnant women with Uzis".'

'It came as just as much of a shock to me,' said Norman. 'I'd ordered *Airfix Monthly* and *Meccano World*.'

'A likely story.' Constable Meek did titterings.

Neville drew Norman a pint of the very best.

'But let us not be distracted from the business at hand.' Constable Meek fingered his brand-new extendible truncheon. 'Should your victims choose to press charges, you'll be looking at a five-stretch, minimum.'

'*Five years?* Cheese!' Neville's face became the mask of fear.

'I love it when their faces do that,' said Constable Mild. 'Makes the job worthwhile, in my opinion.'

'You'll be out in two and a half with good behaviour,' said Old Pete, who had not left his bar stool all day but for the occasional visit to the gents.

'Who did you assault, Neville?' Norman asked as he took

control of his pint and paid for same with the exact amount of pennies and halfpennies.

'I didn't assault anyone,' said Neville.

'He did,' said Old Pete. 'Pooley and Omally. Laid the two of them out, stone cold.'

'You were a witness to this, then, were you, sir?' Constable Meek asked Old Pete.

'Excuse me?' said the ancient.

'You saw the assault occur?'

'You'll have to speak up, my hearing aid is faulty.'

'You witnessed the occurrence!' shouted Constable Meek.

'Did what?' asked Old Pete. 'Pit test the old currants, did you say?'

'That's not what I said.'

'Forget it,' said Constable Mild. 'He's a loon.'

'Up yours, pointy head,' muttered Old Pete.

'What did you say?'

'Excuse me?' said the ancient. 'You'll have to speak up a bit.'

'You're warned,' said Constable Meek to Neville. 'And if your victims do choose to press charges, you're in real trouble. We'll be keeping a close eye on this place. Any more bother and you'll kiss goodbye to your licence and say hello to incarceration.'

And then they left. The two of them. The boys in blue.

'Bastards,' said Old Pete. 'Cossacks.'

Norman tasted ale.

'What?' said Neville. 'What are you looking at?'

'Sorry.' Norman busied himself with further ale-tasting.

'Bop,' went Old Pete, miming mighty boppings with his crinkly paws. 'Just like the Wolf of Kabul swinging Clicki Ba.'

Neville made growling sounds under his breath.

'My glass is unaccountably empty,' said Old Pete, staring into said glass and making a quizzical face. Neville snatched the glass away from the elder and returned it once more to the dark-rum optic.

'Bop?' Norman whispered 'bop' and mimed a muted bopping of his own while Neville's back was turned. 'He really bopped both Jim and John on the head?'

'A real treat, it was.' Old Pete sniggered. 'It's not the sort of mindless violence you see every day, especially not in here. The last time I saw someone get a walloping like that was in one of those dodgy videos you hired me.'

'I didn't know what was on them.' Norman did *sssh-ings* with his fingers. 'They arrived as a job lot. I'd never even heard of a snuff movie. I thought it was, well, about snuff, I suppose.'

Old Pete shook his old and wrinkly head. 'You are a caution, Norman, you well and truly are.'

'If that's a compliment, I'll take it.' The shopkeeper raised his glass. 'Honey catches more flies than vinegar, you know.'

Neville thrust Old Pete's tipple before him and stalked away along the bar to serve a wandering bishop who'd stopped in for a swift one before heading down to the annual congress in the deconsecrated Anabaptist Chapel on the corner of Moby Dick Terrace.

'So,' said Old Pete, 'apart from dodgy videos and girly magazines, how goes the world with you, young Norman?'

'Fraught as ever.' Norman made the face of one who knew the meaning of 'fraught'. 'But I had a bit of luck this afternoon. Answered an ad. A chap giving away crates of computer parts.'

'Giving away?' Old Pete mused upon this concept, but concluded that it meant nothing to him.

'Took me ten journeys in the van.' Norman dragged the last bit of liquid pleasure from his pint glass. 'Couldn't even get the van into my lock-up afterwards.'

'Someone will nick that old van of yours.'

'I can assure you that they won't.' Norman grinned as evilly as his amiable visage would allow. 'It has certain security features built into it. I built them in myself.'

'It will be gone already, then. I have an old handcart I can. let you have at a price that might at first appear reasonable.'

'I'm fine,' said Norman. 'One hand washes the other, you know, and a washed pot never boils.'

'So what are these computer parts? A lot of super-annuated old toot, I'll wager.'

'Well, they're certainly not new. There's nearly forty crates of them, labelled on the side as parts from something called a Babbage Nineteen-Hundred Series.'

Old Pete coughed suddenly into his rum, sending a jet of it up his right nostril to cause him further distress. He coughed and wheezed and Norman took to smiting him between his crook-backed shoulder blades.

'Lay off me, you hoodlum!' Old Pete raised up his stick and Chips bared his teeth towards the Samaritan shop-keeper's ankles.

'I'm only trying to help.'

'Then leave me alone.'

'You seemed to be having some kind of fit.'

'I'm all right.' Old Pete pushed Norman away, took up what was left of his rum and tossed it down his throat.

'Same again for the both of us,' called Norman to Neville.

Neville, who appeared to be having some kind of dispute with the wandering bishop, did not hear him.

'You did say Babbage, didn't you?' Old Pete was almost his old self once more. 'Babbage Nineteen-Hundred Series?'

'That's what it says on the crates.' Norman waved his hands towards Neville. 'Same again over here, Neville, please.'

Neville, however, was still engaged in words with the wandering bishop. Heated words, these seemed to be, although Norman could not quite hear what they were.

'Burn them,' said Old Pete. 'Burn the lot of them now, Norman.'

'That's a bit harsh.' Norman regarded the old scoundrel. 'Every man has the right to worship in the church of his choice. I've nothing against wandering bishops. In fact, I really like their hats.'

'The crates, Norman, you buffoon. The computer parts. If you know what's good for you, you'll burn them all.'

'Burn them?' Norman's face was one of considerable surprise. 'Why would I want to burn the crates?'

'Let's just say that what's in 'em is dangerous. Very dangerous. I know what I'm talking about and I'm giving you sound advice. Trust me, I'm a pensioner.'

'You're drunk,' said Norman. 'Alcohol has addled your brain.'

'Norman.' Old Pete leaned forward on his bar stool and grasped Norman's tweedy lapels. 'You don't know what you've got there. You really don't. I thought all that stuff was done with years and years ago. It mustn't start again. Do you understand me?' And Old Pete shook feebly at the lapels of Norman.

'I don't understand. Calm yourself down.'

Old Pete's fingers trailed away. 'Burn them all. Or by the God of gardeners, *I'll* do it for you.'

And with that said, Old Pete left The Flying Swan, his loyal Chips hard upon his down-at-heels.

The door swung shut upon the decrepit departer and Norman's eyes turned away from it and returned once more to the bar.

Just in time to see Neville striking down the wandering bishop with his knobkerrie.

'I think I'll head off home now,' said Norman to himself. 'Under a ragged coat lies wisdom and there's no peace for the wicked.'

9

Jim Pooley felt decidedly strange. He sat in his bed at the Cottage Hospital and viewed tiny stars and sailing ships and sausages and sprouts.

'I can't imagine why I'm seeing sprouts,' said Jim. 'I'm sure it's the wrong time of year for sprouts.' Jim gingerly fingered his aching head. Jim's aching head was swathed in bandages. To the casual observer it would have appeared that Jim had taken up Sikhism.

'What would I know?' asked the casual observer in the bed next to Jim. 'I only came in here to deliver a parcel and they've taken out my appendix.'

'My head hurts,' said Jim Pooley.

'You're always complaining.' This voice belonged to John Omally, who lay in the bed to Jim's right, the casual observer being in the bed to Jim's left (looking in from the door, of course).

'I am unfailingly cheerful,' said Jim. 'And I never complain,' he complained.

'Then I'll complain for you,' said Omally. 'Even though neither of us is little more than bruised, I'll have that Neville for this. He will pay for the unwarranted violence that he visited upon us.'

'It wasn't his fault, John,' said Jim, who, even on his bed of pain, was still a caring fellow. 'He'd had a rough day. The professor's choice of me as team manager came as just as much of a shock to him as it did to me. I think I'll quit the job now before anything else happens. Will I get redundancy money, do you think?'

'I think you'll get a smack from me if you don't shut up.'

'It's all your fault,' said Jim, sulkily. 'You got me into this mess.'

'I had a dog once,' said the casual observer. 'Used to chase cars.'

'Fascinating,' said Jim.

'Used to catch them, too,' said the casual observer. 'Big dog, it was, the size of a small barn. Or Switzerland.'

'Which ward are we in?' Jim asked John.

'Which one do you think?' John made circular finger motions against the side of his bandaged head.

'Ah,' said Jim. '*That* ward.'

'So, are you a Sikh, too?' the casual observer asked John. 'I see you're wearing the same turban as this bloke.'

'No,' said John. 'I'm a berserker. I suffer from a rare syndrome that manifests itself in bursts of uncontrollable violence when I'm questioned about anything.'

'How did you catch that?' asked the casual observer. 'No, let me put that another way. Very nice to meet you. Good night.' And he turned upon his right-hand side (when looking from the door, of course) and feigned snorings.

'We have to get out of here,' said Jim. 'I dearly need a drink. And a fag, actually.'

'I don't think we'll be drinking in The Flying Swan tonight.'

Jim shook his aching head. 'This is a terrible business, John,' he said. 'To be barred from The Flying Swan – that is as bad as it is possible for things to be.'

'There are many other bars in Brentford, Jim.'

'Take that back,' said Jim. 'There is no other bar like The Flying Swan.'

'You are, of course, right.' John Omally leaned back upon his comfy pillows. 'I think we'd do best to rest up here for the night. Gather our senses. Regain our vitality.' John reached out and pressed the little button on the wall beside his bed.

'What are you doing?' Pooley enquired.

'Summonsing the nurse,' said John. 'Did you get a look at

her through your stars and sprouts? She's a rare beauty. I thought I'd ask her to give me a bed bath.'

'I think I'll get some sleep, then.'

'Good idea, my friend. I'll have the nurse put the screens around my bed. And I'll try to keep the noise down.'

'Good night, then, John,' said Jim.

'Good night, Jim,' said John.

'Goodnight, Ma, goodnight, Pa, goodnight, John Boy,' said the casual observer, who was a fan of *The Waltons*.

Norman should have called it a night and simply gone back home, but somehow he couldn't. He had no idea exactly what had come over Old Pete, nor why the haggard horticulturalist should have got himself into such a state at the mention of the Babbage Nineteen-Hundred Series computer parts. But Norman did feel somewhat excited about all those computer parts, particularly because all those computer parts were the sort of computer parts that Norman could really come to terms with. He'd never really got on with microchip technology. It was all too small. You couldn't tinker at it with a big screwdriver. Valves and diodes and valves and more valves – that was what technology was supposed to be about. That was what it was all about when Norman had been a lad, when he'd read *Popular Mechanics* and *Popular Science*. Not to mention *Modern Mechanix and Inventions* and *Mechanics and Handicrafts* and *Science and Mechanics*. That Hugo Gernsback knew exactly what the future was supposed to look like. It was supposed to look BIG. Huge flying-wing aircraft powered by dozens of propellers, with folk supping cocktails on glass sundecks. And vast cars that seated a dozen well-dressed future folk, who also supped cocktails as they cruised along twelve-lane superhighways. Such cars had big fins on the back and a great deal of chrome. And domes on the top, of course. *Everything* had a dome on top. Your house had a dome on top. And your dog, of course, and you, too, if you were taking your dog for a walk on the moon. Near to the moon base. Which was inside a great big dome.

Norman sighed for this future that hadn't come to pass. Hugo's vision of tomorrow had been thwarted by the coming of the microchip. The future really should have been worked by valves. The future should have been BIG.

And so Norman returned to his lock-up garage.

He upped the up-and-over, switched on the light as it was getting dusky out, then downed the up-and-over and viewed the stacks of crates. It was a nearby viewing. Norman edged around the stacks, avoiding the half-sack of gone-solid cement.

'The thing to do,' said Norman to himself, 'would be to dig into the crates, sort out enough bits and bobs to assemble a complete computer. Then whip them back to the shop in the van and piece them all together. But—'

Norman lifted a suitable tool from a rack upon the garage wall and took to prising the lid from an uppermost crate. 'An instruction manual or book of assembly diagrams would be helpful.'

Norman peered into the crate he had opened: lots of waxed paper and lots of valves. Splendid.

Norman opened further crates and upon his opening of the fifth was heard to cry out (at least by himself) the magic word – Eureka.

'Eureka,' Norman cried out. And he drew into the light afforded by the naked flyspecked dangling bulb a cloth-bound booklet which had inscribed in gold upon its cover the words *Babbage 1900 Series Computer Assembly Manual*.

Norman leafed through the pages, *oohing* and *ahhing* to equal degree. And then he began to open other crates, marvelling at their contents and setting this, and indeed lots of the other, aside.

And when several hours had passed, Norman was done with all of his settings aside. He loaded all he had set aside into a number of emptied crates and loaded these into the back of his Austin A40 van.

And having turned off the light and secured the lock on his lock-up, Norman climbed into his van, donned his Meccano and Christmas-light helmet, keyed the ignition, swore loudly at his van and returned home in time to receive a good telling off for missing his dinner.

Night fell upon Brentford.

Neville evicted the last of his patrons, drew the bolts upon The Swan's saloon bar door, switched off the bar lights and took himself off to bed. Where he spent a fitful night, his dreams beset with images of high-security prisons, where he was banged up at Her Majesty's pleasure in a small and dismal cell, in the company of a tattooed Neanderthal lifer who referred to himself as 'The Daddy' and Neville as his 'bitch'.

Jim Pooley also spent a troubled night. His dreams were of football, with Jim being called on to the pitch to substitute for the Brentford striker who had been shot by a sniper during a penalty shootout with Real Madrid. And Jim was trying really hard to kick the ball, but his feet kept sticking to the turf and the ball wasn't a ball at all, but a sprout. And the Real Madrid goalie certainly wasn't a goalie, he was some sort of dragon.

And Jim kept getting woken up by all this noise coming from the bed to the right of him (when looking from the door). All this grunting and erotic moaning and—

Jim fell back asleep and dreamed some more about football.

Professor Slocombe rarely slept. He sat long into the night poring over ancient and not-so-ancient tomes. He pored over the *Roy of the Rovers* annual and Rommel's *How to Win Tank Battles Bedside Companion* and the autobiography of Alexander the Great and *The Necronomicon* (naturally) and *Death Wears A Tottenham Strip* (a Lazlo Woodbine thriller) and a copy of *Banged Up and Gun Totin'* that had been delivered with his morning paper by mistake. And at four in the morning he slept for an hour in his chair and dreamed an alternative and far cleverer ending to the last episode of *The Prisoner*.

Mahatma Campbell slept and dreamed, but what he dreamed of when *he* slept, only the Campbell knew.

Others slept and dreamed of Brentford. Old Pete, for instance – he slept and dreamed and his dreams were troubled, troubled by memories he had long suppressed. Memories of things which he knew to be true, but had spent a lifetime convincing himself were otherwise.

And Gwynplaine Dhark slept, but didn't dream.

And John Omally eventually slept and did. And his dreams were of a pretty nurse and John enjoyed these dreams.

And so the folk of Brentford slept and mostly dreamed.

And the moon was in its seventh house and Jupiter was in alignment with Mars.

And eventually something *cock-a-doodle-do'd* and a new day came to Brentford.

10

John Omally woke and yawned and wakened not the nurse who slept beside him. Divesting himself of his bandage turban, he slipped from his bed of not-too-much-pain-really and nudged the sleeping Pooley.

The sleeping Pooley woke to find the face of John Omally grinning down upon him.

'Wah?' went Jim. 'What are you doing in my boudoir?'

'You're in the hospital,' John told him. 'Summon up your powers and let's be on our way.'

'Oh yes,' mumbled Jim. 'I remember.'

'Up and at 'em, Mr Manager,' said John. 'The borough's relying on you.'

Jim's mumbling became a groan. 'I really hoped I'd just dreamed yesterday,' said he.

'Well, you didn't,' said John. 'I'll treat you to a breakfast at The Plume, then we'll get down to business.'

'We?' queried Pooley.

'We,' said John. 'We're in this together, I told you, thick and thin. We're the boys, aren't we? The boys from Brentford.'

'There appears to be a penguin in your bed,' said the casual observer, 'from where I'm lying, of course. Which must be on the left, if you're looking from the door. Although I might be wrong.'

'First thing, then,' said John, as he and Pooley took to their breakfasts in The Plume Café, 'is to go to the ground and get you settled into your manager's office.'

'First thing,' said Jim, 'is for me to go to Norman,

purchase my copy of *Sporting Life* and make my selections for the day. And check on the results for yesterday. I might already be a multi-millionaire.'

'No,' said John, a-shaking of his slightly bruised but otherwise undamaged head.

'No?' said Jim, a-shaking of his head in a similar fashion.

'Those days are behind you. You are a man of responsibility now.'

'I don't want this,' said Jim. 'I really don't.'

'You trust the professor, though.'

'He has a rare sense of humour. He might just be winding us up.'

'I don't think so.' John tucked into his double eggs.

'Woe unto the house of Pooley,' quoth Jim, 'for it is surely undone.'

'Another cup of tea?' asked John.

'A mug,' said Jim, taking out a Dadarillo and lighting it. 'I need to keep my strength up.'

There was a degree of unpleasantness.

In fact, it was more than just a single degree.

In fact, there were sufficient degrees involved to construct an isosceles triangle.

Mahatma Campbell, groundskeeper of Griffin Park[*], refused the team's new manager's entrance.

'Open up these gates,' demanded Jim.

'I know you,' spat the Campbell. 'I know you well, wee laddie.'

'Hear that,' said Jim to John. 'The team may not know me, but *he* does. This is *such* a bad idea.'

'The Campbell knows everyone,' said John. 'He knows Professor Slocombe, don't you, Campbell?'

There was more unpleasantness, and much shouting from the Campbell, but eventually much limping off to the

---

[*] For so it is written, that no matter wherever a groundskeeper will be employed, that groundskeeper will *always* be a Scotsman. (Check out *The Simpsons* if you are in doubt.)

telephone and much grudging limping back and even greater grudging unlockings of the gate.

'I willna call ya sir,' the Campbell told Jim. 'And I have this job fer life here. It's in m'contract, so dinna think of sacking me.'

'It was the furthest thing from my mind,' said Pooley. 'Would you kindly lead the way to my office?'

Now, there are offices. And there are *offices*.

Some offices are directors' offices. These are well-appointed offices, they are spacious and luxurious, with a window that occupies the entirety of one wall through which can be viewed panoramic cityscape skylines.

Other offices are poky and wretched, like those of downbeat private eyes, for instance, such as Lazlo Woodbine, the fictional gumshoe created by the mercurial mind of P.P. Penrose (Brentford's most famous and fêted writer of detective 'genre' fiction). Such offices as these have a ceiling fan that revolves turgidly above fixtures and fittings of the direst persuasion: a filing cabinet with few files to call its own; a water cooler that steams gently throughout the summer months; a desk that one would not care to sit at, accompanied by a chair that no one would ever care to sit upon; and a carpet that, should it receive a description, certainly doesn't deserve one.

Jim Pooley viewed the office that was now his own.

'Well appointed,' said Jim, approvingly.

'Poky and wretched,' said John Omally, 'but nothing a lick of paint won't cure.'

'And see, John,' said Jim, 'a desk of my very own. Do you think it has anything in its drawers?'

'I think I'll open the windows,' said John, 'and let the bluebottles out.'

'Isn't it interesting?' Jim sat down in the manager's chair that was now his own and had a little swivel about on it. 'It should be *me* complaining, but it's not. It's you. How would you explain this, John?'

'I'm only thinking of your interests,' said Omally, who certainly was not. 'I want what's best for you. Perhaps we could knock through a wall, put in a Jacuzzi and a sofa bed?'

'I can't imagine why I'd need those.'

'I can,' said John. 'But you certainly have a good view of the ground from here.' John viewed this view through a window that did not occupy the entirety of one wall, but a tiny portion thereof instead. 'You can almost see the full length of the pitch.'

'There'd be a director's box, wouldn't there?' said Jim. 'There's always a director's box. We'd sit in there during a match and drink champagne whilst cheering the team on to victory.'

'You'll be sitting down by the pitch.' John pointed in that direction. 'Encouraging the team to victory.'

'You know what, John?' said Jim, now leaning back in his chair. 'There's no real reason why *I* should do this job at all. *You* could do it. It's only following the professor's instructions, passing the tactics on to the team. And you have plenty of natural charisma. The team would listen to you. Especially the centre forward – I understand that you are not unacquainted with his wife.'

'Oh no,' said John, 'the professor chose you and I agree with his choice. You deserve a chance, Jim. It's your right. I will act as your PA, take away any weight that might bear down upon your noble shoulders.'

'What is a PA?' Jim asked.

'Personal assistant,' said John. 'It's what posh directors have. While they loaf about in their offices and consume liquid lunches, the PAs do all the real hard graft.'

'So what real hard graft would you be doing?'

'Oh, you know, running things generally, things unconnected with the training of the team. Such as the bar, for instance, making sure that it has enough beer beneath its pumps. And the club shop, of course. There are more things that it could be selling than reproduction team shirts. And there's buying and selling of players and all kinds of similar tedious stuff. You don't have to worry about any of that, Jim. I'll take care of the lot of it.'

'You're a saint,' said Jim. 'And you're hired.'

'I'll draw up a contract,' said John. 'You can sign it later. Or I'll sign it for you, to save your precious time.'

'Excellent,' said Jim Pooley. 'So what do you think we should do first?'

'How about a stroll around the grounds?'

It was a sad and sombre stroll, for although it had to be said that Mahatma Campbell certainly maintained a fine pitch (many football pundits agreeing that, but for Wembley, Brentford has always had the finest pitch in the country) the rest of the Griffin Park ground left very much to be desired. It was wretched, it was run down and it was going to pieces. And it was now all Jim's responsibility. And the terrible weight of this responsibility pressed down upon the aforementioned noble shoulders of the lad.

'Those stands don't look very safe,' observed Jim in a mournful tone.

'They just need a lick of paint,' said John, taking a notebook from his pocket and making notes in it with a pencil.

'The toilets really pong,' observed Jim in a nasal tone.

'They just need a scrub down with Harpic,' said John, making further notes.

'The shop is wretched,' observed Jim in a hopeless tone.

'Not for much longer.' John made further notes.

'The bar is really dank,' observed Jim in the tone of a soul that is forever lost.

'It's opening time,' said John, tucking away his notebook.

The Stripes Bar was long and low and loathsome and seemed to lack for everything that made a pub a pub. Behind the jump stood Mr Rumpelstiltskin the barman, a grave and sad-looking fellow who did not ooze *bonhomie*.

'The beer's not very good,' observed Jim a few scant minutes later. 'It's funny how it always tasted better when we'd slip in here for a late-nighter.' Jim's shoulders sank. He was doomed. All doomed.

'I'll sort it,' said John, making further notes. 'You wait until tomorrow.'

'It seems,' said Jim, 'that you *will* be working much harder than I will. But then, as I am contemplating suicide, you may well have to go it alone.'

'Perk up, my friend. We're in this together. We'll succeed.' John raised his glass to Jim and the two men drank in silence.

They drank in silence for some considerable time. This silence was not disturbed by further patrons entering The Stripes Bar.

'Doesn't anyone ever come in here on weekdays?' Jim asked the barman.

'You're the first I've seen in years,' the barman replied. 'I only open up at lunchtimes out of a sense of tradition. Personally, I'd rather be golfing.'

'Doomed, doomed, doomed,' intoned Jim.

'Jim,' said John, and suddenly a very big grin appeared upon his face. 'Jim, do you realise what this means?'

Jim Pooley shook his head. 'That I am doomed?' said he. 'I know.'

John steered Jim away from the dire bar counter to an equally dire yet out-of-ear-shot-of-the-barman corner. 'Jim, *you* are the manager of Brentford United Football Club.'

'Please don't rub it in,' said Jim. 'I'm suffering enough.'

'But Jim, as the manager of Brentford Football Club, you are therefore also the manager of this bar.'

Jim glanced about it in all directions. And Jim did mighty shudderings. 'Doom and gloom and more doom,' said he.

'No.' John shook his head. 'You don't realise it, but you've *really* fallen on your feet here. Jim, this is *your* pub. Neville might have barred us from The Swan, but it doesn't matter now.'

'It doesn't?' said Jim, who was certain that it did.

'It doesn't because you now have a pub of your very own.'

It took Jim a moment or two to digest this intelligence.

But when this moment or two had passed, he stared into the face of his bestest friend.

'A pub of my very own?' mouthed Jim at the enormity of this proposition.

'Perk of the job,' said John. 'And we'll have one over on Neville here.'

'A pub of my very own?'

. 'To manage as you see fit.'

'No,' said Jim. 'No.'

'No?' said John.

'Oh no, John, this is not a pub of *my* very own. This is pub of *our* very own. This is *our* pub.'

John smiled upon his bestest friend. 'I'll get the drinks in, then,' said he.

'On me,' said Jim.

'No, on me.'

'I insist,' said Jim.

'No,' said John, 'I do. Although . . .' John paused.

'What prompts this pausing?' Jim enquired.

'I'm just wondering why either of us should pay. After all, this is *our* pub.'

'Barman,' called Jim, 'two more of same over here, and have one yourself, if you will.'

'Having another?' Neville asked Old Pete. The elder sat upon his usual stool before The Swan's bar counter.

'No,' said Pete. 'I'm all right for now.'

Neville cast a wary eye at Old Pete. 'Not feeling yourself?' he enquired. 'They're still on the house, as if you'd forgotten.'

'I don't want to take advantage.'

Chips looked up at his ancient master and cocked his furry head upon one side.

'Change of heart?' asked Neville. 'I thought you had determined to bankrupt me.'

'I'm sorry,' said Old Pete. 'About yesterday. About taking advantage like that.'

'You *are* ill.' Neville made a face of genuine concern.

Certainly Old Pete was a rogue, but Neville would never have wished any harm to come to him. 'Do you want me to call you a cab, or a medic or something?'

'Don't be an arse, Neville. You're a decent bloke. I wasn't going to ponce free drinks off you for ever.'

'There's something not right.' Neville drew off another rum for Old Pete and placed it before him. 'Do you want to tell me about it?'

'If I did, you'd think I was mad. And you'd never believe me anyway.'

'Try me,' said Neville. 'I'm a publican, after all. I've heard pretty much everything there is to hear during my long years in the trade.'

'You've never heard anything like this, I assure you.'

Neville was intrigued. 'Go on,' he said, 'tell me.'

Old Pete glanced about the bar. It wasn't busy. A salesman travelling in tobaccos and ready-rolled cigarettes chatted with a pimply youth who referred to himself as 'Scoop' Molloy and worked for the *Brentford Mercury*. Office types drank halves of cider and munched on their Lighterman's lunches.

'If I tell you,' said Old Pete, 'you have to promise me that you will never tell another living soul. Can you promise me that, Neville?'

'I can.' Neville licked his finger. 'See this wet,' he said, and then wiped it upon his jacket. 'See this dry. Cut my throat if I tell a lie.'

Old Pete sighed. 'You're a Freemason, aren't you, Neville?' he said.

Neville made a wary face. That was not a question that any Freemason cared to be asked. And it is a tricky one, because if you are, you're not supposed to lie – simply to evade.

'How are your crops at present?' Neville asked. 'How's the Mandragora coming along?'

Old Pete put his hand across the bar counter for a shake. 'Have you travelled far?' he asked.

Neville shook the elder's hand. It was a significant handshake. Both men knew the significance of it. Words were exchanged and these words also were significant.

'I never knew,' said Neville, 'in all these years, that you—'

'I keep my own business to myself, Neville, whereas your Masonic cufflinks are something of a giveaway. But I can trust you. Brothers upon the square, as it were.'

'And under the arch.'

'Quite so.'

'So what is it that you wish to tell me? In complete confidence, of course.'

'How old do you think I am, Neville?'

Neville shrugged.

'I was born in eighteen eighty-five, right here in Brentford.'

'Eighteen eighty-five?' Neville counted on his fingers. 'Why, that makes you—'

'Old enough. Now, you might not believe what I'm going to tell you, but I swear to you it's true. I've spent most of my life trying to convince myself otherwise, but I know what I know. I saw it all with my own two eyes.'

'Go on, then,' said Neville.

'Victorian society,' said Old Pete. 'It wasn't how it's written up in the history books. It was nothing like it's written up in the history books, it was completely different.'

'How?' Neville asked. 'Smellier, more violent? What?'

'Technology,' said Old Pete. 'There was technology back then that nobody knows about now, technology that simply ceased to exist and of which no record survives today.'

'What kind of technology?' Neville asked.

'Electric technology. Have you ever heard of Nikola Tesla?'

Neville shook his head.

'He invented alternating current,' said Old Pete. 'It wasn't Edison who invented that – that's false history. Tesla worked with Charles Babbage, inventor of the computer.'

'I've heard of him,' said Neville. 'He invented the

computer but it was never taken up in Victorian society. He died in poverty. There was a programme about him on the television a while back.'

'He never died in poverty – he was knighted by Her Majesty Queen Victoria in eighteen sixty for his services to the British Empire. With the help of Babbage's computer, Nikola Tesla created a system of towers across the country that broadcast electricity on a radio frequency, no wires. There were flying hansom cabs, electric airships, a space programme. A rocket was going to the moon, but it was sabotaged.'

'You're making this up,' said Neville.

Old Pete glared at him. 'It's true, it's all true. Most houses had electric lighting long before nineteen hundred. And computers. And there were robots, too, powered by broadcast electricity, working as doormen and cabbies, and soldiers as well. The British Empire had conquered almost all of the globe by the eighteen nineties. America had been won back and was a British colony again.'

'This can't be true,' said Neville. 'It would be in history books.'

'It isn't,' said Old Pete, 'because everything changed at the stroke of midnight with the coming of the year nineteen hundred, as far as I can make out. I owned a digital watch, Neville – my father gave it to me when I was ten.'

Neville the part-time barman shook his doubtful head. 'But if this were true, then there'd be some trace of it, surely. What happened to all this amazing Victorian technology?'

'Vanished,' said Old Pete, 'as if it had never existed, at the stroke of midnight with the coming of the year nineteen hundred.'

'But how?' Neville asked.

'Through witchcraft,' said Old Pete, 'as far as I can figure it out. There were rumours that a cabal of witches sought to destroy all Victorian technology. I don't know how, or why, but they wiped it all out.'

'Witches,' said Neville, who was not unacquainted with

several local practitioners of the Craft. 'Witches wouldn't do that.'

'It's what I heard, I can't prove it. I can't prove anything. But I'll tell you this: all that stuff in Victorian science fiction books, H.G. Wells and Jules Verne and so on – it's all true, it was all real. All of it.'

'What?' said Neville. 'Like the invisible man?'

'That was H.G. Wells himself. He was a scientist, not a fiction writer, and I know that for a fact.'

'But this stuff would have been in the newspapers. And newspaper offices have archives.'

'All records vanished with the technology, as if none of it had ever happened, at twelve midnight, coming of the year nineteen hundred. And Norman is in great danger.'

'Norman?' said Neville. 'How does he fit into this?'

'He's come into possession of Victorian computer parts. Babbage Nineteen-Hundred Series computer parts.'

'Then surely these computer parts prove your story. You should be pleased that he's found them. Will you be writing a book? A rewrite of history?'

'Neville, you're a fool. You don't understand.'

'I can't understand if you don't tell me. What's the problem with these computer parts?'

'The computers were part of it. The magic was in the computers, programmed into them. It's evil stuff, Neville.'

'I really don't understand,' said the part-time barman, 'but this is a most extraordinary story. And it's clearly troubling you.'

'It is,' said Old Pete. 'To be frank, it's scaring the very life out of me.'

Neville made a thoughtful face. 'Just one thing,' he said. 'How come only you know about this? If history changed on the stroke of midnight with the coming of the year nineteen hundred, how come no one else who was alive during that period has ever mentioned it?'

'Because all their memories of it were erased. History was changed and it was as if it never ever happened. All the electric technology, all of it, just disappeared and all memory of it, too.'

'So how come *you* remember it?'

'Because I wasn't there when the change came, Neville. I came back afterwards, an hour later, a boy of fifteen, to find my entire world changed – as if everything that had happened had never happened.'

'So where were *you*?' Neville asked.

'I was right here,' said Old Pete. 'Right here, but not right here right now. I was right here several months from now, in Mr H.G. Wells' time machine. I—'

'Have to stop you there,' said Neville. 'Kindly leave my pub, Old Pete, and consider yourself barred for a week.'

'What?' said Old Pete.

And Neville reached for his knobkerrie.

11

Norman hadn't slept at all the previous night. He couldn't – he was far too excited. He just had to put the computer together. Peg had stomped off to the marital bed and she hadn't called down for Norman to join her for a bit of rumpy-pumpy. Which had gladdened Norman, as he'd gone off all that messy stuff many years before.

Norman had been left to his own devices, which were devices of a constructional nature. And the construction details contained within the *Babbage 1900 Series Computer Assembly Manual* were most explicit and exact. They weren't written in pidgin English, as were most of their ilk nowadays. These were written in good old Victorian down-to-Earth straightforwardness. They informed the constructor exactly where to stick each valve and screw on each big fat wire and locate every machined brass bolt, and how to glue and joint each section of the mahogany cabinet that housed the computer screen.

Just so.

And when dawn came up and the bundled newspapers were flung on to his doorstep, Norman was all but finished.

'It's all in the numbers,' said the scientific shopkeeper, who knew what he was all about and what his quest was all about. 'And if the numbers can be found through this, then I'll find them.'

'And if you don't number-up those newspapers, I'll give you the smacking of your life,' said Peg, filling the kitchenette and bringing woe unto Norman.

And then of course there'd been the morning. And Norman had been weary. He'd wondered why Jim and

John had not called in to purchase papers and cigarettes. And then he'd recalled how they had both been hospitalised. And he'd sold a box of chocolates to Bob the Bookie, who, at the mention of Jim's incapacitation, had burst into paroxysms of laughter and purchased several cigars.

And he'd served this chap and the other and he'd really been dying to get back to his computer.

And then at last it was lunchtime.

And Norman turned once more the 'open' sign to its 'closed' side and took himself off to his kitchenette.

And plugged in his Babbage Nineteen-Hundred Series computer.

Then yawned and fell fast asleep.

And as Peg was out, he slept right through the afternoon.

'Ya canna sleep,' said Mahatma Campbell. 'Ya haf ta up an' awa' wi' th' lads.'

'Ooh, ah, wah!' said Jim Pooley. 'What time is it?'

'Seven o'clock in the evening. Ya drank ya sel' to oblivion an' on the firs' day on the job. Y' haf the makins of a firs'-class football manager.'

'I was resting my eyes,' said Jim, a-blinking them.

'Me too,' said John, a-rubbing at his.

'Ya drunken bastards.'

'That's no way to speak to your employer.' Jim rose unsteadily from his seat. Before him, the table spoke of many beers. It spoke in the manner of many empty glasses.

'Did we get through all these?' Jim asked John.

'The barman helped, if I recall,' said John.

'Where is he?' the Campbell asked.

'Gone a-golfing,' said John.

Mahatma Campbell shook his turbaned head. 'You tak' yer shoes off when ya walk on m' pitch,' he told Jim.

'I have no wish to walk upon your pitch,' said Jim.

'You'd better – it's training night. The lads are oot there waiting fer instructions from their new manager.'

'Tell them to take the evening off,' said Jim. 'In fact, tell them to join us in here for a drink.'

'I dinna think so.' Mahatma Campbell handed Jim an envelope.

'What's this?' Jim asked.

'It's for ya, yer name's upon it.'

'It's been opened,' said Jim, observing this fact.

'Correct. I opened it.'

'Why?' asked Jim.

'Because I'm nosy. It's instructions from Professor Slocombe. You'd best be following them, I'm thinking.'[*]

'Ah,' said Jim. And, 'Yes.'

'Let's have a look.' Omally acquainted himself with the envelope, drew out a missive penned upon parchment and read it aloud.

And when he had finished with his reading, Jim said, 'My golly.'

'Your golly?' asked the Campbell.

'Everybody's golly,' said Jim. 'How can I be expected to ask the team to do *that*?'

'I know not,' said the Campbell, 'but for the love of myself, I'm really looking forward to seeing you try.'

The floodlights were on in Griffin Park. The Campbell had switched them on. And it does have to be said that there is a certain magic about a floodlit football pitch. In fact, more than just a certain magic. A floodlit football pitch is BIG MAGIC. Even if you have no liking for the beautiful game.

'Would you look at the size of that,' said John Omally.

'It's grown,' said Jim. 'It was never as big as this at lunchtime.'

'Here,' said John, nudging Pooley's elbow. 'There's the team over there. Would you like me to give you the big build-up?'

'The big what?' Pooley scratched at his head and squinted into the floodlights. 'I think I've gone blind,' he added.

'I'll give you an introductory speech. You'd better take

---

[*] The Campbell's Scottish accent having been established, it can now be taken as read, so to speak.

this,' and John handed the professor's missive to the blinking Jim and strode off to address the team.

The team sat on 'the benches', which is where they sit when they're not doing anything – if they're substitutes, or reserves, or injured players, or whatever. They sit in other places, too, of course, such as the locker room, where they receive their half-time tellings off and their oranges to give them vitamin C. And they also sit in that terrible, Hellish, scary place known as the communal shower (or tub), which it is better not even to think about.

Unless you are of a particular persuasion.[*]

John Omally strode over the pitch and approached the sitters on the benches. The sitters on the benches watched Omally's approach with guarded gazes. One of them spat on to the pitch. Two others stubbed out their cigarettes.

'Brentford United,' said John Omally, bowing low before the sitters. 'I greet you.'

'And who are you, mister?' asked one of Brentford United. The one with the goatee beard.

'I am Mr Pooley's personal assistant,' said John, returning his head to the vertical plane. 'Mr Pooley is your new manager.'

'Oh,' said one of Brentford United. The one with the many tattoos. And he shrugged towards his goateed teammate, who shrugged right back at him. 'Well, I've never heard of *him*.'

So much the better, thought John. 'Then you are all in for a wonderful surprise,' he continued. 'Mr Pooley is the man who is going to take you on to victory this season. To whit, the winning of the FA Cup.'

There was a moment of silence.

This moment was followed by—

'Stop!' shouted John, but his shout was lost amidst the laughter that echoed across the empty pitch, throughout the empty stands and onwards up to Heaven, so it seemed.

[*] Such as a sportsman, perhaps!

Pooley chewed upon his bottom lip and considered having it away upon his toes.

'Stop!' commanded John. 'Cease this frivolity. It is possible for you to win the cup in a mere eight games.'

Between the gales of laughter, the words, 'We all know that, but it's not going to happen,' came from this mouth and that.

'Silence please,' shouted John. Eventually the team came to some semblance of silence. The two smokers took out their fags and lit up once again.

'Wouldn't you like to win the FA Cup?' John asked.

Heads went down and shoulders sagged. 'Every player in every team would *love* that,' said one of Brentford United. The one with the waggly tail.* 'But we know we're beaten. We haven't won a match in two seasons. Our contracts run out at the end of this one and those of us who can't get into other teams will be quitting the game for good.'

'I'm thinking of opening a sports shop,' said one of these fellows. The one with a nose like an engineer's elbow.

'I'm hoping to do some crisp commercials,' said another with very large ears.

John Omally smiled upon the sorrowful, dejected team. 'Imagine,' said he, 'just imagine what would happen if you *did* win the FA Cup. Imagine big cash bonuses. Imagine transfer fees and lucrative merchandising deals, imagine celebrity status, appearing on TV chat shows, opening supermarkets. Imagine those beautiful blonde-haired women who really go for successful professional footballers.'

'I prefer brunettes,' said the one who preferred brunettes, who also happened to be the one with the goatee beard.

'Fame and fortune await you,' said John. 'And bear this in mind – you have nothing whatsoever to lose.'

'Except the next match.'

'Who said that?' John asked.

'I did,' said the one who did.

---

* Which he was saving up to have surgically removed. This player did *not* attend the post-match communal showers.

'Sorry,' said John. 'I didn't see you there.'

'People rarely do,' said the player known as Alan Berkshire, brother to David Berkshire, who served on Brentford Borough Council.

'You are not going to lose the next match,' John informed them. 'Nor the one after that, nor even the one after that. This season you are going to win every FA Cup qualifying game you play. This season you *will* win the FA Cup.'

'Are you that bloke off the telly?' asked one of Brentford United. The one who was having a patio built at the back of his bungalow, but was currently in dispute with the builder regarding the escalating costs.

'What bloke off the telly?' queried John.

'Britain's favourite practical joker,' said the same one. 'Does that *Game For A Laugh* show where he pretends to electrocute people's cats and execute their wives, to great comic effect.'

'Jeremy Paxman,' said the one with the goatee beard.

'Jeremy Irons,' said the one with the nose like an engineer's elbow.

'Iron Maiden,' said the one with the tattoos.

'It doesn't matter who he is,' said John. 'I'm not him.'

'You look a lot like him,' said the one who was having his patio built.

'No he doesn't,' said the one with the tattoos. 'He looks like the lead singer of Iron Maiden – Jack Nance.'

'Jack Nance was a science fiction writer,' said the one with the strange ways about him, who hadn't spoken before. 'You're thinking of Jack the Hat McVitie.'

'No I wasn't, I—'

'Stop!' This 'stop' came not from John Omally but from Jim Pooley, who quite surprised himself with the shouting of it.

'Stop now!' shouted Jim.

And they actually stopped.

'Your new manager,' said John, bowing once more and stepping aside.

Jim cleared his throat and thrust out what he had of a chest.

'Gentlemen,' said he, 'my name is James Pooley and I am your new manager. I am aware that things have not gone well for the team in the past, but these days are behind you now. There is to be a new dawn. A new era. A return to the greatness of former times. If you follow my instructions, I will lead you to victory. Have no doubts regarding this. My word is my bond. I promise that you will win the cup.'

And then further words poured from Jim's mouth, a veritable torrent of words. Mighty words were these, words of a truly inspirational nature. Above Jim, clouds parted in the heavens and a shaft of light beamed down upon him. The words rolled on and on and all who heard these words became transfixed.

The silence that followed these wondrous words was of the variety known as stunned.

John looked from the face of Jim unto the faces of the team. The face of Jim fairly shone and those of his watchers and listeners put John in mind of a painting he had once seen in The National Gallery – *The Adoration of the Shepherds* by Guido Reni.

'Any questions?' Jim asked.

Team heads now shook and team shoulders shrugged.

'Exemplary,' said Jim. 'Now that I have introduced myself to you, I would be grateful if you would reciprocate.'

Heads now nodded. Shoulders, however, still shrugged.

'I'd like to know your names,' said Jim, 'your names and the positions you play.'

'Ah.' Heads now nodded enthusiastically. Looks of enlightenment appeared upon the faces of these heads.

And so Jim Pooley was introduced to the players that were Brentford United.

Ernest Muffler (goatee beard, wife being visited on
    Saturday afternoons by John Omally). Centre forward
    and captain of Brentford United.

Horace Beaverbrooke (tattoos). Left-winger.

Billy Kurton (patio). Right-winger.

Alf Snatcher (waggly tail). Centre mid-fielder.

Morris Catafelto (nose like an engineer's elbow). Right mid-fielder.

Dave Quimsby (very large ears). Left mid-fielder.

Charlie Boxx (the one with the strange ways about him). Left back.

Trevor Brooking (not to be confused with the other Trevor Brooking). Right back.

Alan Berkshire (brother to David Berkshire on the council). Centre half.

Sundip Mahingay (the Indian of the group). Centre half.

Ben Gash. Goalkeeper.

Substitutes:

Don and Phil English (Siamese twins). (Super-subs.)

Barry Bustard (fat bloke).

Loup-Gary Thompson (wolf-boy).

Humphrey Hampton (half-man, half-hamburger).

Jim shook each member of the team by the hand.

And Jim beheld the substitutes.

'Are you the regular substitutes?' he asked.

Don and Phil shook their heads. 'We're on loan from Count Otto Black's *Circus Fantastique*,' they said.

'Explain?' Jim asked Ernest Muffler.

'The club's broke,' Ernest explained. 'None of us are expecting to get paid this season. We're only playing because it would be unprofessional to do otherwise. We can't afford any substitutes. These lads volunteered to substitute for free, for as long as the circus is in town.'

Jim managed a smile at this. 'I think,' said he, 'that it's more than a matter of not wanting to be unprofessional. You all love the club. I know that you do.'

'We do,' said Billy Kurton, 'but we also know a lost cause when we see one. Or,' he paused, 'or, at least we *did* until now.'

'Just so,' said Jim. 'Our cause is not lost. And you will all be paid this season. Full pay.'

A cheer went up from the Brentford team.

'Er, Jim.' Omally nudged Jim's elbow with his own and whispered into Jim's ear, 'Jim, there isn't any money to pay these lads with. All the available money is paying our wages.'

'Then we'll take a cut in salary,' said Jim.

'*What?*' Omally made a horrified face.

'And as my personal PA, whose job it is to take the burden of everyday matters from my shoulders, it will be your job to see that we raise sufficient funds each week to pay the lads.'

'*WHAT?*'

'A special cheer if you will for Mr Omally,' said Jim to the team, 'the man who will be organising the financial wherewithal to pay your wages.'

'Three cheers for Mr Omally,' said Ernest Muffler. 'And make them loud ones, lads.'

And loud ones they were.

Omally glared pointy daggers at Jim.

But Jim wore the face of an angel.

'And so,' said Jim, 'to the training and tactics. For tonight is, after all, a training session, and in order that we dispose of all rival teams that stand between us and the championship, we shall be employing entirely new tactics – tactics that have never previously been employed. We shall take each of our opponents by surprise. Put your trust in me and prepare yourselves for victory.'

Horace Beaverbrooke lit up a cigarette. Jim stepped forward and plucked it from his fingers. 'Not during training sessions,' he said. 'Now, if you would kindly divide yourselves up into two teams, substitutes included. A short kick-around is in order so that I can gauge your relative skills.'

The team didn't move.

'Go to it,' said Jim and he clapped his hands together.

And so the team went to it.

John and Jim settled on to the bench and watched them go to it. Jim lit up a Dadarillo Super-Dooper King.

'Your speech was truly inspired, Jim,' said John. 'I wouldn't have thought you had it in you.'

'I don't think I did,' said Jim. 'The words just came out of my mouth.'

'As did the ones about *me* raising the funds to pay the team.'

'John,' said Jim, 'we have our own pub now, and our own gift shop. I feel confident that you will find ways to provide for the team.'

'I wish I could share your confidence.'

'We'll succeed,' said Jim. 'I just know that we will. Now, let's watch our team doing its stuff.'

And so they watched.

And so they flinched.

If a special prize was to be awarded for ineptitude and downright uselessness in a football side, there was no doubt in the minds of either John or Jim that this special prize would be unanimously awarded to the lads of Brentford United.

'They're useless,' said John, as sportsmen blundered into one another, tripped over the ball and avoided every tackle as if it were a beast of prey. 'They can't play at all. The fat bloke from the circus just put the ball past the Brentford goalie.'

'There are certain weaknesses,' said Jim.

'Certain weaknesses?' hooted John. 'These lads couldn't kick a hole through an ozone layer.'

Jim produced from his pocket a whistle. An Acme Thunderer.

'Where did you get *that* from?' John asked.

'My pocket,' said Jim, and he put it to his lips and blew.

Play came to an end and the players limped from the pitch, puffing and panting and looking for the most part near to death.

'Well done,' said Jim. 'Five minutes to gather your breath and then we will work upon the new tactics.'

'We usually go to The Stripes Bar for a pint about now,' said Trevor Brooking*. 'It's a dangerous thing to overtrain. You could tear a hamstring, or pull a ligament or get a groin strain, or something.'

'That seems reasonable,' said Jim. 'When do we play the first FA Cup qualifying match?'

'Saturday,' said Ernest. 'Against Penge.'

'Saturday?' Jim all but swallowed the cigarette he was puffing upon. '*This coming Saturday?*'

'It's an away game,' said Ernest. 'We'll need to hire a coach.'

Jim looked at John.

And John looked at Jim.

'Best make a note of that,' said Jim wearily. 'Hire a coach, John.'

John made a note of that.

'So,' said Jim, as brightly as he could, 'the pints will have to wait. Back on to the pitch and we'll get straight to work on the tactics.'

'But, Boss,' said Alf Snatcher, whose waggly tail was troubling him.

And although Jim liked the sound of 'boss', he did not like the sound of the 'but'.

'But me no buts,' said Mr Pooley. 'We have a match to win.'

High in the corner of the south stand, unseen by team and boss alike, Professor Slocombe sat and watched the tactics being put into operation.

And Professor Slocombe smiled unto himself, leaned upon his ivory-topped cane and whispered, 'Good boy, Jim. We will succeed.'

And high in the corner of the north stand, equally unseen and even unsensed by the professor, another sat. He sat half-

---

* Not to be confused with the other Trevor Brooking.

in and half-out of the floodlight's glare. The half of him that was in shadow was not to be seen at all, but the half of him that was to be seen, the lower half, was all in black, a blackness that was two shades darker than the blackest black yet known. And this blackness came and went, as if going in and out of focus. And strange unearthly sounds issued from the half that was not to be seen. Coming from the mouth-parts. Probably.

And the sounds that were issued were the sounds of words.

But not of any language known to man.

The translation of these words, had a translator been present to do the translating thereof, would have been as follows, for they came in answer to those spoken by the professor. To wit, 'We will succeed.'

And these words that came in answer, in this unknown tongue, meant, 'Oh no you won't.'

12

Norman, having slept throughout the afternoon – much to the distress of his customers, who had been unable to effect entry to his shop – was awakened at six by the return of his wife.

Who gave Norman a thrashing.

The evening meal was a sombre affair, lacking for sparkling conversation and gay badinage. But then it always did. And upon this particular evening, Norman felt this lack most deeply.

Wouldn't it be wonderful, he thought to himself as he munched upon the fish and chips his wife had sent him out for, to have one of those marriages where you actually got on with your wife? Were friends with her, and woke up without the dread of what might lie in wait for you during the coming day. Indeed, awoke with the prospect, well founded, that sex might await you before you even got up for the breakfast that had been cooked for you.

Such marriages did exist, Norman felt certain of it. Not that he actually knew anyone who had one of these marriages, but they must exist. Somewhere.

Norman finished his fish and chips, scrunched up and binned the papers and heard his wife, Peg, slam the back door behind her as she went off for her weekly tuba lesson. He sighed, then smiled as he settled himself down in front of his newly constructed computer, which had by now grown comfortably hot, having been left on throughout the afternoon.

'It never rains, but it pours,' said the shopkeeper. 'But a bird in the hand is worth two in Shepherds Bush.'

And Norman tapped at the antiquated keyboard, which was a glorious affair fashioned after the old-fashion of a manual typewriter, with raised brass keys with enamelled lettering upon them, and wondered how, exactly, you worked a computer.

'Manual,' said Norman, reaching for the cloth-bound copy of *The Babbage 1900 Series Computer Assembly Manual*. 'It will all be in the manual.'

And, of course, it was.

'Ah,' said Norman. 'Cable into the phone socket. Interesting concept.' Norman gazed towards his telephone. It was a fine Bakelite affair that had served the Hartnel clan well ever since its installation in the late 1930s. It didn't have a socket, as such, though, just a big black box where it was wired into the wall. A big black box that had the word 'DANGER' printed upon it and a kind of lightning-flash motif. Norman took out his screwdriver and tinkered with this box.

And in less time than it takes to call an ambulance for someone who has been electrocuted as a result of tampering with something electrical that they really shouldn't have tampered with, but slightly more time than it takes to recover from such an electrocution and do the calling yourself, Norman was all cabled up with only the minimum of fingertip charring and singeing of the wig.

'Piece of cake,' said Norman, applying himself once more to manual and keyboard. The valves hummed away nicely, projecting an amber glow through the air holes in the back of the mahogany cabinet that housed the monitor screen and making that electrical toasty smell that is oft-times referred to as ozone, but is probably Freon. And then things began to appear upon the monitor screen.

Norman viewed these things and purred his approval.

They all looked very exciting, but he didn't know what they meant. They were definitely symbols of some sort, row upon row of them, travelling sedately across the screen. Mathematical symbols? Norman certainly hoped so. If he was to come up with The Big Figure, the number of it all, the very number of existence – perhaps, Norman mused, the mathematical equation that was the Universe, or even God himself – then row upon row of mathematical-looking figures doodling their way across the screen was probably as good a place as any to start.

Norman continued with his viewing, and with his musing also. It was a private and personal kind of musing. And it ran in this fashion: perhaps, Norman's musing went, going outright for The Big Figure was overly ambitious. It was not so much that he lacked the confidence to go for The Big Figure – far from it, Norman had every confidence in what he might personally achieve. All things *were* possible, to Norman's mind. All things *could* be achieved if he, Norman, put his, Norman's, mind to these things. That others thought him a dreamer did not enter into it. People were always saying that this can't be done, and that can't be done, and that to achieve big ends required vast organisations with vaster budgets. Norman pooh-poohed such narrow-mindedness.

But perhaps he should take things a bit at a time on this particular project, because it was, after all, a very BIG project. And if he did manage to come up with The Big Figure before anyone else did and could patent it, it would put him in a very powerful position. A kind of King of the World position, The Big Figure giving its discoverer all but limitless power, assuming that it did actually exist and that it was actually possible to discover it. And then actually do something with it.

Norman ceased his musing; such musing was not helpful. Such musing inspired doubt. Better just to get on with the project, find The Big Figure and then cock a snoot to the lads at The Flying Swan who had doubted his ability to do so.

Norman consulted the manual once more. 'Oh, I see,' said Norman. 'It's a computer program, loading itself up.' Pleased that he could at least understand the basic concept of what was going on, Norman left the computer to be going on with whatever it was going on with and went off to make himself a mug of tea.

He returned, tea mug in hand, to discover that the computer had done whatever it wanted to do and now awaited his instructions.

'All right,' said Norman, 'let's see what you can do.' And he began to type: *If one man can dig a hole six foot deep and three foot square in two and a half hours, how many men would it take to make fifteen such holes in forty-five minutes?*

Norman shook his head. Surely that was too easy for a calculating machine. *Multiply this figure by the area of a lean-to shed and the angle of a ship upon the horizon.*

'No,' said Norman. 'I won't know whether it gets the answer right or not. There has to be a way of testing this machine's abilities. Oh, what's this?'

The computer screen now lit up with the words 'TECHNICAL SPECIFICATION: TESLA BROADCAST POWER SYSTEM'.

'I never asked for that,' said Norman. 'I wonder what that might be.' There was a key marked 'ENTER' upon the keyboard and Norman gave this a tap. Figures and diagrams and tracts of printed text now appeared upon the screen. Norman read the printed text and Norman's eyebrows rose.

'Tell me,' said Norman, 'that this isn't what it appears to be.' But there was no one present to tell Norman otherwise.

'It's a plan for a device,' said Norman, 'that can broadcast electricity on a radio frequency, without cables. But no such device exists, surely – or ever has existed.'

Norman now jiggled the little brass mouse about, scrolling words and diagrams and technical bits and bobs up the screen. 'Patented in eighteen sixty-two,' read Norman. 'Patent, the property of Charles Babbage and Nikola Tesla. Babbage! And this is a Babbage computer. A Victorian computer. This can't be right. Although . . .' Norman cast his inventor's eye over the diagrams and technical bits and bobs. 'This Broadcast Power System looks as if it might actually work – it's really a very simple system. But I'm sure there's no record of this. There's never been "broadcast electricity". Something like that would revolutionise everything.' Norman scrolled on. Plans appeared for electric automobiles that ran without batteries, drawing their loco-motive power from broadcast electricity received upon radio waves. And electric airships. And flying hansom cabs. And automata.

'Oh my goodness,' said Norman. 'The Motherlode. The works of Victorian inventors that somehow were never brought to fruition. The work of unrecognised geniuses – much like myself, in fact. And all this has lain locked away for nearly a century, waiting . . .' Norman paused. 'Waiting for *me*,' he continued.

The training session had reached its conclusion, and there had been no fatalities. No heart attacks, no mental break-downs, very little in the way of swearing and no one so badly bruised as to need assistance when leaving the field of play.

'You've all done very well,' Jim told them. 'You can all take a shower, if you fancy that kind of thing, and then join myself and Mr Omally in The Stripes Bar. The first pint is on me.'

As there were no shower enthusiasts, Jim led the sweaty team off to the bar.

'I think that all went rather well,' said Jim when he had acquainted himself with a pint. 'What do you think, John?'

'It's undoubtedly a new approach.' Omally settled him-self on to an uncomfortable chair and supped upon his second-rate ale. 'I'm even looking forward to Saturday. I can't wait to see what Penge makes of it.'

'Don't forget that you're in charge of hiring the coach,' Jim told him.

'I'll have a word with Big Bob Charker who runs the Historic Tour of Brentford bus. He'll be grateful for the business and he owes me a favour or two.'

'And the fund-raising to pay for the team's wages?'

'I have an idea for that. Friday night will be Benefit Night, right here in our personal pub.'

'Tomorrow night is Friday night,' said Jim. 'It will surely take powers greater than your own to organise a Benefit Night in a single day.'

'Trust me,' said Omally. 'I'm a PA.'

Pints sank and more were ordered.

And paid for by the members of the team.

Omally engaged the conjoined twins in conversation, subtly steering the dialogue towards a particular area of their lives that was of particular interest to himself.

Jim sat chatting to Ernest Muffler, whom John seemed anxious to avoid, for some reason.

'We really can win this,' Jim told him.

Ernest offered Jim a guarded, doubtful glance.

'It's true,' said Jim. 'Powers greater than our own are at work to aid us to victory.'

'Have you ever heard of a thing called a group dynamic?' Ernest asked him.

'Is it one of those Californian things where blokes take their clothes off and hug trees in a forest?' Jim asked him in return.

'No,' said Ernest, now offering Jim another kind of glance.

'No,' said Jim. 'I don't mean that I . . . I mean, well . . . no, I *don't* know what a group dynamic is.'

'It's something to do with motivating a bunch of people, getting them all to work together for a common goal, that kind of thing.'

'That's the kind of thing I'm trying to do,' said Jim.

'Well, you'll have a hard time doing it with this bunch,' said Ernest. 'They'll do what you tell them, to some extent, especially as you're actually going to pay them, but you can't really trust them. They're all up to something.'

'Everybody seems to be.' Jim took further sup upon his substandard pint. 'But surely none of them will do anything to sabotage the team's chances of success.'

'I'm sure they'll all try their hardest to win if they all actually turn up for the game. I did hear you say something about a Benefit Night tomorrow evening to raise money for our wages.'

'You can consider your wages paid,' said Jim, all but finishing his substandard pint.

'And I appreciate that. But if you have a Benefit Night for the team tomorrow evening, the team will be expected to attend. It would be impolite not to. So they'll all get pissed and have hangovers on Saturday morning.'

'Ah,' said Jim. 'I see. That's what you'd call a dilemma, isn't it?'

'Happily though,' said Ernest, rising from Jim's table and taking himself off to the toilet, 'it's your dilemma, not mine.'

Jim now sat and stared gloomily into what was left of his substandard pint. This really was all too much. All too much of everything. Especially responsibility. Jim's brief flirtation with responsibility had never led to a lasting relationship. Jim considered that being responsible for himself alone was a full-time job in itself. And one which, of course, left no time for any other kind of full-time job. But to have all this so suddenly and unceremoniously dumped upon his shoulders, even with all of Omally's boasts of selfless support and the professor pulling the strings, as it were, was, Jim considered . . .

All too much.

'Those twins lead a most remarkable sex life,' said Omally, placing a newly drawn pint before Jim and settling himself into Ernest's uncomfortable chair. 'I think I might consider joining the circus.'

'I think I might come with you,' said Jim. 'I don't think I can go through with this.'

John patted Jim upon his sagging shoulder. 'Perk up, my friend. The first day on the job is always the trickiest.'

'And you would know this from experience, would you?'

John Omally scratched at his curly bonce. 'Well, I've heard it said,' said he. 'I don't think I've ever actually lasted for more than a single day in what they call regular employment.'

'We're doomed,' said Jim.

'Now don't start that again. We're *not* doomed. We have the professor to aid us. And our own pub, Jim, don't forget that. And when Neville finds The Swan empty tomorrow night, he'll rue the day that he bopped us on the head.'

'We might have to cancel the Benefit Night,' said Jim and he went on to explain why.

John gave the matter a moment's thought. 'Have no fear,' said he. 'I'll take care of it,' and he gave his nose a significant tap. 'Now, is there anything else that troubles you?'

'Well,' said Jim, taking a big breath. 'There's . . .'

'No,' said John, putting his tapping finger to Jim Pooley's lips. 'Drink your ale and stop worrying yourself. We'll come through this and we'll come out on top. Trust me, I'm a—'

'I know,' said Jim. 'A PA.'

'No,' said John. 'A Brentonian. And we lads can get through anything.'

Professor Slocombe descended at length from the south stand of the football ground. Behind and beneath the stand, just along from The Stripes Bar, there existed a rude hut constructed of railway ties, daub and wattle, canvas and corrugated iron. To the first and passing glance, this curious dwelling resembled little other than a stack of debris, carelessly discarded. And to the second and third glances also. For this was the way that the Campbell preferred it. For this was the Campbell's home.

Professor Slocombe knocked upon a section of corrugated iron. It was a 'certain' knock. There was a certain pattern to it. The section swung aside, a hand beckoned greeting and Professor Slocombe entered the Campbell's dwelling. The Campbell closed and secured his secret door.

'Seat yourself,' said he.

The dwelling was spacious within. Remarkably so. And remarkable, too. Many candles lit a single gallery. The undersides of the stand seating above gabled its ceiling. Flagstones paved its floor. And then there was the Gothic. There were tapestries and hunting trophies, shields and claymores and antlered heads. The look of all and sundry of it was one of a Scottish laird's hunting lodge. Or something to do with *Highlander*.

A great fire blazed in the rough stone fireplace, but where the smoke went was anyone's guess.

Professor Slocombe lowered his fragile frame into a crofter's chair before the fire. Mahatma Campbell decanted a measure of Scotch into a goatskin goblet and placed it in the scholar's hand.

'If I might say so,' said he, 'you took your time.'

Professor Slocombe smiled. The Campbell seated himself in a great chair opposite, took up a poker and gave the fire a stabbing with it.

'You remain most loyal,' said Professor Slocombe. 'How many years is it now?'

'Too many.' The Campbell spat into the fire. 'But I keep the watch. And if this Pooley is your man, then I'll keep a watch on him, too.'

'I would appreciate that.' Professor Slocombe tasted the Scotch. It tasted mighty fine. 'Jim is a good man. I would not want any harm to come to him.'

'Does he know what he's dealing with?'

'No.' Professor Slocombe shook his head.

'Then you're sending him to his death.'

'Not with you here to protect him.'

Mahatma Campbell took up Scotch of his own and threw it down his throat. 'One of them was here tonight,' he said, 'in this very stadium.'

'No.' The face of Professor Slocombe became grave. 'Whilst I was here? I felt nothing.'

'They're cunning. And new, these – a different breed. Even blacker than the ones before.'

'Even blacker.' Professor Slocombe's fingers tightened around his goatskin goblet. 'I shall have to be more vigilant.'

'You're vulnerable away from your manse. But wherever you are, I'll not be far from your side.'

'Protect Jim,' said the professor. 'Perhaps you should go to him now.'

'The danger has passed. But they're watching. You

shouldn't have left it so long. If they take the football ground, then it's the end for us all.'

'They'll never take the football ground,' said the professor.

'But you could have stopped all this months ago, paid off the club's debts. You've enough in your coffers.'

'I had to wait. There are certain predestined events that have yet to occur. It is all part of my plan.'

'And this clown Pooley, he is part of your plan?'

'We will only have one chance at this.' Professor Slocombe turned his goblet between his slender fingers and considered the flames of the raucous fire. 'You and I both know the date.'

'It's written into my very soul,' said the Campbell. 'To know in advance the date of the Apocalypse is a sombre enough matter by any reckoning.'

Professor Slocombe put a finger to his lips. 'Hush,' said he. 'Not even here.'

'I can speak here well enough, Professor, there's none that can hear me but yourself.'

'I would prefer that our conversation remained, how shall I put this, cryptic and enigmatic.'

The Campbell spat once more into the fire. 'Perhaps in some Hollywood thriller or mystery novel, but I am a plain man and I speak plain words.'

'You may look like man,' said Professor Slocombe, 'but you and I both know that you are not one.'

'Be that as it may. But I, like you, am sworn to serve and protect this borough. The forces that seek to destroy it are beyond the ken of the normal Brentonian, who goes about his business in ignorance of their very existence.'

'And that is how it will remain. As it always has been and as it always will be.'

'Secrets, secrets, secrets. It's always secrets.'

'Magic must always remain secret, the preserve of the few – for good or evil.'

'You should tell the world, Professor, all that you know.'

'And the world would not believe me, but in telling all,

my powers would be dissipated. But not so those of our mutual enemy. The King of Darkness thrives upon disbelief. You know that, Campbell.'

'You could at least warn the people somehow.'

'No.' Professor Slocombe arose from his chair, his ancient limbs click-clacking. 'The football ground and what lies beneath it must remain untouched. I will play my part in seeing that this remains so. And you will play your part also.'

'As I always have,' said the Campbell. 'I am sworn to serve you.'

'I know that. And if we achieve our ends without anyone else being aware of our genuine motives, so much the better. Brentford retains its football ground and a team that might go on to further success. And the Powers of Darkness are forestalled until another day.'

'And the Apocalypse?' the Campbell asked.

'Postponed,' said Professor Slocombe. 'Indefinitely.'

'I certainly hope you're right.'

'I enjoin with your hopes.'

John Omally zipped up his trousers. As the bog in The Stripes Bar had been flooded – something to do with Billy Bustard, apparently – John had slipped out to make his ablutions elsewhere.

And he had been doing so against this old pile of corrugated iron and debris beneath the south stand when he'd heard these muffled voices.

And so, whilst peeing, he had pressed his ear to the corrugated iron and overheard a certain private conversation.

And now he heard the words, 'Goodnight to you, Campbell.'

And John Omally made it away.

Lightly and upon his toes.

13

John Omally for once didn't sleep at all well. He slept alone, in the bed that was his own, which at least made a change for him. But he slept most uncomfortably. John Omally had much on his mind.

He was puzzled and disturbed by the conversation he had overheard between Professor Slocombe and Mahatma Campbell. What had that all been about? The Apocalypse? The King of Darkness? Things that were blacker than black? Something beneath the football ground that had to remain undisturbed? And what had he, Omally, got Jim into? Mahatma Campbell was to protect Jim – from what? The blacker-than-blackers?

Omally had considered having it out with the professor, but that would have taken more nerve than even he possessed. Omally revered the ancient scholar, and trusted him also. But if Jim was being used as some kind of pawn in some cosmic good-versus-evil game, then John could not be a party to that. Jim was his bestest friend.

John Omally just didn't know what to do.

And when folk just don't know what to do, they always do one of two things: the wrong thing, or nothing at all.

John decided on doing the latter.

Because John, like Jim, now had responsibilities. And to John, these were probably even more irksome than they were for Jim, for while Jim was at least responsible for himself, John was totally irresponsible. Although basically a good man, John Omally did do a lot of things that were not entirely good. They weren't terribly bad, but they certainly weren't good, either.

'I'll try harder,' said John, as he fought to get some sleep. 'And I'll work hard, I really will.'

And then the thought of all the work that lay ahead of him kept him even wider awake.

He'd taken on a lot here. Certainly he hadn't taken it on out of a spirit of altruism. Rather, he had to admit – at least to himself, where no one else could hear him – that he had done it from greed, for the many potential pennies that might be made if the unlikely event of Brentford winning the FA Cup was to occur. There was Jim's bet with Bob the Bookie, for one thing. And even if the team didn't succeed, there would be the profits from the Omally-improved Stripes Bar, and the Omally-improved gift shop, and countless other nice little earners that were sure to present themselves to the aspiring entrepreneur who had a hand in running a football club.

But now . . .

But now it was a case of right here – right now.

John had to organise a Benefit Night for the following evening and fill The Stripes Bar up with folk who were prepared to dig deeply into their pockets for a worthy cause that all considered lost. John took some comfort in the fact that he had made a single telephone call that evening, from The Stripes Bar, and it might just be that this telephone call would prove its worth upon the following morning.

But it was all rather scary, this responsibility lark.

And so John Omally did not sleep comfortably in his bed and did not greet the morning with a smile.

Norman did.

He was up with that lark that always gets up early, because Norman had a phone call of his own to make – to the Patent Office. Norman had all these plans that he'd painstakingly copied from those that had appeared on his computer screen, and Norman meant to find out whether any of the marvellous Victorian inventions pictured in these plans had ever received a patent.

Because if they hadn't . . . !

Norman hoisted the bundle of newly delivered *Brentford Mercurys* on to his counter, took out his reproduction Sword of Boda paper knife, cut away the twine bindings, pressed apart the waxed brown paper and exposed the day's front-page news.

'A hard rain's gonna fall!' exclaimed the shopkeeper, in no small surprise, as he read the headline: BRENTFORD DESTINED TO WIN FA CUP.

An hour later, Neville read this selfsame headline and the text that was printed beneath it. And Neville the part-time barman ground his teeth and loosened an expensive filling.

And at approximately the same time, Bob the Bookie viewed the front page of the *Brentford Mercury* and did grindings of *his* teeth, loosening an even more expensive filling.

And shortly after that, Jim Pooley, a man for whom sleep was becoming little more than a precious memory, also read this headline and the text that was printed beneath it. Jim read it whilst sitting in his office and wondering what he should be doing with himself for the day. And Pooley smiled hugely unto himself and said, 'Nice one, John, you're certainly doing your job.'

'Your job,' said Lily Marlene as she turned up her well-lashed eyes from the newspaper towards the customer who now stood before her counter in The Plume Café, 'is apparently personal assistant to Brentford's new manager, "a gentleman" – and I quote from the *Mercury* – "who is employing a revolutionary approach to the beautiful game, honing the team to perfect fitness and investing them with a will to win that will make them unbeatable this season".'

'This is apparently the case,' said John Omally, smiling his winning smile.

'All rather sudden, isn't it?'

'Grasp the nettle,' said John, miming the grasping there-of. 'Seize the moment and things of that nature, generally.'

'And yet the last time we met, you were buying dodgy fags off a dodgy salesman.'

'All above board,' said John. 'Would you care for a few packs to put behind the counter?'

Lil shook her peroxide head, showering John with pheromones. 'And I quote,' she continued, ' "Mr Omally is organising a fund-raising *Night of the Stars*, a charity auction with A-list celebrities and live music from 'name bands'. A splendid time is guaranteed for all." '

'Stripes Bar tonight,' said John. 'It will be my honour to act as your escort, if you would deign to grace this auspicious occasion with your divine presence.'

'John,' said Lily Marlene, 'this is one bash I wouldn't miss for the world.'

'Splendid,' said John. 'I'll be round here at seven-thirty to drive you there myself.'

'I didn't know you had a car.'

'I don't,' said John, 'but I've got a big whip.'*

'A whip-round?' said Mr Kay of Kay's Electrical Stores in the High Street. 'Naturally I'm aware of the concept. It's just that I've never actually . . .'

'For the club,' said John Omally, who now stood before Mr Kay's counter. 'Every tradesman, and woman, is putting in. I've just come from The Plume – Lily is offering her support.'

'Oh,' said Mr Kay, and he sighed. 'Lily,' he said, in a sighing voice.

'It's called sponsorship,' John continued. 'You get to have your establishment advertised upon the team's shirts. That's the kind of advertising that money just can't buy.'

'But I thought you said—'

'I don't want your money,' said John.

'You don't?' said Mr Kay.

'No,' said John. 'Perish the thought. All I want is *that*.'

---

* The old ones *are* the best.

'What is *that*?' asked Jim Pooley of the man who now stood before his desk.

'It's a mobile phone,' said John Omally. 'I acquired it from Mr Kay in the High Street.'

'A mobile phone?' Pooley drew back in horror. 'I've heard about those lads,' he said. 'They fry your brain with microwaves. Otherwise normal individuals turn into burbling fools the moment they put one of those things to their ear. They feel compelled to call people simply to inform them of their whereabouts. They will be the death of us all. Throw the thing away, John, while you still have the power to do so.'

'Enough of your nonsense, Jim. This little baby is all charged up and ready to bring fortune to the both of us.'

'I am afeared,' said Jim. 'Use it out in the open, lest the death rays penetrate my groin.'

'No,' said John. 'I've read that an independent committee formed from employees of the mobile phone companies has declared these contraptions to be absolutely harmless.'

'Well, don't blame me if you end up speaking in a high voice and feeling the urge to ride Marchant side-saddle.'

'I'll use it outside, if it bothers you so much.'

'It does, and who do you intend to call on it anyway?'

'A-list celebrities. Name bands. All manner of folk.'

'May God go with you, then.'

'Thank you, my friend.'

Now, there are friends who have friends, who have other friends of their own (some of whom, no doubt, live by a river) and John Omally had cultivated many friendships in his time – mostly, it is true, with the female of his species. John had an awful lot of numbers in his little black book and the battery of his new mobile phone *was* all charged up.

Lunchtime found John still making phone calls. He sat now in The Stripes Bar, in the corner he had marked out as his office, in a chair he had acquired from Goddard's Home-Furnishing Stores in the area of the High Street known as the Brentford Half-Acre. Mr Goddard had loaned the comfy recliner (the 3000 series Royal Damask model) in return for having his company logo printed upon the team's shirts. The chair was a plug-in jobbie with a footrest that went up and down to offer support for the varicosely inclined and a vibrating doodad built into the seat for those who were otherwise inclined. John had the remote control in his phone-free hand and John's feet were going up and down.

'So let me get this straight,' John was saying, 'you said to Val Parnell that if your name didn't go above the jugglers, you would not appear.'

John listened as further words poured into his ear.

'And do you think you can get all three Beverley Sisters?' he enquired.

Jim Pooley drank at the bar counter. He had no wish to interrupt John in the course of his business.

'He's certainly doing his stuff, isn't he?' Jim said to Mr Rumpelstiltskin.

'He's switched breweries also,' said the barman. 'We'll have Large here on the hand pump by this evening.'

'Bliss,' said Jim.

'You reckon?' The barman shrugged. 'He's ordered enough beer for tonight to slake the thirst of the Queen's Own Regiment of Foot, Fowl and Four-by-Two, and it's not on sale or return.'

'Beer never is,' said Jim.

'The sort I always ordered was.'

Jim shrugged also.

'And crisps,' said the barman. 'I never trouble with crisps. Too messy, crisps. They get in the carpet. I can't be doing with crisps.'

Jim cast a shufty around and about the dire establishment. There was nothing that crisps could do to make it any worse than it already was.

'And peanuts,' said the barman mournfully. 'And he's hiring in extra bar staff. Women, I'm told.'

'Stop now,' said Jim. 'You'll spoil the surprise.'

'And bunting.'

'Stop, please.'

'I don't know where *you* are going to find all the money.'

'Definitely stop,' Jim told him. 'All will be well.'

'I'm thinking of running away with the circus,' said Mr Rumpelstiltskin.

'Am I speaking to *the* Tom Jones?' Jim heard John Omally say.

'And who exactly am *I* speaking to?' Norman asked.

He was in his kitchenette and his telephone wasn't working properly. He'd had to wire it back into the box into which he'd wired the Internet cable of his computer and there had been some more scorching of the fingertips involved.

'Ah yes,' said Norman. 'The Patent Office, Mr Parker . . . Pardon? Oh yes, I see, Percy Parker the patents person – rolls off the tongue, doesn't it? I said, "It rolls off the tongue." Yes. Listen, I have to talk to you about a number of inventions. I want to know whether patents have ever been taken out on them. Pardon? Oh yes, I see, you're the man to ask. Right then. Sorry, what? Ask you then? Yes, I will.'

'Will I *what*?' Neville stared across the saloon bar counter of The Flying Swan at Old Pete, who stood smiling before him. 'I thought I told you that you were barred for a week.'

'You did,' said Old Pete, who today actually smelt of old peat, for he had been turning his allotment beds.

'And you want me to do *what*?' Neville asked.

'Just put one of these up in your window and a bundle of these on your counter.' Old Pete proffered papers.

'Are they pamphlets?' asked Councillor Doveston, who had just popped in for a swift half-dozen before settling in for his afternoon snooze.

'Flyers,' said Old Pete, thrusting one in the councillor's direction.

'About bees, by any chance?'

'The Brentford Bees,' said Old Pete. 'There's a benefit

fund-raising night this evening at The Stripes Bar. John Omally had these pamphlets run up on the library photocopier. I'm giving them out in return for free entrance to the event. Cheap beer and A-list celebrities.'

'Out of my bar!' cried Neville.

'Excuse me?' said Old Pete.

'You heard me.' Neville reached for his knobkerrie. 'Traitorous knave!'

'Now, let me get this straight,' said Old Pete. 'Are you refusing to display the poster and hand out some flyers?'

Neville's face was a sight to be seen. And not a very pretty one. 'Out!' he roared.

'You are saying,' said Old Pete, unflinchingly, 'that you do not wish to offer your support to an enterprise that might save Brentford football ground?'

'I . . .' said Neville. 'I . . . never—'

'You wish to number yourself amongst the vile would-be despoilers of our borough who seek to destroy our glorious heritage?'

'I never said that.' Neville shook from Brylcreemed head to carpet-slippered toe.

'I'm glad to hear it,' said Old Pete. 'I dread to think of how dire the consequences might be for you if you had.' He mimed once more the throwing of a rope over a high beam.

'Give them here,' snarled Neville, 'and then depart.'

'Are you not going to offer me one for the road?'

'Get out.'

Old Pete chuckled as he shuffled away. 'Don't forget to put up the poster,' he called upon his departure.

'I know it's a bit of a departure from the norm,' John Omally was saying into his mobile phone, 'but please bear with me on this, there is a good reason for it.'

Words of affirmative reply were evidently spoken into John's ear.

'Thanks very much and see you later.' John switched off his mobile phone and slotted it into the top pocket of his jacket. 'All done,' said he.

Jim viewed his bestest friend from the bar counter. 'All done?' he said.

John pressed a button on his remote control and lowered his feet to the unspeakable (but crisp-free) carpet. 'All done,' he said. 'Everything arranged.'

'For tonight? You've done it all?'

'You won't be disappointed. We should be able to raise enough money to pay the team's wages for the next couple of months.' John sauntered up to the bar.

'If I possessed a hat, I would take it off to you,' said Jim.

John Omally saluted him. 'You do your job and I'll do mine,' said he.

'You're really enjoying this, aren't you, John?'

John ordered two pints from Mr Rumpelstiltskin, who didn't waste his time asking for the money. 'We'll pull this off,' John told Jim.

'I wish I shared your confidence.'

'You just wait until tonight.'

'It's going to be a good bash, is it?'

'I think I can promise you,' said John Omally, raising his pint, 'a night to remember.'

'Kenneth More starred in *A Night to Remember*,' said Jim Pooley. 'It was all about the sinking of the *Titanic*, if I remember correctly.'

14

P.P. Penrose – Brentford's most famous son, creator of Lazlo Woodbine, the twentieth century's most beloved fictional genre detective, polymath and genius, and a man who would die before his time in a freak accident involving a vacuum cleaner and a pot of fish paste – had been big in the sixties.

In the music industry.

P.P. – or Vain Glory, as those who knew then knew him – had been the lead singer of that seminal sixties prog-rock ensemble The Flying Starfish From Uranus. Who, through a number of personnel changes (due to what is known in 'the biz' as 'musical differences') later became The Plasma Jets, and later still Citizen's Arrest, and later later still Dada Black Sheep. And later later later still, and probably most famously of all, the seventies supergroup The Rock Gods.

And although old rockers really should know when to call it a day, consign the Wem Vendetta speakers to the garage, fold up the stage clothes that no longer look quite so convincing now that snake hips have swelled from adder to anaconda, they really can't.

There is simply too much of a buzz to be had from getting up on the stage and doing it one more time.

Being an author is a fine enough thing, of course. There are few finer callings. It is a precious thing, a special thing, to bring joy into the hearts of readers. Who could ask for anything more?

Well.

There is that buzz.

That buzz that can only really be attained by being up on

stage bawling into a microphone and working up a good old sweat.

And there is the 'woman thing'. The 'fan-woman thing'. Because, let's face it, how sexy is it being an author?

Well, obviously quite sexy – some might say *very* sexy – but never on the scale of being a rock star. And call it weird and wonderful, or call it something else entirely (possibly due to the water and the direction it goes down the plug-hole) but there are very few rock bands (given, of course, that the members actually manage to go on living) that don't continue to go on playing.

Certainly they may be reduced to the pub circuit, or one of those terrible multi-band retro tours that always seem to involve Nick Heywood or Tony Hadley somewhere on the bill.[*] But they do go on playing.

Folk *do* remember them.

Folk *do* turn up for the gigs.

Which is where the 'fan-woman thing' comes into it. (Or vice versa!)

Many of the giggling, screaming girlies who dampened the seats in those bygone days of slim-hippedness have evolved into rather fine-looking middle-aged ladies, most of whom have also taken that other revolutionary step from married woman to divorcée. And they do tend to turn up at the reunion concerts.[†]

Which can be pretty cool if you're a middle-aged (and several times divorced) author who's looking to pull.

It had been far less difficult than Omally had supposed to enlist the services of The Rock Gods for the Brentford United Benefit Night. Nor, indeed, several other name bands from the past.

'Don Omally?'

A large and horny hand fell upon the shoulder of Omally,

[*] Up at the top, probably.
[†] The term 'reunion concert' is mostly a misnomer. It means that the band that have been playing endlessly and relentlessly for the last three decades have got a new gig in a town they haven't played before.

who was sitting in his office at The Stripes Bar, and the son of Eire looked up to gaze upon its owner.

'Tim McGregor,' said the owner of the hand, now putting it forward for a shake. John Omally shook this hand.

A big hand it was, and horny with it. '*John* Omally,' he said. 'I was speaking to you earlier, I believe.'

'On the Nina[*],' said Mr McGregor. 'I'm the road manager of The Rock Gods. I've a van full of mosh[†]. I'll be needing someone to give me a hand unloading it.'

'Jim here will give you a hand,' said Omally.

'Hang about,' said Pooley, who was lounging near at hand with glass in hand and didn't feel too handy. 'I'm the manager of a football team, not a roadie.'

'Look at the time.' John Omally displayed a wristlet watch before Jim. It was a brand-new wristlet watch. It had been given to John by Mr Ratter, who ran the jeweller's shop in the High Street, in return for an endorsement on the team's shirts. 'It is six-thirty of the evening clock. I have so much here still to organise.' John made expansive gestures.

Jim took a glance about The Stripes Bar. Aside from himself, John, Mr McGregor and Mr Rumpelstiltskin, it was somewhat deserted and looked no more in need of organising than it generally did.

'I can't do it all myself,' said Mr McGregor. 'If it's too much trouble, then stuff it. We're doing this for free and if you can't be arsed to—'

'It's all right.' Jim put up his hands. 'I'd be pleased to assist you. The Rock Gods, did you say? The *real* Rock Gods?'

'How many Rock Gods do you know?'

'Well,' said Jim, 'there's—'

'Don't even start,' John told him. 'Just go and help the man unload.'

Pooley hastened, without haste, to oblige.

---

[*] Rockney rhyming slang – Nina Simone: telephone.
[†] Rockney rhyming slang – mosh pit: kit.

The van stood in the car park outside. It was a very knackered-looking old van, a van that had clearly seen a lot of action. The words 'THE ROCK GODS' had been spray-painted on the sides, although some wag had scrawled out the letter 'R' and substituted a 'C'. Jim viewed the van and sighed. A life on the road with a rock-and-roll band, that really would be something. Mr McGregor flung open the rear doors to reveal a considerable amount of mosh.

'Coo,' said Jim. 'Do you really need all that stuff?'

'What would you prefer, mate? Unplugged? A bunch of Marshas[*] sitting on stools, strumming acoustic guitars?'

'Perish the thought,' said Jim. 'But it all looks rather heavy.'

'Yeah, don't it?' Mr McGregor smiled upon the heavy-looking equipment. 'And heavy makes you happy, as we used to say.'

Jim tried to smile upon Mr McGregor. There was a fair amount of this fellow to smile upon. He had very big hair, which was very dark and very tied back, and he was dark of eyebrow and long and plaited of beard. And he was generously muscled: big and burly were his shoulders, large and rippling his biceps. And all the bits that were visible, bulging from his vest and shorts, were colourfully tattooed with designs of the Celtic persuasion.

'What are you smiling at?' asked Mr McGregor. 'You ain't a Leo[†], are you?'

'Certainly not,' said Jim. 'I'm a Piscean.'

'Then help me *fish* out that Marshall amp and we'll get on *swimmingly*.'

And so, puffing and blowing and trying very hard not to complain at all, Jim Pooley helped Tim McGregor unload the van.

'You see,' said Tim in reply to some question that Jim

---

[*] Marsha Hunt: fool (probably).
[†] Leo Fender: bender.

hadn't asked him, 'it all gets a bit tricky. Mr Penrose wasn't the original lead singer of The Rock Gods. That was Cardinal Cox.'

'Wasn't he in Sonic Energy Authority?' Jim asked.

'Not originally – that was Phil "Saddle-Sniffer" Cowan. The Cardinal was the original lead singer with The Gods, so when he split with them due to musical differences they discovered that he'd copyrighted the name, so they changed it to The God Rockers, which wasn't too good, then later to The Gods of Rock – that was when Mike 'Damp-Trouser' Simpson was lead singer. But he died in a freak accident involving a three-in-one hair trimmer and a pot of fish paste.'

'Where is this leading?' Jim asked as he struggled to unload yet another big, dark loud-speakerish jobbie.

'There's three bands,' said Mr McGregor, taking up his end of same in a single hand and all but heaving Pooley from his feet, 'all called The Rock Gods, all doing the club circuits up north. Each band has one of the original line-up. And they're all Ravis[*].'

'Even this one?'

'This one's probably the worst. I've been with them for twenty years now. I only do it out of *schadenfreude*. I love to see the looks on the faces of the punters, who've usually coughed up twenty quid a head, when the band lurch into their first number and the punters find out just how bad they are. And I like the rioting, too, gives me a chance to keep my hand in with the old martial arts[†].'

'No?' said Jim and he made a horrified face.

'Only winding you up,' said Tim. 'They're a great band. They'll see you all right.'

'I'm glad to hear it,' said Jim, straining to keep his end of the big, heavy speaker jobbie off the ground.

'As long as their needs are met, they'll be fine.'

---

[*] Ravi Shankar: wanker.
[†] Not to be confused with Marshall amps.

'I'm very glad to hear it.' Jim continued with his struggling.

'I'm very glad to hear *you* say *that*,' said Tim, who appeared to be carrying his end with little more than one finger. 'Personally, I find all this "pandering to the needs of musicians" stuff a pain in the backstage*. They get above themselves. They all need a good smack in my opinion.'

Jim Pooley's fingers were now giving out.

'Not much further,' said Tim.

Jim continued with his strugglings. 'What exactly did you mean about "pandering to their needs"?' he asked, when he could find the breath.

'You've not read the riders, then? Your mate Don has the list.'

'I've not seen any list. What's a rider?' Jim had a serious wobble on. 'We'll have to put this down or I'm going to drop my end.'

'Give it here.' Tim took the heavy-looking speaker jobbie, lifted it from Jim's hands and humped it effortlessly on to the stage. 'That's the last of it,' he said.

'Did you really need my help?' asked the exhausted Jim.

'Not really,' said Tim, 'but I enjoy the company and the conversation. Life on the road can be lonely at times.'

Pooley shook his head. 'What is on the list?' he asked.

'Oh, you know, all the usual stuff. White African lilies in the dressing room. Three bowls of Smarties, with all the red ones taken out. The services of an acupuncturist and a foot masseur. Canapés, whatever they are, and—'

'Don,' called Jim, across the bar.

It does have to be said that the plain folk of Brentford, the plucky Brentonians, *do* like an event. And they *do* like to dress for an event. Especially a star-studded event. And so, all over the borough, folk were togging up in their bestest duds, slicking back their barnets in the case of the gents, and primping about at theirs in the ladies'. So to speak. Shoes

---

* Backstage pass: arse.

were being polished and mothballs plucked from the pockets of suits that hadn't seen action since the last time a relative died (so to speak, also).

Lily Marlene put her high-heeled sneakers on her feet and her wig hat on her head. Small Dave, Brentford's pint-sized postman, ironed his man-sized turnups and Soap Distant (Brentford's resident hollow-Earth enthusiast) took a bit of spot remover to his going-out Wellington boots. Old Pete pinned his 14–18 medals of valour to the breast pocket of his dress uniform and Councillor Doveston stuffed pamphlets into every pocket he possessed. The Campbell tucked a claymore into his belt, a dirk into his sock, a pistol into each of his shoulder holsters and a stun grenade into his sporran.

Neville the part-time barman looked gloomily upon his empty bar. He was still wearing his carpet slippers.

Jim Pooley went home for a wash and a change of clothes.

And the clock ticked on towards the hour of eight.

Which was kick-off time for the Benefit Night.

Omally regarded his wristlet watch. 'It's nearly eight,' he said to Rumpelstiltskin the barman.

'Don't blame me,' said that man. 'I don't make the rules. I'm not God, you know.'

'I'll have another pint of something,' said Tim McGregor. 'What do you recommend?'

'Large,' said John Omally. 'Pour the man a pint, please, barlord.'

'Have you got the opossum?' Tim asked Omally.

'Certainly not,' said John. 'I always use a condom.'

'Most amusing,' said Tim, accepting the pint that was drawn for him. 'The opossum that Mr Penrose likes to pet in the dressing room before he goes on. It was at the top of the list of riders. Well, under the lady-boy.'

'Ah yes,' said John. 'The list of riders.'

'Was that "ah yes" as in yes, you've got it? Or just "ah yes", you vaguely remember the list?'

'Ah yes,' said John. 'Hello, who's this?'

A long, thin fellow with an exciting shock of bright red hair had entered The Stripes Bar, looking somewhat lost.

'Can I help you?' John called to him.

'Tom Omally?' asked the man.

'John,' said John. 'I think there must be something wrong with my mobile phone.'

'Oh, right,' said the long, thin fellow. 'Well, I've got the Beverley Sisters outside in my van. Could someone help me unload them?'

Jim Pooley was having a bath. Jim was trying very hard to remain cool, calm and collectable. It wasn't easy. But then this *was* John's responsibility. If anything went wrong to-night, then he, Jim, was not to blame for it. Even though the responsibility for everything that went on with the club now lay with him, John and he were a partnership and *this* was all down to John.

Jim doodled about a bit in the bath water. He'd play it cool, have a good soak, tog up, slowly stroll down to The Stripes Bar, catch the action, press the flesh, do a bit of networking (Jim had once heard this phrase used), put names to faces (also this one) and if all went well . . .

Take the glory.

And if all didn't go well . . .

Know where to lay the blame.

'Don't worry,' Jim told himself. 'All will go well. John knows how to organise things. Not that I've ever seen him organise something like this before, but he'll be fine. It will all be fine. It will, it really will.'

'They're dead,' said John Omally.

'That's not an expression I like to use,' said the long, thin fellow with the exciting shock of bright-red hair. 'Resting between engagements is the way I like to put it.'

Tim McGregor peered in through the open rear doors of the knackered old van that was now parked next to his knackered old van. 'They do *look* dead,' he said.

'They're living legends,' said the long, thin fellow. 'They're the Beverley Sisters. My name's Howard, by the way.'

'Is that hyphenated?' asked Tim.

'No, it's Welsh.'

'But they *are* dead,' said John Omally. 'They're preserved corpses. They're mummies.'

'I thought they were sisters,' said Tim.

'Technically speaking, they're not entirely dead,' said Howard, 'although I have to confess that *he* is.' And Howard pointed a long and twiglike digit over the shoulders of the three Beverley Sisters, who sat in their glittering stagewear staring sightlessly into space, towards . . .

'That's Tom Jones,' said Tim. 'The Rock Gods once supported him in Abergorblimey in Wales. No, they were Citizen's Arrest then. Tom made the lead singer – Kevin 'Pud-Puller' Smith, it was then – flush the bog for him after he'd had a Gordon.'[*]

'Tom Jones is dead?' said John Omally. 'This is news to me.'

'Died in a car crash in Nevada in nineteen eighty-three. The CIA put out a hit on him due to his involvement with a covert operation that sought to liberate the captive space aliens from Area Fifty-one.'

'You can't put dead rock stars on stage,' said John.

'Tom's never really been *rock*,' said Howard. 'He's more pop and ballad. But of course you can put them on stage, it's done all the time. Animatronics, remote control, recorded tapes. How do you think that Cher goes on and on, always looking the same?'

'Dead?' said John. 'You're telling me that Cher's dead, too?'

'I always thought she was,' said Tim.

'Please keep out of this,' John told him. 'But how come you have Tom Jones's body in your van?'

'You phoned me up, asked for him to appear. He's just

[*] Gordon Giltrap: crap (and how true).

finished his latest British comeback tour and I was boxing him up to return him to the States, so you caught me at the right moment. You're not in the biz, are you?'

'Who's that?' John pointed.

'Tina Turner,' said Howard, 'but you can't have her tonight. One of her legs has come off and I've got to glue it on again.'

'This is absurd,' said John Omally.

'It's business.' Howard shrugged. 'After Elvis snuffed it, along with Marc Bolan in the same year, the music industry decided that although sales figures went up after well-known musical figures died, there was more money to be made if they "kept them alive" indefinitely. My dad worked in Hollywood as a special-effects man. EMI employed him to wire up Tina and Tom after they died at Nutbush City Limits in a freak accident involving some green, green grass of home and a pot of fish paste.'

'Was there any CIA involvement in that?' Tim asked.

'Funny you should say that,' said Howard.

'I thought so,' said Tim.

'And they really look convincing when they're on stage?' John asked. 'Even though they're dead?'

'That would appear to be the case, wouldn't it?' said Howard.

'Then we'd better get them unloaded before anyone sees us.'

'Fair enough,' said Howard. 'Would you like Cliff as well? I brought him along on the off chance.'

And so they came, if not in their thousands, then at least in their hundreds – the plain folk of Brentford, the plucky Brentonians, dolled up and dressed to kill. John Omally sat at the door, taking the money.

'You got the Beverleys,' said Old Pete, viewing the hastily penned poster that now adorned the wall behind John. 'I thought they were dead.'

'Free admission,' said Omally. 'Move through, please.'

'Can we get autographs after?' asked a lady in a straw hat.

'If I'd known Tom Jones was going to be here, I'd have worn a pair of knickers to throw on the stage.'

The Rock Gods now sat in their dressing room. It wasn't a dressing room as such; it was Jim Pooley's office, which was better than some dressing rooms, but not as good as most. And it was now a very crowded dressing room/office. Howard was testing out the Beverleys with his remote control. Tom Jones was propped up by the window. And an all-girl funk/soul band rejoicing in the name of Stevie Wonderbra were going through a workout routine, much to the pleasure of Tim McGregor. And Tony Hancock. And then there were the jugglers. The Rock Gods weren't happy.

'Where's my opossum?' asked P.P. Penrose (lead singer).

'And where's my lady-boy?' asked Captain Venis Wars (bass guitarist).

'And my Smarties without the red ones?' asked Steve 'Chucky' Wykes (lead and rhythm).

'And my two ounces of Moroccan Black?' (Jah Dragon on drums.)

Tim McGregor finished off his seventh pint of Large. 'Guess who I just shagged in the back of a van?' he asked.

'Tina Turner?' said Captain Venis Wars.

Tim McGregor grinned.

The Stripes Bar was now filling up. Rather well. All the team were there, dressed in a selection of suits supplied to John Omally by Mr Gavin Armani, who ran the men's outfitters in the High Street, in return for an endorsement on the team's shirts. They were shaking hands with all comers and draining pints of Team Special that Omally had laid on especially for them.

'I have great hopes for this evening,' said Ernest Muffler. 'Things are going to change, we are going to succeed.'

'The builders didn't turn up today,' said Billy Kurton. 'My patio's never going to get finished.'

'When we win the cup,' said Morris Catafelto, scratching

at that nose of his that so resembled an engineer's elbow, 'you'll be able to buy a hundred-acre estate in Spain and patio over the whole blinking lot.'

'Do you really believe we'll win?' asked Trevor Brooking (not to be confused with the other Trevor Brooking). 'I mean, let's be sensible here, those tactics we practised – they're not exactly orthodox, are they?'

'They're great,' said Ben Gash, the goalkeeper. 'They keep you buggers well away from my end of the pitch.'

'Listen,' said Dave Quimsby, 'I can hear a lark rising in Candleford[*].'

'Will there be chicken on a stick?' the lady in the straw hat asked Omally. 'I do like chicken on a stick.'

'Please move along, madam,' Omally told her. 'You're holding up the queue.'

'Canapés are so important at a function,' said the lady, 'especially one where Tom Jones is going to appear. Chicken on a stick there should be. And mule fingers to dip in your soup.'

'And strained crad,' said a gentleman with a whiskered face. 'The lady in the straw hat is correct. Is the meal included in the price of admission?'

'I once had sprouts dipped in chocolate and deep fried,' said the lady. 'But that was at a wedding in Tierra del Fuego. They really know how to live, those Tierra del Fuegans.'

'You think *they* know how to live,' said the bewhiskered gentleman. 'I once attended the ordination of a wandering bishop in Penge—'

'I've heard it's a very nice place,' said the lady. 'But I've never been there myself.'

'Very nice,' said the gentleman. 'And you should have seen the dips they had, and tasted them, too. There was super gnu and trussed snapping toad and creamed jack-anapes and—'

---

[*] Dave is the one with the exceedingly large ears. In case by chance you might have forgotten. As if!

'Uncle Tom Cobbleigh and all?' asked the lady.

'No,' said the gentleman.

'So I said to Val Parnell,' said Tony Hancock, who'd tired of Jim's office, to Alf Snatcher, who tired easily of sitting due to his waggly tail, 'if my name does not go above the jugglers, I will not appear.'

'I once asked my wife,' said Alf, 'what her favourite sexual position was and do you know what she said?'

Tony Hancock shook his head.

'Next door with the neighbour,' said Alf.

'Old Pete,' called Omally to Old Pete, who was loafing about close at hand, 'will you take over on the door for me? I have to get things organised inside.'

Old Pete smiled the smile of one who had been loafing about close at hand awaiting the opportunity to make the acquaintance of the ready cash. 'It would be my pleasure,' he said.

John Omally bagged up what money he had already taken, stuffed it into the poacher's pocket of his jacket, left his seat on the door and took himself inside.

The Stripes Bar was now very full. In fact, it had never known such fullness before. Mr Rumpelstiltskin stood behind the bar, a frozen, terrified figure. The bar staff John had engaged for the evening were, however, going great guns. These were young bar staff.

And female.

Tracy waved a delicate hand towards John. 'Good do, innit?' she called.

John gave Tracy the thumbs up. 'Make sure the team get as much of the Team Special as they want, on the house,' he called back. And John's eyes fell upon the breasts of Tracy and verily the sight thereof brought joy unto John. For John had made intimate acquaintance with these breasts in times past, and hopefully would do so again in times soon to come. 'Speak to you later,' called Omally. 'I have to get things started.'

John Omally eased his way through the crush, mounted the stage and took up the microphone. He blew into it and did the old 'one-two-one-two'.

Feedback flooded The Stripes Bar and brought the crowd to attention.

'Good evening, all,' said John, in the manner of the now legendary Dixon of Dock Green.

'Nice start,' said Constable Meek, who had come along in plain clothes to 'observe the proceedings'.

'Eh?' said Constable Mild, whose clothes weren't quite so plain and whose tie would have caused a riot in Tibet.

'Welcome, each and all,' said Omally. 'Welcome and thank you for attending this Night of the Stars to raise funds for our club and team. I feel confident in saying that you are about to enjoy a night to remember.'

'Kenneth More was in *A Night to Remember*,' Old Pete said to Small Dave as he relieved him of his entrance fee and pocketed same. 'It was all about the *Titanic*, if I remember correctly. And I do, because I went down on it.'

15

Norman regarded his reflection in the dressing-table mirror of the marital bedroom. 'Pretty damn hot to trot,' said the shopkeeper, grinning and straightening his wig. 'A regular dandy.'

The mothballs were out of the pockets of his granddaddy's double-breasted evening suit. This suave apparel now graced Norman, who took a little bow before the mirror.

'My lords, ladies and gentlemen,' said Norman, 'and indeed Her Majesty the Queen, it is with great pleasure that I receive this Nobel Prize for Services to Mankind. So great, however, is my wealth now that I couldn't possibly accept the cheque.'

'What are you babbling about?' The voice of Peg swelled from the *en suite* bathroom that Norman had constructed in the wardrobe.

'Just singing, my dear. Are you almost ready to go?'

'I'll be ready when I'm ready and not a moment before.'

'Time heals all wounds,' said Norman. 'And it's a small world. Although I wouldn't want to have to paint it.'

'What was that?'

'I said "take your time".'

'Don't worry, I will.'

Norman grinned at his reflection. If only she knew, he thought, if only she knew. But she wasn't going to know, because he was not going to tell her.

Norman had slipped out during the afternoon to the local Patent Office (next to the town hall, in the building with the weathervane shaped like a DNA strand on the top) and there had registered five (count them!) five brand-new never-before-registered patents. And if all went well, and Norman could think of absolutely no reason why all should not go well, he would very shortly be very, very, very rich indeed.

'I shall buy a castle,' whispered Norman to his reflection. 'An old castle on top of a hill, with a laboratory in it. And I'll have all manner of equipment sparking out all over the place and those big we-belong-dead levers that you throw and there—'

'What was *that*?'

'Nothing, dear. There I will uncover the formula, The Big Figure. I think I'll go water-skiing, too, I've always fancied that.'

'Fancied *what*?' Peg appeared from the *en suite*. She wore the gold figure-hugging strapless Lurex number she had worn upon the night Norman met her, in that time so long ago, at The Blue Triangle Club in Ealing Broadway. On a Tuesday night in May, with Jeff Beck on stage and Norman full of Purple Hearts. The gold Lurex figure-hugger hugged somewhat more than it used to. Peg had let it out, inserting gussets of the pink gingham persuasion, which lent her the appearance of an exploding cushion.

'How do I look?' Peg asked.

'Like an expl . . . Like a vision,' said Norman.

'Yes.' Peg viewed the area of herself that the dressing-table mirror was capable of reflecting. 'Like a vision.'

'From the Book of Revelation,' whispered Norman. 'Shall we be off?'

Off and running, up upon the stage at The Stripes Bar, were a local tribute heavy-metal band called IRONIC MAIDEN (in capital letters). They were *very* loud. The crowd pressed themselves back from the stage, feet were trampled upon, drinks spilled and voices raised.

These raised voices went unheard.

'I quite like *them*!' bawled Mr Rumpelstiltskin towards Old Pete – the noise of the band had raised the barman from his vertical coma.

'I've got my deaf aid switched off,' the oldster replied. 'You'll have to shout. Give me a large dark rum and put it on Mr Omally's bill, I'm on the door.'

Mr Omally was up in Mr Pooley's office. It was a very, very, very crowded office. John could but barely squeeze himself into it. 'The jugglers go on next,' he said. 'Can anybody hear me? Where *are* the jugglers?'

'They're practising over there,' Tim McGregor told him, 'with bits of the Beverley Sisters. And I'll tell you something else.'

'If you must,' said John.

'The Rock Gods aren't happy,' said Tim. 'No opossum. No lady-boy. No dancing dwarves. No angel fish in an aquarium shaped like a handbag. No—'

'Have Stevie Wonderbra arrived?' John asked.

'Yeah,' said Tim, 'but there's something not quite right about them.'

'I saw them play at The Shrunken Head a couple of weeks ago,' said John. 'I hope they're wearing the same short skirts.'

'The one that was standing next to me taking a pee in the gents was,' said Tim.

'Eh?' said Omally.

A knocking sounded at the office door. John wriggled about and managed to winkle it open an inch or two.

'The Count Basie Orchestra,' said a dapper fellow beaming through the crack at John. 'Can we come in?'

Jim Pooley awoke to find his bath water cold. 'By Crom,' said Jim, who occasionally favoured some Robert E. Howard, 'I must have dropped off. I work too hard. Better get off to the gig.' Jim tried to rise from his bath, but, strangely, he could not.

'That's odd,' said Jim. 'Must have a bit of pins and needles in the old pegs. Probably stress-induced. It's like that for we high-powered business types. I hope my hair doesn't go white – although I wouldn't mind a bit of greying at the temples. Very Stewart Granger.' Jim struggled to rise once more. And found to his horror that not only did his legs not work, but his arms weren't working either.

'Either you come out, or we come in,' the fellow from the Count Basie Orchestra called through the door crack.

'I can't get out,' John called back to him. 'This room appears to have reached critical mass.'

'Can you pass out our bowls of jelly babies, then?' called the fellow. 'The ones with the black jellies taken out. I mentioned them in the list of riders.'

'Can't seem to get to them right now,' called John. And, 'Not now, madam,' he continued, as one of the Stevie Wonderbras squeezed forcefully against him.

'Sorry,' said the Wonderbra. A rather tall Wonderbra. With a rather deep voice for a girlie.

'Get the orchestra on stage,' John called through the door crack. 'I'll be with you as soon as I can.'

'Mr Omally,' called the voice of Howard, 'do you have any superglue? This Beverley's head keeps falling off.'

IRONIC MAIDEN came off stage to very little applause. They made Devil-horn finger gesturings towards the crowd and headed for the bar. The Count Basie Orchestra began to set up their music stands and tune their instruments.

Sitting behind the moneymaking table on the door once more, Old Pete stuck his wrinkled mitt out for money. 'It's a fiver,' he said, 'for the boys of Brentford.' And then he looked up at the latest arrival.

The latest arrival looked down upon Old Pete. Not that the ancient moneytaker could see the new arrival's eyes. These were hidden, along with his face, in the shadow of the new arrival's broad-brimmed black hat.

It was a *very* black hat.

It matched in blackness the blackness of the new arrival's long black coat, which swept the ground, showing only the toes of his very black boots.

Old Pete shuddered, as one does when someone 'walks over your grave'.

The figure of darkness dipped into an atramentous pocket with a nigrescently gloved hand and drew out a five-pound note. He held this towards Old Pete who viewed it with a rheumy eye. The figure made curious gurgling sounds, which might have passed for speech. Old Pete took the fiver.

It was cold and damp.

But a fiver *was* a fiver and Old Pete pocketed same.

'Go through, please,' he said in a tremulous, whispery tone.

'Help!' The voice of the incapacitated Pooley had a tremulous tone to it, too, but there was nothing whispery about it.

'Help!' Jim cried. 'Man in trouble here. Not waving, but drowning – well, not drowning as such, but *HELP!*'

But his voice echoed emptily; Jim's landlady was no longer in the house. She had dolled up and offed herself to the big event at the football ground.

'Help!' wailed Jim. 'Somebody help. Something very odd and scary has happened to me.'

'There was something very odd and scary about that fellow,' said Old Pete, shuddering once more. 'Oh hello, who's this? Watchamate, Norman.'

'Watchamate, Old Pete,' said Norman.

'And who is this you have with you? Mae West, as I live and wheeze.'

'Shut your trap, you superannuated turd,' said Peg.

'I love it when you talk dirty.' Old Pete sniggered.

'Two,' said Norman, digging in his pockets for change and then recalling that he'd left his wallet behind in the bedroom. 'Oh dear.'

'Oh dear?' asked Old Pete.

'I seem to have left my wallet behind.'

'You can owe me,' said Old Pete. 'Don't worry, I won't forget. And Norman . . .'

'Yes?' said the suave-looking shopkeeper.

'Did you destroy all that stuff in your lock-up, like I asked you to?'

'Well,' said Norman, 'now that you ask . . .'

Old Pete smiled upon Norman. The smile quite put the wind up the shopkeeper. 'Never mind,' said Old Pete. 'Did you come here in your van, by the way?'

'Actually, we did,' said Norman. 'Why do you ask?'

'No reason. Go on through, have a good time, stay late.'

'Thank you, Old Pete,' said Norman.

'Get a move on, you,' said Peg.

'Move,' shouted John. 'Move back so I can get out of the door.'

'We're all a bit jammed,' said Tim. 'Careful now, you almost spilled my pint.'

'I have to get out of here.' John pushed and shoved.

'Careful where you're pushing, mate,' said the surprisingly tall Stevie Wonderbra. 'You nearly elbowed me in the nuts.'

'We could pass you over our heads,' said Tim, 'to the window and you could climb out. There's a fire escape – I was sick on it earlier.'

'By Crom,' said John Omally.

The Count Basie Orchestra launched into a Robert E. Howard swing number. Not a lot of people are aware that as well as penning the now legendary Conan the Barbarian series, Robert E. Howard also played tenor sax with John Steinbeck's Jumping Jazz Cats in the nineteen thirties. Something to do with authors not pulling as many women as jazz musicians in the nineteen thirties. Probably.

'I know this one,' said Councillor Doveston to Mr Rumpelstiltskin the barman. 'It's about bees.'

'It never is,' said the barman. 'It's about the silent-screen actress Theda Bara. Howard was in love with her. Her name is an anagram of Arab Death, you know.'

'The production department at Fox thought that up,' said Councillor Doveston. 'And I should know, I was one of them. A *Thedaoptrus barata* is a kind of bee, a bit like a Klaatu Baradu Nikto, but with more stripes.'

'You live and learn,' said the barman, ignoring the many pleas that were coming at him for some service at the bar. 'Which is to say that some folk live and learn. Me, I know nothing.'

'He looks to me like a man who knows nothing,' said a casual observer who had recently escaped from the 'special' ward at the Brentford Cottage Hospital. 'But then, what would *I* know? I'm psychotic, me. Anyone got a handbag I could have a poo in?'

'I'm in the poo here,' called Jim Pooley, 'and growing very frightened. Won't someone help me, *please*?'

'Is Jim Pooley here?' Professor Slocombe asked Old Pete.

'Haven't seen him, Professor,' replied Old Pete, 'but I expect he's inside, putting his weight to the bar counter lest it collapse unexpectedly.'

'I'll just have a word with him, then.'

'Fiver admission,' said Old Pete. 'Please, sir, if you will. Good cause and all that.'

'Good cause indeed.' Professor Slocombe drew out a medieval chain-mail purse and counted coins from it.

'I've no change for golden guineas,' said Old Pete.

'Then keep the change – and, Peter?'

'Yes, sir.'

'Best put back the thirty-five pounds that have *accidentally* fallen into your waistcoat pocket.'

'Yes, sir, I will indeed.'

'And, Peter, it might prove necessary that I visit you in the near future with regards to certain herbs that you grow upon your allotment patch.'

'Ah,' said Old Pete, and a certain significant look was exchanged between the two ancients. 'I am always at your service, sir.'

'That is good to know.' Professor Slocombe smiled, extended his hand and had it shaken in a significant fashion.

★

Professor Slocombe entered The Stripes Bar. It was very, very, very, very crowded now, but a path cleared before him.

'Has anybody seen Jim Pooley?' asked the professor.

Jim Pooley hollered some more and then took to listening. Surely that creaking sound was the hinges on the front door. And a slam. And yes, footfalls in the hall.

'Help!' Jim resumed his hollerings. 'Upstairs here, me, Jim Pooley. Down but not out. But trapped in my bath. Please help me.'

'Thanks for your help,' called John Omally, gaining the fire escape and all but slipping to his death upon vomit. 'Jugglers next, then Stevie Wonderbra, then the Beverleys, then The Rock Gods. Then, er, well, Tom Jones for the finale, I suppose.'

'We're bigger than Tom Jones,' squeaked P.P. Penrose, whose face was pressed against the upper windowpane of the raised-at-the-bottom-bit window. So to speak. And very badly, too.

'Taller, maybe,' called the voice of Tim McGregor. 'And less dead, perhaps.'

'And *where* is my opossum?' demanded P.P. Penrose.

'See you later.' John made his slippery way down the fire escape.

'Escape,' whispered Jim, as footfalls fell footsteplike upon the stairs. 'In here,' he shouted. 'Help me, please.'

The Count Basie Orchestra played a jazz classic about fire escapes, bath tubs and . . .

'Bees,' said Councillor Doveston.

'Ernest Hemingway wrote that song,' said Rumpelstiltskin. 'He used to play sax with Evelyn Waugh.'

'Waugh?' said Councillor Doveston. 'What was he good for? Absolutely nothing. In my opinion.'

'If I had an opinion,' said the casual observer, 'it would be that the barmaid over there looks as if she'd know her way around the inside of a string vest.'

'What has a string vest got to do with anything?' asked Councillor Doveston.

'Well, Evelyn Waugh invented the string vest, didn't he? While he was at the Somme. Or was it the hammock?' The casual observer scratched at his head. Casually.

'It was another author who invented the hammock. Some thriller-writer chappie.'

'Dashiell Hammock?' Rumpelstiltskin suggested.

'Could somebody please serve us? I'd like to open an account,' said Norman. 'A pint of Large for me and a—'

'Nose bag for your horse?' asked the casual observer, casually observing Peg.

To any observer, casual or otherwise, Jim Pooley was clearly in distress. He appeared frozen into his bathwater.

A knock came at Jim's door.

'Enter, please,' called Jim. 'And please help me.'

The door swung open and a certain blackness entered Jim Pooley's rooms.

The jugglers wore black, and gold, and silver, too. Leotards they wore, and little pom-pommed slippers on their feet. They'd made it through the window and down the fire escape and as the Count Basie Orchestra left the stage (after an encore, which was an old George Orwell number) to riotous applause, the jugglers were doing what they did best. Or, at least, what they did second best, for they were accomplished installers of double-glazing during weekdays.

Juggling. Of course.

'I've never been a big fan of juggling,' said Barry Bustard, circus fat-boy and Bees substitute, to Don and Phil the conjoined twins (who were drinking doubles[*]). 'Too much danger of stuff falling on you.'

'Depends what's falling on you,' said Don.

[*] Ho ho ho.

'Or *who*,' said Phil.

'It's why I never travel by air,' said Barry.

'No, that's because you're too fat to get into a seat,' said both Don and Phil.

'That, too, but aeroplanes crash. I went to America once to tour with Barnum's circus. I didn't take a plane, though. I was smart, I went by ship.'

'How did the tour go?' Phil asked.

'No idea, I never got there.'

'Why?'

'Because the ship sank.'

'You'd have been better off going by plane, then.'

'No, I wouldn't – the ship sank because the plane fell on it.'

A fire extinguisher fell on the head of one of the jugglers.

'I thought he was being somewhat overambitious there,' said Councillor Doveston to Mr Rumpelstiltskin. 'Do you have any objection to me handing out a few pamphlets while I'm here?'

'I'm beyond caring, me,' said the barman. 'I really do think I'll join the circus.'

'Have any of you seen Jim Pooley?' asked Professor Slocombe.

Jim Pooley looked up at his potential rescuer. 'Thank God you've arrived,' said he. 'I am stuck here, and most indecently, too. Who . . .'

Jim's look became a stare. This stare became a look once more. It was a look of horror.

Something black, blacker than black, loomed large over Jim. It was all shadows and darkness and a strange smell came to the nostrils of Jim.

It was the smell of the grave.

'I . . .' said Jim. 'Oh dear God, help me, someone.'

A voice spoke unto Jim, but in a language Jim did not understand. If he had been able so to do, then he would have known the words that were spoken.

Those words were: 'There is no help for you.'
Then the figure of darkness plunged forwards.
And forced Jim's head beneath the cold bath water.

16

John Omally was back upon the stage. 'A big hand for the jugglers,' he said, as a couple of chaps from the windscreen-wiper works who knew first aid (because they'd been on the course, because it got you off work and you got an extra five pounds a week for being a safety officer) fanned at the face of the unconscious juggler and offered him a glass of water (they hadn't paid much attention while on the course).

'Next up,' said John, 'is another local band. They're going to be big – and I should know, as I have lately become their manager. Please give it up–' (John had heard this expression used upon a Yoof TV programme) '–for Stevie Wonderbra.'

And John Omally left the stage.

But not, as in the case of Elvis, the building.

Professor Slocombe caught John's attention as he left the stage. 'John,' said the professor, 'where is Jim?'

'Skiving off,' said Omally. 'Went home for a bath, leaving me to do all his work for him. You should give me his job, Professor. I wouldn't say a word against Jim, of course, he's my bestest friend, but the responsibility is too much for him. Perhaps we could draw up a contract and—'

'Silence.' Professor Slocombe put his finger to his lips and John fell silent. 'I believe Jim to be in danger,' the professor said.

'Danger?' said John. 'Jim?' said John. 'What danger? What can I do?'

'Just carry on with what you are doing. I will attend to what must be done. The evil is amongst us here, I believe.'

'Evil?' said John, recalling the conversation that he had overheard between the Campbell and the professor. The one he had really been meaning to pluck up enough courage to ask the professor about. 'What evil is this?'

'I will be keeping an eye upon you,' said Professor Slocombe. 'You have nothing to fear.'

'*Me*?' said John. '*I* have nothing to fear?'

Jim had only known true fear on one previous occasion.

And *that* had involved drowning.

It was when Jim had, as *he* told it, *fallen* off the pier at Brighton.

Jim had been a teenager in the days of the Mods and the Rockers. Jim had gone to Brighton with his teenage sweetheart Enid Earles to have one of those dirty weekends that Brighton is famous for. Jim had really loved Enid Earles. They'd been at Grange Junior School in South Ealing together and had met again at The Blue Triangle Club on the night Jeff Beck played there. Jim had thought that it would take a lot of persuading to get Enid to go down to Brighton with him. Jim had called upon all of his powers of persuasion to assist him. And Jim being Jim, and being the big romantic that he was, he had even bought Enid an engagement ring from Mr Ratter's jewellery shop in the High Street.

In case it was needed.

Enid, however, had gone remarkably willingly. Somewhat *too* remarkably willingly, as it happened. Enid had really been up for a dirty weekend in Brighton.

Although, as it turned out, not necessarily with Jim.

They had taken an evening stroll upon the pier, which was a very romantic thing to do, in Jim's opinion. Enid had imbibed somewhat too freely of Babycham in the pier bar. And there had been this young hobbledehoy from Canvey Island there with his mates, and they had been Mods – Ivyshop loafers, parkas, the whole business. And they had come down on their motor scooters.

Jim and Enid had come on the train.

And there had been some unpleasantness in the bar.

And there were a lot of Canvey Island Mods and only one of Jim.

And the Canvey Island Mod squad had thrown Jim off the end of the pier.

And Jim couldn't swim.

And Jim had sunk beneath the waves and the last thing he'd seen was the face of Enid, laughing at him. The Canvey Island Mod was kissing her neck.

And the fear of impending death had been so great.

And the water had been so cold.

And Jim had woken up in the back of an ambulance.

But there was no ambulance now to wake up in.

And Jim's head was beneath the cold bath water.

And there was no breath left in the lungs of Jim Pooley.

And he could see once more the laughing face of Enid Earles.

'A G and T,' said Enid Earles to Tracy the temporary barmaid at The Stripes Bar. Enid was married now, with three kids. She hadn't married the Mod from Canvey Island, though. She had married the butcher's lad who had got her up the duff at an offal-rendering convention in Isleworth. She'd put on a lot of weight since her teenage years, but this hadn't lessened her enthusiasm for dangerous sexual liaisons with strangers.

'What danger?' John spoke closely into the ear of Professor Slocombe. Stevie Wonderbra were making a whole lot of noise now – though good noise it was, all funk and soul and everything.

'That lead girl singer has an Adam's apple,' Old Pete, now up at the bar for a doorman's freeman, observed, for although his hearing was ropy, his eyesight was acute.

'Just trust me,' said the professor. 'All will be well.'

'But you said Jim was in danger,' said John. 'What kind of danger? Real danger? Is someone trying to kill him?'

'Calm yourself, John. No one is going to kill Jim Pooley.'

Hands clapped together in wild applause. Stevie Wonderbra waved and wiggled their hips about.

'That bass player's legs need a shave,' Old Pete observed.

'Tell me what is going on,' said John to the professor.

'Now is neither the time nor the place.'

'I'm going to Jim.'

'Stay here, beside me. All will be well.'

'Well, well, well,' said Old Pete, drawing out his pocket watch and perusing the face. 'Ten o'clock already.'

Now, there are sometimes moments of silence even in the most crowded bar. Generally these occur at precisely twenty minutes past the hour, or twenty minutes to. Why this is, nobody knows, though many have their suspicions. However, upon this particular evening, the moment of silence occurred on the stroke of ten.

And from the distance somewhere came a sound: a dull but powerful thump, it was. It rattled the optics behind the bar.

'What was *that*?' was the question that issued from many mouths.

'Sounded to me,' said Dave Quimsby, whose very large ears rarely failed him, 'to be the sound of a lock-up garage in Abaddon Street exploding. Third from the bottom end.'

Norman heard the words of Quimsby, as indeed did many other folk. Norman turned his eyes upon Old Pete.

'Don't you turn your eyes upon me,' said the elder. 'I told you those computer parts were dangerous.'

Norman opened his mouth to issue accusations but thought better of it and tried once more to open an account at the bar.

Peg was chatting with Scoop Molloy from the *Brentford Mercury*.

'Yes,' Scoop was saying, 'apparently it's a sure thing. The team's tactics have been formulated by an international expert. It's just a matter of the team turning up and going through the motions, really. The *Brentford Mercury*'s name is going on all the team's shirts. Cost an arm and a leg, but what publicity, eh?'

Peg viewed the chatty young man. She'd noticed that he had a nice little bum.

Scoop Molloy viewed Peg. He'd always had this thing for fat women.

'You have magnificent tits,' said Scoop Molloy.

'Would you care for a shag?' asked Peg.

'Now, don't call me crude,' said Old Pete to Councillor Doveston, 'but between the two of us, I'd shag *that*.'

'I do call you crude,' said the councillor. 'But what is it that you'd shag?'

'Any one of them,' said Old Pete, pointing a wrinkly paw towards the side of the stage. 'The Beverley Sisters.'

'Why are they in wheelchairs?' asked the councillor.

'Saving their legs for the dancing, I expect. I can never remember their names though, can you?'

'Larry, Curly and Mo,' said Councillor Doveston.

'I won't be a mo,' said John. 'I'm just going to check the pumps – can't have the beer running out, can we?'

'You weren't thinking of running out yourself, were you, John?' Professor Slocombe asked.

'Perish the thought,' said John and he pushed his way into the crowd.

Stevie Wonderbra had finished their set with a Stevie Wonder number.[*]

Howard wheeled the Beverleys across the stage, set them

---

[*] Lest the reader think that the opportunity for another running gag about musically inclined authors was passed up here, let it be said that Stevie Wonder began as an author, but changed his mind and became a musician instead. Something to do with him not being able to see the typewriter keys. Or something.

in a row, adjusted the microphones before them, then climbed down and began to jiggle with his remote control.

John made his way to the door and prepared to take his leave at the hurry-up.

But, to John's consternation, the door was closed and apparently locked.

'That's probably a breach of fire regulations,' said John, rattling the door. 'No, hang about, this door bolts from the inside, and it's not bolted.'

John rattled at the door once more, but the door remained firm. It wasn't going to budge. 'Someone's jammed it from the outside,' was John's opinion, and he made off in further haste to seek another exit.

'Oh, they're up,' said Councillor Doveston, 'although they do look a bit shaky on their pins.'

'They still look good for their ages,' said Old Pete. 'What do you think they must be in years, now? Seventy? Eighty?'

'Eighty at least,' said the councillor. 'And do you know,' and he spoke behind his hand, 'I seem to recall that *I* shagged the one in the middle about fifty years ago. I was greatly attracted to her beehive hairdo. I was in the music biz then, you know. I was one of Johnny Kidd's original Pirates.'

'You *too?*' said Old Pete.

The door at the other end of the bar was closed, too, and John Omally couldn't open it. Sounds, however, came from beyond this door. John recognised these sounds: they were the sounds of passion. John put his ear to the door.

'Do it to me, big boy,' he heard the voice of Peg urging.

'Open this door!' shouted Omally.

The sounds of passion died. The sound of a trouser zip being pulled up was faintly to be heard.

'I know you're out there,' called Omally. 'Open the door, this is an emergency.'

Sounds of the door being rattled now came to John and he did some rattling of his own. But this door, like the last, would not be opened.

'Rear door,' said John to himself. 'Door leading to the fire escape.' And John was off on his frantic way once more.

'Great to see them once more,' said Councillor Doveston. 'They haven't lost their old magic, have they? They wobble a bit, but they can still belt out a number.'

'So which one did you say you'd shagged?' Old Pete asked. 'Larry, was it, or Mo?'

'Not sure now,' said the councillor, 'but I recall that she was a bit curly, if you know what I mean.'

Norman, who had given up on getting a drink for himself, was tucking into whatever anyone put down near him. 'You have no respect for women,' he told Councillor Doveston.

'That's true,' said the Councillor, 'but I display no prejudice. I have no respect for men, either. Bugger off.'

'Women are precious,' said Norman. 'Well, some of them are.'

'I respect bees,' said Councillor Doveston, 'and I'm getting up a petition to save the *Africanus psychopathia*.'

'That's the killer bee,' said Norman. 'Why would you want to save *that*?'

'Bees only sting you if you upset them. Here, have a pamphlet. You send me a quid and you can adopt a bee from one of my hives. You get an adoption certificate and everything.'

'That sounds like a sound business proposition,' said Old Pete.

'Would you care for a pamphlet, then?'

'No,' said Old Pete, 'but my bog is full of bluebottles. Bung us half a quid and you can have the lot. I'll even paint stripes on them, if you want.'

John Omally wanted out. He wanted to get to Jim. Jim was in danger. Big danger. And John would never be able to forgive himself if something was to happen to Jim. Something that he, John, could have stopped from happening.

The door that led to the fire escape would not be opened.

John fought with this door. This was the last door. There was no other way out of The Stripes Bar. The door remained impervious to John's assault. It was a sturdy door, as were the others, made sturdy to withstand the attentions of the light-fingered gentry who targeted the rear doors of licensed premises.

Regularly.

'Open!' shouted John, kicking at the door.

A curious gurgling sound caused John to turn his head.

A gaunt, black figure looked down upon him.

'Door won't open,' said John. 'Give me a hand, please.'

The gaunt, black figure extended a hand. Clothed in a black leather glove, it was. The forefinger of this hand waggled at John and the blackly hatted head slowly shook.

'Who are you?' asked John. And then a certain coldness entered his being, a certain feeling of dread, of not-rightness. And a smell entered the nostrils of John.

And it was the smell of the grave.

'What is that smell?' asked Councillor Doveston.

'Beer,' said Norman. 'Team Special, all the team are guzzling it down.'

And so the team were, and singing, too, a limerick kind of a song about a young girl from St Mawes.

'Not *that* smell,' said Councillor Doveston. 'It's a kind of electrical smell.'

'Ah,' said Norman, 'an electrical smell. Let me have a sniff.' And he sniffed. 'Definitely an electrical smell. Ozone, that is – or possibly it's called Freon – but it's one of my favourite smells.'

'It's growing a bit strong,' said Old Pete, 'and my sense of smell has been somewhat impaired since I had my nose blown off at Ypres in the first lot.'

'They did a good job sewing it back on,' said the councillor. 'I lost a kneecap at Gallipoli, or was it Skegness? Anyway, I put it somewhere.'

'It *is* getting strong,' said Norman. 'It seems to be coming from the equipment on the stage.'

'It's coming from one of the Beverley Sisters,' said Dave Quimsby. 'I can hear things popping in her neck – like transistors, I think.'

'The Beverley Transistors?' said Old Pete. 'That doesn't sound right. Which one is it coming from?'

'Larry, I think. Yes, definitely. You can see a bit of smoke now.'

Old Pete stared. And Councillor Doveston stared. And Mr Rumpelstiltskin stared. And Norman stared. And so did Dave Quimsby.

And so did the lady in the straw hat.

Who hadn't said anything much for a while.

'That Beverley Sister is on fire,' she said.

And even though she hadn't said anything much for a while and had indeed uttered only six words now, they were potent words. Or at least one of them was.

And that one was the word 'fire'.

'Fire exit,' said John. 'Must get out of the fire exit.'

He could have said anything, really, such as 'get away from me', which would have been equally appropriate.

The figure in black plunged forward at John.

'Get away from me!' shouted this man, putting up his fists. The figure was upon him, engulfing him in a terrible blackness. John swung fists, but to his further horror, for horror it was that now filled his being, he found his fists to be swinging at nothing at all.

A cold, black force surrounded him, pressed forward upon him, smothering, consuming. But John could not strike it down. The figure was more like a fog than a man – a stifling, suffocating fog.

'Help!' cried John, but somehow the blackness swallowed up his words.

'Help!' cried someone else. And someone else cried, 'Fire!'

Fire! Fire! Fire! The word was repeated by mouth after mouth. And indeed a fire there was.

A Beverley floundered about on stage, smoke issuing

freely from the cleavage of her pink chiffon gown. Howard tapped madly at the remote control and the Beverley took to beating at her chest, in the manner once favoured by Tarzan.

'For the love of God,' cried Norman, 'put her out, someone.'

'I think the fire extinguisher got broken when it fell on the juggler's head,' said Mr Rumpelstiltskin. 'Throw your beer. Everyone throw your beer.'

'Get real,' said Ernest Muffler, as folk took to panicking all around and about him. 'Throwing beer is a last resort, surely.'

'I'll save you, love,' said Old Pete. 'Chips,' he told his half-terrier who, although not having received a previous mention, was nevertheless, as ever, at his side, 'go and piddle on the lady.'

Chips slipped his collar and hastened to oblige.

Larry Beverley, however, now appeared to be beyond even Chips' piddling, even though the dog *was* a prolific footpath-fouler. Larry Beverley was now well ablaze. She – or possibly it is more tasteful to refer to *she* as *it*, considering that there wasn't really too much of the original *she* involved – stumbled about on the stage, flaming away like a good'n and bashing into The Rock God's speakers, setting them afire.

'Fire!' The word was now a scream. And the stampede had begun. Folk did as folk always do in such a situation: panic and put themselves first.

'Don't panic!' Mr Rumpelstiltskin shinned up on to the bar counter. 'Nobody panic,' he shouted. 'Everything will be all right.'

'That's impressive,' said Old Pete, who hadn't left his barstool, 'taking control like that. I wouldn't have thought he had it in him.'

'This bar is fitted with a fire-defence system,' shouted Mr Rumpelstiltskin, which lessened the panic, the pushing and the shoving somewhat. 'It will come on in just a moment and extinguish the flames.'

'Sprinklers,' said Norman. 'Good fire security that. No-body panic.' He joined his voice with Mr Rumpelstiltskin's. 'The sprinklers will kick in in a moment.'

'Better than sprinklers,' said Mr Rumpelstiltskin. 'It's a halon system – American chum of mine put it in.'

'Halon?' said Norman. 'That's not for public places. That gas is deadly if you breathe it in.'

'Panic!' shouted Mr Rumpelstiltskin. 'To the exit doors, everyone.'

And he launched himself from the bar counter into the pushing, shoving crowd.

Who had now reached the exit doors.

The exit doors that would not open.

John Omally, swallowed up in darkness, was pressed against one of these very exit doors.

Kicking, stamping, screaming, panicking, the crowd surged towards the exit doors – but only those before the bar counter. John was on his own. On stage now, all three Beverleys crackled and flared. Amps and speakers took fire.

The flames licked at the low ceiling, licked at the halon system.

It was mayhem now. It was fear and horror.

Death by fire or suffocating gas.

Crushed folk were passing from consciousness. The weak were being trampled by the strong.

And . . .

'Stop!'

A voice rang out above the screams and cries of horror and pain. A single voice that spoke with authority. And something more.

'Stop!'

The crowd seemed to freeze.

And to turn.

And to look.

Towards . . .

Professor Slocombe.

The ancient scholar stood upon the stage, the flames roaring about him.

'Cease!' Professor Slocombe flung out his fragile arms. A wave of force swept the length of the bar. The flames to either side and behind him froze. Became still. And vanished away.

'And *open*!'

The exit doors burst from their hinges, flinging themselves away from the building. Folk fled, but somehow in a more orderly fashion. They helped up their fallen comrades, comforted the weak. They fled with dignity.

Professor Slocombe leapt down from the stage.

It was an impressive leap. Old Pete, who had not left his barstool, was mightily impressed by it. For one thing, it was the grace of the leap – it appeared to be in slow motion. And the very scale of the leap, too, for it was a leap that travelled the entire length of the bar.

'Unhand that man.' The voice of the professor rang out once more. Old Pete gazed towards the subject of this command, but could see nothing. Nothing but a curious darkness that seemed to engulf the rear fire door beyond the bar counter.

'Release him, I say.' The professor, his feet now once more upon the floor, upon the unspeakable carpet, raised his hands above his head. And to Old Pete's amazement the area of darkness at the door appeared to coalesce into the figure of a man. And behind this man another figure appeared – that of John Omally. And John Omally sank to his knees and then fell forward on to his face.

And then Old Pete – and indeed Councillor Doveston, who had also remained upon his barstool, for, being ancient, as was Pete, what chance would they really have had by joining in with the panicking? And also, it had to be said, Norman, who had been cowering and constructing for himself a makeshift gas mask from ale-soaked beer mats – each and all of these three were forced to shelter their eyes from the glare.

It began as sparklets of light issuing from the fingertips of

Professor Slocombe. And these sparklets grew into a blinding light and this light swept towards the figure of darkness that now stood defiantly before the professor.

And so the three observers did not see the gush of rainbow colours as the figure of darkness dissolved into absolute nothingness.

17

John Omally awoke, coughing and gagging, to find himself no longer in The Stripes Bar but in the study of Professor Slocombe, sprawled upon an overstuffed *chaise-longue*.

John caught his breath and coughed and gagged some more. And then words came to him and John managed, 'Jim. Where is Jim?'

'Jim is fine,' said the professor. 'Have no worries for Jim.'

'I do.' John tried to rise, but fell back in exhaustion.

'He's fine,' said the voice of Mahatma Campbell. And John looked up to see this fellow standing framed in the opening of the professor's French windows. Mahatma Campbell held in his arms the prone and lifeless-looking body of Jim Pooley.

'Jim!' cried John. 'What have you done to him?'

'He'll be fine,' said the Campbell. 'I got to him in time.' And he carried Jim to a fireside chair and dropped him into it.

'Careful,' said John, coughing somewhat more.

'I'll raise Jim to consciousness,' said the professor. 'And I think some drinks are called for.' And he rang the little Burmese brass bell upon his desk.

'Drinks,' said John, 'and an explanation also. What have you got us into, Professor? That man who attacked me – he wasn't a man.'

'All in good time,' said the professor.

'Now is the best time there is.'

'Then at least wait until I have awakened Jim.'

★

Gammon brought drinks upon a tray: a large decanter of whisky and four large glasses.

Professor Slocombe drew Jim Pooley into consciousness. Jim spewed water then took to coughing and gagging.

'A spell of disablement was placed upon him,' said the Campbell as he sampled Scotch and found it pleasing. 'A darkster entered his dwelling and pushed his head 'neath his bathwater. I'd been keeping an eye out as you told me to, Professor. I crept up upon it and struck its head from its shoulders with the claymore you'd blessed for that purpose.'

'What is going on here?' Omally demanded to be told.

'When Jim is his old self again,' said the professor.

'I almost am,' said the sodden and shivering Pooley. 'I will be when I've had a glass of Scotch. And Christ's cap and old brown dog!' exclaimed Pooley. 'I'm naked.'

'We did observe that,' said John, 'but I, for one, was too polite to mention it.'

'You?' Jim gawped at the Campbell. 'You carried me naked through the streets of Brentford?' Jim covered himself with a velvet cushion.

'I'll have Gammon bring you some clothes.' Professor Slocombe reached towards his brass bell.

But Gammon was already standing in the inner doorway. 'I felt that our nudist guest might feel the need for these,' he said, proffering a set of silk pyjamas and a dressing gown.

The fire blazed away in the fireplace and offered warmth to Jim, who sat before it cradling his glass of Scotch in trembling fingers, well dressed in PJs and a dressing gown, but still in a state of shock and no small terror.

'I am so sorry,' said Professor Slocombe. 'I never thought it would come to this. Well, not quite so soon, anyway.'

'Not so soon?' said Omally. 'You set us up for something terrible. You betrayed our trust in you.'

'I know it appears that way, but it was not my intention.'

Jim looked towards John. It was quite clear to Jim that something terrible had happened to John also.

'Sorry I missed the Benefit Night,' said Pooley foolishly. 'How did it go? Did you raise a lot of money?'

'He's in shock,' said Omally. 'Look what you've done to him.'

'I am sorry,' said Professor Slocombe, easing himself into the fireside chair opposite Jim. 'The two of you deserve an explanation and I will give it to you. You will not like it, but I will give it to you just the same.'

'What about the team?' Jim asked. 'They didn't get too drunk, did they, John? They'll be all right for tomorrow's game?'

'They're fine,' John assured Jim. 'They didn't get drunk at all. I had the brewery knock up a special batch of non-alcoholic beer – Team Special. The team may have thought they were getting drunk, but they weren't.'

'You're a genius,' said Jim. 'Where am I, by the way? This doesn't look like my bedroom.'

'He *is* in shock,' said Professor Slocombe. 'Perhaps we should speak of these matters on the morrow.'

'We'll speak of them now,' said John. 'You have put the life of my bestest friend in danger – and my own, but that is by the by. Tell us what is going on and what you have got us involved in.'

'Indeed. Mahatma, if you would be so kind, would you kindly refresh the glasses of my guests?'

Mahatma Campbell poured Scotch for John and Jim.

'What I am about to tell you,' said Professor Slocombe, 'is the truth as far as I know it to be. You may choose not to believe it. Indeed, the Buddha himself said, "Doubt everything and find your own truth." But I say unto you, I believe this to be the truth.'

'Go on,' said Omally.

'Firstly,' said the professor, 'it is essential that Brentford United win the FA Cup. This is what it is all about.'

John Omally sighed, loudly and pointedly. And he coughed a little, too, as he still had a cough or two left in him. 'Let me get ahead of you here,' he said. 'Are you suggesting that whatever attacked me and attempted to murder Jim has something to do with football?'

'In a manner of speaking, yes.'

'Oh,' said John. 'So what attacked us, demons raised by a rival team? What would that team be, then – Hell United?'

'Hull United?' said Jim. 'Are we playing them tomorrow? I thought it was Penge.'

'Why don't you take a little sleep, Jim?' said John. 'I'll wake you up when all this is over and take you home.'

'It would probably be better if both of you spent the night here,' said Professor Slocombe.

'Better and better,' said John. 'Get your head down, Jim, and keep it down until morning. I'll mind your Scotch for you.'

'I can mind my own Scotch, thank you,' said Jim. 'How were The Rock Gods? Were they good?'

'Fair to middling,' said John. 'You didn't miss much. Now please go on, Professor.'

'Thank you, John. When I said that in a manner of speaking this is all about football, what I meant by it is that this is all about football grounds. And magic. And the forces of evil. And the past, as we understand it, not being what we understand it to be.'

'What could be clearer?' said John.

'I will start at the very beginning,' said the professor, 'when God created man and placed him in the Garden of Eden.'

'Have to stop you there,' said John. 'I am not unacquainted with scripture. I know both Old and New Testaments well.'

'The Garden of Eden,' said Professor Slocombe, 'was right here – right here in Brentford.'

'Perhaps I shouldn't have stopped you just there,' said John. 'I should have let you build up to that.'

'I was planning to do it in a most dramatic way.'

'The Garden of Eden was right here?'

'Right here.'

'Right here,' repeated John. 'And do you know what?'

'What?' Professor Slocombe asked.

'That's the biggest load of old rubbish I have ever heard in my life. Apart from the time Jim told me that he had acquired a goose that laid golden eggs.'

'It did,' said Jim. 'Sporadically.'

'It was a chicken,' said John. 'And this is a turkey.'

'Where?' Jim asked, looking around. 'What kind of eggs does *it* lay?'

'Fried ones, probably. But this *is* rubbish, Professor. I want the truth from you. Something terrible happened tonight. You owe us the truth.'

'I am telling you the truth. You know that I am working upon my book – *The Complete and Absolute History of Brentford*. I have uncovered many strange things regarding the borough. This is perhaps the strangest, but this is what all this is about. The biblical Eden was here, John, right here in Brentford.'

'Are you serious?' John stared at the antiquated scholar. 'You *are* serious, aren't you?'

'If the Garden existed, it had to be somewhere.'

'In a somewhat more southerly and sunnier clime, I had been led to believe.'

'It was here,' said the professor, 'where the football ground now stands.'

'So what is it that lies beneath the turf?'

'Ah.' Professor Slocombe smiled. 'You show your hand, John. How much did you overhear of my conversation with Mahatma Campbell?'

'Not enough to understand what's really going on.'

'Then let me put this to you as simply as possible. Yes, something does exist, imprisoned beneath the football ground, something that must not be released upon mankind.'

'What?' John asked.

'The serpent,' said Professor Slocombe.

'The serpent? The serpent that tempted Eve? The Devil?'

'Not the Devil. Not Satan. Satan, as we know him, is Lucifer, the morning star, the fallen angel. This is a more ancient evil – the original evil that is responsible for the original sin.'

'And it's under the football ground?' John's voice lacked somewhat for conviction.

'The serpent never left Eden,' said Professor Slocombe. 'You know your scripture. God punished the serpent, cursed it to crawl for ever upon its belly. And he confined it also, that it might never leave Eden.'

'And someone wants to dig it up? Is that what you're saying? If I believed for a moment what you're saying, which I'm most uncertain as to whether or not I do.'

'You have experienced the evil,' said the professor.

'I certainly have, but who sent this evil to attack Jim and me? The serpent – is that what you're saying?'

'A magician,' said the professor, 'as skilled in the Black Arts as I am in the White. Whether I am his equal or not I do not know. Myself and the Campbell here are guardians, guardians of Eden. It is our duty to protect the borough, indeed the world, you might say, because there is no telling what horrors might be unleashed should the serpent be released from its bonds.'

'Why would God let that happen?' John asked. 'If he boxed up the serpent, the serpent will stay boxed up. That's my opinion.'

'God does tend to take what our American cousins would refer to as a rather "hands-off approach" nowadays,' said Professor Slocombe, acquainting himself with further Scotch. 'You will notice that although there was the Old Testament and the New Testament, there was never a third book in what would surely have been a best-selling trilogy. God does *not* interfere in the affairs of man in the way he did in biblical times. He has retired from all that kind of business.'

'You know him well, then?' said Omally.

'I'd like to say that we were on chatting terms,' said Professor Slocombe. And then his voice rose harshly. '*But that would be really stupid.* Pardon me.'

'Consider yourself pardoned,' said John. 'So, and please let me get this straight in my mind, the serpent of Genesis is trapped in Eden, which is now underneath Brentford football ground, and an evil magician – and I'm one step ahead here – my guess is that he controls the Consortium that seeks to purchase the ground.'

Professor Slocombe nodded. 'His name is William Starling. I know nothing of his origins. There seems to be no record of his birth. He appeared, as if out of nowhere, some five years ago and during that time has amassed a vast business empire. He is a very powerful black magician.'

'And he is intent upon releasing the serpent upon mankind?'

'In a word, yes.'

'Yes,' said Omally, thoughtfully and slowly. 'And you, knowing all this – and, I suspect, knowing in advance that the only way Brentford Football Club could be saved was if the team were to win the FA Cup – saw to it that Jim was given the job of manager, putting him directly in the line of fire of this demonic magician!'

'In the same word,' said the professor. 'And that word is yes.'

'Why?' John asked. 'Why Jim? What has he ever done to you?'

'I haven't done anything,' said Jim. 'Were the Beverley Sisters good, John? Sorry I missed them.'

'I would not let any harm come to Jim,' said Professor Slocombe.

'Harm did come to Jim – and to me, too.'

'We will be more vigilant in the future.'

'There will be no future,' said John. 'We quit.'

'We?' said the professor.

'Jim and me.'

'What am I quitting?' Jim asked. 'Have I got a job?'

'You did have, but you haven't now. Come on, Jim, we're leaving.'

'I really wouldn't do that, John.'

'You betrayed us.' John dragged himself from the *chaise-longue* and pointed an accusing finger at Professor Slocombe. 'You literally sentenced Jim to death.'

'Jim is a good man, John.'

'I know he is a good man. He's my bestest friend.'

'I need you,' said the professor, 'both of you. I would have willed it differently. I had hoped that neither of you would ever have found out the truth, that I could have protected you from it. I underestimated my opponent. For this I apologise to both of you.'

'Well,' said John, 'we're still on our way. Enough of this.'

'You cannot leave, John, not without protection.'

'Then give us your protection and set us free from this madness.'

'You will prosper when we succeed.'

'Profit no longer enters into this. Life is more valuable than profit.'

'And there you have it.' Professor Slocombe smiled. 'In your goodness, John. You are a rogue and no doubt about it, but the moment you regained consciousness you thought of Jim rather than yourself. I could not have chosen better in this borough than the two of you. You care for each other, and for Brentford – and for the world, too, I think.'

'Of course I care,' said John. 'But—'

'I will care closely, John, for the two of you. This must be done. I ask you – no, I beg you, to help me in this.'

'You *beg* me?' said John.

'On my knees, if necessary.'

'No,' said John, 'that won't be necessary. That would be undignified. I would never ask that of you.'

'Then you will assist me in this most important matter?'

John shrugged. 'Do I really have any choice?' he asked.

'You always have a choice.'

John turned towards Jim. 'I know you are hardly *compus mentis*,' said John, 'but what are your thoughts on this?'

'Zzzzzzzz,' said Jim Pooley.

18

Jim Pooley awoke to a sunshiny Saturday morning.

Jim Pooley awoke to find Gammon smiling down upon him.

'Wah!' went Jim. 'What are *you* doing in my boudoir?'

'Coffee and croissants, sir,' said Gammon, removing the silver dome from an eighteenth-century croissant dish and wafting delicious smells in Jim's direction.

'What am I doing *here*?' Jim asked, a-blinking and a-rubbing of his eyes. 'I am at the professor's house and . . .' Jim did pullings at himself. 'These aren't my pyjamas,' he continued. 'My pyjamas have the A Team on them.'

'You imbibed a little too freely last night, sir. The professor was pleased to put you up.'

'Oh,' said Jim. And, 'How kind,' said Jim. And, 'Pour me a coffee then, please,' said Jim also.

Gammon obliged and then bowed himself from the bedroom.

Jim sat up and sipped coffee.

'Imbibed too freely?' Jim shook his head from side to side. He didn't have a hangover. What time had he and John left The Stripes Bar? Jim now cocked his head upon one side. What time had he actually arrived at The Stripes Bar? And what had actually happened at the Benefit Night at The Stripes Bar?

Jim Pooley made a very grave face. He had absolutely no memory of the evening before.

Scoop Molloy's memories of the evening before had been put down upon paper even before the evening before was done. Scoop had viewed the smoke and the exploding exit doors and the fleeing folk through the rear window of Norman's van in the car park, where he and Peg had retired to make the beast with two backs after John had disturbed their earlier tryst outside the fire exit. Scoop had been forced to excuse himself from the frantic coitus. He was a professional. The news always had to come first.

So to speak.

And upon returning to the offices of the *Brentford Mercury* with many pages of purple prose, he had been granted that moment so beloved of newsmen throughout the ages: that moment when they can cry, 'Hold the front page!'

And, to his chagrin, Scoop discovered that the front page was already being held for information that was coming in regarding a lock-up garage in Abaddon Street that had apparently been destroyed by a terrorist bomb. The headline 'BIN LADEN ATTACK UPON BRENTFORD' was already being set up in six-inch Times Roman lettering.

'You'll have to put your piece on the sports page,' Badger Beaumont, the *Mercury*'s inebriate theatre critic, told him. 'I was there, at the scene of the outrage, walking my old brown dog, and I got my headline in first.'

'But I have "HUNDREDS FLEE IN TERROR",' said Scoop, 'and I saw all kinds of weird stuff going on in The Stripes Bar after the fleeing was done. I peeped in through the doorway.'

'Sorry,' said Beaumont. 'That's journobiz, I guess.'

'But,' said Scoop. 'But . . .'

'Butter?' asked Professor Slocombe. 'For your toast, Jim?'

Jim now sat, with John, at the professor's breakfasting table in his marvellous conservatory. It was one of those wonderful Victorian jobbies with all the cast-iron fiddly bits and the brass handles on the walls that you turn to engage complicated mechanisms which open upper windows. And there was all manner of exotic foliage and rare blooms perfuming the air, and it was all very blissful.

And Jim was in a state of some confusion.

'I can't remember anything,' said Jim, accepting butter for his toast that he might enjoy a second breakfast, as in the manner of Hobbits. 'I remember going home for a bath and that's it. Waking up here this morning is the next thing I remember.'

Omally cast a cautious glance towards the professor.

A knowing one was returned to him.

'I expect it will all come back to you in time,' Omally told Jim, although John's fingers were crossed beneath the table. 'But suffice it to say, it was a most profitable night. We took almost two thousand pounds on the door alone. I haven't checked the bar takings yet, but we have more than enough to pay the team for the next few weeks.'

'Oh my God,' said Jim. 'The team – did they all get drunk?'

'No,' said John. 'I told you, I—'

'You told me what?'

'Nothing,' said John. 'The team all drank the Team Special ale I had the brewery lay on for them. It was non-alcoholic. They'll be fine this morning.'

'Where are my clothes?' Jim asked.

'I'm having them cleaned for you, sir.' Gammon poured Jim further coffee. 'You were a bit sick.'

'Oh my God once more,' said Jim. 'Not *here*? I'm so sorry, Professor.'

'You have nothing to be sorry for, Jim. You acquitted yourself in a gentlemanly manner.'

'But I can't understand why I can't remember anything.'

'It's all for the best, Jim. Trust me on this.' John raised his coffee cup to Jim. 'Think only of today, Jim. Today is going to be a big day for Brentford United.'

Jim felt his stomach knotting. The prospect of the forthcoming match was terrifying in the extreme.

'Do I *have* to go?' Jim asked.

'You certainly do,' said Professor Slocombe. 'But have no fear, I will be going with you.'

'You will?' said Jim.

'I will, and I will be sitting beside you on the bench.'

'That makes me feel a good deal better. What about the bus, John?'

'All arranged,' said John Omally, dabbing a serviette about his laughing gear. 'Big Bob Charker will pick us up from your place at ten.'

'Will I have to walk home in these PJ's?' Jim asked.

'I will fetch you some appropriate daywear, sir,' said Gammon.

And the new day came to Brentford.

To find many in the borough most unwilling to greet it.

The 'STRIPES BAR HOLOCAUST', as it would come to be known due to the six-inch Times Roman headline on the rear sports page of the day's edition of the *Brentford Mercury*, would linger long in the memories of those who had been there to experience it. And those who had been there would speak of their experiences again and again over the coming weeks, each lingering long upon the gory details and even longer upon whatever deeds of personal bravery they claimed to have performed.

But upon this particular morning, all concerned were laying long in bed, trying to sleep the whole thing off.

Big Bob Charker, Brentford's tour-bus driver, had always been an early riser and today was no exception. He was already at the depot polishing his bus.

The depot was more of a shed than a depot. In fact, it *was* a shed – a shed large enough to house a bus, but a shed more so than less. It was an aged shed that had once been an engine shed in the days when steam trains still ran from Brentford Station, days that were now far gone.

The yard, ex-railways and now the property of Brentford Magical History Tours, Ltd. looked just the way such a yard should look: decoratively decked out in rusted ironwork of the corrugated persuasion and flanked around by tall fences topped with razor-wire. A sign on the gate read 'BEWARE THE SAVAGE DOGS THAT ROAM THESE PREMISES BY NIGHT' and a great many of those corroding oil drums that always look as if they must contain something very, very dangerous indeed.

Big Bob Charker was a man of biblical proportions and spoke in a manner appropriate to his stature.

'Dost thou truly think the team will win through to the FA Cup Final?' he asked Periwig Tombs, the mechanic, who was wiping his hands upon an oily rag, as mechanics will do whenever they are given the chance.

'Nope,' said Periwig. 'Why do you ask?'

'Because John Omally spake unto me as one who hath the wisdom of Solomon, and did persuade me to provide free transport for the team in return for an endorsement upon their raiments.'

'Woe unto your house, then, Big Bob,' said Periwig sarcastically. 'For surely it was written that he who giveth his services freely goeth without beer, but still must render unto his mechanic that which is owed unto him. Weekly.'

Big Bob placed his official cap upon his head. 'Verily I say unto you,' he said, 'that should the team fail to gain victory over the Pengeites, then lo, they will be walking home.'

'I'm not walking home in this,' said Jim. 'I look like Bertie Wooster.'

John Omally cast an eye over Jim's apparel, which consisted of a three-piece, plus-fours suit of green Boleskine tweed. 'To be honest,' said John, his fingers crossed once more, but this time in his pocket, 'it rather suits you, makes you look, how shall I put it . . .'

'A prat?' Gammon suggested, tittering behind his hand.

'A character,' said John. 'Football managers are noted for their eccentricities – weird haircuts, unkempt eyebrows, odd regional accents, a penchant for blonde Swedish television presenters.' John made a wistful face at the thought of the latter. 'And ill-fitting nylon tracksuits. You'll cut a dash in that outfit. In no time folk will be copying you. You could well become a fashion icon.'

'Do you really think so?' Jim did a foolish kind of a twirl.

'Absolutely,' said John, bravely keeping the straightest of

faces. 'Now we really must be going. Big Bob will be on his way.'

And Big Bob was.

He drew the big bus to a halt before Jim's lodgings and tooted the horn. Jim – who had, upon his return home in the company of John, been somewhat surprised to find that there were no clothes missing from his inextensive wardrobe and was demanding explanations, as well as stuffing his wallet and cigarettes into the pocket of his tweedy plus-fours and getting himself into a state and receiving no satisfactory replies to his endless questions – was hustled by John from the house and out into the street.

'Sodom and Gomorrah!' went Big Bob, taking in Pooley's apparel. 'Surely thou art Bertie Wooster himself.'

'Morning, Bob,' said John, smiling up and into the cab. 'Looking forward to watching the team put paid to Penge?'

'Fear the wrath that will surely visit their failure,' said Big Bob in ready reply.

'I'll take that as a yes, then,' said John. 'All aboard now, Bertie.'

'What did you say?' Jim asked.

'I said, "All aboard, it's nearly ten-thirty."'

'You certainly did not.'

John and Jim climbed aboard.

'Can we go on the top deck?' Jim asked. 'Sit at the front? We can stomp our feet over the driver's head until he comes upstairs and threatens to chuck us off.'

'Sit there.' John indicated the bench seat next to where the conductor would be standing, had there been a conductor to stand there.

'Spoilsport,' said Jim, slumping down sulkily and taking out his cigarette packet.

Big Bob glanced back at him through the little glass hatch at the rear of his cab. 'No smoking downstairs,' he told Jim.

John made his way to the driver and handed him a list of the team's addresses. 'As fast as you can, please,' he told Bob.

'You should have arranged that the team all meet up at

the football ground,' Jim told John upon his return. 'We could have picked them all up in one go.'

John shook his head. 'I don't trust them,' he said. 'This way we can beat upon their doors and shout up at their bedroom windows. We'll shout loudly, and they'll feel too guilty to refuse us.'

'You don't miss a trick, do you, John?' said Jim.

'I've missed one or two so far,' said John in an enigmatic manner, 'but I won't be caught out again.'

'Don't forget to pick up the professor,' said Jim.

'He's second to last on the list.'

And it *was* a struggle. And they *weren't* keen. But, one by one, John and Jim winkled them out. They all looked in a bit of a state.

They all looked rather hungover.

'I thought you said . . .' said Jim.

'I *did*,' said John, and he addressed the team and the substitutes who now filled most of the bus's lower deck. 'I have something of which to inform you all,' said John.

'Oh yes?' came mumblings from here and there.

'None of you actually has a hangover,' said John.

There were mutterings at this, and the word 'bollocks' was brought into service.

'No,' said John, as Big Bob took a corner sharply and nearly had him off the bus. 'The Team Special beer that I had laid on for you was non-alcoholic. I did it for your own good, so that you would play at your best today.'

There were further mutterings, and then someone said, 'We know.'

'Who said that?' John asked.

'Me,' said Dave Quimsby. 'And don't shout so loud, I've got a hangover.'

'You have *not* got a hangover,' said John. 'It was non-alcoholic beer.'

'It may have been at The Stripes Bar, but it wasn't at The Beelzepub.'

'What?' said Omally.

'After all the fire and chaos . . .' said Dave.

'Fire and chaos?' asked Jim.

'Fire and chaos,' said Dave. 'Gwynplaine Dhark from The Beelzepub turned up at the ground. In this very bus, actually . . .'

'What?' said John once more.

'Short-notice booking,' Big Bob called back through his little glass hatch. 'He had to pay double.'

'Gwynplaine Dhark took us all for a celebratory drink at his pub,' said Dave. 'On the house. We didn't get home until after *three*.'

'Treachery!' cried John. 'Sabotage!'

'Not so loud!' cried all and sundry. Especially Dave Quimsby.

'This is bad,' said Jim. 'This is very bad.'

Big Bob brought the bus to a halt at Professor Slocombe's house and Jim helped the ancient scholar aboard.

'We've been sabotaged,' Jim told the professor. 'Gwynplaine Dhark took the team back to his pub for a late-nighter. They've all got hangovers.'

'So much the better,' said Professor Slocombe.

'So much the *what*?' said Jim.

'Trust me.' The ancient fellow tapped at his ancient nose. 'I think I'll go and sit upstairs now,' he continued. 'I've always wanted to sit at the front and stomp my feet over the driver's head until he comes up and threatens to throw me off.'

There was one more stop to be made before the trip to Penge proper began. And this was at Mohammed Smith's Sports Shop in the High Street. John had done a deal with Mr Smith. It was a sponsorship deal.

Bing and Bob made many 'road' films, but they never made *The Road To Penge*. Although they should have, because it would have been a goodie.

There are so many exciting places to pass through on the

road from Brentford to Penge. There's Kew, Barnes, Putney, Wandsworth, Clapham, Streatham, not to mention West Norwood.

But as for Penge itself, well, what can be said about Penge? Well, it's sort of Sydenham. And Sydenham is Crystal Palace, because the Crystal Palace was rebuilt upon the hill there when the original Crystal Palace in Hyde Park was demolished.

For those interested in the architecture of football stadia, the Penge ground was designed by Sir Giles Gilbert Scott, the legendary designer of the K2 red telephone box. Who also invented Blu-Tack, Velcro and the jumbo jet.[*]

It is a truly magnificent stadium constructed from cast iron, teak and glass, with a saucer dome rising above four segment-headed pediments, reminiscent of the tomb of Sir John Sloane in St Pancras Churchyard and capable of seating nearly two people.[†]

'Behold the stadium,' said Omally, as Big Bob drew up the big bus before it.

'My goodness,' said Jim, 'but surely that's a telephone box.'

'Next to the telephone box, Jim.'

'Ah,' said Jim. 'That's a fine-looking stadium.'

'Park the bus around the back please, Bob,' said John.

'I wilst in but a moment,' said Big Bob. 'But first I'm going upstairs. If the professor doesn't stop stomping his feet, I shall cast him forth from the bus.'

'Is it just me,' said Jim, 'or do we live in rather weird times?'

'It's just you,' said Big Bob. 'I'll park around at the back. Verily.'

Penge had been having a good run of luck over the last few seasons. They'd won games and managed to run at a profit

---

[*] No he didn't. [Ed.]
[†] Surely that's a telephone box? [Ed. again.]

and they'd used this profit to do what is all-important in the world of the football club: buy in top talent.

Over the preceding six months they had taken on a new barman, a new plumber in residence, a replacement Scottish groundskeeper (the old one having run away to join the circus) and still had enough money left over for the manager to acquire a new bungalow, a new Ford Escort and a new mistress, who was a blonde Swedish television presenter.

And they had really smart shirts and a really smart changing room.

The Scottish groundskeeper led Jim, John, the professor, the Brentford team, its substitutes and Big Bob Charker to his office. 'You'll have to change in here,' he told the team. 'We dinna hav' a visiting-team dressing room – we knocked the wall out and extended the bar.'

'Perk up,' Jim told the team, who looked anything but perked up (hence his telling). 'It doesn't matter where you change, it's what you do on the pitch that counts.'

'I think I'll probably throw up on the pitch,' said Alf Snatcher, waggling his waggly tail beneath his tracksuit pants. 'Or even here, at a pinch.'

'Why is it that I lack for confidence?' Jim whispered to John.

'I've no idea, my friend. Shall I pop into the bar and get us in a couple of beers?'

'Good idea.'

'And a small sweet sherry for me,' said Professor Slocombe. 'My feet are sore from all that stomping.'

Penge even had a resident jazz band. James Barclay's Rhythm Boys, they were called. They were a marching band, and they marched up and down the pitch belting out a selection of tunes which might possibly have been penned by present-day authors who were hoping to break into the music biz, but, given the law of diminishing returns, were equally possibly just old Kenny Ball numbers.

'Wasn't that an Anne McCaffrey tune?' Jim asked John, who now sat next to him 'on the bench'.

'No,' said John. 'And we'll hear no more about it.'

James Barclay's Rhythm Boys lined themselves up in the middle of the pitch and to the great applause of the crowd (which numbered between two folk and several thousand, depending upon where you happened to be sitting) heralded the arrival of the opposing teams.

'Showtime,' said John Omally, sipping on a pint of ale. 'Rubbish ale, by the way.'

'Are we really going to be able to pull this off?' Jim asked Professor Slocombe, who sat next to him sipping sherry.

'You gave them the pep talk before you came out here, and most inspired it was.'

'Yes,' said Jim, 'it was, wasn't it? I don't know how this stuff comes into my head.'

Professor Slocombe tapped once more at his slender nose. 'Enjoy the game, Jim,' said he. 'Oh, and feel free to do a lot of shouting at the team as they play. They won't be able to hear you, but they'll appreciate it all the same. And it is expected of you.'

'What should I shout?' Jim asked.

'I expect you'll think of something.'

And on they came, the Penge team resplendent in their colours of beige, light tan and buff (these being the new black this season. But as Wimbledon play in blue, which is often the new black also, it doesn't really matter).

And the Brentford team in . . .

The crowd exploded into laughter.

'Oh my God,' cried Jim. '*What* are they wearing?'

'It's the new kit,' said John. 'I did a deal with Mohammed Smith at the sports shop.'

'They're wearing kaftans,' said Jim. 'They look like the cast of *Hair*.'

'I thought the cast of *Hair* were mostly naked,' said John.

'And what are those patches that are sewn all over the kaftans?' asked Jim.

'Advertising logos, Jim. Sponsorship deals, endorsements,

you know the kind of thing. I needed kaftans to fit them all on. I've got almost every shop in Brentford signed up.'

'You crammed a lot of work into a single day.'

'The Miracle of the Mobile Phone.' John whipped this item from his pocket.

'Don't put that thing near me,' said Jim.

The crowd had not ceased in its laughter at the Brentford team. And it looked very much as if the Brentford team was all for fleeing back to the groundskeeper's office.

'They're laughing at us,' said Jim.

'They'll be laughing on the other side of their faces come half-time,' said John.

'How *do* you do that?' Jim tried to frown on the other side of his face but could not.

'One more pep talk required,' said Professor Slocombe. 'Go to them, Jim.'

'What will I say?'

'You'll find inspiration.'

And Jim did. He gathered the team about himself. He spoke honeyed words. Magical words. A very great many words. And they seemed to work. He even got one of those Maori war chant kind of jobbies on the go.

He patted backs and returned to the bench.

'I don't know where I find it,' said Jim, 'but I find it.'

'You certainly do,' said John, exchanging secret smiles with the professor.

And then the ref blew his whistle and the game was on.

To this day, no one knows *exactly* how it was done. The game was not recorded for television transmission and so no visual evidence remains to be analysed by football pundits. There were members of the press there, but they gave conflicting accounts of the game. And as for the crowd, well, a crowd of folk will rarely agree upon anything. Except to being stirred up by a single individual into doing something stupid.

And so *exactly* what happened upon that fateful afternoon in Penge must remain for ever a matter of debate.

Except for one detail.

And that one detail was beyond debate.

For that one detail was the final score.

It was the greatest defeat that Penge had ever suffered, greater even than the infamous 'Day of Shame' when they were hammered five-nil by Orton Goldhay Wanderers. An occasion the ignominy of which was added to by Penge's then manager and latterly convicted serial killer Wally 'God-Told-Me-To-Do-It' Tomlinson, whose excuse for the team's defeat was that they had contracted a dose of the King's Evil at Madame Loveridge's whorehouse in Pimlico.

'Eight-nil.' Jim Pooley counted eight goals on to his fingers. Jim was somewhat far gone in celebratory drink now. He was on the tour bus that Big Bob was driving back to Brentford. Big Bob was singing. The team was singing.

Up on the top deck, John, Jim and Professor Slocombe were drinking champagne.

'Eight-nil.' Jim counted his fingers again, just to be sure. 'They were all hungover and they still thrashed Penge eight-nil.'

'I feel that we can chalk the tactics up as a success,' said Professor Slocombe.

'I think the kaftans helped,' said John.

'Impossible,' said Jim. 'I must be dreaming this.'

'The price of endorsements upon the team's strip has just doubled,' said John. 'No, let's be fair to the shopkeepers of Brentford – trebled.'

'I'm not sure that Paine's Undertakers should have such a prominent position on the backs,' said Professor Slocombe.

'Eight-nil,' said Jim, losing count of his fingers. 'Brent-ford won eight-nil.'

19

Scoop Molloy had not attended the match. He'd spent the day 'following up leads' regarding the terrorist bombing of Norman's lock-up garage and the queer events that had occurred at The Stripes Bar the previous night.

But he wasn't getting anywhere.

He did, however, receive an 'on-the-pitch' account of the match from the *Brentford Mercury*'s new self-appointed roving sports correspondent, Mr John Vincent Omally, via John's mobile phone, from the top deck of Big Bob's bus. It was a very full and glowing account of Brentford's remarkable victory.

Scoop would have loved to tell the *Mercury*'s editor to hold the front page, but the *Mercury* didn't come out on Sunday, so there really wasn't any point.

But word of the victory did reach Brentford before the team returned. Omally made copious phone calls, and the team returned to an impromptu victory parade.

True, few of the revellers who had attended the Benefit Night at The Stripes Bar were there to wave Union Jacks and throw rose petals, but the plain folk of Brentford, the plucky Brentonians who had been hoping and praying a little, too, thronged the streets. And the bunting was up.

'Good grief,' said Jim, making a bewildered face at the cheering crowds lining the Ealing Road. 'This is beyond belief.'

'Take a bow, Jim,' said John, waving somewhat. 'You've played your part in this triumph.'

'I really don't think I have.'

'The only way is up,' said John. 'We'll triumph.'

'Take a bow, Jim,' said Professor Slocombe.

Jim rose unsteadily from his seat and bowed towards the crowds.

'I know my opinion isn't worth much,' said a casual observer peering up from the roadside, 'but isn't that Bertie Wooster?'

There was dancing in the streets of Brentford upon that Saturday night, and the team all got very drunk again.

John and Jim did what came naturally to them and headed off for a drink. They bade their farewells to Professor Slocombe, but, to Jim's alarm, found themselves now in the company of the Campbell.

'I'll come along, if it's all right with you,' said the mystical highlander.

'It's not,' said Jim.

'It is,' said John.

'It is?' said Jim.

'It is – the Campbell is now your, er, *minder*, Jim. A successful football manager always has a security man to protect him.'

'From *what*?' Jim asked.

'Oh, you know, overattentive fans, the gentlemen of the press. You'd be surprised.'

Jim Pooley shrugged. 'So where are we drinking? The Stripes Bar, our own personal pub?'

'Ah, no,' said John. 'The Stripes Bar is currently undergoing renovations.'

'Would this be something to do with the fire and chaos that you seem disinclined to speak to me about?'

'Possibly so,' said John. 'Let's go to The Flying Swan.'

'The Swan? But we're barred from The Swan.'

'My, my,' said John, 'by what would appear to be sheer chance, we find ourselves right outside that very pub.'

'He'll club us down,' said Jim. 'He will employ his knobkerrie once again.'

'Have a little faith, Jim,' said John. 'I'll sort it.'

Jim took out his packet of Dadarillos and lit one up.

'You smoke too many of those,' said John.

'They calm my nerves and keep me mellow.'

'You chain-smoke the damn things.'

'Let's go somewhere else,' said Jim.

'No, my friend, we're going in here.'

'But we've got our own pub and you said—'

'I can't be having with loose ends,' said John. 'Nor can I bear to be barred from any bar in Brentford. It's a matter of principle.'

'Oh dear, oh dear, oh dear,' said Jim.

Trade was good in The Flying Swan. Saturday night was always Neville's busiest, but tonight surpassed the usual. Neville was hoping it would make up for the previous night, when he had done precisely *no trade at all*.

Neville did not own any Brentford Football Club team flags, but he had managed to find, in the beer cellar, a number of Charles and Diana wedding flags and these now hung behind the bar. And as there had been no time to take on extra bar staff, Neville was very busy. And *very busy* can sometimes mean *very stressed*.

This was one of those sometimes.

Neville espied the approach of Jim and John, closely followed by the Campbell, and Neville's good eye widened. And as John and Jim reached the bar counter, Neville's mouth did also.

'Out of my bar,' quoth the part-time barman.

'Let's not be hasty, now,' said John.

'Empty,' said Neville. 'Last night my bar was empty.'

'It's pretty full now,' said John.

'It will be emptier by two in just a moment. No, make that *three* – take that weirdo with you.'

'Oh,' said John. 'Ouch,' and he clutched at his forehead.

'That's where you'll get it,' said Neville, 'if you don't leave now.'

'That's where I have already received it,' said John. 'My solicitor is suggesting that I sue for damages. I found the figure *he* suggested preposterous, but then considering that I have always wanted to live the now legendary life of ease, I am tempted to let him go ahead with the lawsuit.'

'Do your worst,' said Neville.

'So you are really throwing us out?' said John.

'Do you have any doubt about this?' Neville sought his knobkerrie.

'I'm leaving,' said Jim. 'I don't wish to be smote a second time.'

'You stand your ground,' John told him. 'Neville, I know we have had our differences, but—'

'Differences?' The part-time barman's face began to turn that terrible whiter shade of pale once more.

'But there is nothing to be gained by petty feuding and the holding of grudges. Hence, I am willing to forgive and forget,' John continued.

Pooley flinched and Neville ground his teeth, loosening yet another filling to add to the previously loosened one, which had not as yet received the attention of the dentist.

'What I am saying to you, Neville,' John continued, 'is that you should be thanking us rather than behaving in this discourteous manner.'

'*Thanking* you? *Thanking* you?'

'Can I have some service over here?' asked a lady in a somewhat charred straw hat.

'Thanking us.' John risked a lean across the bar counter and a conspiratorial tone. 'Thanking us for saving your bacon.'

'My *bacon*?' Neville shook and rocked and the sound of the grinding of his teeth was hideous to the ear. One hundred yards away in The Four Horsemen, Dave Quimsby heard them and shuddered.

'Think about this, Neville,' said John. 'Who was it who appointed Brentford's new manager? The manager who has led them to an eight-nil victory over Penge?'

'Eh?' said Neville.

'You,' said John. 'And look, here is Brentford's new manager offering to favour this particular bar, out of all the bars in Brentford, including *his own*. What kudos, having the Brentford manager patronise your pub.'

'What?' said Neville, in a creaky kind of voice.

'An absinthe spritzer and a pale ale and Pernod,' called the lady in the charred straw hat. 'And make it snappy, or we'll take our business elsewhere.'

'You should take your due credit,' said John to Neville. 'You deserve praise. And to be honest, I don't know how well it would go down with the locals if they were to find out that you'd barred Brentford's manager. Excuse me, madam,' John said to the lady, 'but did I hear that you were thinking of taking your business elsewhere, because—'

'Stop!' cried Neville. 'Enough. Enough.'

John viewed the trembling barman. He wasn't enjoying doing this to Neville. Well, actually he was, because Neville *had* bopped both he and Jim upon their heads. 'What do you say?' John asked, sticking his hand out for a shake. 'Let bygones be bygones and all prosper from the glories that lie ahead for the team and the borough?'

Neville sighed. It was a deep and tragic sigh, but if all the truth was to be told, Neville was very pleased to have John and Jim once more in his bar.

'Bygones be bygones,' said Neville wearily and with that he shook Omally's hand.

'And Jim's, too,' said John. And Neville shook Pooley's hand also.

'Splendid,' said John, a-rubbing of his palms together. 'Then three pints of Large, please Neville.'

'All right,' said Neville and he set to pulling the pints. 'But there is only one thing that I want to know.'

'Which is?' asked John with caution.

'Why is Jim dressed as Bertie Wooster?'

And so the celebrations proper began, much to the pleasure of Jim Pooley, who found his hand being endlessly shaken, his back being endlessly patted, pint after pint being placed before him and kisses being planted on his cheeks by numerous female football fans. John, who was not averse to bathing in a bit of reflected glory, engaged the kiss-planters in conversation and added several numbers to his telephone book.

At a little after nine, Norman Hartnel entered The Flying Swan. Norman was carrying two duffel bags and Norman had a big grin on.

'Evening, John, Jim, Neville,' said Norman when he had fought his way to the counter.

Heads nodded and glasses were raised. 'You look very full of yourself, Norman,' said John. 'Come to toast the team's success and buy the men who brought it to fruition a pint or two?'

'Come to do a bit of celebrating myself,' said Norman, 'on my own account, for I shall shortly be rich beyond the dreams of Avril.'

'It's avarice,' said John.

'Then you haven't met my cousin Avril,' said Norman. 'But enough of that. I have, but yesterday, taken out five original patents. You had best shake my hand now, because it will be far too busy receiving awards in the future to be available for shaking then.'

'I am intrigued,' said John.

'Me, too,' said Jim.

'And what happened to you last night?' Norman asked Jim. 'You missed all the mayhem and magic at The Stripes Bar.'

'I did?' said Jim, casting a suspicious glance towards Omally.

'Forget all that,' said John. 'Tell us what you've been up to, Norman.'

'I heard your lock-up was blown up by Al Qaeda,' said Neville, sticking two olives into a pale ale and Pernod.

'Al who?' Jim asked. 'What team does he play for?'

'We're not on one of those right now,' said John. 'Tell us what's what, Norman.'

'About the lock-up?' asked the shopkeeper. 'It doesn't matter, it was insured.'

'About whatever you've invented that is going to bring you untold wealth,' said John.

'Ah, that.' Norman unshouldered his duffel bags and placed them upon the bar counter. 'Wireless transmission of electricity,' he said. 'Which is to say, electricity without cables beamed from one place to another upon a carrier wave. It will literally revolutionise everything.'

Neville the part-time barman scratched at his head with a cocktail stick and nearly put his good eye out. *Wireless transmission of electricity*? That rang a bell somewhere. Someone had mentioned something about that to him recently. Neville tried to recall just who it had been.

'Does this involve microwaves?' Jim asked fearfully. 'Like in portable telephones?'

'No,' said Norman. 'It's all very simple. Would you care for me to demonstrate?'

'I wouldn't miss it for the world,' said John, as yet another young woman came forward to offer Jim a kiss.

'I'll be getting all that soon,' said Norman, unpacking his duffel bags. 'A king's chaff is worth other men's corn. And I'm thinking of getting one of those special wheelchairs like Stephen Hawking has, with the voice box and everything.'

'Why?' John asked, as he watched Norman setting up strange contraptions upon the bar counter.

'Just trying to think of things to spend my money on.' The strange contraptions that Norman was now setting up were mostly constructed from Meccano. They resembled two little towers surmounted by silver Christmas-tree decoration balls. One of the little towers had a hand-crank attached to it and what looked like a tiny generator. The other was simply attached to a light bulb on a stand.

'Put that one at the other end of the bar,' Norman told Omally.

'Is this safe?' Neville asked. 'There won't be any explosions or loss of life or anything? I can't be having with that in my bar.'

'It's perfectly safe.' Norman took hold of the little tower with the hand-crank. 'I will turn this handle and charge up this tower, and the electricity will be transmitted to the other tower and light up the light bulb.'

'No offence, Norman,' said John, 'but that is *most* unlikely.'

'Nevertheless it will occur, as surely as a trained dog needs no whistling.'

The crowd in The Flying Swan, which had been conversing and hubbubbing and singing, too, and chanting *Brent-Ford*, *Brent-Ford* from time to time also, had been doing less of the conversing, hubbubbing and so on and so forthing also with the setting up of Norman's little towers.

The crowd was growing *interested*. Heads were turning, elbows nudged elbows. A certain hush was descending upon the saloon bar of The Flying Swan.

'It seems you have an audience,' said John.

'Wonderful,' said Norman and he turned to address the crowd. 'Ladies and gentlemen,' he said, 'what you are about to witness is something that you will never have seen before, something that will change the very face of civilisation: the wireless transmission of electricity. I will crank up this tower here. The crank powers this little generator, which in turn charges up the capacitor. When it's completely charged up, I throw this switch.' Norman turned and pointed and turned back once more. 'And the electricity will be transmitted through the air to that tower at the other end of the bar and will light up the light bulb.'

'For what it's worth,' said a casual observer. 'I—'

'Are we all ready?' Norman asked.

Heads nodded. The word in the bar was yes.

'Then I shall crank.' And Norman cranked. He cranked and he cranked and then he cranked some more. And then he said, 'That should be enough. Would you like to count me down? It makes it so much more exciting.'

Shoulders shrugged and then the countdown began. Necks craned to see what would happen. Folk at the back leaned upon shoulders and stood upon tippy-toe.

There was a general air of *expectation*.

'Three . . . two . . . one . . .'

And Norman threw the switch.

And then there was *ooohing* and *aaahing* and then there was silence.

For nothing whatever happened.

'Cop-out,' called someone.

'Load of old toot,' called someone else.

'No, hold on, hold on,' Norman called back. 'I'll just make an adjustment or two. It must work. I obviously haven't charged up the capacitor enough. It needs a lot of energy – after all, the electricity does have to travel through the air.'

Norman took to cranking some more. He cranked and he cranked and he cranked. He cranked as one possessed. Sweat appeared on the shopkeeper's brow and his face became crimson. His breath came in short pants. His short pants came in a gingham design.

'There,' gasped Norman, when he could crank no more. 'One more time, if you will. Three . . .'

The crowd, enlivened by drink and celebratory *bonhomie*, joined Norman in his second countdown.

'Three . . . two . . . one . . .'

And Norman flicked the switch.

There was a moment of absolute silence. But this moment was too short to be truly registered by those present, especially because what happened next caught them somewhat unawares and unprepared.

There was a flash, as of lightning, and a sort of a blue arc. It travelled through the base of the Meccano tower, which Norman had neglected to insulate with rubber feet, and it travelled to the brass rail that ran along the edge of the mahogany bar counter. The brass rail that Norman was holding on to. And it travelled to Jim Pooley who was leaning upon Norman's shoulder and from there to John who was leaning upon Jim's and from there it travelled every which way, with the exception, so it seemed, of the other tower, to which was connected the light bulb.

And electricity travels fast.

And it travels, also, with vigour.

★

There is a story, the authenticity of which has yet to be verified, that some years ago a group of Russian scientists drilled a five-mile-deep bore hole in Siberia during a study of plate tectonics. According to this story, their drill bit broke through the ceiling of some underground cavern and a microphone (upon a *very* long cable) was lowered into the void.

The scientists claim that what they heard, relayed to them from this microphone, was the sound of millions of souls screaming in torment.

The scientists had unwittingly drilled into Hell.

No recording of this hideous cacophony of the damned has ever been played to the general public.

But if it were, then it is odds-on that the sound would be all but identical (although somewhat louder, due to the greater numbers involved) to that which was now to be heard within the saloon bar of The Flying Swan.

It was one Hell of a collective scream.

Bodies shook and quivered, eyeballs rolled back into heads, teeth chattered and hair rose upon craniums to such effect that had another casual observer entered the bar at that very moment, he (or she) would have been convinced that he (or she) had entered the Don King lookalike convention.

And sparks flew.

Let us not forget the sparks.

They flew from fingertips and earlobes and privy members, too. And pints of ale bubbled on the bar top and optics shattered and . . .

Norman found himself barred from The Flying Swan.

20

Kevin Hurst, the ambulance driver from Brentford Cottage Hospital, offered Neville the bitterest of glares.

'Twice in one week,' he said. 'What goes on in this bar? And what is this, anyway – a Don King lookalike convention?'

A thin haze of pale blue smoke still hung in the air of the saloon bar – a saloon bar whose patrons now sat slumped in attitudes of despondency, or lay upon the floor in attitudes of unconsciousness.

Neville, who had escaped electrocution by merit of being on the other side of the bar and consequently touching no one, was hardly able to speak.

Constables Russell Meek and Arthur Mild however, who had lately arrived on the scene, had plenty to say.

'Quietly patrolling, we were,' they told Scoop Molloy, who had his pencil and notebook out, 'when we observed the premises illuminate with a fearsome fulguration. Unthinking of our personal safety, we pulled many from the jaws of death. There'll be medals in this for us, I wouldn't wonder.'

Scoop scribbled away in his notebook. 'Fearsome fulguration. Jaws of death,' said he. 'I like that.'

'My mobile phone,' croaked John Omally. 'He blew up my mobile phone.'

'And singed my suit,' whinged Pooley.

'It's what you call a glitch,' Norman explained.

'And how come *your* hair isn't standing up?' a lady in a charred and elevated straw hat asked Norman.

John and Jim decided to call it a night. It had been an

exciting day for the both of them, and enough was definitely enough.

'I will see you on the morrow,' said John, when they reached Jim's lodgings.

Jim patted down his hair and cracked his knuckles and licked at his charred fingers. 'I thought arresting Norman was somewhat overzealous on the part of those policemen,' he said.

'They'll probably let him out in the morning. You have a good sleep now, Jim. I'll meet you tomorrow lunchtime in The Swan and we'll discuss what is next to be done with the club.'

'And you can tell me everything that really went on last night,' said Jim. 'And don't think I'll forget to ask you about it.'

'Goodnight to you, Jim,' said John, heading off for home.

'John,' Jim called after him. 'Aren't you forgetting something?'

'Is it further congratulations you're looking for?' enquired John, turning back.

'No,' said Jim. 'It's *him*.'

'Him?' John asked.

'Him,' said Jim. 'You, Mr Campbell. Goodnight to you, too. Go along with John.'

'I'm staying,' said the Campbell.

'You're not staying with me.'

'I'll be here, outside your door, maintaining the vigil.'

'I'd rather you just went home, thank you very much.'

The Campbell sat down upon the pavement. 'Away to your bed, wee laddie,' said he. 'I'll see that no harm comes to you.'

'John,' said Jim, 'I don't like this, John.'

'Humour him,' said John. 'He has your interests at heart.'

'But it's not right. It's indecent somehow.'

'Goodnight to you, Jim,' said John once more.

Jim Pooley shrugged. 'Goodnight to you, John,' said he. 'And goodnight to you, Campbell,' he said also.

★

The night passed without incident, and presently changed into coming day.

Lunchtime of this coming day found John and Jim *and* the Campbell, who had maintained his vigil outside Jim's lodgings throughout the night, once more in the saloon bar of The Flying Swan.

Neville did not greet his now unbarred patrons with a smile and a merry quip. Neville was very down in the dumps.

'Why me?' he asked. 'My only desire is to serve fine ale and maintain a happy bar. What have I done to bring all this down upon me? Have I offended the Gods in some way? Tell me, won't somebody tell me?'

'You've done nothing,' said John, accepting the ale he had ordered and paying for same with the exact amount of pennies and halfpennies. 'You're a good man, Neville. I'm sure you find favour in the eyes of your Gods.'

'I'm seriously thinking about running away with the circus,' said Neville.

'Strike that thought from your mind,' said John. 'You are the finest barman in Brentford – probably in the country.'

'You really think so?' Neville preened at his lapels.

'Certainly,' said John. 'Do you think you could open a window? It's still a bit whiffy in here.'

Neville sloped off to open a window.

'He sat outside my place all night long,' Jim whispered to John, turning his eyes towards the Campbell, who sat by the door polishing his claymore with his kilt. 'He fair puts the wind up me, John. Couldn't he be your minder for a while?'

'Take it like a man, Jim,' said John. 'You are a man of responsibility now. And there's a Wednesday-night game coming up. You should be applying your mind to this.'

'I don't think I'll survive the season, John. This is all too much for me.'

'You'll be fine. Let's take a seat yonder. There are matters to be discussed.'

'Such as what actually happened on Friday night.'

'Oh, that, of course, but first things first. On the strength of the team's great victory, I think we can bring in some big outborough money. People like to associate themselves with winners. I have one or two ideas that should bring us in a good many pennies.'

'John,' said Jim, 'there is something you're not telling me, something that has to do with the real reason why that lunatic in the kilt is following me around. I demand to be told, John. You're my bestest friend. Please don't lie to me.'

'Jim, just concentrate on the matters at hand.'

'Tell me now, John, all of the truth – or although we have been lifelong friends, I will walk out of this pub right now and I swear that I will not see you again.'

John Omally took in breath. 'Now, Jim,' he said. 'Don't be hasty, now.'

'I mean it, John.'

Omally took a large swallow of ale. 'All right,' said he. 'I'll tell you. You won't like it and you'll be very angry and feel that you have been betrayed – that's the way I felt. But you deserve to be told and I've not been happy keeping it from you. You are my bestest friend.'

'I really don't like the sound of this.'

'Then don't make me tell you.'

'I have to know, John, and you know that I have to know.'

'All right,' said Omally. 'Let us sit over in the corner. I'll get us in more ale.'

'At *your* expense? Now I really *am* worried.'

'Go and sit in the corner.'

Jim went and sat in the corner. John joined him in the company of further ales.

And then John told to Jim everything that the professor had told to John. And John told to Jim everything that had really happened to Jim.

And John omitted nothing.

And Jim chain-smoked cigarettes until John had eventually done with his telling.

And Jim was not a happy man.

And then John stared into the face of Jim Pooley, a face that was bereft of colour, and John said unto Jim, 'Are you all right?'

And Jim could not speak for a moment. And it was a long moment. But when Jim was able to speak, he simply said, 'Yes.'

'Yes?' said John. 'Is that all you have to say on the matter?'

'No,' said Jim, 'I have much to say. I must say thank you to the Campbell for saving my life and I will have much to say to the professor. But for all that you have said, let me ask you this: do you actually believe it?'

'I believe what I saw with my own eyes and what I experienced. I have never been so afraid in all of my life, which is one of the reasons that I didn't want to tell you. It is all so fearsome, Jim.'

'What are we going to do, John?'

'I really wish I knew.'

'But if these dark, black things are really out to kill us—'

'I know, my friend. But the Campbell will protect you.'

'And what about you? Who's going to protect you?'

'I trust the professor. We'll come out of this in one piece.'

'It's absurd,' said Jim. 'It's beyond absurd. And above that it's unfair that we should have been dragged into this.'

'I think you're taking it very well.'

'I don't think it's fully sunk in yet.'

'I think we should just get on with doing what we're doing – stick with trying to take the club to victory and leave all the magical stuff to the professor and the Campbell.'

'You don't think that perhaps we'd both be better off just running away?'

'To where? Brentford is our home. I don't know about you, but I have no wish to leave it. I like it here. I love it here.'

'Yes,' said Jim, 'me, too. This is all very hard to take in. *Very* hard. It's not exactly your everyday problem, now is it?'

Omally shrugged and shook his head.

'And the more I think about it, the more I think that you are going about all this in the wrong way.'

'How so?' John asked.

'Because of the scale of the problem, John. This is big, really big. Brentford hadn't even played a single FA Cup qualifying game before these monsters were dispatched to kill us. Now Brentford *has* won a game, and handsomely, too. So what's next? More assaults upon us, I would guess, more attempts upon our lives.'

'That will probably be the case.'

'And this Consortium that wants to take the football ground – it is run by some satanic magician, this William Starling character?'

'He would seem to be the villain of this piece,' said John.

Jim Pooley shrugged and continued, 'How much power does this character have? A lot, would be my guess, and with every success the team has, he will throw more and more monsters at us.'

'The professor will protect us.'

'And who will protect the professor?'

'Ah,' said John. 'Good point.'

'They'll beat us,' said Jim. 'They'll kill us, and the professor, too. We can't just sit around waiting for this to happen. Well, *you* can, if you want, but I won't. We're sitting targets, John, they'll get us sooner or later. There could be thousands of them. You hear talk about Satanists and Black Magic covens, that they're everywhere. Anyone could be a member. I've seen movies like this – you don't know who to trust.'

'Stop this now,' said John. 'Let's just do our jobs.'

'No,' said Jim. 'If we do that, then we're doomed. If we're involved in this, and seemingly we are, then *we* have to do something about it in order to protect our own lives. I trust the professor, the same as you do, but he's a frail old man, not a superhero. We're still young men, John. *We* should be doing something.'

'But what?' John drained away further ale.

'Get them before they get us,' Jim Pooley suggested.

'What are you suggesting?'

'Know your enemy,' said Jim. 'I read that somewhere. Let the hunted become the hunter. Things of that nature, generally.'

'There is a wisdom in your words, Jim Pooley.'

'Thank you,' said Jim, finishing his pint. 'The only question is, what should we do, and to whom?'

'Surely that's *two* questions.'

Jim ignored this remark. 'What do you know about this Consortium, John?' he asked.

'Probably as much, or as little, as you do. It's a big multinational affair, property development. The headquarters are in Chiswick.'

'Just down the road,' said Jim. 'Which makes a lot of sense.'

'It does?'

'If the ultimate goal of the character who owns this Consortium is to release the old serpent that is imprisoned beneath Brentford's football ground, then it's unsurprising that the headquarters would be nearby rather than, say, in Rio de Janeiro.'

'Ah yes,' said John. 'I suppose it would.'

Jim raised an eyebrow at John.

'I'm really glad I told you all about this,' said John. 'We work really well as a team.'

'Hm,' went Jim. 'Well, that's where we should start – at their headquarters. And today.'

'Today?'

'It's Sunday,' said Jim. 'Offices are closed on Sunday – a good time to have a little look around, I would have thought. See what might be seen. Find out what might be found out.'

'You really *are* on the case, Jim.'

'I don't want to die, John. The prospect of impending death does tend to concentrate the mind.'

'So are you suggesting that we break into the offices?'

'Would *I* suggest a thing like that?'

'I'm beginning to wonder whether I really know you at all,' said John.

'We could pay the offices a little visit. I feel confident that you could talk our way in.'

John Omally put his hand out for a shake.

'Let's take a trip to Chiswick,' said John.

'Let's lose him first,' said Jim, rolling his eyes once more towards the Campbell.

John and Jim went off to the bog and left The Swan via the window. They shinned over the rear wall and had it away on their toes.

'We'll take the bus,' said Jim.

'We'll take Marchant,' said John.

Marchant was still in Jim Pooley's allotment shed where John had left him when he stored the cache of Dadarillos – a cache that Jim was digging into once again.

'We'll never make any profit from those,' John told Jim. 'You'll soon have smoked them all.'

'I'm not too happy about travelling on that bike of yours,' said Jim, filling his pockets with packs of cigarettes. 'That bike hates me.'

'The lad's all right,' said John, stroking Marchant's saddle. 'He'll see us all right, too, won't you, Marchant?'

The bicycle kept its own counsel.

'Let's get this done,' said John, leading it from Jim's shed.

The journey to Chiswick was uneventful but for the occasional tippings of Jim from the handlebars of Marchant. At length, the offices of the Consortium rose up in the distance. When the distance became the near-at-hand, the very scale of these offices revealed itself to be . . .

Awesome.

'By the hoary hosts of Hoggoth,' said Jim, who favoured a *Dr Strange* comic. 'That is a very big building.'

'And very black, too,' said John. 'All black, in fact.'

'There'll be a doorman or a security guard or something,'

said Jim, as Marchant unexpectedly applied its front brake and spilled Pooley once more to the road. 'You do the talking.' And Jim picked himself up from the gutter.

The architectural style of the Consortium's offices had a certain familiarity about it. In fact, it resembled a gigantic telephone box of the Giles Gilbert Scott persuasion.

Although all in black.

A broad span of black basalt steps swept up to a grandiose entranceway. John parked Marchant and he and Jim looked up at the imposing structure.

'That's a very imposing structure,' said John. 'This organisation is worth a *lot* of money.'

'Let's not be intimidated,' Jim told him. 'Size isn't everything.'

'No, but it does give one an edge.' John squared his shoulders, which didn't need much of a squaring. 'Let's get this done,' said he.

Jim gave John a thumbs-up and the two set off up the steps.

Vast doors of polished black glass slid soundlessly to either side at their approach and the two friends entered the building. They found themselves in an entrance hall of heroic proportions, decked out in the classical style.

There were couches that spoke of the Ottoman Empire.

And mosaics that sang of the glories of Rome.

Columns that whispered of nights in Byzantium.

A sampler that said there was no place like home.

'Very swell,' John observed.

'Very cold.' Jim hugged at his arms.

'That would be the air-conditioning. I've been thinking of having it installed in your office.'

'Have you, now?'

'Might I be of assistance to you gentlemen?' The voice was thin and reedy and male, which came as a slight disappointment to John, who had been hoping for a female receptionist. 'Over here, if you will.'

A tiny man sat behind an enormous reception desk that

murmured of Mount Parnassus, clearly upon a very high chair – he was a veritable elf, all pointy chin and pointy nose and long and pointy ears.

He pointed a pointy finger at John. 'What do you want here?' he asked.

'Inspectre Hovis of Scotland Yard,' said John Omally, whipping out his wallet and flashing what Pooley recognised to be John's Roy Rogers Appreciation Society sheriff's star at the bewildered elf. 'And this is my partner, Sergeant Rock.'

'He looks more like Bertie Wooster,' said the elf.

'I don't,' said Jim. 'I'm not wearing the plus-fours suit today.'

'It must be the haircut, then. What do you gentlemen want?'

Omally cleared his throat and spoke with the voice of authority. 'Kindly gather all staff who are presently within the building and lead them to the car park,' he said.

'I fail to understand.' The receptionist scratched at his pointy head.

John leaned forward across the desk and whispered the word 'bomb'.

'Bomb?' The receptionist's eyes bulged from their sockets and his mouth dropped open, exposing pointy teeth.

'Alka Seltzer,' said Jim.

'Al Qaeda,' said John. 'We have received a tip-off from ZZ-Nine, Above Top Secret Department. This building has been targeted. We are here to search for and disarm the bomb.'

'No, no, no.' The pointy little man shook his pointy head. 'No terrorist could have infiltrated these offices. That is impossible.'

'I'd love to spend time discussing it with you,' said John, checking his wristlet watch, 'but by my reckoning there is less than half an hour before . . .' And he mimed the explosion of a very large bomb.

'I must telephone for confirmation.' Pointy fingers reached towards a desktop phone.

'Evacuate the staff before you do,' John told him. 'I'm sure you wouldn't want their deaths on your conscience.'

'No, certainly not.' The pointy man dithered.

'Time is ticking away,' said John.

'There's no one in the building but me. I must phone for confirmation.'

'Nobody but you?' John made the face of one appalled. 'What kind of security is that for an establishment such as this?'

'There is sufficient security, I can assure you.' The pointy man's eyes became narrow, hooded slits. 'Might I see your badge of authority once more? It seemed to me to be a—'

But the pointy man said no more, because John Omally had punched him right in his pointy chin.

'Was that really necessary?' Jim climbed forward over the reception desk and viewed the unconscious figure of the tiny pointy man that now lay on the floor beyond. 'You might have killed him.'

'I didn't hit him that hard.'

'But he's only little.'

'He'll be fine. Come on, Jim, this was your idea, remember?'

'Perhaps it wasn't such a good idea.'

'It *was* a good idea. Have another fag and calm your nerves.'

'Good idea.'

Omally shinned over the reception desk and rooted about in search of keys, which he soon discovered.

'Where should we begin our search?' John asked. 'Start at the top, do you think?' He flourished a key, attached to which was a black metal tag with the words 'Penthouse Office' inscribed upon it.

'The only way is up,' said Jim. 'Shall we take the lift?'

'I think that would be the thing to do.'

The lift was one of those glass-cylinder jobbies and it travelled upwards with a giddying swiftness.

'It does seem rather odd,' said Jim, as he clung to a handrail and tried to stop his knees from knocking together. 'A Diddy Man on the desk and not an armed guard with an Alsatian to be seen.'

'Overconfidence,' said John. 'These fellows think themselves untouchable.'

'Perhaps.' Jim held his nose and swallowed air. 'I'm going to be sick,' he said.

'Puff upon your fag and stop complaining.'

And then the lift stopped.

Very suddenly.

'We're trapped!' cried Jim. 'We're doomed. We'll plummet to our deaths.'

And the lift doors opened and a mechanised voice announced, 'The Penthouse Office, please mind the gap.'

'Poltroon,' said John. 'Come on.'

The corridor was swank, in a jet-black marbley kind of a way that babbled of Babylon. And it was cold, too.

Jim blew onto his fingers. 'I think I've got altitude sickness,' he said. 'Do you think we need oxygen masks up here?'

'Jim,' said John, 'you are priceless.'

'Thank you very much,' said Jim.

'Aha.' A door loomed before them and a big one, too. John presented the key to its lock.

'You don't think we should knock first,' Jim asked, 'in case there's anybody home?'

'No,' said John, 'I don't.' And he turned the key and pushed open the sizeable door.

Beyond lay a terrible room.

It glowed in the light of many candles, uniformly black and arrayed in elaborate *torchères* fashioned in the likenesses of naked men thrown into attitudes of appalling agony. Jim caught sight of these and Jim was ready for the off.

'Steady now, Jim,' said John. 'We weren't expecting a cosy parlour.'

'What are those?' Jim asked, and he pointed.

Omally entered the terrible room and viewed what was to be seen.

'Cabinets,' said he, 'glass cabinets filled with what look to be fossils. Come and have a look, Jim.'

Jim entered upon unsteady legs. 'It smells bad in here,' he said. 'It smells of . . .' he paused as terrible memories returned to him.

'It smells of the grave,' said John.

Jim peeped into a cabinet. 'What are they fossils of?' he asked. 'I've never seen anything like these before. They're like octopuses, but with wings.'

John shrugged. He had seen something more interesting. At the centre of the terrible room stood a kind of altar, heavily carved with scenes of damnation, tormented forms twisted in anguish, demonic creatures and fallen angels of Hell. Upon this altar there rested a red velvet cushion, and upon this cushion, a thing of great beauty indeed.

It was a gemstone the size of a golf ball. It glittered and twinkled and seemed to radiate a curious light of its own. John cast a covetous eye over it.

Pooley said, 'What do you think is in there?'

John turned away from the altar. 'In where?' he asked.

'Behind those big doors,' said Jim, pointing to a pair of very big doors set into the furthest wall. Elaborately carved were these doors, with further scenes of Hellish horror. 'Strongroom, do you think?'

John approached the doors. 'No sign of a lock,' said he. 'Let's have a look.'

Pooley drew back. 'I don't think so, John,' he said. 'This place reeks of evil and I have a very bad feeling that something really ghastly lurks beyond those doors.'

'Well, there's only one way to find out.' And with reckless abandon, John Omally put his weight to the great doors and eased them slowly open.

Beyond lay another room.

And John looked in.

And Jim looked in.

Then John looked at Jim.

And Jim looked at John.
And then they both turned hard upon their heels.
And ran screaming in terror for their lives.

21

Professor Slocombe looked grimly upon the two white-faced and shivering men who sat in the armchairs to either side of his fire. The elderly scholar poured two large glasses of Scotch and pushed these into the trembling hands of his guests.

'What you did was beyond reckless,' he told them. 'And I blame *you* for this.' The professor turned to confront the Campbell, who stood beside the French windows, his hand upon the pommel of his claymore. 'To let them slip away from you like that—'

'They left their ales half-drunk,' said Mahatma Campbell.

'Yes.' The professor smiled wanly. 'That would probably have fooled me, also.' And he turned back to his ashen guests. 'Tell me what you saw,' he said.

Jim's teeth chattered noisily.

John said, 'I don't know. But it was horrible. Terrible.' And he hid his eyes with his free hand and poured Scotch down his throat with the other.

'You said something about tentacles,' said the professor, 'and bat's wings and eyes.'

'T-t-too much,' stuttered Jim. 'Too much to think.'

'I see.' The professor took himself over to one of the burgeoning bookcases and withdrew a slim volume bound in yellow calfskin. He leafed slowly through this and then he held the open book towards Jim. 'Is this what you saw?' he asked.

Jim glanced at the page and went 'Aaaagh!'

'I thought as much.' Professor Slocombe closed the book. 'What is it?' John asked. 'You know what it is.'

'This book,' Professor Slocombe tapped at the volume, 'is a first edition signed by the author – with a dedication to myself, I am proud to add. It is the work of one Howard Phillips Lovecraft. The illustration was drawn by the legendary Count David Carson. It is Lord Cthulhu, the Great Old One.'

Jim's glass rattled against his teeth. 'It was a monster from Hell,' he managed to say.

'Not from Hell,' said the professor, 'but from a time when the universe was chaos. When God said, "Let there be light," the Great Old Ones, the lords of chaos and terror, were banished. Cthulhu and his kingdom sank into the ocean depths, where they were to remain for ever – not dead, but forever dreaming, dreaming of their return to rule the world of men. Legend has it that Cthulhu can only be raised by a powerful spell activated by a sacred stone known as the Eye of Utu. But as legend also has it that the Eye is hidden where no man can find it, I am at a loss to understand how Starling achieved his evil ends.

'Most believed Lovecraft to be either mad or possessed of an overly morbid imagination, and Cthulhu and the Eye nothing but myth – a fireside tale to trouble the sleep of children. But it would appear that the sceptics were sadly mistaken, and that what I always suspected to be the case is indeed reality. This William Starling has somehow raised Cthulhu from sunken R'leah and brought him to the very heights of Chiswick.'

'Real bomb,' chattered Pooley. 'Real bomb, John, blow the monster up.'

'I'm with you there, my friend,' said John.

'No.' Professor Slocombe raised a slender hand. 'You two will not return to that building. I forbid it.'

'That thing is evil.' Jim slurped down further Scotch. 'Pure evil. We felt it. I all but pooed myself.'

'I think you did poo yourself a little,' said John, 'by the niff of you.'

'Shut up, John. It must be destroyed, Professor.'

'Oh, yes, indeed it must, but that is for myself and the

Campbell and others that I can call into service to deal with. You must continue with your work: taking the team on to victory.'

'Forget that,' said Jim. 'That doesn't matter anymore.'

'On the contrary, it matters more than ever. Griffin Park must remain inviolate. The serpent must not be released.'

'Blow up the Consortium building,' said John. 'That will sort everything out. Could I have some more Scotch, please?'

'Getting your strength back, are you?' The professor poured John another Scotch.

'Me, too,' said Jim, finishing his.

Professor Slocombe obliged. 'We cannot blow up the Consortium's headquarters,' he said. 'It is in the heart of Chiswick – hundreds of people could be killed. It is unthinkable.'

'That creature is unthinkable,' said Jim. 'And impossible, too. This is Brentford, Professor, the real world. This kind of stuff does not belong in the real world. The real world is buses and babies and bedtime. It isn't *this*.'

'Bedtime?' said John.

'I couldn't think of anything else beginning with "b".'

'Breasts,' said John. 'Boobs, bosoms, b—'

'Shut up, John, this is serious.'

'I know, my friend, I know.'

A brass candlestick-style telephone upon the professor's desk began to ring. The old man stared at it in alarm.

'Your phone is ringing,' Omally said.

'It shouldn't do that,' said the professor.

'It's what they do,' said John. 'I had one of my own that did, but Norman blew it up.'

'This one should not ring, John, because this one isn't plugged in.'

'Ah,' said John Omally.

Professor Slocombe sat down behind his desk, took up the telephone receiver and put it to his ear. Words came to him and the old man's face became pale. At length he replaced the receiver and his fingers trembled as he did so.

'Who was it?' John asked.

'William Starling,' said Professor Slocombe, pouring Scotch for himself. 'The managing director, chairman and owner of the company that calls itself the Consortium. He wishes to have a meeting with me.'

Pooley was staring at the telephone. 'How did he do that?' asked the puzzled Jim, 'if there are no wires?'

'He wants back what you stole from him.' Professor Slocombe stared hard at John Omally.

'Stole?' And then John's fingers tightened on his bulging trouser pocket.

'You brought it here,' said Professor Slocombe, 'to *my* house, and I was unaware.'

'It just sort of fell into my pocket. Heat of the moment. He can have it back, I don't want it.'

'Show it to me, John.'

'Yes, sir.' John fished into his pocket and brought out the gem – the golfball-sized gem that had rested on the cushion upon the dreadful altar in the terrible room. It glistened and flickered; rays of light seemed to emanate from it.

'I never saw you nick that,' said Jim.

'It is a very pretty thing,' said John.

'And very deadly,' said the professor. 'Place it upon my desk, John, please.'

John arose from his seat and did so. 'Is it important?' he asked.

'Important?' Professor Slocombe smiled. 'Your light-fingeredness may well have saved all of our lives.'

'Really?' said John. 'Well, naturally . . .'

Professor Slocombe now began to laugh. 'You do not have the faintest idea as to what you have here, do you, John?'

'Something valuable, I think.'

'Something beyond value. You will recall what I told you about the raising of Cthulhu, regarding the Eye of Utu?'

John nodded.

'This,' said Professor Slocombe, 'is the Eye of Utu.'

★

The metal shutter slid aside and an eyeball peered in through the eyehole and into the prison cell.

Where Norman sat, the very picture of dejection.

'On your feet, prisoner,' called the voice of Constable Meek. 'You're going home.'

Norman dragged himself to his feet, which wasn't easy, for his knees were still numb and his finger-ends likewise. Constable Meek dragged open the door and grinned upon the slammed-up shopkeeper.

'Peg?' said Norman. 'Has Peg bailed me out?'

'No,' said the constable. 'Some big swell from the city.'

Norman shook his bewigged, befuddled head. 'I don't know any big city swells.'

'Well, he knows you and he's outside in his car. You're being chauffeured home.'

'Oh,' said Norman. 'It's a long straight road that has no turning.'

'Yeah, and a trouble shared can get you five years in Strangeways.'

Norman took up his jacket from the bed and shrugged it on.

'Normally,' said Constable Meek, 'myself and Constable Mild would give you a summary beating with our trunch-eons to teach you the error of your ways and to discourage you from further wrongdoing, but Constable Mild has the day off and it's no fun doing it on your own.' Constable Meek handed Norman his duffel bags. 'Go forth and sin no more,' he told him.

The Sunday sunlight was bright to Norman's eyes as he left the confines of the Brentford Nick. He did a bit of blinking and a car beeped at him.

Norman looked towards the car that stood at the kerb-side. It was a very posh-looking car, very long and shiny-black. An electric window in its rear compartment swished down.

'Mr Hartnel?' called a voice, and a posh voice it was. 'Mr

Norman Hartnel, not to be confused with the other Norman Hartnel?'

'That's me,' said Norman.

A long rear door swung open. 'Please step inside,' called the voice.

Norman shrugged and did so. The door swung shut behind him. 'Electric door,' said Norman, much impressed.

'Please sit yourself down, Mr Hartnel.'

Norman sat himself down upon a comfy seat upholstered with the skin of some endangered species.

'Comfy seat,' said Norman, patting same. 'Thank you very much.'

'My card.' A gloved hand passed a business card to Norman. Norman took the card and smiled towards the owner of the hand. He was a most impressive figure – clearly tall, although sitting down, young and with striking features. He had a head of the blondest hair and eyes of the deepest blue and when he smiled he showed off teeth that really were the whitest of whites.

'I am very pleased to meet you,' said this fellow, now putting forward his gloved hand for a shake.

Norman shook it. 'I don't understand,' said he.

'Patents,' said the fellow in his very posh voice. 'You have recently registered five original patents.'

'Yes,' said Norman proudly. 'Yes, I have.'

'And these were entirely your own work?'

'Well,' said Norman guardedly, 'I think you'll find that no one has registered them before. But how did you know about this?'

'My company,' said the gentleman, 'deals in acquisitions. We acquire patents and develop new products. We developed Blu-Tack, Velcro and the jumbo jet. Not to mention the Octotron.'

'The Octotron?' asked Norman.

'I told you not to mention that.'[*]

'Sorry,' said Norman.

---

[*] God bless you, Spike Milligan. Wherever you are.

'All new patents go into a government database, and my company is privy to that database. I had some difficulty in locating you. I called at your address. Your wife – Peg, is it?'

Norman nodded dismally.

'She told me that you were incarcerated. She didn't seem to know anything about your patents. She was most surprised when I informed her.'

Norman groaned.

'Are you all right?' asked the gentleman. 'Would you care for some champagne?'

'Yes, please,' said Norman.

The gentleman tapped buttons upon a little keypad arrangement on his seat arm. A cocktail cabinet slid out from somewhere and opened. The gentleman took from it a bottle of vintage Krug and popped the cork. Then he poured out two full glasses and handed one to Norman.

'Bottoms up,' said the shopkeeper, downing champagne.

'To you,' said the gentleman, sipping his.

'So you want to buy my patents?' said Norman. 'They're worth a great deal of money, I know that.'

'A very great deal,' said the gentleman. 'You will be a very wealthy man.'

'I'd quite like a car like this,' said Norman. 'What would one of these cost, do you think?'

'I'll let you have this one, if you'd like it.'

'Wow,' said Norman.

'I have contracts already drawn up, if you'd care to peruse them.'

'I certainly would.' Norman finished his champagne. 'The bubbles go right up your nose, don't they?' he said. 'Could I have some more?'

'Help yourself to the bottle.'

'Thank you very much indeed.'

The gentleman took papers from a glossy executive case and passed these to Norman. Norman put down the champagne bottle and perused the papers. 'That is a good many papers to peruse,' said he.

'You will no doubt want a solicitor to look through them.'

'Oh,' said Norman.

'Oh?' said the gentleman.

'Well,' said Norman, 'naturally I assumed that you were intending to ply me with champagne in order to get me to sign away my patents for peanuts because I'd failed to look at the small print.'

'You are most astute, Mr Hartnel.'

'Not really,' said Norman. 'It's just what always happens in the movies.'

'More champagne?'

'Yes, please.' Norman took up the bottle once more and refilled his glass.

Professor Slocombe refilled John Omally's glass. 'This puts us in a far more powerful position,' said he. 'William Starling called me, using this defunct telephone to impress me with his powers, but *he* called *me*. I deduce from this that he believes that *I* dispatched you two to his headquarters upon a mission to purloin the Eye of Utu, a mission that you successfully accomplished. We now have a certain degree of bargaining power.'

'Destroy it,' said Jim. 'It is in your hand, Professor. If it is as powerful as you say, and as valuable to them, grind it to smithereens.'

'Tempting as that is, Jim, I do not feel that by doing so we would benefit.'

'Well, you can't just give it back to him,' said John.

'A deal might be struck. But, as is said, he who dines with the Devil must do so with a very long fork.'

'Probably said by Norman,' said John.

'It's us,' said the suddenly enlightened Jim. 'You're going to bargain with him – the Eye in return for him making no further attempts upon our lives.'

'It seems the most logical thing to do,' said the professor. 'I involved you in this, so I must do whatever I can to protect you.'

'But how can you trust him?' asked Jim. 'If he gives you his word, how will you know whether he will keep it?'

'The Brotherhood of Magic,' said Professor Slocombe, 'whether white or black, exists within a certain framework. There are rules to every game, rules that must be obeyed. A magical oath, once sworn, cannot be broken, save at the great expense of he that breaketh it.'

'But that thing,' said Jim, 'that thing in the building—'

'One *thing* at a time, Jim. If we obtain a truce from Mr Starling, his promise that he will make no further attempts upon your lives, then you can concentrate upon the job at hand – protecting Griffin Park. I and my associates will deal with Lord Cthulhu.'

Jim threw up his hands, all but spilling his Scotch (but not quite). 'It all seems terribly complicated,' he said. 'And if you'll pardon me saying this, aren't we missing something obvious?'

'Enlighten me,' said the professor.

'Well,' said Jim, 'all right, if the team wins the FA Cup, then Griffin Park is saved and the Consortium cannot dig it up and release the serpent. But why are they even bothering to attempt to buy the ground in the first place? Why don't they just sneak in one night with a load of shovels and simply dig up the blighter?'

'Good point,' said John. 'Jim has a good point there, Professor.'

'He does, John, and I will tell you why they cannot do this. It is not a matter of simply digging up the serpent. If it were, then they would have done so already. The serpent remains constrained through the will of God. A digger and a spade would not be sufficient.'

'Then what would?' Jim asked.

'Something,' said the professor, 'beyond more than, if I might misuse the word, mere magic. And something that will involve more than a furtive overnight dig. I suspect, and it is only a suspicion, that it would involve the employment of some kind of alternative technology, some kind of energy – although I know not what.'

'And where would this Starling acquire such alternative technology?' Jim asked.

'I have no idea, Jim, but if it exists, then I have no doubt that if he has not already acquired it, he most certainly will.'

'Yes,' said Jim, 'but where from?'

'Possibly anywhere, Jim. Possibly from right here.'

'Right here,' said Norman. 'Can you drop me off right here?'

'This isn't your shop,' said the gentleman.

'No, it's The Flying Swan,' said Norman, who had quite forgotten that he had been barred. 'I think I might down a celebratory stiff one or two before I go home.'

'And face your lady wife.'

'Something like that, yes.'

'Then I shall say farewell to you, Mr Hartnel. It has been a pleasure to make your acquaintance. Have your solicitor go through the contracts tomorrow. I will telephone you tomorrow evening and hopefully we will have a deal.'

'Hopefully,' said Norman.

The electrically operated rear door opened and Norman stepped from the car.

'I am very excited about your patents,' said the gentleman. 'I make no secret of the fact. They offer, how shall I put this, an alternative technology to the world. We can expect most astonishing things to occur through their employment.'

'The biggest fish swim near the bottom,' said Norman, 'and a cheerful look makes a dish into a feast.'

'Quite so.'

'Well, it's been a pleasure to meet *you*.' Norman peered at the gentleman's business card. 'Mr Starling,' he said.

22

Professor Slocombe removed himself from his study.

'Where has he gone?' Jim asked the Campbell.

'To meet with that blackguard Starling, I'm thinking, to strike a deal in exchange for the Eye.' The Campbell waggled his claymore towards the sinister gem that twinkled on Professor Slocombe's desk.

'Then we must go with him.' John Omally leapt to his feet, spilling precious whisky as he did so.

'You can't go with him. He'll not be leaving the house.'

'Then Starling is coming here?'

The Campbell shook his turbaned head.

'Then I don't understand you,' said Omally.

'They'll not be meeting in the flesh,' said the Campbell, which really didn't help matters.

'I know what he's going to do,' said Jim. 'He can really do it?' Jim addressed this question to the Highlander.

'Aye,' said Mahatma Campbell.

'Incredible.' And Jim shook his head. 'All my life I've wanted to do that.'

'You'll have to enlighten me, please,' said John. 'This conversation appears to be in code.'

'Astral travel,' said Jim. 'The professor will put himself into a mystical trance and his ectoplasmic spirit form will leave his physical body and travel to the meeting with Starling.'

'Right,' said John. It was a definite kind of 'right'.

'It's true as Jim says it,' said the Campbell, helping himself to another treble Scotch.

'After you with that decanter,' said John. 'But leave his body? That is the stuff of fantasy fiction.'

'That would be irony, would it, John?' said Jim. 'Considering what we've just been through? But I did it once, left my own body.'

'After ten pints of Large, with the wind behind you.'

'I did, John. I really did.'

John's glass was refreshed with Scotch. And Jim's glass took refreshment, too.

'*You* left your body?' said John. 'I have heard of such things. Were you in a car crash or something?'

'John, you've known me all my life. Have I ever been in a car crash?'

'Not that I know of.'

'Then let me tell you what happened. Remember yesterday, when you told me all about what was going on and what had really happened to me on Friday night and you said that I took it very well?'

'You did,' said John, 'ridiculously well, and then you came up with the plan to visit the Consortium building. Rather a bold plan, I considered, for one so normally timid as yourself.'

'I'm not timid,' said Jim, 'I'm just cautious. But the reason I took it so well is because somehow I've always been expecting something like this to happen. I've always believed in this kind of stuff.'

'It's the first I've heard of it.'

'Because I knew you'd laugh.'

'I'm a Catholic,' said John. 'You'd be surprised at all the old rubbish we Catholics believe in.'

'No, I wouldn't. But this kind of thing has always fascinated me and I always hoped it would be real. You see, when I was a child, my dad gave me a copy of Lobsang Rampa's book *The Third Eye*. It's the autobiography of a man who grew up in a lamasery in Lhasa, Tibet. He became a lama and learned to open the third eye in his forehead. And he could see people's auras and indulge in astral travel and even levitate.'

'Sounds most unlikely,' said John.

'And, sadly, so it proved to be. Years later the book was

revealed to be a hoax written by Cyril Henry Hoskins, a plumber from Plympton.'

'Tough luck,' said John.

'But it didn't put me off,' Jim continued. 'And when I was a teenager I discovered Dr Strange in Marvel Comics – the original series, drawn by the now legendary Steve Ditko. Dr Strange learns all the stuff that Lobsang—'

'Cyril,' said John.

'Yes, that Cyril said he'd learned. He battles Baron Mordo and the Dread Dormammu. And I really, really wanted to do that, and every night I would lie naked on my bed and try to leave my body.'

'I've never heard it called that before,' said John, doing a Sid James snigger.

'Don't be crude.' Jim sipped further Scotch. 'But every night I tried, concentrating really hard. And then one night I actually did it.'

'You left your body?'

'Floated right out of myself. It was very scary at first. I sort of hung there above my bed, looking down at me, which I can tell you is very strange, because I didn't look the way I thought I looked.'

Omally shook his head and rolled his eyes.

'Because,' said Jim, 'we only see ourselves in mirrors, and that's the wrong way round. That's not the way we look to other people. We see ourselves in photographs, but that's not the same, either.'

'Nice touch,' said John.

'What?'

'I said "nice touch". That little detail adds a bit of authenticity to your ludicrous tale.'

'It's all the truth. I looked down upon myself and I was connected to my body by a silver cord. And when I got over being so scared, I went out for a fly. I went straight through the bedroom wall and up the street and along the Ealing Road, floating, swimming through the air at the height of the top of the lampposts. It was incredible. And when I got to the football ground I saw this boy, a ginger-haired boy, and he was sitting right on the top of one of the floodlights.'

Omally shook his head, but Jim continued with his tale.

'So I swam on through the air,' Jim continued, 'and joined this boy on top of the floodlights. And I said to him, "Why did you climb up here? It's really dangerous." And he said, "I didn't climb up here, I flew like you. I'm astral travelling, too." Apparently he'd always been able to do it. We arranged to meet again the following night and he said he'd fly with me to Tibet.'

'And did you?' John asked.

'No,' said Jim. 'The next thing I knew it was morning and my mum was bringing me a cup of tea and I was still lying on top of the bed in my nudity.'

'You dreamed the whole thing,' said Omally.

'No,' said Jim. 'It was real.'

'It was a dream, Jim. Just a dream.'

'No, John, it was real, because that very morning I saw the ginger-haired boy.'

'Really?' said John. 'And he confirmed your meeting with him the night before?'

Jim shook his head. 'I was on the number sixty-five bus, going off to an interview for a job at George Wimpeys, which happily I didn't get. The bus pulled up outside Norman's shop – this was when Norman's dad was still alive – and at the bus stop stood Norman, and the ginger-haired boy was there beside him. And he saw me through the window and raised his thumb and mouthed the word "Tibet". But the bus was full and it pulled away from the stop before I could jump off, so I didn't get to speak to him.'

'So Norman saw this ginger-haired boy. Did he know him?'

Jim shook his head once more. 'I asked Norman later. I said, "Do you know that ginger-haired boy who was waiting at the bus stop with you this morning?" And Norman said, "There wasn't any ginger-haired boy. I was all alone at the bus stop." '

John looked hard at Jim. 'Is that the end of the story?' he asked.

'That's it.' Jim shrugged. 'And it's all true, I promise you. I never managed to do the astral-travelling thing again, so I never saw the ginger-haired boy again and I never flew to Tibet. But I still try, on the rare night that I go to bed sober.'

'You should have come to the professor,' said the Campbell, 'when you were a lad. If he'd believed you to be sincere, no doubt he would have taught you the technique.'

'Do you really think so?'

'No,' said the Campbell. 'I'm pulling your plonker. He'd never train a twat like yourself.'

'Thank you very much indeed.'

The inner door of Professor Slocombe's study opened and the ancient scholar stood framed in the opening. His face was grey and he looked more frail and fragile than ever before. His delicate fingers trembled and his old head rocked gently upon his slender neck.

Omally hastened to guide the old gentleman into a fire-side chair. 'Are you all right, sir?' he asked. 'You look all but done.'

'All *is* done,' said Professor Slocombe, accepting John's glass of Scotch and tossing it back in a single gulp. 'The deal is done.'

'You met with Starling?' Jim asked.

'In my astral body, Jim. And your words came to me and offered me some comfort. Had I met with him in my physical form he would have killed me. His accomplices were awaiting my arrival.'

Jim Pooley made a fearful face.

'Fear not,' said Professor Slocombe. 'All is done. Starling will trouble you no more.'

'You didn't—'

'No, Jim, I didn't kill him. He is a powerful magician, very strong with spells. But I extracted from him a magical oath in return for the Eye. He has promised that no more attempts will be made upon the lives of yourself and John.'

'And you trust his words?' asked Jim.

'By breaking a magical oath he would forfeit his powers. But he will not swerve from his goal. He intends to acquire the football ground and to loose the serpent. I suspect that we may be visited by Lord Cthulhu's dark and scaly minions, intent upon some kind of sabotage or another. But no more attempts will be made upon your lives.'

'So we're free men?' said John. 'We're safe?'

'You are safe,' said the professor, 'and we may still succeed. Seven more games and Brentford wins the cup.'

'It all sounds so very easy when you put it like that,' said Jim.

'It will not be easy. We must remain on our guard, and I will arrange for certain herbal preparations that will offer extra protection. It will not, as I say, be easy, but we will succeed. And now I suggest that you fellows go off about your business – football club business. I am weary and sorely in need of rest.'

'Yes,' said Jim. 'Well, thank you, Professor. Thank you for everything.'

'It is I who should thank you, Jim. I am responsible for the dangers to yourself, for which I am truly sorry. I will do whatever I can to make it up to you.'

'Will you teach me the secrets of astral projection?' Jim asked.

'No,' said Professor Slocombe.

'Oh,' said Jim.

'Just one thing,' John said. 'What about the Eye? Is Starling coming here to reclaim it?'

'No need,' said Professor Slocombe, and he gestured to his desk. The Eye of Utu was no longer there to be seen.

23

Richard Gray leafed once more through the documents that had been placed before him. He made some marginal jottings with his fountain pen and then replaced its top and returned the pen to the topmost pocket of his topping suit.

'Mr Hartnel,' said Mr Gray, leaning back in his leather-upholstered chair and gazing across his expansive desk towards the shopkeeper who sat before him. 'Mr Hartnel, I have been Brentford's solicitor in residence for thirty-five years. I knew your father and, if you recall, I drew up the prenuptial agreement that your fiancée demanded.'

Norman nodded dismally. He recalled that all too well.

'And you have since come to me on many occasions, mostly, I recall, in the hope of securing financial backing for one of your, how shall I put this, *imaginative* inventions. How goes the Hartnel Grumpiness Hyper-Drive, by the way?'

'Very well, actually.' Norman smiled towards the solicitor, who did not return this smile. 'I had to really shout at it this morning – I think there's a bit of dirt in the carburettor.'

'Quite so. Suffice it to say that you have called upon me on many occasions, and here you are once more, upon this Monday morning, calling upon me with this –' Mr Richard Gray cast Norman's contract towards Norman. '– and asking me to, how did you put it? "Give it a quick once-over, because a trouble shared is a trouble halved."'

Norman's head bobbed up and down in the manner of a felt dog in a Cortina rear window.

'What *exactly* do you expect me to say about *this*?'

'That it's sound,' said Norman. 'That I'm not going to be diddled out of my millions.'

Mr Richard Gray took up his desk calendar. It was one of those Victorian ones, with the little rollers with little brass knobs that you turn to alter the date and the day. 'Am I misreading this?' he said.

'I don't think so,' said Norman. 'Why?'

'Because surely it must say April the first. Because surely this must be an April Fool's Day jape.'

'I assure you, it is *not*,' said Norman.

'Then you are telling me that you hold five original patents?'

'I have them here in one of my duffel bags,' said Norman. 'Would you care to take a look?'

'Certified by the Patent Office? Stamped with their official seal?'

'Yes,' said Norman. And he drew out these items, somewhat crumpled due to their duffel-bag confinement and passed them across the expansive desk and into the manicured hands of Brentford's solicitor in residence.

This man now examined these plans and documents and seals of certification. And then he sat back once more in his leather-upholstered chair.

'You are telling me,' he said, 'that this is really *real*?'

Norman's head nodded once more.

'But . . .' The solicitor perused the plans and the documentation and the contracts and anything else that he might possibly have previously overlooked.

'But?' Norman asked.

'But this is . . .' The solicitor's voice trailed off.

'Are you all right?' Norman asked.

'Yes, yes.' Mr Gray raised a manicured hand. He tapped at a little desk console. 'Ms Bennett,' he said.

'Yes, sir,' came a breathy feminine voice, a breathy feminine voice that Norman recognised to be that of the breathy feminine receptionist who had ushered him without charm into the solicitor's office. 'Ms Bennett, do we still have that bottle of champagne left over from the Jimmy Bacon case?'

'The one the gang gave you for getting him off the charge of indecent assault against the usherette of the Odeon cinema? And he was bloody guilty, you know that.'

'Quite so, Ms Bennett, but do we still have it?'

'It's in the fridge, next to your inflatable love trout.'

'Hush.' Mr Richard Gray fluttered his fingers. 'Please bring in the bottle and two glasses.'

And presently Ms Bennett entered the office of Mr Richard Gray. She was a stunner, was Ms Bennett, one of those curvy blonde bombshells of a type that have gone out of fashion, but really, truly should not have.

'There you go,' said she, leaning over Norman, who vanished in the shadow of her bosom, and placing the bottle of champagne and the glasses on to the expansive desk.

'That will be all,' said the solicitor in residence. 'Back to your desk, now.'

'No champagne for me, then?' The bosom unshadowed Norman. The shapely legs were near enough for him to ogle shamelessly.

'Return to your desk, please,' said Mr Richard Gray.

Norman watched Ms Bennett depart, and sighed a little as she did so. He'd seen Ms Bennett in The Flying Swan once, in the company of John Omally.

'Champagne?' said Mr Richard Gray.

'Does this mean that the contract is A-okay?' asked Norman.

'Mr Hartnel,' said Mr Gray, uncorking the champagne and caring not one hoot for the fact that it spilled all over his expansive desk, and indeed his topping suit. 'Mr Hartnel, what you have here is a contract drafted by the Consortium, a multinational concern headed by William Starling – whom, rumour has it, is shortly to be awarded the Order of the Garter by Her Majesty the Queen, God bless her.'

'I met him yesterday,' said Norman. 'Very charming fellow.'

'A contract,' the solicitor continued, 'that will be activated upon Cup Final Day, although I cannot understand why that should be.'

'Me neither,' said Norman, 'but these things take time, I suppose. He'll probably want to count all the many millions, make sure I'm not short-changed.'

'Undoubtedly so.' Mr Gray rolled his eyes.

More damn eye-rolling, thought Norman.

'Undoubtedly so,' Mr Gray continued, 'but on that date, the Consortium will take control of your patents and you will receive a twenty-three-million-pound advance.'

'That's what I thought it said,' said Norman.

'Against a fifty per cent royalty on your patented inventions. And given the groundbreaking nature of your inventions and the fact that they will totally revolutionise transport, telecommunications, power supply and just about everything else on the planet, I would estimate that within five years you will be one of the two richest men on Earth, Mr William Starling being the other.'

'You don't think that I should hold out for a better deal then? Say a sixty per cent royalty?'

Mr Gray, who was sipping champagne, coughed into it. 'Excuse me,' he said, drawing a shirt cuff sporting a Masonic cufflink over his mouth. 'To bring these plans of yours into actuality will require a financial investment of millions. To have been offered a fifty per cent deal is beyond the wildest dreams of any inventor. History is being made here, Mr Hartnel, right here in this office.'

'Splendid,' said Norman, sipping his own champagne. 'This isn't as good as Mr Starling's champagne,' he added.

'Mr Hartnel, you will soon be able to purchase every bottle of champagne in the whole world, should you so wish it.'

'I don't think I would,' said Norman. 'My fridge isn't all that big.'

'Then buy another one. Buy ten – buy a thousand.'

'I wouldn't know where to put them all.'

'Quite so. Then let us get down to business. More champagne?'

'I haven't finished this one yet.'

'Then do.'

Norman did.

Mr Gray refilled his glass. 'To business,' he said once more. 'I am honoured that you have chosen me to represent you. You will, of course, need a great deal of legal advice during the coming months and years. There will be a lot of paperwork and a man of boundless wealth such as yourself would not wish to be burdened with it. But have no fear, I will take care of this tedious business for you. I will draw up an agreement of exclusivity.'

'What is that?' Norman asked.

'Nothing to trouble yourself about. Simply an agreement, a gentlemen's agreement between the two of us, that I am your sole representative in all forthcoming legal matters. Your *man*, in fact. I will handle all your business, that you might enjoy the fruits of your labours, to whit, your enormous wealth.'

'That's very kind of you,' said Norman. 'So the contract is A-okay, is it?'

'There is no small print. It is a thoroughly honest contract, with no legal loopholes and no danger to yourself of being swindled.'

'Splendid,' said Norman, gathering up the contract and his plans, patents and whatnots and so ons and ramming them back into his duffel bag.

'I'll draw up the agreement now,' said Mr Gray. 'A trifling point-five of a per cent and all your legal troubles will be forever behind you. This is your lucky day, Mr Hartnel. More champagne?'

'No thanks,' said Norman. 'I have to get back to the shop. Peg thinks I'm in the toilet – I climbed out through the window.'

'It will take no more than a moment to draw up the agreement.' Mr Gray took out his fountain pen once more.

'Well,' said Norman, rising to his feet and shrugging, 'thanks very much for the offer, but I don't think I'll bother. If the contract is A-okay, that's enough for me.'

'Oh no,' said Mr Richard Gray. 'Oh no, oh no, oh no. You have no idea of all the seemingly insurmountable problems that lie ahead of you. I can deal with them all. I *am* your man. I am your *man*.'

'I'll be fine, thanks,' said Norman. 'Twenty-three million will be more than enough to be going on with. I'm not a greedy man.'

'But . . .' Mr Richard Gray now clawed at the air, almost in the manner of a drowning man. 'No, wait. You can't leave. You *can't*.'

'I have to get back,' said Norman. 'The lady outside said there was a twenty-five-pound consultancy fee. I paid her in cash. Thanks for your time. Goodbye.'

And with that, Norman left the office of Mr Richard Gray. And Mr Richard Gray opened his office window and threw himself out of it.

On to the dustbins outside.

For the office was on the ground floor.

'Mr Hartnel,' said Ms Bennett as Norman was leaving the building, 'the office intercom was still on and I couldn't help overhearing your conversation with Mr Gray.'

'Better an egg in peace than an ox in war,' said Norman.

'I do so agree,' said Ms Bennett.

'You *do*?' said Norman.

'I *so* do. And I love the way you said it. You're a very assertive man, Mr Hartnel.'

'I am?' said Norman, adjusting his wig.

'You are. And a very handsome one, if I dare say so.'

'Well,' said Norman, 'there's no harm in daring.'

'Perhaps we might go for a drink at lunchtime?'

'Why?' Norman asked.

'Well.' Ms Bennett threw back her blondey hair and thrust out her preposterous bosoms. 'To get to know each other a little better, perhaps.'

'I'd like that,' said Norman. 'What shall we say? One o'clock in The Swan, would that be all right?'

Ms Bennett left her chair and moved to sit upon her desk, where she crossed her shapely legs in a most provocative fashion. 'I'll be looking forward to it,' she said.

'Looking forward to the match on Wednesday, Neville?' asked Old Pete, reacquainting himself with his favourite stool in The Swan's saloon bar.

'I'm damn sure I barred you for a week,' said the part-time barman.

'What's a week between old friends?' Old Pete grinned a toothless grin. 'And you barred Norman, too. I think I'm losing the plot. I heard you have unbarred John and Jim.'

'Yes,' said Neville, 'well—'

'And a very wise move on your part. A large dark rum, if you will. I have the exact change.'

Neville drew off a large dark rum for the antiquated horticulturalist. 'What match is this you're talking about?' he asked.

'The team's next match, against Orton Goldhay Wanderers, the legendary thrashers of Penge upon their legendary Day of Shame. Should be a good'n.'

'And you'll be there, will you?'

'In spirit,' said Old Pete, 'but out of loyalty to yourself and The Swan I'll be drinking here rather than in The Stripes Bar.'

'Cheese,' said Neville.

'And I have something for you.' Old Pete rooted about in his tweedy pocket. 'As a token of our longstanding friendship, as it were.'

'Oh,' said Neville. 'What's that then?'

'Mandragora,' said Old Pete. 'The crop has come in. The first batch is on the house, Neville.' And Old Pete passed Neville a bag of what looked to all the world to be Mary Johanna herself.

'This place is a crack den,' said a casual observer.

'Back to the Cottage Hospital with you,' said Neville, showing the casual observer the door.

'This stuff,' said Old Pete, 'will make you a god-damn sexual tyrannosaurus. Just like me.'

'I don't think so.' Neville pushed the bag back across the mahogany bar counter.

'Give it a go,' said the elder, pushing it back. 'Two tea-spoons in your morning coffee. Trust me, it will perk up your old chap no end.'

'My old chap does not need perking up.'

'Neville,' said Old Pete, 'I have no wish to be crude here, but when was the last time you had a shag?'

'That is none of your business.' Neville made an appalled face and pushed the bag back towards Old Pete.

'Not in my living memory,' said Old Pete, 'and my living memory goes back one heck of a long way.'

'I'm a busy man, Pete. I have no time for trivial dalliances.'

'I see you ogling the office girls that come in here at lunchtimes, but you don't have the courage to ask them out. You're afraid that your old chap will let you down.'

'Lies,' said Neville. 'Damned and filthy lies.'

'Try it,' said Old Pete, pushing the bag once more in Neville's direction. 'What have you got to lose?'

'I *don't* take drugs,' said Neville, pushing it back.

'It isn't drugs,' said Old Pete, pushing it back at Neville once again. 'It's a natural herb extract. You'll thank me for it, Neville, you really will.'

Neville gazed down upon the little bag. 'No,' said he.

'Go on, Neville. Trust me, I'm a horticulturist.'

Neville sighed, took the bag and placed it upon a shelf behind the bar, amongst the Spanish souvenirs.

'Good boy,' said Old Pete.

'I'm not going to take it,' said Neville.

'Of course you're not.' Old Pete finished his large dark rum. 'Same again,' he said, 'and have one yourself, on me.'

'One for yourself?' said John Omally.

He and Jim stood in The Stripes Bar. It was a Stripes Bar that was still undergoing redecoration. Hairy Dave and Jungle John, Brentford's builders in residence, were bashing away with the three-knot emulsion brushes and spreading paint in most places other than on the walls.

'I'm cutting down,' said Jim. 'Make mine a half.'

'Two more pints over here, please,' John told Mr Rumpelstiltskin.

Mr Rumpelstiltskin drew off two pints of Large.

'A shame about the Beverley Sisters catching fire like that,' said Jim as he took his up.

'Swings and roundabouts,' said John, 'but at least The Rock Gods escaped unscathed. I'm sure I can persuade them to attend another Benefit Night, although I'm not so sure that I'll be able to provide an audience. Shall we adjourn to my office? It escaped the worst of the holocaust.'

John and Jim adjourned to John's office in The Stripes Bar and sat themselves down, John upon his comfy recliner.

'Do you really think we're safe?' Jim asked.

'If the professor says we're safe, we're safe.'

'I hope so.'

'And the Campbell is no longer following you around, which must prove something. Jim, we are presently weird-free. Nothing else weird is going to occur, nothing else preposterous.'

'I really *do* hope so.'

'Perk up, Jim.' John raised his glass. 'We're back in the game. There are pennies to be made, games to be won and a betting ticket in your pocket that will take us both to wealth.'

'If Brentford wins seven games on the trot.'

'Trust the professor's tactics. So far, so good.'

'But another game on Wednesday – so soon.'

'It's hard work in the big league, but the payoffs are more than favourable. Now, about these strippers.'

'Strippers,' said Jim. '*Strippers?*'

'Strippers,' said John. 'I thought I might engage some for lunchtimes in here, to bring in a bit of trade.'

'Neville won't take kindly to that.'

'I have not entirely forgiven Neville for bopping us on the head. But this is business, Jim. We need the money to pay the team.'

'I've been wondering about my wages, John. When do

you think I'll be seeing any? I'm all but broke and my landlady is all for casting me into the street.'

'What? The manager of Brentford United? I'll have words with that lady. You leave it to me.'

Jim shrugged and sighed. 'So, strippers it is,' he said in a hopeless tone. 'What else?'

'More sponsorship. I have a new mobile phone.' John flourished same and Jim flinched. 'And new stock for the club shop. You can leave all that to me, I'm on the case.'

'And me?'

'You just enthuse the team, pass on the professor's tactics – do your job. We'll succeed. I have every confidence that we will.'

'We can but try,' said Jim Pooley. 'But see, who is this?'

Jim pointed and John followed the direction of his pointing.

'It's Small Dave,' said John, 'Brentford's dwarfish postman, locally known as a vindictive grudge-bearing wee bastard with nasty warty little hands.'

'I know who he is,' said Jim, 'and his horrid warty little hands fair put the wind up me. But what is he doing here?'

'Good day, each,' said Small Dave, waddling over.

'Good day, Dave,' said John.

And Jim did likewise.

'Thought I'd just pop in,' said the diminutive deliverer of the Queen's mail. 'Tell you a bit of hot news.'

'Really?' said Jim. 'What news is this?'

Small Dave made gagging sounds in his throat. 'My voice departs me,' he whispered. 'My throat is parched.'

'Pint of Large over here, please, barman,' Omally called. 'Courtesy of the management.'

'Cheers,' said Small Dave. And upon receiving his pint, he said 'cheers' once again and climbed on to a chair to address his benefactor. 'He's back,' said the small one.

'Who's back?' Jim asked.

'Archroy is back.'

'Archroy?'

John looked at Jim.

And Jim looked at John.

'Archroy is back?' said Jim.

'That's what I said.' Small Dave took up his pint in his two tiny hands, which Jim and John refrained from gazing upon, and gulped away the better part of it. 'Arrived this morning, looking very full of himself. Well tanned he is and wearing a pith helmet.'

'He's been gone for ages,' said Jim. 'How long has it been?'

'Eighteen months,' said Small Dave, finishing his pint. 'Went in search of the Ark of Noah that supposedly rests upon Mount Ararat, which is now buried in the ice.'

'And did he find it?' asked Jim.

'Apparently not. The borders are closed – there was some unpleasantness – so he set sail for other parts.'

'He's a nutter,' said John. 'Always was. A dreamer, even when we were back at school together. He goes off on his wanderings in search of mythical artefacts and always comes back empty-handed.'

'Not this time,' said Small Dave, rattling his empty glass upon the table. 'This time he's hit the motherlode. Oh no, my voice is giving out again.'

'One more, then,' said Omally, calling out to Mr Rumpelstiltskin for more. 'But this had better be good.'

'Oh, it is.' Small Dave awaited the arrival of his new pint and, upon its arrival, continued with the telling of his tale. 'He got blown off course somewhere in the Adriatic. Got washed up upon an island.' Small Dave went on to name the island.

'Never heard of it,' said John.

'That's because it's not on any modern map. Did you ever see that film *Jason and the Argonauts*?'

'One of my favourites,' said Jim. 'A Ray Harryhausen.'

'That's the one,' said Small Dave.

'Ah, yes,' said Jim, 'and that island is where Jason captured the Golden Fleece.'

'You are correct,' said Small Dave. 'And that's what Archroy's done.'

'What has he done?' John asked.

'He's found the Golden Fleece and he's brought it back to Brentford.'

John looked at Jim once more.

And Jim looked back at John.

'On your way, Dave,' said John Omally. 'And give that pint to me.'

'I'm not kidding, lads,' said Small Dave, clinging on to his pint. 'He really has found it, and it really is magic. Remember the warts?'

'What warts would these be?' asked John, as if he didn't know.

'As if you don't know,' said Small Dave. 'All over my hands. Well, look at them now.' And Small Dave held up his hands. 'He laid the Golden Fleece upon me and all my warts vanished away.'

And John beheld the hands of Small Dave.

And Jim beheld these hands also.

And lo, these hands were free of warts.

These tiny hands were wartless.

'Now let me just quote you, John,' said Jim. 'Nothing else weird is going to occur, you said. Nothing else preposterous.'

Norman drank that lunchtime in The Flying Swan, in the company of Ms Bennett. Later, the two of them took a little drive in Norman's van.

And what went on in that van, somewhat later, when it was parked-up in a quiet cul-de-sac, would have been considered by John to be more than quite preposterous.

24

Archroy did not pop into The Stripes Bar for a pint or two to celebrate his unexpected return to Brentford. Neither did he pop into The Flying Swan. Which was probably a good thing, because Neville was having a bit of trouble with the brewery.

It was Tuesday now and Neville was cringing at the unexpected and truly unwelcome arrival of the brewery-owner's son, Young Master Robert.

Young Master Robert paced up and down The Swan's saloon bar, turning occasionally to glance at Neville before pacing on.

'Everything is in order,' Neville told him. 'The books balance, as near as books can balance. Trade is good.'

'Really?' Young Master Robert ceased his pacing and turned his visage fully upon Neville. 'Words reach my ear,' said he, 'words to the effect that The Stripes Bar has engaged the services of a lunchtime stripper.'

'No,' said Neville. 'Really?'

'Trade appears somewhat slack in here at the present,' said the young master. 'And the present is lunchtime, is it not?'

'They'll be in soon,' said Neville. 'They always are – young pasty-faced office types. We get through a lot of cider.'

'But not today, apparently.'

'They'll be in.'

'Then perhaps I'll wait and say my hellos.'

'Cheese,' said Neville.

'Needs a pep-up,' said Young Master Robert. 'This place needs a pep-up, something to draw in the punters.'

'We have regular trade,' said Neville. 'This is a highly respected establishment, very popular with the locals.'

'A lot of no-marks.' Young Master Robert paced up to the bar counter and sat himself down upon Old Pete's favourite stool, which was unusually empty. 'I hear that the team actually won a match on Saturday.'

'Indeed,' said Neville, 'and I am responsible for appointing the new manager, not that I wish to take any credit. Although if any is going, I will receive it without complaint.'

'Needs a pep-up,' said Young Master Robert. 'Needs a new look.'

'It really doesn't.' Neville found himself wringing his hands. He thrust these wringing hands into his trouser pockets. 'It's perfect as it is. It couldn't be more perfect.'

'New look,' said Young Master Robert. 'Pep-up. Vodka and Slimline.'

Neville hastened to oblige. 'Please don't do anything to the décor,' he begged the young master as he presented him with his drink.

'One thing at a time,' said the brewery-owner's one and only boy-child. 'Let's start with the bar staff.'

'Oh no,' said Neville. 'You're not going to sack me?'

'Oh no, not yet, but the place needs a little colour. And if The Stripes has strippers, then The Flying Swan needs ladies, too.'

'Not strippers,' said Neville. 'Anything but strippers.'

'Not strippers, but female bar staff.'

Neville flinched, horribly. He'd never met a woman yet who could draw a decent pint.

'Female bar staff?' he said in a tremulous tone.

'*Topless* female bar staff,' said Young Master Robert.

'By the shades of the seraphim,' said Jim Pooley, for Dr Strange Comics were rarely far from his mind these days, 'that lady has very large bosoms.'

'*Very* large,' said John Omally. 'I agree that she doesn't have much of an act, just sort of crawls on to the stage and tries to stand upright, but it works for me.'

John and Jim viewed the stripper, as did the large male contingent that thronged The Stripes Bar. Which included, upon this occasion, the now legendary Ivor Biggun.

'A decent turnout for a lunchtime,' said Jim.

'It's a wonder what a few posters will do,' said John.

'Neville is not going to like this.'

'He's a professional. He understands the spirit of healthy competition. Hey, look, here's Norman. And who's that with him? I know that woman.'

'Hello, lads,' said Norman, mooching up to the bar counter. 'This is my business associate, Ms Bennett.'

'We've met,' said John, putting out his hand for an intimate shake.

'Have we?' said Ms Bennett, declining the offer of John's hand.

'Champagne,' said Norman, 'if you have any.'

'Of course we have.' John drew the attention of Mr Rumpelstiltskin, which was difficult as the barman's eyes were fixed upon the bosom of the stripper. 'Champagne over here.'

'She's nearly up,' said Mr Rumpelstiltskin. 'No, she's down again.'

'Champagne,' repeated Omally.

'Cheers,' said Norman. 'And get in further glasses. You can have some, too.'

'So what are we celebrating?' Omally asked.

'My patents,' said Norman. 'I am shortly to be very rich indeed.'

'This would be the electrical business that nearly killed us all in The Flying Swan, would it?' said John.

'I've done a deal,' said Norman. 'Signed the contracts yesterday evening.'

Mr Rumpelstiltskin uncorked a bottle of warm champagne and decanted it into champagne flutes and into John and Jim's pints. 'Can I have a glass myself?' he asked. 'I've never tasted champagne.'

'Knock yourself out,' said Norman. 'A friend in court is better than a penny in a purse.'

'We're getting married,' said Ms Bennett.

'You're *what*?' said Omally.

'I'm divorcing Peg,' said Norman. 'I haven't actually broached the subject with her yet. She doesn't actually believe in my patents – happily. Even though the chap who's bought them mentioned them to her on Sunday, she still doesn't believe in them. Unlike Yola here.'

'I believe in you,' said Ms Bennett, giving Norman's crotch a loving tweak. 'You're a wonderful man, Norman.'

'We're soul-buddies,' said Norman. 'We were made for each other. We're going to buy a castle together.'

'And a yacht,' said Ms Bennett. 'And Argos.'

'Argos?' asked Jim.

'It's a retail outlet,' said Norman, 'with very competitive prices. It has its own catalogue. Yola likes the jewellery section.'

'Well, I wish you both the best of luck,' said Jim, raising his glass in salute.

'Norman,' said John, 'do you think I might have a small word with you?'

'You might,' said Norman, tipping champagne down his throat, 'so long as it's very small indeed.'

'In private,' said John.

'I have no secrets from Yola,' said Norman, and Yola snuggled against his chest and gave his bum a pat.

'Naturally not.' Omally made smilings at Yola that were not returned to him. 'But it is a personal matter. If you'd be so kind as to indulge me.'

'A trouble shared *is* a bird in the bush,' said Norman, removing his person with difficulty from Yola's caresses and following John to his office.

'Sit yourself down,' John told him and Norman did so in John's lounger. 'Norman,' said John, seating himself, 'Norman, how long have we known each other?'

'Since we were wee small boys together,' said Norman.

'Yes.'

'With holes in our socks and tears in our trouser seats.'

'Quite so.'

'Playing conkers and scrumping apples.'

'This is true.'

'Filling our mouths with gobstoppers and slipping in through the back doors of the Odeon for Saturday morning pictures.'

'Yes, I remember it well.'

'Playing "knock down ginger" on Mrs Smith's door and—'

'Shut up, Norman, please.'

'Oh,' said Norman.

'My point is,' said Omally, 'that we have known each other, man and boy, for a good many years and I am proud to call you my friend.'

'No,' said Norman.

'No? No, I'm not your friend?'

'No,' said Norman. 'As in no, you can't borrow a fiver.'

'I wasn't going to ask you for a fiver.'

'Not a *tenner*, surely? Have you no shame?'

Omally sighed a deep and truly heartfelt. 'I wasn't going to ask you for any money at all – unless, of course, you'd care to invest a couple of million in a football club.'

'I might well do that.' Norman swigged champagne. 'But I don't get my money until Cup-Final Day. I'll certainly give it some thought, though.'

'This isn't about money,' said John. 'Well, in a manner of speaking it is, but it isn't that I want to take your money. It's about her.' Omally gestured in a subtle and understated manner towards Ms Bennett.

Ms Bennett waved back at John, incorporating into this wave a subtle and understated two-fingered 'Harvey Smith'.

'Norman,' whispered Omally, 'would you say that I knew something about women?'

'If it makes you happy,' said Norman. 'You know something about women. There, I've said it. If that's all you wanted, I'll be on my way now.'

Omally made an exasperated face. 'Norman, I'm trying to save you a lot of pain and anguish here – and a lot of money, as well.'

Norman's glass was empty and the shopkeeper turned it between his fingers. 'What *are* you trying to say?' he asked.

'She only wants you for your money, Norman.'

'Who does?' Norman asked.

'Yola – Yola Bennett.'

Norman made the face of surprise. And then the face of doubt. This face of doubt became the face of grave concern.

'You're just jealous,' said Norman, which went to prove that faces can be misleading.

'No, it's not that. I promise you it's not.'

'She loves me,' said Norman. 'She said that she loves me.'

'It's your filthy lucre she loves. She'll suck you dry, Norman.'

Norman stared hard into the face of Omally. 'Suck me dry?' he said.

Omally nodded.

'What, every night?'*

Omally would have thrown up his hands, but one was holding his Large-and-champagne shandy. 'When you get your money,' he said, '*if* you get your money, you can have your pick of women. Thousands of women. You could have your own harem.'

'In my castle?'

'Certainly. Or have an extension built.'

'So what you're saying is that I shouldn't tie myself down just yet?'

'That sort of thing. Don't make any rash commitments.'

'I see,' said Norman. And he nodded, thoughtfully.

'Word to the wise, that's all.' And Omally tapped at his nose.

'Don't tap at my nose like that,' said Norman.

'I wasn't. I was tapping at *my* nose.'

'Oh yes, so you were.'

'So you'll bear in mind what I said.'

'I will,' said Norman.

---

* The old ones are still the best.

'And you won't do anything silly, like get engaged to Yola or anything?'

'Ah,' said Norman.

'*You haven't!*'

Norman grinned towards John. 'No,' said Norman in a whispery tone, 'I haven't. Nor do I intend to. I'm not stupid, John. I know exactly what she's up to, but I'm presently getting the best sex I've ever had in my life, so I think I'll just stick with it for now, if that's all right by you. Care for another?'

And with that said, Norman returned to the loving arms of Yola Bennett.

Jim Pooley joined John at his office table. He sat himself down and said, 'All right?'

Omally shrugged and shook his head.

'Did you put Norman right on that gold-digger?'

'I don't think he needed putting right. That shopkeeper has more savvy than a Sainsbury's cold-meat counter. I think we've sorely misjudged that fellow.'

'Oh,' said Jim. 'That's a shame, because it occurred to me that we might ask him to invest some money in the club.'

'Forget it,' said John.

'Shame,' said Jim, 'because the stripper's got herself upright and she wants paying.'

'I'll get it to her later.'

'And the Campbell has just brought me this.' Jim proffered an envelope. 'More tactics from the professor, I think. The Campbell said we should put the team through their paces tonight in preparation for tomorrow's game.'

Omally pulled out his new mobile phone. 'I'll call them all up, then,' said he. 'Leave it to me, my friend.'

At seven o'clock, the team assembled themselves upon the hallowed turf of Griffin Park. Jim marched up and down before them, smiling encouragement.

The team returned his smile to him in a somewhat sheepish fashion.

'Is everything all right with you chaps?' asked Jim.

Shoulders shrugged and mumblings were all the rage.

'You look a tad, how shall I put this, *uncertain*.'

Ernest Muffler spoke. 'Perhaps if you'd like to count heads,' said he.

'Count heads?' Pooley shook his. 'Okey-dokey.' And Jim counted heads. 'Someone's missing,' he observed. 'Who's missing?'

'It's Billy Kurton,' said Ernest.

'Our right-winger. Where is he?'

'Gone,' said Ernest. 'Upped sticks and gone.'

'*What?*' said Jim.

Ernest raised his palms. 'Went round there earlier. The folk next door said a removal van came in the middle of the night. They said he owed a lot of money to the builders for his patio.'

'Terrible,' said Jim.

'I know. I've seen it – it's a terrible job, pointing all over the place. And level? It's like a humpback bridge with the mumps.'

'I don't mean *that*. I mean it's terrible that we've lost our right-winger.'

'It will put us at a bit of a disadvantage,' said Ernest, 'when it comes to us scoring goals.'

'Right,' said Jim, 'but we won't be disheartened.'

'We *won't*?' said Ernest.

'We won't,' said Jim. 'A temporary setback. We'll put in one of the substitutes until we can purchase a new right-winger.'

'We'll have a crack,' said Don and Phil, the conjoined twins.

Jim made a truly thoughtful face. 'You are absolutely certain that you qualify as *one* player?' he said.

'We only have one passport,' said Don.

'And one birth certificate,' said Phil.

'And one pair of trousers,' said Ernest, 'although they have four legs in them.'

Jim perused the new tactics, penned upon parchment by Professor Slocombe. He'd spent half the afternoon trying to memorise them, but had failed dismally. 'All will be well,' said Jim. 'Trust me on this. We will be on home ground, cheered on by our loyal supporters. And with these new tactics *I* have formulated, we shall triumph. Now, they might at first seem somewhat complicated, but put your trust in me and follow them to the letter and I guarantee that we will succeed.'

'You promise?' said Ernest.

'You have my word.'

'He hasn't let us down so far,' said Dave Quimsby. 'The boss knows what he's doing.'

'Thank you, Dave,' said Jim. 'Now, how best to explain this, I wonder? Ah yes, have any of you ever seen a chorus line dancing? Like the Tiller Girls? Remember them?'

Blank faces gazed back at Jim.

'Right,' said Jim. 'Well, form yourselves into a line, arms about each other's waists, like so. Yes. No, not like that. And . . .'

It did take some hours. And to the casual observer who might have been looking down from the stands, it certainly didn't look like football.

'It looks more like origami to me,' said the casual observer. 'But then what do I know, I'm still on the run from the men in white coats.'

But the team worked hard, and Jim worked hard, and at length all was achieved in the unorthodox manner in which it was desired that it should be achieved.

'That's it, then,' said Jim, panting for breath. 'You've all done very well. Do it like that tomorrow and we will win the match.'

'With a bit of luck,' said Dave.

'Oh yes indeed,' Jim agreed. 'With a bit of luck, we will.'

'So you won't let us down, Boss?' said Dave.

'Of course not,' said Jim.

'There, lads,' said Dave, 'I told you he wouldn't let us down.'

'Of course I won't,' said Jim. 'Did you think I would?'

'I didn't,' said Dave, 'but some of the others were doubtful.'

'Shame on you,' said Jim to the others.

'They said you wouldn't do it.'

'Of course I will,' said Jim. 'Do what, by the way?'

'Do the thing that brought us luck last time.'

'Ah,' said Jim, 'the pep talk on the field of play. Have no fear on that point.'

'No, not that, Boss. The lucky thing. The thing that brought us luck, that made us win last time. Sportsmen are superstitious, you know that, and once a thing is done once and it works, it becomes a talisman – a token of good luck.'

'Well, whatever it was that I did, I promise I will do it again,' said Jim. 'What was it, by the way?'

'Wear your lucky Bertie Wooster suit,' said Dave.

25

Scoop Molloy had been given a special pass by John Omally that gave him access to Griffin Park's executive box.

Now, there are executive boxes and there are executive boxes. Happily, time and space forbid a prolonged monologue upon the disparities. However, let it be said that Griffin Park's executive box did not rank amongst the higher echelons of the executive box world.

'This is not so much a box,' Scoop observed, 'it's more of a carton.'

'I have a new carpet on order,' said John, 'and new seating also and a bar will shortly be installed.'

'And then there'll be no room for anyone.'

'It's not normally so crowded.'

But tonight it *was*. Because tonight the home team, who had so recently wrought desolation upon Penge, had drawn something of a crowd. And the executive box was packed to capacity and beyond with all the local sponsors of the team.

Mr Goddard was there. And Mr Paine, the undertaker. And Mr Ratter, the jeweller. And Mohammed Smith from the sports shop. And Mr Kay, of Kay's Electrical Stores. And a good many others who had coughed up their hard-earneds to have John put their logos upon the team's kaftans, and who were all entitled, by merit of their sponsorship, to a seat in the executive box. And there were others, too, others who really shouldn't have been there. Others who didn't deserve to be there, but who had demanded that because of 'their rank', they should be there.

These others were Town Councillors Vic 'Vanilla' Topping, Doris Whimple and David Berkshire (David Berkshire was hard to spot, but he was in there somewhere). These town councillors had decided that they had better make an appearance, in the pretence that they supported the team. Omally had been all for sending them packing, but Jim, being Jim, had let them stay.

'Shift along,' said the voice of Norman Hartnel as the scientific shopkeeper elbowed his way into the crush. 'Give my girlfriend a seat.'

'Who let you in?' John Omally asked.

'Jim did,' said Norman. 'I've decided that I will invest in the club when my money comes in. In fact, I've decided to buy it.'

'That's all very well,' said John, 'but—'

'I bunged Jim one hundred pounds up front, to seal the deal, as it were.'

'Where did you get one hundred pounds?'

'Insurance money for my lock-up. I'm glad I had that terrorist-attack clause written into my insurance policy. It always pays to think ahead, doesn't it?'

'Apparently so.'

'I've brought my own champagne,' said Norman, proffering the bottle, 'so you don't need to buy me any.'

'Ah,' said Mr Ratter, who was getting somewhat squashed, 'the champagne. You did mention champagne, didn't you, Omally?'

'I'll get to it,' said John. 'And for God's sake don't all stamp your feet when the team scores or you'll find yourselves down in the cheap seats.' And with that he eased himself out of the executive box and went off in search of Jim.

Jim was to be found in the changing rooms, giving the team a pep talk. It was a most inspired pep talk this evening, which likened the noble game of football to a beautiful garden that had to be nurtured and cherished, its darling buds and precious blooms coaxed into being. And so on and so forth and such like. Most of it didn't mean much to the team, but Jim's words flowed over them, wonderfully, magically. Into Jim's head and out of Jim's mouth, these wonder words got the job jobbed.

'Sporting your lucky suit, I see,' said John when Jim had done with his wondrous words.

'Lucky suit,' said Jim and he said it slowly and with thought.

'Or so I heard,' said John, with haste. 'Is everything hunky-dory?'

'Our rivals are changing next door – the Campbell is looking after them.'

'Lucky them.'

'And the BBC? You said you were making phone calls on your portable telephone. Are the BBC going to cover the match?'

'Ah,' said John.

'Ah?' said Jim.

'Well, I had a bit of trouble with the BBC. They said that they were covering a match involving a team called Manchester United tonight. Some bunch of Northerners.'

'So they won't be covering us?'

'Sadly, no. But I got the next-best thing.'

'And what is that?'

'The voices of Free Radio Brentford.'

Jim made groaning sounds. 'Those mad blokes – Terrence Jehovah Smithers and the Second Sponge Boy?'

'They're cult figures. They have a lot of something called "street cred".'

'And what does that mean?'

'I've no idea,' said John, 'but they're very popular. They'll be covering the match live, and their portable transmitter is very powerful. They say they'll turn it up full blast and it will cut into every radio and TV channel in a five-mile radius. Think publicity, Jim. Think further sponsorship.'

'Oh dear, oh dear, oh dear,' said Jim.

'The professor is waiting for you on the bench,' said John. 'Oh yes, and he told me to mention that –' Omally perused his wristlet watch '– it's five minutes now to kick off.'

'Four minutes now to kick off,' said Terrence Jehovah Smithers. 'Should we go live, do you think?'

'Give it another minute or two,' said the Second Sponge Boy. 'We're all linked up, aren't we?'

The two of them lay commando fashion, in the company of many cans of lager on the roof of the executive box. They had microphones strapped about their necks and headphones on their heads. Cables ran from their portable transmitters, conveying their words to a knackered VW camper van that kept constantly on the move through the eveningtime streets of Brentford. From this van their words would be broadcast to each and every thing of an electrical nature within a five-mile radius, including pop-up toasters, hairdryers and items from the Ann Summers catalogue. It was all very hi-tech, bought-over-the-Internet and utterly illegal.

Terrence Jehovah Smithers and the Second Sponge Boy, cult figures and local legends, were not, as such, much to look at. They were slim and pale and pinched; they wore baggy trousers and training shoes (although neither of them were actually sportsmen) and the 'hoodie' – a kind of hooded jerkin much favoured by the criminal underclass in order to evade recognition on CCTV.

'Let's go for it,' said Terrence. 'The teams are coming on to the pitch.'

The Second Sponge Boy clicked on his microphone and spoke the words, 'Go live,' into it.

In the rear of the ever-moving camper van, a fellow who in legal jargon is known as 'an accomplice' pressed a button upon a small black box and replied with the words, 'You're on.'

'Good evening, all,' said Terrence, 'and welcome to the big match.'

And all over Brentford – and, in fact, for a five-mile radius – his words poured forth from every television set and radio set and crystal set and—

'Oh my goodness,' said Peg, who, left to her own devices at home, was enjoying one of these devices. 'Who's in there?'

And moving swiftly on.

'I'm Terry,' said Terrence.

'And I'm Sponge,' said Sponge Boy.

'And we're broadcasting to you live from Brentford, where giant-slayers the Bees are preparing to make short work of Orton Goldhay Wanderers.'

'Very short work,' said Sponge Boy, 'positively dwarf-like. And the teams are marching out on to the pitch, the home team in their distinctive stylish kaftans—'

'It's what everybody will soon be wearing this year,' said Terrence.

'Is it?' said Sponge Boy.

'It is.'

'Well, I won't be.'

'Just get on with the commentary,' said Terrence.

'Absolutely. The home team – deprived, I understand, of their right-winger, Billy Kurton, but with a most unique substitute in the twin figures of Don and Phil English, who, I am told, are currently appearing in Count Otto Black's *Circus Fantastique* on Ealing Common.'

'Were you paid to say that?'

'Of course I was.'

'Then open up a beer.'

Beers were opened and guzzlings were done.

'The home team,' said Terrence. And he proceeded to name the home team and sing their praises.

'And the other mob,' said Sponge. 'And the ref is tossing the coin. And the home team have won the toss.'

On the bench, Jim Pooley eyed Professor Slocombe.

'Did you?' he asked.

Professor Slocombe smiled back at Jim. 'As if I would,' he said.

★

'And what is this?' said Terrence. 'What kind of formation would you call that, Sponge Boy?'

'Well, Terry, as you know, you have your four-three-threes, your three-three-fours, your two-four-fours and your four-four-twos. And, of course, if you're into DIY, you have your two-by-one.'

'I know a song about that,' said Terrence.

'Me, too,' said Sponge Boy. 'Positively Eurovision.'

'So what would you call the formation the home team are employing tonight?'

'A ten-zero-zero, I suppose,' said Sponge Boy.

'And let's see how it's going. They're dribbling the ball between them. Cardinal Cox, Orton Goldhay's left-winger, has come in for a tackle. Now they've closed ranks into a sort of circle formation and they're moving forward . . . ah . . . and now they've broken into a kind of dance. What kind of a dance would you say that was, Sponge?'

'A kind of Russian dance, Terry, in a circle. Positively Cossack.'

'Orton Goldhay are massing their forces now. All their players are trying to kick their way into the circle.'

'Now that's fouling, Terry. The ref won't have that.'

'No he won't, Sponge, he's showing them all the yellow card.'

'But Brentford are still moving forward, if in a sort of circular pattern.'

'It's very graceful, though, isn't it? That's a sort of square-dance formation now, isn't it?' said Terrence.

'More of a line-dance, I'd say. That Mahingay is very light on his toes for a Sikh.'

'Not as light as that Dave Quimsby.'

'I heard that,' said Dave Quimsby. 'I hope you're not implying that I'm a poof.'

'They've almost reached the box,' said Terrence.

'Very nice for them,' said Sponge Boy.

'And the Orton Goldhay team are in the box, too. They're confused. The goalie is confused. He's running from side to side.'

'Positively crablike, Terry.'

'Oh and there it goes. The ball is in the air. The crowd is on its feet. And *IT'S A GOAL!*'

'Oh, and what a goal, Terry. And a victory dance, too. What kind of dance would you say that one was?'

'The macarena, Sponge Boy.'

'The macarena,' said Jim. 'Did I say anything to you about doing the macarena?'

Jim was in the changing room now. The team was in the changing room now. It was half-time now. The team were eating their oranges. Now.

'Did I say anything to you about doing the macarena?' Jim asked once again.

'No,' said Alf, 'you didn't.'

'Then why did you do it?'

'Well, Boss, we got carried away, what with the early goal and everything.'

'And so what happened next?'

The lads' heads went down.

'They scored two goals, Boss. On the trot.'

'On the trot,' said Jim. '*Two goals*. And so what happened next?'

'You shouted at us, Boss.'

'And I heard you, Boss,' said Dave Quimsby, 'and I passed it on.'

'You did,' said Jim. 'And so what happened next?'

'We scored three more,' said Alf, 'on the trot, while doing the Wall Street shuffle.'

'You did,' bawled Jim. And he flung his hands into the air.

There was almighty cheering and Jim was lifted shoulder-high. Which was a pity as the ceiling was low and Jim's head hit it with force.

'Are you all right, Boss?' asked Trevor Brooking[*], fanning at the semi-conscious Pooley with a programme.

'I'm fine, I'm fine,' said Pooley, who wasn't. 'Perhaps a

---

[*] Not be confused with the other Trevor Brooking.

tad confused. Go back out there and give 'em Hell. What are we?'

'We are the lords of the dance, are we,' went up the chorus.

'Oh yes we are,' said Jim.

'And it's coming up to the second half, Terry,' said Sponge Boy. 'Would you care to make any considered observations regarding the team's performance during the first half?'

'Not many, Sponge. They were strong, I thought, on the modern dances, particularly the twist and the watusi. But they were definitely weak in the old-time numbers. Their waltz lacked for finesse and the tango would have been spoiled altogether if it hadn't been for the English brothers, who I felt gave a spirited interpretation, especially when they neatly covered that professional foul on Orton Gold-hay's striker Micky Carroll.'

'Do you think we'll be seeing any free-form in the second half?'

'Self-expression through the medium of dance?'

'That's the kiddie,' said Sponge Boy.

'I shouldn't think so. My guess would be that they might go for a conga.'

'But that's only your guess.'

'Or possibly the birdie.'

'One of my all-time favourites.'

Brentford's glory boys left out the lambada. They turned down the tango, they shunned the shimmy, they side-stepped the sand dance and avoided the vogue. They pooh-poohed the polka, shirked the shake, dodged the disco, bypassed the bumps-a-daisy, spurned the salsa, flouted the flamenco, rejected the rumba and baulked at the bolero—

They even nixed the knees-up, Mother Brown.

'It's the Tennessee wig-walk, Terry.'

'No one remembers the Tennessee wig-walk, Sponge.'

'Then they're walkin' the dog.'

'I beg to differ with you, Sponge, I think you'll find they're doing the Lambeth Walk.'

'It's definitely a very "walk"-orientated dance.'

'Perhaps they're doing the "Walk of Life" by Dire Straits,' said Terrence.

'Perish the thought, but whatever they're doing, it's *ANOTHER GOAL!*'

The home crowd were doing all manner of dances.

The executive boxers did the March of the Mods.

'Don't do that,' shouted Omally. 'The floor will go through.'

'They're certainly leading Orton Goldhay a merry dance, Sponge.'

'They certainly are, Terry, positively lurch-puddle-like.'

'And that would be, Sponge?'

'It's an Armenian folk dance that my nana taught me when I was a child.'

'I thought your Nan was a Jamaican Rastafarian?'

'Still is, Terry Babylon, still is. Ai.'

Now, to cut a long and what might otherwise become tedious story short, and to avoid further references having to be made to *Roget's Thesaurus* and *The Complete History of Dance* by P.P. Penrose—

The Brentford Bees went for the Border morris dance, possibly because the Morris Minor has always been the vehicle of choice amongst Brentonians, or possibly for certain esoteric reasons known only to Professor Slocombe. But the *Brentford Mercury* of the following morn told the whole story of the team's second glorious victory beneath the banner headline:

BERTIE'S BOOGIE BEES
10-2 VICTORY DANCE

Scoop Molloy dictated this piece from his bed in Brentford Cottage Hospital. He concentrated upon the details of the match specifically, rather than dwelling for *too* long upon the confusion and chaos that had ensued when the floor of the executive box fell through, disgorging its exclusive load on to the cheap seats below. Or even on the police assault that was made upon the ground by the Special Forces Unit, dispatched to arrest the Voices of Free Radio Brentford, who had disrupted all telecommunications and broadcasting networks over a five-mile radius, bringing minicabs and emergency services to a standstill.

Scoop never even mentioned the rioting because he was already in hospital by then. The rioting had been started by the Orton Goldhay supporters and they had eventually been brought to book by the far greater numbers of Brentford supporters.

Although, unfortunately, not before they had smashed every shop window in Brentford High Street and engaged in frenzied looting.

No, Scoop stuck to the details of the match, and Brentford's second glorious victory – which took them one step closer to winning the FA Cup.

26

Neville the part-time barman retrieved the morning's copy of the *Brentford Mercury* from one of the hanging baskets of Babylon that prettified The Swan's front wall.

He growled towards the receding figure of Zorro the paperboy as he pedalled away on his bike, tucked the paper beneath his arm and stood for a moment drawing healthy draughts of Brentford air up the unbunged nostril of his hooter.

And then, turning on a carpet-slippered heel, Neville returned to the saloon bar, where he drew himself a measure of breakfast and perused the day's front-page news.

Much of it wasn't news to Neville. He hadn't attended the match himself, his bar-keeping duties having prohibited this. Not that it would have hurt if he had gone – The Swan had known little business that evening. And what Neville hadn't seen, he'd heard. The match, for instance, had been broadcast to him through the jukebox. The rest he'd just *heard*: the police-car sirens, the ambulance bells, the sounds of breaking glass and mob rule; the words of the riot act being read by Inspectre Sherringford Hovis through the police bullhorn; the sounds of the tear-gas shells being fired. And so on and so forth and such like.

Neville couldn't help but manage a small grin.

He wasn't a vindictive man, far from it; he was a good man, pure and simple, but this was all getting somewhat out of hand. Football in Brentford had never been quite like *this* before.

Neville gave the front page further perusal. He'd wondered what the big crash had been. The floor of the executive box collapsing into the stand below, that was it, eh? Neville shook his noble head. Pooley and Omally would soon have the entire stadium down and save the Consortium the cost of a bulldozer.

Neville grinned a bit more. And it wouldn't be *his* fault. He'd appointed Pooley manager, certainly, but that was as far as it went. And if the walls did come tumbling down, well, it couldn't be helped. And Neville *would* get his shares from the Consortium, so he *could* purchase The Flying Swan and run it entirely *his* way.

Which would certainly please the patrons.

So no harm done. Really.

Neville further perused. There was a great deal of detail regarding the extraordinary tactics employed by the home team to achieve their decisive victory.

'The cancan,' Neville read. 'The floppy-boot stomp.'

The part-time barman gave his head further shakings.

Where was this all going to end?

What possibly could happen next?

'Mr Neville, is it?'

Neville jumped back. He hadn't heard anyone enter the bar.

'Oh, Mr Neville, I'm sorry, did I startle you?'

Neville focused his good eye upon—

And Neville let out a gasp.

Before him stood possibly the most beautiful woman he had ever seen in his life. She was tall and shapely, with long auburn hair and the most remarkable emerald eyes. Her facial features seemed delicately carved, as from ivory; her mouth was wide and upturned at the edges into a comely smile. She wore a pink T-shirt, the shortest of skirts and undoubtedly the highest of heels, which probably accounted for her height. And she had . . .

'By the Gods.' Neville raised his hands to his face and peeped through his fingers.

She had a truly stunning pair of breasts.

'She's always creeping up on people.'

Neville's mouth fell open. The woman's mouth hadn't moved when she spoke these words.

'I'm over here.'

Neville turned his head and all but fainted from the shock. There was another one of them, identical to the first. Neville's brain flip-flopped about in his skull. Two of them. Identical. There had to be an obvious explanation for this. Clones, that's what they were, grown in some secret government research laboratory beneath Mornington Crescent Underground Station.

That had to be it.

'We're the new bar staff,' said the first clone.

'I'm Pippa,' said the second clone.

'And I'm Loz,' said the first.

'Bar staff,' whispered Neville.

'Bobby from the brewery sent us,' said Pippa.

'To pep the place up.' Loz looked all around and about. 'It's a bit of a dump, innit?'

'It serves,' said Neville, straightening his shoulders and his clip-on bow tie. 'It's a traditional hostelry.'

'We'll soon liven it up,' said Pippa. 'Do you want to show us how those beer-pump thingies work?'

Neville groaned, internally. He was no misogynist, was Neville, he wasn't anti-women or anything. Nor was he one of those fellows who avowed that 'a woman's place is in the home'. Oh no, Neville had always considered that women should be treated as equals. They should be allowed to go out and work. Nay, they should be encouraged to do so. Let them pull their weight and do their fair share of the graft, rather than loafing about at home watching daytime TV and breeding babies. Let them work if they so wished.

But not in a bar.

And certainly not in *his* bar.

And then there was that other thing. That other thing that Neville never spoke about. That personal thing. That private thing. That thing about *him* and women. That thing about his problem with women.

That, pure and simply, they terrified him.

Neville had never been a ladies' man. He lacked the confidence, he feared rejection, he feared for his performance, sex-wise, feared, that he might be scorned and laughed at. So he kept his distance. He worked in an environment where he was safe, where there was a sturdy counter between him and the world of women. And where the world of women did not encroach too freely.

Certainly women drank in The Swan, but they were far outnumbered by men. And it was usually men who bought the women drinks, so Neville could remain uninvolved.

'Hello,' said Loz. 'Anybody home? You seem to have drifted off somewhere, Mr Neville.'

'No,' said Neville, doing further straightenings. 'I'm fine. A lot on my mind. A very responsible job, keeping bar. A lot of technical details.'

'I'm sure we'll soon figure it all out,' said Pippa and she leaned forward across the bar counter, her breasts provocatively caressing the polished bar top. And Loz did likewise and Neville took a big step back.

Colliding with the optics.

'Have you worked in a bar before?' he enquired, clinging to his dignity as a drowning man will cling to the matchstick of proverb.[*]

Loz shook her beautiful head. 'Not *behind* one,' she said, 'but we've danced in lots. We're pole-dancers.'

'You don't look Polish,' said Neville.

Loz looked at Pippa.

And Pippa looked at Loz.

And both laughed coquettishly.

Neville clutched at his heart.

'So do you want to show us how these pump thingies work?' Pippa asked once more.

'And should we take our tops off now, so we can all get the feel of things for the lunchtime session? Mr Neville? Are you all right? Wake up, Mr Neville.'

'Are you all right, John?' asked Jim Pooley, looking up from his office desk, upon which rested the morning's copy of

---

[*] Should such a proverb actually exist.

the *Brentford Mercury* and tapping the ash from his smoking Dadarillo into the ashtray shaped like a football boot. A cup of tea steamed at his elbow and a smile shone out from his face.

'I've just come from the Cottage Hospital.' John sat himself down in the visitor's chair before Jim's desk and availed himself of Jim's cuppa. 'I think I've managed to talk them out of suing, although those town councillors were pretty surly. But no one seems too badly hurt, except for Mr Ratter, who fell on to a casual observer in the crowd.'

'Didn't that cushion his fall?' Jim took back his tea and sipped at it.

'The casual observer blacked Mr Ratter's eye.' John re-availed himself of Jim's tea.

'Harsh,' said Jim. 'But you're all right?'

'I wasn't in the box when it collapsed. I was being interviewed by constables Mild and Meek, who were making enquiries regarding the Voices of Free Radio Brentford.'

'You denied all knowledge, of course.'

'Of course. They said they'll be coming back later to speak to you about it.'

'You didn't put *me* in the frame?'

'Of course I didn't. I think we can expect a visit from the Health and Safety people also. I'll do my best to keep them at arm's length.'

'If it's not one thing, it's another,' said Jim, but he said it with a certain brightness in his voice, with a certain unfailing cheerfulness. He took his teacup from John's fingers, but found it was now empty.

'Still,' said John, turning the newspaper towards himself and running an eye across it, 'you seem perky enough. "Bertie's Boogie Bees", eh – you're making a name for yourself.'

'My name isn't Bertie, but I know what you mean. I'm really beginning to enjoy this, John. It's a great old game, this football lark.'

'The shopkeeping victims of the executive-box catastrophe might not agree with you, what with them also having had their shop windows broken and their premises looted and everything.'

'These things happen,' said Jim, puffing contentedly on his Dadarillo. 'There's nothing new about football hooliganism.'

'There is in Brentford.'

'Then it's a cross we'll have to bear. You could suggest to them that they get shutters for their windows.'

Omally made a face.

'You already made the suggestion?' said Jim.

'The club is paying for these security improvements,' said John. 'I had no choice. But don't worry, I don't think they'll sue us for compensation or anything. It was an accident, wasn't it? And accidents *will* happen. And I did warn them not to stamp their feet. I'm sure it won't cost too much to cobble together a few window shutters.'

Jim Pooley ground out his cigarette. 'And where are we going to find the money?'

'Perhaps we could get an advance from Norman.'

'I'm not going to be put off,' said Jim, 'no matter what. After all the chaos and bloodshed last night I know I should be, but I'm not. We won again, John – ten-two. We're heading for the record books here. The only way is up.'

'If I wore a hat,' said John, 'I'd take it off to you.'

'We're going to win this thing, John. I feel it in my fingers.'

'Do you feel it in your toes?'

'I do. So you'll probably want to start making some more calls on your portable phone.'

'Will I?' John asked. 'And is there any more tea?'

'You will,' said Jim, 'and there isn't. Firstly you must get on to Hairy Dave and Jungle John, Brentford's master builders, and have them come and fix the executive box's floor. And the other thing.'

'Other thing?' John asked.

'We need a new right-winger,' said Jim, 'what with Billy Kurton upping sticks and having it away on his toes.'

'Buy a new player?' John all but fell backwards from his chair. 'Have you gone insane? We don't have the money for that.'

'Then you'll have to find some. Those Siamese twins looked pretty puffed after the match. I don't think they can take much more.'

'But . . .' said John. 'But—'

'But me no buts,' said Jim. 'We're a team, aren't we? You said so yourself. Together we will triumph. Here, take a look at this.' Jim rose from his chair and drew John's attention to a large chart pinned to the wall.

'Nice,' said John. 'It covers that damp patch well.'

'It's a fixtures chart,' Jim explained. 'FA Cup fixtures. The team will have to play a lot more than seven games this season, but it's only the Cup-qualifying games that matter. It works like this.' And Jim proceeded to explain to John *exactly* how it worked.

Now, if anyone has ever tried to explain to you the rules of backgammon, or bridge, it's the same kind of thing. It's even more complicated than the offside rule.

'Ah,' said John, when Jim had done with his explaining. 'It all makes perfect sense. It's quite simple, really.'

Jim cast John that *old-fashioned* look.

'What?' said John.

'Never mind,' said Jim. 'But as you can see, there's a lot of away games and we must be prepared.'

'Right,' said John.

'Right,' said Jim.

'Anything else you can think of?' John asked.

'Not really,' said Jim.

'Right,' said John once again.

'Right indeed,' said Jim.

There was a pause. A moment of silence.

John perused his wristlet watch. 'The bar's open,' he said.

★

The saloon bar door of The Flying Swan wasn't open, even though it was now five past eleven.

The door of Neville's bedroom wasn't open, either. It was similarly locked. Neville sat upon his bed and Neville had a big sweat on. Downstairs, he knew, downstairs in *his* saloon bar, were two young women. Two beautiful young women. Two beautiful young women who were stripped to the waist.

Neville shuddered. His fingers trembled. These trembling fingers poured a trembling but substantial measure of his private stock of whisky into a glass that would have held his false teeth, had he worn any. Which he didn't, for his teeth were all his own. Neville upended the glass into his mouth and gulped back the contents. What was he going to do? He couldn't go down there and stand at the bar, *his* bar, with *those things* bobbing away on either side of him. He'd faint again. He knew he would. Well, faint again *again*. Because he had re-fainted after the first time, when Pippa and Loz had loomed over him trying to bring him round by fanning him with the T-shirts they'd removed.

'What am I going to do?' cried Neville.

But answer came there none.

'I could run.' Neville's good eye turned towards his wardrobe and the battered suitcase that gathered dust upon its top. Slip out, over the back wall, make a run for it.

Neville shook his head. Fiercely. No, that wouldn't do. The Swan was his life. He wouldn't be driven from it by two pairs of breasts. It was unthinkable.

Sadly it wasn't unthinkable, because Neville was thinking it.

'What am I going to do?' Neville took up his pillow and hugged it to his own bosom. 'What am I going to do?'

And then something caught the part-time barman's good eye. Something that had been under his pillow. Something that he had all but forgotten about. He'd put it there for safekeeping. And because, in its plastic bag, it had looked very suspicious behind the bar amongst the Spanish souvenirs. It had looked, in fact, like drugs.

Which somehow, in a way, was what it was: the bag of Mandragora given to him by Old Pete.

Neville took up the bag, opened it and sniffed at its contents suspiciously. What had that old villain said? *That stuff will make you a god-damn sexual tyrannosaurus. Just like me.* Neville quite liked the smell. It smelt fruity. But what, *exactly*, did it really do? Did it really prolong active life, increase virility, put a spring in your step and lead in your pencil?

What if it did?

Neville took a deep breath through his mouth and blew it out of his unblocked nostril. It might be just what he needed – a bit of a sexual pick-me-up, or at least something that would lift his spirits, take the edge off his blind terror, simply give him confidence. What would be the harm in taking it? Old Pete wouldn't poison him, that was unlikely.

Although.

Neville held the packet at arm's length. The oldster had a wicked sense of humour. This fruity-smelling herbal something might prove to be a powerful laxative.

'No,' said Neville, drawing it near to himself once more and giving it another sniff. 'He prides himself on his horticultural knowledge. If he says that this stuff does what he says it does, then it will do what he says it does.'

And with that said, Neville emptied a small quantity into his false-teeth-glass-if-he-wore-false-teeth-which-he-didn't. And topped the glass up with whisky.

'Tell you what,' said Neville, steeling himself and tipping in at least half the remaining contents of the bag. 'In for a penny, in for a pound. There's no point in going off half-cocked, is there?'

272

27

Norman felt remarkably chipper.

Which was odd, considering.

Considering the punishment he'd taken when the floor of the executive box had given way.

Norman distinctly remembered falling through. And coming into contact with the concrete of the stand below. And then the other shopkeepers coming into contact with *him*, as they, too, plummeted downwards. And Norman also remembered the sounds, those terrible sounds of his own bones breaking – his wrist bones and his ribcage, and his jaw, as well.

He could remember all this. And then things went a bit hazy.

Norman stood behind the counter of Peg's Paper Shop and felt at himself. Gingerly. He wasn't even bruised. How could that be? By all accounts he should surely be dead, but he wasn't. How *could* that be?

Norman scratched at his wig and sought an answer. There was something, he was sure of it. He did have some recollections. A face swam into Norman's thoughts, if faces could but swim. And this face was the face of Archroy.

Archroy.

'Yes,' whispered Norman. 'I think I do recall, after all.'

He could see the face of Archroy gazing down at him. It was a face displaying an expression of concern. And a voice, too – Archroy's voice. And the voice said, 'Don't worry, old chap, you'll be all right. You're not going to die.'

'Die?' whispered Norman. 'I *was* going to die.'

And the shopkeeper remembered something else, amongst all the chaos and the screaming and the people running in all directions (well, one direction each). Something Archroy had put over him. Something woolly and warm and golden and twinkling.

And then that was it.

And Norman had woken up in his bed with not a bruise or a bit of his person broken.

And Peg had actually let him sleep late, until nearly half-past ten. Which was decidedly odd in itself. Beyond odd, in fact. Little less than unnerving.

'Odd,' whispered Norman. 'Most odd. I will have to speak to Archroy of this. I've heard that he's definitely back in the borough.'

'What are you whispering about?' boomed the voice of Peg.

'Nothing, my dear, nothing. In fact, I'm just popping out for a moment. I won't be more than five minutes.'

'You'd better not be.'

Norman slipped off his shopkeeper's coat and slipped from the shop. He crossed the road and entered the phone box (a red K2 designed by Sir Giles Gilbert Scott) and from here he phoned the offices of Mr Richard Gray, Solicitor of Law.

Ms Yola Bennett answered the phone.

'It's me,' said Norman.

'Norman,' said Yola. 'My love, how are you?'

'How are *you*?' Norman asked. 'I woke up in my bed this morning, but I don't remember getting home. Things are a bit confused. Were you injured?'

'I wasn't in the box when the floor fell through, I was downstairs in the bar. I couldn't find you in all the confusion. They said you were taken to the hospital, but you weren't. I've been so worried.'

'Well, I'm fine,' said Norman. 'Not even a chafing. Would you care for a lunchtime shag, I mean drink?'

'I can't get away this lunchtime. We've got a lot of

bandaged-up town councillors here, all intent on suing the club for compensation.'

'Oh,' said Norman. 'Well, perhaps tonight? I'll call you later.'

'E-mail me,' said Yola. 'You do have a computer, don't you, Norman?'

'I certainly do.'

'Then take down my e-mail address and e-mail me.'

'Right,' said Norman, and he took out a sharpened pencil and a bit of old till receipt that he had been saving for a rainy day and took down Yola's e-mail address. 'Got it,' said Norman, when he had done so.

'Lovely,' said Yola. 'And Norman.'

'Yes?'

'Love you.'

'Mmm,' went Norman, replacing the receiver.

Norman stood before the phone box, taking in the sunshine and the healthy Brentford air. He really should go straight back to the shop. That would be the best thing to do.

But then, as chance would have it, if such a thing there really is as chance, Norman chanced to see a distinctive form marching up the Ealing Road. Decked out in pith helmet and safari suit and jungle boots, this distinctive form was none other than Archroy himself.

'Archroy himself,' said Norman, as he watched the distinctive form vanish into the saloon bar of The Flying Swan. 'A five-minute conversation with that lad wouldn't hurt.'

But then Norman's eyes strayed once more towards Peg's Paper Shop.

But then Norman shrugged. 'If wishes were butter cakes, beggars would bite,' said Norman.

It was nearing twelve of the midday clock now and The Swan hadn't, as yet, got into its lunchtime trade.

As Norman entered the bar, his eyes adjusting to the transition from bright sunlight to 'ambient bar glow', he did not espy all too many patrons.

At the bar counter sat Bob the Bookie, Old Pete, Councillor Doveston (who had not been up in the executive box as he wasn't too good with stairs) and Archroy. And that was it, for the saloon bar was otherwise deserted.

'Good morning, each,' called Norman, making his way towards the bar.

But no head turned and no greetings were returned to him.

'Please yourselves, then,' said Norman, climbing on to the barstool next to Archroy. 'A pint of Large, please, Neville. *Oh my God!*'

They were there. Before him. Beyond the bar counter and before him. Breasts. Big breasts. Big *bare* breasts. Two matching pairs of Big Bare Breasts. Norman stared at these big bare breasts. He gawped at these big bare breasts. These big bare breasts consumed all of Norman's vision, as they similarly did the vision of the other patrons who sat transfixed before the bar counter.

'Boo-boos,' said Norman. 'Big boo-boos.'

'Pint of Large was it, my luv?' asked Pippa. 'My name's Pippa, by the way.'

'Norman,' said Norman, breathlessly. 'Norman Hartnel, not to be confused with the other Norman Hartnel.'

'Pleased to meet you, Norman. Is this the Large?' Pippa ran her hand up and down the enamel pump handle in manner suggestive of . . .

'Yes,' gasped Norman. 'That's the one.'

Pippa took up a dazzling pint pot, held it beneath the Large pump and cranked out foam and bubbles. 'There's something wrong with this pump,' she said, and she wiggled her bare bosoms about. Wiggled *bare bosoms*, right there, behind the saloon bar counter of The Flying Swan!

'I'm hallucinating,' said Norman. 'I must have concussion from the fall I took. Or possibly I've developed X-ray vision. Yes, that might be it.'

'They're real,' said Archroy, turning a grin towards Norman. 'They're the Real McCoy. And good day to you, old chap. No ill effects from last night, I trust?'

'No,' said Norman. 'And welcome back, Archroy. And I have to talk to you about that.'

'Later, old chap. But for now, why not just sit back and enjoy the view.'

'The view?' said Norman.

'The view,' said Archroy. 'And believe me, I speak as one who has seen views. I have seen views and I have seen *views*. The sunrise over Kathmandu reflected in the sacred Ganges. The mists upon the peak of Kanchenjunga, rolling down towards Nepal. The glories of fair Atlantis and also the glories of Rome (which are of another day, of course). But I have to say that, but for the bare-naked lady-boys of Bangkok, this is an unparalleled view.'

'Yes indeed,' agreed Norman. 'But where's Neville?'

Pippa presented Norman with a pint of froth. 'It's got a bit of a head,' said she, 'but it will settle down.'

'I hope it will soon,' said Norman, plucking at his trouser front.

'Naughty boy,' purred Pippa.

'But where's Neville?'

'He hasn't come down from his bedroom yet. He was taken a bit poorly earlier. Loz and I had to open up for him.'

'But Neville would never be late in opening up,' said Norman.

'Well, he was today. How much is Large? Do ya know?'

Considering his pint of froth, Norman named a figure that was well below the actual asking price and paid with the exact coinage.

Pippa rang up 'no sale' on the cash register and pocketed Norman's pennies. Then she wiped herself down with a bar cloth, much to the joy of her beholders.

'Good day, each.'

The eyes of the beholders drew away from the beauty that was being beheld by them and beheld . . . Neville.

And the eyes of the beholders blinked and did the now legendary double take. Neville appeared somewhat . . .

Different.

He was not in his regular barman's apparel – the slacks,

the button-collared shirt and dicky bow. This was a new and hitherto unseen Neville. Although always smartly turned out, this was something more.

The part-time barman sported, and that *was* the word, a brightly checked sports jacket and a dashing red silk cravat. And his hair was all quaffed up at the front and he wore a pair of—

'Sunspecs,' said Norman. 'You are wearing sunspecs.'

'They're Ray Bans,' said Neville. 'I generally wear them when I'm driving.'

'But you don't have a car.'

'Anyone waiting to be served? Here, my dear.' Neville took a glass from Pippa's hand and applied a practised hand of his own to the beer pump. 'Yours, Norman?'

Norman considered the pint of froth that stood before him, pushed it aside and said, 'Mine.'

'Are you all right?' asked Old Pete.

'Never better,' said Neville, and he lifted his sunspecs and winked his good eye at the ancient. 'Never better. Does anyone else need serving?'

'Me,' said Bob the Bookie.

'And me too, old chap,' said Archroy.

'Archroy,' said Neville, 'they told me you were back in town. I'm most pleased to see you.'

'And me, you,' said Archroy. 'And your new bar staff also.'

'Yes,' Neville grinned. 'Lovely ladies. Lovely ladies.'

And Old Pete and Councillor Doveston and Bob the Bookie and Norman and Archroy looked on in horror as Neville stepped between his new bar staff and smacked each of them on the bottom.

During the lunchtime session, Norman spoke unto Archroy regarding what had occurred upon the previous evening and received in return an explanation that he considered truly fantastic – an explanation which involved the now legendary Golden Fleece.

At two-thirty, Neville called 'time', much to the further horror of his patrons.

'Important business regrettably forbids me from continuing this session,' Neville told them.

'Then you bugger off to it and leave the girls to serve us,' countered Old Pete.

'This important business involves the lovely ladies,' said Neville. And he raised his Ray Bans and winked his good eye once more.

'To The Stripes Bar, lads,' said Old Pete.

And that was that.

And Norman returned to Peg's Paper Shop.

'And where have you been?' Peg demanded to be told.

'Some important business came up,' said Norman.

Peg waggled a forbidding digit towards her errant spouse. 'Well, you can stay here now,' she told him, 'because I'm going out. It's Townswomen's Guild afternoon again.'

'Time certainly flies,' said Norman, 'but heals all wounds as it does so.'

'Moron,' said Peg in a voice so loud that it rattled the humbugs in their jars. 'I'll be home about midnight.' And she left in a huff*, slamming the shop door behind her.

'Midnight,' said Norman. And he stroked at his chin. 'Perhaps I will invite the vivacious Yola here for the evening. In fact, I definitely will.' And he took out the e-mail address that he had scribbled down earlier in the telephone box.

Norman looked at it thoughtfully.

'E-mail,' said Norman, and there was some degree of doubt in the tone of his voice. 'I know of it, naturally. And my computer *is* wired into the telephone socket.'

Norman considered his fingers. The electrical burns had all but healed up now. 'There shouldn't be much to this e-mail business.'

Norman turned the 'open' sign to its 'closed' side, bolted the shop door and then sneaked away to his kitchenette-cum-computer-workstation area. The machine was still

---

* A size-eighteen pink gingham one, with a matching snood.

humming away. He'd never got around to switching it off.

'But that's good for computers,' said the shopkeeper, seating himself before the screen. 'Or at least that's what I've heard.' He reached forward to tap at the keyboard and then took to howling in pain.

The keyboard was very hot indeed.

Norman left his seat and returned at length in the company of a pair of gardening gloves, which he donned.

'To continue,' he said, and he tapped at the keyboard.

A logo appeared upon the screen, a gorgeous sepia-coloured Victorian-style logo, all noble heroic figures in Grecian garb and British Bulldogs and lions and scenes of industry and Queen Victoria's head. And the words 'BABBAGE NINETEEN-HUNDRED SERIES' in Times Roman lettering. And lots of those little icons and tool-bar jobbies all around the edge of the screen.

Norman moved the brass mouse about and a little arrow moved upon the screen in time to his movings. Norman clicked upon a random icon. The Babbage logo disappeared and Norman found himself confronting a big list of items, which appeared to be that of the computer's potentialities.

'Hmm,' went Norman, 'interesting. But where would the e-mailing bit be?' And he did the scrolling thing he'd learned when going through the Babbage plans. The list moved up the screen, on and on and on it went. Norman stopped at intervals, read things aloud, scratched at his wig in wonder and scrolled on.

'If I didn't know better,' said Norman, when much further scrolling had been done and the list showed no signs whatsoever of coming to an end, 'I would say that this is all some kind of formula. And not just any formula, but some kind of magical formula. Most odd. Although . . .' Norman cocked his head upon one side. 'No,' said he, 'this is too absurd even to contemplate.' He cocked his head upon the other side. 'It couldn't be. It surely couldn't be.'

Norman did a bit of scrolling back. A lot of scrolling back. 'They are,' he said. 'They really are.'

He drew himself closer to the screen, as close as the radiating heat would allow, and studied the list more carefully. They *were* the names, they really were. And beside them the formulae, the equations, the numerical equivalents. 'They have to be,' he said and he did rackings of the brain. Bits and bobs came back to him about a science fiction story he'd read many years ago. He couldn't recall the author's name, but he felt certain that the story had been called 'The Ten Million Names of God'. Or possibly it hadn't, but that was what it had been about – this theory that God had ten million different names and as soon as mankind had worked out all of them, that would be it for mankind, or mankind would ascend to the status of the angelic hosts or something similar. And there had been this fellow who had been working all the names out with the aid of a computer program. And when he'd finished, the sky had gone out and the world had come to an end. Or something. Norman could not remember exactly what.

But this, surely, was such a list.

The names of God. With their numerical equivalents . . .

Which, when all put together . . .

'Would give you The Big Figure,' said Norman, 'The Big Figure that I was originally searching for that would be the answer to everything – which was the reason why I assembled this computer in the first place.'

Norman sat back upon his kitchen chair, now in a state of considerable confusion. How could this be?'

Coincidence? This was surely well beyond all that.

What, then? Fate? Act of God?

Norman did some more wig-scratching. There had to be an answer. Assuming that he was right. Norman applied his gloved fingers to the gently steaming keyboard.

'REVIEW PRESENT END OF LIST,' typed Norman, for he could think of no better way of putting it.

The names and numbers whirled up the list, on and on and on until finally settling. Norman viewed the last name on the list. And as he did so, another one typed itself beneath it, and then another.

'Those names are . . .' Norman paused. '*Modern* names,' he said, with considerable emphasis. 'Which means . . .' He sat back once more. 'Which means that the computer program that's cataloguing the names is still running. It's been running ever since I first turned on this computer. It must be downloading all the modern names through the Internet connection. Which means . . .' Norman did further rackings of the brain.

And would probably have gone on to perform many further *further* brain rackings had not an event occurred that was of such singularity and drama as to cause him considerable distraction and derail whatever trains of thought might have been emerging from the tunnels of his mind.

There was a sudden rush of force, a fearsome pressure that toppled Norman from his chair and sent his wig a-winging it away. And there was a light. A really bright light. And into Norman's kitchenette came something as from nowhere, swelling, expanding, then crashing and smashing.

And then the lights went out for Norman and things went very dark indeed.

28

Norman awoke to a short, sharp shock: a glass of cold water thrown into his face.

'Awaken, fiend!' a voice commanded.

'Fiend?' said Norman. 'What?'

'Look into the face of your nemesis.'

'Hold on there,' cried Norman, floundering about. 'Don't hurt me.'

'Hah! The fiend grovels. He shows no bravery now.'

'No, he don't, gov'nor. Gawd pickle me plums if he does.'

Norman peeped through trembling fingers. Two figures stood over him, a man and a boy: a portly, well-dressed man and a ragged, ill-washed boy.

'Who are you?' whispered Norman. 'Where did you come from?'

'As if you do not know,' said the portly man.

'As if you don't,' said the ragged boy.

'I don't,' whimpered Norman. 'I truly don't.'

'We know you, sir,' said the portly man. 'You are the King of Darkness, the Evil One himself, and so must be destroyed.'

'No,' wailed Norman. 'I'm not. I'm truly not. I'm just a shopkeeper.'

'Prepare to die. I would strongly suggest that you commend yourself to your maker and beg his forgiveness for your numberless transgressions.'

'But I haven't, I mean, sometimes, but only a bit . . .' Norman now found himself looking into the muzzle of a pistol. 'No,' he howled. 'Don't shoot me.'

'It is better than you deserve. But first . . .' The gun

barrel swung away from Norman. There was a deafening gunshot. Norman's computer exploded.

'You shot my computer.' Norman made feeble attempts at rising.

'Stay down,' the portly man commanded.

'But you . . . I mean . . . You . . . I mean . . . Why?'

'Articulate, ain't he, gov'nor?' said the ragged lad. 'Gawd taint me tadpole if he ain't. And he ain't.'

'Why . . . Who . . . *What?*' whimpered Norman. And he pointed feebly to the *What?* in question.

It was a goodly sized what, a big, Victorian goodly sized what, and it now filled much of Norman's kitchenette. It was like unto a large overstuffed leather armchair mounted upon brass runners and surrounded by all manner of wondrous brass equipment, and involving a good many valves. The whole thing was surmounted by a kind of helicopter-blade arrangement.

'What is *that*? And how did you get it into my kitchenette?' And, '*Cough, cough, cough.*'

Norman took to considerable coughing. Thick black smoke was now billowing freely from his bullet-scarred computer. Norman took to fanning at his face.

The portly gentleman fanned at his. 'That, sir,' said he, between fits of coughing, 'is my Time Machine. And I am Herbert George Wells of Wimpole Street, London.'

'Time Machine?' Norman coughed some more. 'Herbert George Wells? You're H.G. Wells. *The* H.G. Wells.'

'Your nemesis, you fiend.' The gun barrel was once more pointing towards Norman's face.

'There's been some kind of mistake.' Norman covered his face. 'You've got the wrong man. I'm innocent.'

'Enough of your duplicity. Confess your sins and die like a man.'

'I'm innocent.' Norman assumed the foetal position.

'Then die like the dog that you are.'

Norman heard the cocking of the pistol and then he heard the sound of the gunshot. And then he heard nothing more at all.

29

H.G. Wells said, 'Oh, calamity.'

Winston said, 'Sorry, gov'nor, but I couldn't let you top him.'

The window of Norman's kitchenette was now open. The computer's fire had been extinguished and the smoke had cleared.

'But my Time Machine.' Mr Wells wrung his fingers. 'The bullet ricocheted through the mechanism. It has been destroyed . . . entirely.'

'We can fix it, gov'nor. But I couldn't let you top him, truly I couldn't. It would've bin murder most foul.'

'But he was running the computer program, the signal emitted by which enabled us to locate him through time. He *must* be the one.'

'Be honest, gov'nor. Does he look like the King of Darkness to you?'

'The Devil takes many forms, Winston.'

'Yeah, but they're mostly rulers of nations – dictators, according to you. This bloke's a nobody.'

'I resent that,' mumbled Norman. 'I mean, sorry, don't kill me. I'm innocent.'

'He's a non-such, gov'nor.'

'Then he's an agent of the King of Darkness.'

'I'm a shopkeeper,' moaned Norman. 'My shop is next door. See for yourself.'

'You were running the computer program,' said Mr Wells, 'activating the terrible spell that would wreak havoc upon mankind.'

'I didn't know what it was. I left the computer on. It was running itself.'

'A likely story.' The gun was once more pointing in Norman's direction.

'I'm just a shopkeeper. A nobody, like that dirty little urchin there says.'

'Urchin?' said Winston.

'The computer was in an old store,' Norman explained, 'in crates. I reassembled it. I didn't know what it would do. Although . . .'

'Although *what*?'

'Nothing,' said Norman. '*Although* I wasn't expecting *this*, perhaps.' He raised himself to a kneeling position, sought out his errant wig and repositioned it upon his shaken head. 'Is that *really* a Time Machine?' he asked. 'How *exactly* does it work?'

'It no longer works,' said Mr Wells, lowering his pistol.

'Perhaps I could mend it for you,' Norman suggested.

'*You*?' The gun was once more pointing in Norman's direction.

'I have a Meccano set. You'd be surprised what I can do with it.'

'Meccano set?' said Mr Wells. 'I invented the Meccano set.'

'And Velcro, too,' said Winston. 'Mr Wells invented that. And Blu-Tack. And the jumbo jet.'

Norman was now almost on his feet. 'It really *is* a Time Machine,' he was saying. 'That's exactly the way a Time Machine should look. And you *really are* H.G. Wells?'

'And I'm Winston,' said Winston. 'Mr Wells' personal assistant.'

'He's nothing of the kind,' said Mr Wells. 'He's a common little thief who entered my house when I was putting my machine into operation, climbed aboard without me seeing him as I travelled into the future, and has been plaguing my existence ever since.'

'You like me really, gov'nor. I'm a lovable rogue. And I've helped you out of more than a scrape or two, Gawd nip at me 'nads if I ain't.'

'Well, I never did,' said Norman. 'A stitch in time saves two, as it were.'

'Enough of this idle discourse.' Mr Wells puffed out his cheeks, which were of the ruddy persuasion. 'I am here upon a sacred mission. I have no time for trifles.'

'I quite like trifle,' said Norman.

'Me, too,' said Winston. 'And humbugs.'

'I've got jars of humbugs in my shop,' said Norman. 'And blackjacks and gobstoppers and—'

'Cease this idle prittle prattle. My machine must be repaired. Even now, in some future time, the computer program might be running again.'

'I don't think you have that quite right,' said Norman, helpfully. 'If it's in some future time, then it can't be running "even now", can it?'

'It can if you possess a Time Machine. Now cease your stuff and nonsense, or I will shoot you through petulance alone.'

'Sorry,' said Norman, now fully in the vertical plane, 'but if the computer program has been destroyed, and it does look very destroyed to me—' Norman viewed his burned out computer '— then your work here is done and you can return in glory to the past — as soon as the Time Machine is fixed, and I'm certain that I can help you to mend it. Do you have a set of plans with you?'

H.G. Wells shook his head. Sadly.

'Well, never mind,' said Norman. 'A trouble shared is a trouble halved. And half a sixpence is a threepenny bit.'

'There's truth to them words, gov'nor,' said Winston. 'Now, about them gobstoppers.'

Norman looked over at Mr Wells, who was ruefully considering his ruined Time Machine. 'Is it all right if I give Winston some gobstoppers?' he asked.

'Do whatever you will,' said Mr Wells, prodding at the bullet hole.

'This way, Winston,' said Norman.

'The way I see it,' said Jim Pooley, propping up the counter of The Stripes Bar, 'as long as I keep following the professor's instructions for the team's tactics, we'll win the FA Cup and the black magician and his henchmen won't get their evil hands on the football ground and set free the biblical serpent.'

'Will you please keep your voice down, Jim,' John told him. 'You have imbibed too freely, in my considered opinion.'

'This is only my seventh pint,' said Jim. 'I'm fine.'

'Well, keep your voice down anyway. There's no telling who might be listening.'

'They're all watching the stripper, John. No one's paying us any attention.'

'Well, keep it shushed. I've just seen Archroy. I'm going over to say my hellos. Will you be all right here on your own?'

'I'll chat to Mr Rumpelstiltskin.'

'But not about *private* matters, eh?' John tapped at his nose.

'Absolutely not.' Jim tapped at his. And John made off through the crowd.

'Enjoying yourself, Mr Pooley?' asked Mr Rumpelstiltskin, sidling over. 'Everything meeting your approval?'

'Everything's fine,' said Jim. 'Another pint, if you will.'

'Certainly, sir.' Mr Rumpelstiltskin drew Jim off another pint of Large. Jim accepted it with gratitude, but it really didn't taste as good as those drawn in The Swan. Exactly why, Jim had no idea, but it just didn't.

'But everything *is* okay, isn't it, sir?' Mr Rumpelstiltskin asked.

'Everything's fine,' said Jim. 'And less of the "sir". I can't be having with the "sir". Call me Jim.'

'Just as long as you're happy, Jim.'

'And why shouldn't I be happy?'

'Oh, no reason. Just talk. Things blokes say in pubs. You know the sort of thing.'

'I don't,' said Jim, settling into his pint.

'Rumours, then,' said Mr Rumpelstiltskin. 'And what with all that weird stuff happening on the Benefit Night.

And the team actually winning for a change. And what I just overheard you saying to Mr Omally.'

'Take no notice,' said Jim. 'Of anything. Just do your job and I'll do mine and everything will be fine.'

'Oh yes, *Jim*. Certainly. But you know how people are. And about *your* job – there's rumours about that. Well, let's face it, I've known you and Mr Omally for years, coming in here to drink after hours. Have you *ever actually had* another job before this one?'

'Many,' said Jim. 'Many, many, but none like this. What about you? Have you always been a barman?'

Mr Rumpelstiltskin shook his head. 'I was a professional dog-walker once.'

'And what does that entail?'

'Walking dogs for people who can't be bothered.'

'Really?' said Jim. 'And was there money in that?'

'There was for a while, before the authorities found out.'

'Is professional dog-walking illegal, then?'

'Not as such, but what *I* did was.'

'I'm intrigued,' said Jim. 'What happened?'

Mr Rumpelstiltskin did lookings to either side to assure himself that he wasn't being overheard. 'It was all Norman's fault,' he whispered.

'Norman Hartnel? Not to be confused with the other Norman Hartnel?'

'Same fellow. I had this van, see. Picked up the dogs each day, put them into the van, drove them to the park and walked them. Then one day Norman happens by the park and asks me what I'm doing with all these dogs. So I tell him. And Norman says, "That's a waste of energy." Which it was, because they used to drag me all over the place. Norman says, "Those dogs should be working for *you*," which had me a bit baffled. He came down to the park the next day and told me that he'd worked out a plan for me that would not only save me energy, but get the dogs to generate energy for me.'

'Whatever did he mean?' Pooley asked.

'I had no idea, but he explained it to me. Put the dogs

inside big wheels, he said, like hamster wheels, and connect these wheels up to generate electricity.'

'That sounds like Norman,' said Jim. 'And it sounds like a good idea, actually.'

'That's what I thought. And Norman built the wheels for me, out of Meccano. There was a lot of Meccano involved. We put a can of dog food in front of each wheel and the dogs ran and ran, for most of the day. The power they generated provided the electricity for my home.'

Jim Pooley laughed. 'It's pretty brilliant,' said he.

'That's what I thought. Then Norman had this other idea, that he said would save me money on buying the dog food and generate enough electricity to power the entire street. He said he'd go into business with me and build all the extra wheels.'

'You were going to take on more dogs?' said Jim.

'No,' said Mr Rumpelstiltskin. 'Not dogs, other animals. Norman had this idea about perpetual motion. He said he had a "spin" on it. It would be called *Pet*ual Motion.'

'Go on,' said Jim, already halfway through his pint.

'It wouldn't just be dogs, you see, there'd be a whole series of wheels, starting out big, then getting smaller, then big again, positioned in a circle. We built them in a rented warehouse down by the docks. It worked like this: there were six wheels; in the first there was a dog, and in the one in front of the dog there was a cat – so the dog chased after the cat, see. And the cat ran away from the dog, so both wheels turned.'

'Go on,' said Jim once again.

'In the wheel in front of the cat there was a wheel with a mouse in it. And in the wheel in front of that, an elephant.'

'An elephant?' said Jim. 'Where did you get an elephant from?'

'We, er, borrowed one from the zoo – we couldn't think of anything else that would run away from a mouse.'

'I understand,' said Jim. 'Go on some more.'

'We got a lion in front of the elephant, to run away from that, and a buffalo in front of the lion, to run away from that, and then we were back to the dog in the circle, you see, in front of the stampeding buffalo in the wheel behind it. All in a circle, they all ran and ran. *Pet*ual motion. Powered the entire street.'

'And then the police arrived,' said Jim.

'Exactly,' said Mr Rumpelstiltskin. 'There was a right fuss. Norman and I were lucky to stay out of prison.'

'This is the first time I've ever heard this story,' said Jim, 'and I certainly never read about the case in the news-papers.'

'It was a very long time ago. We were teenagers then. And I bet you never read the papers when you were a teenager.'

'Only *Sporting Life*,' said Jim. 'But you do have to hand it to that Norman. He certainly does come up with some inventive ideas.'

'Do you really think he's going to make millions out of those patents he claims to have?'

Pooley shrugged. 'It all seems a bit doubtful, doesn't it? I mean, can you really imagine Norman doing something that would gain him a place in history?' And Pooley laughed.

And Mr Rumpelstiltskin laughed.

And Winston the ill-washed youth laughed also, although in Norman's shop.

'These are brilliant gobstoppers,' he said.

'Have more,' said Norman. 'Put some in your pocket for later.'

'Thanks,' said Winston, digging into the jar and filling his pockets.

'Tell me about you and Mr Wells,' said Norman. 'I mean, this is incredible, you both appearing here, now, in my kitchenette. And thank you for nudging his elbow and saving my life.'

'I could see you ain't the King of Darkness, gov'nor. Not with them patched elbows.'

'But what *is* all this business about the King of Darkness?'

'Mr Wells' sacred mission. It happened by accident. He just wanted to try out his machine, see if it really worked. He was to present it before Queen Victoria the next day. Perhaps he will go back to the same time that we left, after he's finished his mission.'

'But this King of Darkness?' Norman persisted.

'Well, it happened like this. Like you heard, I snuck aboard his Time Machine when it was taking off. Yeah, I was in his house on the nick, I admit it. We landed the first time about five years in the future from now.' Winston took his shabby self over to Norman's front window and peered out through the grimy pane. 'It's all *very* different then than it is now, Gawd flatten me ol' fella if it ain't. There's technology, see, like you ain't got now, at this time, but like we had back in the Victorian days. Wireless transmission of energy, it was, electricity without wires.'

'Ah,' said Norman. 'That.'

'Flying hansom cabs,' Winston continued, 'and a space programme. But none of that survived – it's as if it all vanished. But it will come back. It will be everywhere in a few years from now. And the one who brings it back, that's the King of Darkness – the Devil in the shape of a man. He wants to rule the world, you see, and hasten the Apocalypse. And Mr Wells has this bee in his bonnet that somehow it's all his fault and he has to stop it.'

'I really don't think I understand any of this,' said Norman. 'Why *exactly* did you and Mr Wells appear in *my* kitchenette, right now?'

'Because you were running the computer program, the King of Darkness's computer program, with all the magic in it and all the nicked plans. Mr Wells did all these mathematical calculations – he worked it out.'

'Nicked plans?' said Norman in as normal a tone as he could muster up. 'What is this about nicked plans?'

'All the technical gubbins – the wireless transmission of energy, all that stuff. The stuff that was somehow vanished out of history so that the King of Darkness couldn't get his evil hands on the plans and do all the awful stuff that he would do with them if he got hold of them, if you know what I mean.'

'He sounds a very bad sort, this King of Darkness fellow,' said Norman.

'He is.' Winston stuffed another gobstopper into his mouth. 'Mr Wells is determined to stop him, so he zeroed in on the computer program. The computer is destroyed now, so that should be that for now, in this time.'

'Right,' said Norman. 'That's that, then.'

'So if we can fix up the Time Machine, we'll go home in it.'

'I'll help you,' said Norman. 'I'm sure together we can fix it.'

'You're a good bloke, Norman, I can see that.'

'Thanks,' said Norman.

'I mean, you're not an agent of the Devil made flesh, is ya?'

'Of course I'm not,' said Norman.

'Of course you're not,' said Winston, thrusting yet another gobstopper into his mouth, but still managing to speak somehow. 'You wouldn't do anyfink that would help the King of Darkness gain control of the world, would ya? Like bunging him the plans for the supertechnology?'

'I certainly would *not*.' Norman crossed his heart. 'Just one thing,' said he.

'Yeah,' said Winston, with difficulty.

'Do you know the identity of this Devil-made-flesh chap?'

'Of course,' said Winston. 'We've already been to his time, five years in the future. We had to scarper back here quick – he nearly did for Mr Wells.'

'So,' said Norman, 'what *is* his name?'

'William Starling,' said Winston.

30

Old Pete sat before his allotment hut upon a battered campaign chair. The chair had seen many campaigns and Old Pete had seen them with it. Old Pete's hut was of the corrugated-iron variety, with a pitched roof, curtained windows and a rather elegant porch that the oldster had added to make it stand out from the many similar sheds that bespotted St Mary's allotments.

Not that there had been any need to, for Old Pete's patch was a sufficient cornucopia to draw the eye on any day of the week. Even including Tuesdays.

He grew the most wonderful things.

Amorphophallus titanium rose erect and proud from iron tubs and *Rafflesia arnoldi*, which the natives of its native Sumatra believe is pollinated by elephants, covered many feet of ground. *Lycopodium sp*, the plant that Druids grew to bring good favour, blossomed alongside *Lunaria annua*, which was said to have the power to unshoe horses that stepped upon it. There was *Ferula asafoetida*, which wards off the evil eye, and something known as the Tree of Life, upon which bloomed certain fruit that Old Pete was disinclined to harvest.

All in all it was a garden unlike any other, with the possible exception of those belonging to Professor Slocombe, or Gandalf.

It was all rather special.

Old Pete took a sniff at the air. Fragrances of stinkhorn and stenchweed and arse violet filled the ancient's nostrils. He took from the tweedy pocket of his elderly waistcoat an antique pocket watch and shone a torch upon its pitted face.

Eleven-fifteen of the evening clock. Old Pete shivered somewhat. He replaced his watch, switched off his torch and turned his jacket collar upwards. And then he shivered again. But it wasn't from the cold. Old Pete ground his dentures together, rooted about between his feet, drew to his lips a tin can and took a swill of sprout brandy. It tasted good. The crop had come in early this year and the still that Old Pete illegally maintained within his hut had performed its duties well. The old one sighed and took another swill. He was not a happy fellow, Old Pete was not. He would be a happier fellow were he able to sit here, undisturbed, for another hour swilling sprout brandy and then take himself off to his bed. But Old Pete knew in his antiquated bones that this was not to be.

He knew, he just knew, what was about to occur.

He had tried for so long, for all these long long years, to put the past behind him, and indeed the future, if that was possible. But he knew that this was the night, the night he had dreaded all these years. It would happen tonight, or it would not happen at all.

Sounds came to Old Pete upon the gentle Brentford breeze, sounds that he knew well enough – the sounds that he had been dreading.

The sounds of swearing and of engine noise.

'Get a bl★★dy move on, you b★st★rd!' shouted Norman.

'Is this appalling language really necessary?' asked Mr Wells.

'I'm sorry, Mr Wells,' said Norman, 'but if I don't shout at this van it will *not* work.'

'Technology ain't up to much nowadays,' observed Winston from the back of Norman's van.

'It's the Hartnel Grumpiness Hyper-Drive,' Norman explained. 'The engine is powered by negative energy. There's so much of the stuff about, and none of it being put to good use.'

'And where exactly are we now?' asked Mr Wells.

'Turning into the allotments,' said Norman. 'Go on, you sh★tbag!'

'The allotments,' said Mr Wells as Norman's van bumped through the open gates on to the rutted track beyond.

'Like I explained to you,' Norman continued, 'Peg will be home any time. I couldn't have her finding you two and the Time Machine in her kitchenette. You know what women are like, they ask all kinds of uncomfortable questions and they'll rarely take even a well-told lie for an answer.'

'And so we are coming to your allotment patch.'

'To my allotment *shed*, yes. We can hide the Time Machine inside and you and Winston can sleep in there for tonight. Tomorrow I'll arrange for board and lodgings at Madame Loretta Rune's in Sprite Street. She's a Spiritualist, but she takes in lodgers. You'll get bed and breakfast.'

'Ah,' said Mr Wells as his head struck the van's roof. 'Spiritualism, is it? I have some interest in that myself. I am currently investigating the case of the Cottingly Fairies. Two young girls have taken photographs of fairies, you know. Very interesting case. I am an expert on this subject.'

Norman swung the steering wheel. 'You're a useless swine!' he shouted.

'How dare you!' said Mr Wells.

'The van, sir, not you. Faster, you f★ckwit!'

'Quite so.'

'Although.' Norman's van ploughed down a row of beanpoles, destroying Mr Ratter's potentially prizewinning crop. 'Although, I think you'll find that it was Sir Arthur Conan Doyle who investigated the Cottingly Fairies.'

Winston chuckled.

'Why chuckle you?' Norman asked.

'Because Mr Wells *is* Sir Arthur Conan Doyle. It's his pen name when he dabbles in a bit of fiction.'

'A mere hobby,' said Mr Wells. 'The world will remember me as a great scientist, and a saviour of mankind.'

'But you don't look anything like Sir Arthur Conan Doyle,' said Norman, as Mr Kay's cabbages went the way of all flesh.

'False moustache,' said Winston. 'Not to mention the hat.'

'The hat?' said Norman.

'I told you not to mention that.'

'Ah,' said Norman. Thoughtfully. 'Well, we're here now. Would you like to get out?'

'Not really,' said Mr Wells. 'I would prefer to repair to Madame Rune's for a cognac and a cigar, before turning in for the night.'

'Nevertheless,' said Norman, 'this, I regret, is where you will be staying tonight.'

Amidst much grumbling from Mr Wells and immoderate chuckling from young Winston as he shinned over the passenger seat, the three debouched from Norman's knackered van and into the moonlit allotments.

'You're a very nice van indeed,' said Norman, 'and I love you very dearly.' The van's engine died and its lights went out.

'And what now, gov'nor?' Winston asked.

'That's my hut over there,' said Norman. 'The one with the solar panels and the wind-farm attachment on the roof. We'll unload the Time Machine and drag it inside.'

'Just one thing,' said Mr Wells.

'Yes?' said Norman.

'Well,' said Wells, 'I appreciate that you wished to remove us and my machine from your kitchenette before your wife returned home, in order to avoid having to answer any difficult questions.'

'This is true,' said Norman, opening the rear doors of the van. 'A good wife makes a good husband, but a woman scorned is a mischief unto sparrows.'

'Possibly so, but that said, how will you explain to her the fact that you had to demolish much of the rear kitchenette wall, which you did in order to remove my machine from your premises?'

'She wants an extension building,' said Norman. 'She's been wanting it for years. I'll tell her I started tonight, to surprise her when she got home.'

'Nice thought, gov'nor,' said Winston. 'You'll probably get yourself a shag out of that.'

Norman shuddered. But as with Old Pete, this wasn't from the cold. 'It never rains but it pours,' said he. 'Please give me a hand with the Time Machine.'

It was a struggle.

But then isn't getting a Time Machine out of a van and dragging it into an allotment shed always a struggle?

Norman unpadlocked his shed and threw open the doors. They were double doors. Norman had a very large allotment shed.

'This is a very large allotment shed,' said Mr Wells.

'It's really a lock-up garage,' said Norman. 'I bought it in instalments and installed it here.' Norman laughed foolishly, although for why, no one understood.

'There are certain things every man needs,' said Norman, once the Time Machine had been dragged within, the doors closed and the lights switched on. 'A lock-up garage, an allotment shed and a wife who is always eager to please her husband sexually. Two out of three and you can chalk your life up as a success.'

'And I am expected to sleep *here*?' Mr Wells made a most disdainful face.

'It's the best I can offer you for now.'

'I am not accustomed to camping out in such wretched hovels as this. Take me at once to Madame Rune's.'

Norman did a bit of pensive lip chewing and then rephrased a careful suggestion. 'I feel it would be safer this way,' said he, 'for yourself and your youthful ward here. I am not precisely clear as to what *exactly* the computer program was doing. Nor, in truth, do I think that I want to know. But as you were able to, how shall I put this, zero in upon it when I perused the program, do you not think that this King of Darkness of yours might similarly be able to do so?'

'Undoubtedly.'

'Might he not suspect that you, his archenemy, had a hand in the destruction of the program?'

'Undoubtedly also.'

'Then he might wish to exact revenge.'

'Ah,' said Mr Wells.

'And you are presently unable to evade him due to the fact that your Time Machine is disabled.'

'Ah,' said Mr Wells once more.

'So perhaps it would be best if you took refuge here in this secret hideaway for the night.'

'Hm,' said Mr Wells. 'Perhaps you are correct. But only for tonight, though.'

'Only for tonight,' said Norman. 'Then I'll sort out proper accommodation and we'll get your machine working and you can be off on your way back home, having thwarted the evil schemes of the King of Darkness.'

'All right,' said Mr Wells. 'I will put up with the discomfort for tonight. The computer program is destroyed and as soon as the Time Machine is made serviceable once more, Winston and I will return to the nineteenth century.'

'For the busy man time passes quickly,' said Norman. 'I'll say goodnight to you, then. There are a couple of sleeping bags over here. I'll be back in the morning with some breakfast.'

'Goodnight, then,' said Mr Wells.

'Ta-ta for now,' said Winston.

Norman left his allotment shed, returned to his van, shouted abuse at it and drove homeward.

Winston unrolled the sleeping bags and he and Mr Wells settled down for an uncomfortable night.

Moonlight shone in through the window of Norman's lock-up garage/shed and lit upon the faces of the getting-off-to-sleepers. Mr Wells huffed and puffed and grumbled to himself, but eventually took to snoring. Winston went out as a light will do and lay, bathed in moonlight, making one of those angelic-sleeping-child faces that even the naughtiest and most impossible children always seem capable of making.

A shadow briefly crossed the face of the angelic sleeper. It was the shadow of Old Pete.

The elder peeped in through the window and viewed the sleeping child.

Old Pete drew a deep and silent breath. 'So it was all true,' he whispered to himself. 'All the vanished Victorian technology. All true. As true as it is that the child sleeping there is none other than myself. I never liked being called Winston. I'm glad I changed my name to Pete.'

31

Jim Pooley awoke to another Saturday morning. Jim eased himself gently into wakefulness in that practised manner of his and lay, taking in the ceiling and gauging the potential measure of the day. Jim's waking eyes strayed towards the chart that he had Sellotaped to the bedroom wall above the fireplace.

The FA Cup fixtures chart.

This chart had a lot of crossings out on it now, and a lot of arrows scrawled hither and thus. And a lot of circles about the name Brentford United. The team were going great guns now. As a result of the professor's continuing missives and Jim's instructions to the team, things were really rocking and rolling. Four FA Cup qualifying games they'd played now and had won every one of them. Decisively.

Jim viewed the other wall. The wall by the door. The door with all his press cuttings affixed to it, and the magazine front covers, too. The ones that had him on them. *Him*. Jim Pooley of Brentford. There he was on all those covers, in his Bertie Wooster suit, giving the big thumbs-up. *FHM*, *Loaded*, *The World of Interiors*, which had done a feature on his kitchenette. And *House and Garden*, which had struggled, although quite successfully in Jim's humble opinion, to get a two-page spread out of his window box. He even featured on the cover of this month's *Cissies on Parade*, although why that should be, Jim wasn't precisely sure.

But he was quite the man about town now. He'd even been invited for a night out at Peter Stringfellow's club, which Jim had found rather noisy and crowded – although

Omally, who had gone along with him, had added many telephone numbers to his little black book.

Jim stared at all the glossy covers and the press cuttings. It wasn't right, Jim knew that it wasn't right. It wasn't real. Although folk kept telling him that it was, it was all stuff and nonsense really. *He* had little to do with the team's success. He was just a pawn in some terrible game being played out between Professor Slocombe and William Starling. He was right in the middle, in the firing line – although no one was actually firing at him at the moment. And for that fact he knew he should feel grateful and be enjoying himself.

But Jim was not enjoying himself. He didn't want to be this person. He just wanted to be Jim Pooley, man of the turf, investor in the Six-Horse Super Yankee.

All he really wanted was just to be left alone to be Jim.

Jim Pooley sighed. Why did life have to be so complicated?

John Omally awoke in his own cosy bed, in which he was alone upon this Saturday morning. John had sworn off the women for more than a week now, which was quite a big thing for him. It had not exactly been a voluntary swearing off, though; it was more that he just didn't have the time. There was simply too much club business to be dealt with.

John had always been of the opinion, as have many, that people tend to make simple matters difficult. He believed that things could be dealt with simply, that every problem had a simple solution. Certainly John had held to this opinion because he had rarely encountered any situations that were actually difficult, up until recent times. He had always sidestepped them.

Now, however, everything seemed to be difficult.

The town councillors who had received injuries when the floor of the executive box collapsed had decided to sue the club for damages. Their solicitor Mr Gray, an unwontedly vicious individual who Omally surmised must have received some slight or missed some business opportunity to have put him into such a vile frame of mind, was going all out for many thousands of pounds. John hadn't mentioned this to Jim for fear of upsetting the lad. And then there was The Stripes Bar. It should have been raking in the money, what with the strippers and everything, but it wasn't prospering. Neville had drawn the clientele back to The Flying Swan, which was infuriating.

The club shop was doing well, though, knocking out many, many team kaftans, but the money coming in was hardly covering all the expenses of keeping the club going.

Such as paying the players.

And there was a big problem with the players.

Before every FA Cup qualifying game, one of them had dropped out, vanished, had it away on their toes for financial or personal reasons. Horace Beaverbrooke had apparently run off with a lady tattooist. And Trevor Brooking, not to be confused with the other Trevor Brooking, had got so fed up with people confusing him with the other Trevor Brooking that he had given up football for life and opened a sports shop.

Or so they said. In Omally's opinion, they had simply lost their nerve.

The substitutes – Don and Phil English, Barry Bustard and Loup-Gary Thompson – were doing their best, but soon the team would be coming up against the BIG OPPONENTS, the big-league fellows. A bunch of circus performers, no matter how well intentioned and aided by the professor's magical tactics, could not survive against these.

Omally did sighings. Why did life have to be so complicated?

Norman awoke to find Peg snoring as noisily as ever beside him. Norman made a face of displeasure. He'd been dreaming about Yola Bennett, about doing certain things to Yola Bennett. But Norman hadn't had any time recently to do these things to Yola Bennett in anything other than his dreams.

Norman's waking hours had been rather busy.

And Norman's waking hours had not been happy for the lad.

Norman was feeling bad. Norman was feeling guilty.

He should never have claimed that those inventions he'd discovered on the Victorian computer were his own. He should never have claimed the patents. And he should never have sold the rights on these purloined patents to William Starling.

Norman felt wretched. He was not by nature a dishonest man. He was a good man. But he was also a human man. He was a greedy man. He had clearly done a very bad thing. A truly bad thing, if the future of mankind had anything to do with it.

But had it really been his fault? Norman tried to convince himself that it had not. He had been seeking The Big Figure, hadn't he? Which was why he'd answered the ad for the free computer parts and assembled the computer in the first place.

Norman did silent sighings. All that fitted, but rather too well. It was as if a hand greater than his own had had a hand in it. So to speak. It wasn't his doing, it wasn't just a coincidence – he'd been drawn into all this.

And what of Mr Wells and Winston? Norman was currently forking out his pennies and pounds to pay for their accommodation at Madame Loretta Rune's. And Mr Wells, posing as Norman's visiting Uncle Herbert, had become a regular patron at both The Flying Swan and The Stripes Bar, running up monthly accounts that Norman was also forced to cover.

And of course, Norman had been spending all of his free time at his allotment shed/lock-up garage trying to fix the Time Machine, which was one reason why he had had no time to see Yola Bennett. Christmas had come and gone now and so had the New Year and what did Norman have to show for all the work he'd been doing on the Time Machine?

Well, not very much, as it happened.

He'd had it all to pieces. In fact, it was now little more than pieces, but how it worked was still a mystery; and to add mystery to mystery, Mr Wells seemed to have no idea how it worked either. Which was rather strange, considering that he claimed to have built it.

As far as Norman had been able to make out, the Time Machine contained no internal mechanisms. There were some levers, but these seemed merely to enter a box which contained . . .

A sprout.

A sprout, yes!

Norman had examined this sprout. There was nothing immediately 'special' about this sprout, although there was definitely something 'odd'.

Norman had, upon first taking this sprout up in his fingers, felt an almost irresistible compunction to thrust it into his ear. He had imagined that the sprout was speaking to him. Norman had hastily thrust the mysterious sprout into the half-consumed jar of pickled onions that he had half-consumed and hastily screwed down the lid.

Norman was mystified.

Mystified, guilty, running out of cash and wondering about his wife, who seemed to be spending more and more time in the company of Scoop Molloy, cub reporter from the *Brentford Mercury*.

Norman did more silent sighings. Why did life have to be so complicated?

Neville the part-time barman awoke with a great big smile upon his face. It was a blinder of a smile and it really lit up the publican's normally paler-shade-of-white visage. Neville stretched out his arms and brought his hands down gently.

On to shoulders.

Female shoulders.

To Neville's right there lay a woman. A naked woman.

And to Neville's left, another one.

Alike, were these, as two peas in the proverbial pod.[*]

Naked ladies in Neville's boudoir.

One naked lady called Loz.

[*] Or metaphorical. Or neither.

And another one called Pippa.

Neville smiled some more and waggled his toes about. This was all right, this, this being a ladies' man. He should have got into this kind of thing years ago. Why hadn't he done that?

The smile faded slightly from Neville's face. He knew full well why he hadn't. But he was doing it now, making up for lost time. And in a big way, too. Two ladies. Two bare, naked ladies. And he hadn't disappointed either of them. He was a Goddamn sexual tyrannosaurus.

Neville made a thoughtful face, although it still had a bit of a grin left on it. He knew full well that it wasn't him, wasn't *really* him. It was all down to Old Pete's Mandragora. That stuff made Viagra look like spray starch.

And it was undoubtedly addictive. Neville was now downing a packet a day, and Old Pete was upping the price with every delivery. He was even talking about cutting Neville's supply completely because he had 'more important matters on his mind'.

More important matters than Neville's sex life?

What could possibly be more important than that?

And then there was the other business.

The other business, which involved Young Master Robert, the brewery-owner's beloved only son. He had further plans to liven up The Swan.

Neville's smile all but left his face. All but.

Why did life have to be so complicated?

Pippa awoke and her hand brushed lightly against Neville's todger.

'Stuff complications,' said Neville.

Arising, as one would, to the occasion.

32

Big Bob Charker hummed an Old Testament ditty. It was the one about Moses riding his motorbike.* He steered the big open-topped bus on to the Great West Road and took to the putting down of his foot.

Above Big Bob, Jim Pooley stomped his feet – but lightly.

'I feel a winner coming on,' said Jim to John Omally.

'I'll bet Bob the Bookie didn't give you good odds.'

'The man refuses to take any bets from me now, which I'm sure can't be legal.'

'I'm impressed that he has not dispatched a hit man to rub you out and relieve your body of the betting slip that will shortly be bringing us fortune.'

Jim Pooley shivered. 'Not even in jest, John, not even in jest. But he has offered to buy the ticket back from me for a thousand pounds.'

'You told him into which part of his anatomy he could insert his offer?'

'In the politest possible manner. I lay my bets in Chiswick now – but well away from the Consortium building.'

It was John's turn now to shiver. 'That creature we saw there still gives me nightmares. And the thought that Lord Cthulhu's dark and scaly minions might at any time put in an appearance does little to ease my concerns.'

'I'm sure the professor's on the case,' said Jim.

'Let's hope so.'

---

* 'And the roar of his Triumph could be heard throughout the land.' Exodus (somewhere or other).

Jim Pooley stretched out his arms and let wind slip through his fingers. 'It can't go on like this,' he said.

'Like what?' Omally asked.

'With one of our star players absconding before each and every game. I see we have Humphrey Hampton, the half-man, half-hamburger, on board today. And no Morris Catafelto.'

'He's having a nose job, I understand.'*

'It can't go on,' said Jim.

'I think their nerve just goes, Jim. It's the stress of all the winning – they're not used to it. It's too much for them.'

'But we can't end up with a team solely composed of circus performers. It's not professional.'

'They're professional performers. And the circus hasn't objected to them taking the time off.'

'It won't do,' said Jim. 'You must buy us more players.'

'With what, my friend? With what?'

Jim sighed. 'Why does everything have to be so complicated?' he asked.

Omally shrugged. 'Good question,' he said.

Big Bob turned on to the motorway: today the team were playing in the North. London suburbs fell astern and countryside appeared all around. Jim looked fearfully at this countryside because, as has been said, no traveller was Jim. 'This is a very large park,' said he.

'Do you want to sit downstairs?' John asked.

'I do, please. I think I'm getting a nosebleed.'

The team were already in their kaftans, kaftans that now weighed heavily with all manner of advertising logos.

Jim viewed these with interest. Many of them were new to him. 'What's an Arab strap, John?' he asked.

'It's for sport,' said Omally, which had a basic accuracy.

'And a Klismaphilia Specialist?'

'Enjoy the view, Jim.'

---

* He was the one with the nose like an engineer's elbow.

'It's more park. And surely it's getting darker.'

'We're travelling north, Jim – the nights are longer here.'

'Burnley,' said Jim. 'Where exactly on the map is Burnley?'

John Omally shook his head. 'A little to the left of Leeds, I believe,' he said.

Charlie Boxx* touched the hem of Jim's raiment. 'Boss,' he said, 'the lads are wondering about the language problem.'

'The what?' Jim asked.

'Well, the Northerners, Boss. They don't speak the Queen's English, do they?'

'Do they, John?' Jim asked.

'In a manner of speaking. I have a phrase book.' John took it from his pocket and handed it to Jim. Jim leafed through it.

'It's all about flat caps and whippets and going-to-the-foot-of-our-stairs,' said he.

'Sorry,' said John, reacquiring the phrase book and repocketing same. 'That's the Yorkshire one. This is what you need.' He handed yet another book to Jim.

'Surely this is Klingon,' said Jim.

'It's basically the same. Trust me, I'm a PA.'

Jim now shook his head and addressed the team over the tour-bus microphone. 'Gentlemen,' said he, 'we are travelling north into *terra incognita*, into realms hitherto untravelled by Brentonians. We are pioneers, trailblazers, a bit like the Pilgrim Fathers. We will bring the Gospel of Brentford unto these heathen hordes.'

'Yea, verily,' enjoined Big Bob.

'Steady on,' said John.

'What I say unto you,' Jim continued, 'is be not afraid. We have practised our tactics – well, all of us but for Mr Hampton here who is replacing Alan Berkshire, who we didn't know had gone missing until I did a headcount.'

Omally groaned. Another one had lost his bottle.

---

* The one who had strange ways about him.

'So please help Humphrey out and give him a round of applause for stepping in at such short notice.'

The team gave Humphrey a round of applause.

'Thanks very much, I'll do my best,' said the human half of the half-man, half-hamburger.

The other half said nothing.

'What I am saying to you,' Jim continued, 'is that you have nothing to fear but fear itself.'

'I hear you, Boss,' said Dave Quimsby. 'But then I'd hear you if you were a mile away. What is your point, exactly?'

'I am saying,' said Jim, 'that we have nothing to fear.'

'But we're not afraid,' said Sundip Mahingay (the Indian of the group). 'I follow Guru Maharugo Rune. I do not even fear fear itself.'

'Quite so,' said Jim.

'And I'm not afraid,' said Charlie Boxx. 'I fear only the radiator that comes on before six in the morning.'

'Yes,' said Jim. 'But—'

'Jim,' said John, putting his hand over Jim's microphone, 'they're not afraid. Only *you* are afraid.'

'I'm not afraid,' said Jim. 'The sky's growing very dark, though, don't you think?'

'It's smoke,' said John. 'From the mills. Or the mines, or suchlike.'

'I'm just trying to encourage the team.'

'You're putting the wind up them. Stop now.'

Jim made a pouting face. 'Carry on, lads,' he called. 'There's nothing to be terrified of, really.'

'Stop it *now*.' John put his other hand over Jim's mouth. 'Have a little pick-me-up. I've brought a hip flask.'

The sky continued to darken as the bus moved on up the M something-or-other, through wild moorlands now where the plaintive howls of feral whippets reached the ears of Dave Quimsby.

John perused his wristlet watch and urged Bob Charker onwards.

'What time starteth the match?' enquired the big one through his little panel.

'Seven-thirty,' said John. 'Evening game. We have plenty of time.'

'The bus needs diesel and the team the bread of life.'

'Lunch, do you mean?'

'I doeth,' quoth Big Bob.

'Well, when you see one of those motorway service station jobbies, pull in.'

'Three-sixteen,' said Big Bob.

'You mean ten-four,' said John. 'Like "it's a big ten-four" in those American trucker movies.'

'I mean, John, three-sixteen,' said Big Bob, 'as on those cards that members of the audience hold up during American wrestling matches.'

'So,' said Barry Bustard to Alf Snatcher, 'this duck goes into the Jobcentre.'

'Duck?' said Alf.

'Duck,' said Barry. 'And he's looking for a job, but the bloke behind the counter says that there aren't many jobs for ducks. But if the duck fills in a form, then he'll let him know if anything comes up. So the duck fills in the form—'

'How?' asked Alf.

'Doesn't matter,' said Barry. 'Let's say that the Jobcentre bloke fills in the form for him.'

'Fair enough, then, go on.'

'So the duck goes home. And the very next day the Jobcentre bloke answers the phone and it's Count Otto Black's *Circus Fantastique* and they're looking for a duck. Six-week tour, three shows a day, two hundred quid a week and all found.'

'All what?' asked Alf.

'Food and board,' said Barry.

'Fair enough, go on.'

'So the Jobcentre bloke phones up the duck and says—'

'How did the duck pick up the phone?' asked Alf.

'He had a friend,' said Barry. 'A monkey. The monkey answered the phone for him.'

'Fair enough, go on.'

'So the Jobcentre bloke says, "You'll never guess what. I've just had a call from Count Otto Black's *Circus Fantastique* and they need a duck. Six-week tour, three shows a day, two hundred quid a week and all found—" '

'And the duck says, "That's no good for me, I'm an interior designer!" ' said Alf.

'You've heard it,' said Barry.

'I know the duck,' said Alf. 'He redesigned my sitting room.'

Barry Bustard sighed.

'Are there any jobs going in the circus for tailed men?' asked Alf.

The bus turned on to a slip road leading off the motorway.

'Are we nearly there yet?' Jim asked.

'He's stopping for diesel,' John told Jim. 'And lunch. And beer. Northern beer, which many speak of highly.'

'Ah,' said Jim.

The sign said 'Services One Mile' and Big Bob took this sign at face value. The big bus found its big wheels upon country road and as it was now three-thirty in the afternoon, and they *were* in the North and night was beginning to fall, Big Bob switched on the headlights.

'What is *that*?' Jim asked, pointing out and upwards through a window.

'The aurora borealis,' said John. 'Don't let it bother you, Jim.'

'It's very pretty,' said Jim. 'Are we nearly there yet?'

'Soon.'

Big Bob squinted through the windscreen and set the wipers working. 'It groweth somewhat foggy,' said he.

What merry converse there had been on the bus, and there hadn't been much since Pooley's pep talk, now ceased altogether and the team peered out through the windows at little other than darkness and fog.

'I think we should go back to the motorway,' Jim Pooley called through Big Bob's little hatch.

'These lanes be too narrow,' the big one called back. 'I canst not turn the bus around.'

Jim affected a gloomier countenance. 'I wish the professor had come this time,' said he.

'Perk up, Jim,' John told him. 'A couple of pints of Northern brew will raise your spirits.'

'We're lost,' said Jim. 'I know we are. The bus will run out of diesel and we will be stranded and we'll miss the match and we won't win the FA Cup and the Consortium will acquire the ground and loose the old serpent and the world as we know it will come to an end.' Jim's hands began to flap and he made to rise from his seat to begin turning around in small circles, with hands all a-flapping, as was his way when caught in moments of terror.

'Sssh,' said John. 'Calm down and be quiet, or I will be forced to give you a smack.'

'We're doomed,' whispered Jim, hands flapping faster, his bum gaining liftoff.

Omally raised a fist.

'Aha,' cried Big Bob. 'Yonder shineth lights. I behold a diesel pump and a pub thereto.'

'Nobody panic,' cried Jim. 'Everything is going to be all right.'

'Buffoon,' said John Omally.

Big Bob drew the big bus to a halt and viewed through the fog the pub sign that swung in a creaky kind of fashion. 'The Slaughtered Lamb,' said he. 'I'll fill the tank whilst thou drink not only water, but take a little wine, for thy stomach's sake.'

'Three-sixteen,' said John Omally.

The team climbed down from the bus, hugging themselves for warmth, and Jim Pooley led them to the alehouse. He pushed upon a rugged door of panelled oak, and this door opened before him. Beyond lay the interior of a tavern that surely had not changed for several centuries. It was all oak beams and benches. Sawdust carpeted the floor and ancient fellows in cloth caps tugged upon tankards of ale and offered crisps to their whippets. Behind a rugged bar counter stood the lord of this domain: a barkeep who wore a soiled leather apron and bore an uncanny resemblance to the late, great Michael Ripper.

Jim Pooley whistled. 'Good grief,' said he.

And then Jim stepped aside to avoid being trampled in the rush to the bar.

Many pints were ordered but the barkeep stood resolutely behind his counter, regarding all with a quizzical expression.

'Allow me,' said Jim, elbowing his way into the crush and consulting his Klingon phrasebook.

'Zoot a roony gabba gabba hey,' declared Jim.[*]

'Fourteen pints of Old Dog-Gobbler, then, is it?' said the barkeep.

'Zipperdee do dah,' said Jim.[†]

'And a packet of pork-scratchings.'

'Kree-gah, Bundolo!'[‡]

'And a handbag full of cheese?'

'Yes, please,' said Charlie Boxx.

The beer came in pewter tankards, the pork-scratchings in plastic packets and the handbag in a basket with a side salad. The team descended to the benches and took sup with relish.[§]

John and Jim did leanings at the bar.

'We don't have many sand-dancers calling in this way,' the barkeep observed as he viewed the team's kaftans. 'Are you a fan-club party bound for the Wilson, Kepple and Betty convention in Huddersfield?'

'It's a football team,' said Jim. 'Brentford United.'

'*The* Brentford United?' The barkeep eyed the team. 'By the Gods, 'tis true. And you, yourself, my son has your

---

[*] For the *Klingon Dictionary* is copyright, so you can't quote from it.

[†] This armature leans at forty-five degrees.

[‡] Make that fourteen.

[§] Or hickery dickery duck, in the alternative Klingon tongue.

picture on his wall and has taken to the wearing of the green tweeds. You're Bertie.'

'Jim,' said Jim. 'The name's Jim.'

'Well, 'tis a pleasure to make your acquaintance, Jim. I'm so sorry that I didn't recognise the team at once, but it is beyond belief that you should be here, in my pub. I can't believe it.' The barkeep stuck out his hand for a shaking and Jim took this hand and shook it. It was a cold and clammy hand, and when Jim had done with the shaking of it, Jim wiped his hand upon a tweedy plus-foured trouser leg.

'You're up against Burnley tonight,' said the barkeep. 'Do you fancy your chances?'

Jim made an 'O' with his right thumb and forefinger.

'You'll score no goals,' said the barkeep. 'Shame.'

'No,' said Jim. 'We'll win.'

'And you deserve to – you are the greatest, up from nothing and heading for glory. Might I ask you a favour?'

'You might,' said Jim.

'Would it please you if I treated the team to a round of drinks? It would be my honour.'

'Would that include the manager?' Jim asked.

'And his PA?' John Omally added.

'I would be doubly honoured.'

Another round was served. And packets of pork-scratchings liberally distributed. And Charlie Boxx received a holdall full of crabsticks as a main course.

Jim soon warmed to Old Dog-Gobbler, which, although lacking the subtle nuances of Large, embodied the richer qualities of medical alcohol and poteen, and had a decent head on it, too.

'We mustn't drink too much,' he told the barkeep. 'We have a match to play.'

'And to win,' said the barkeep, raising a pewter tankard of his own and draining its contents to the dregs. 'But you're only round the corner – the ground is but two miles on, so you can have another round, on the house.'

'Really?' said Jim.

'Might I come with you?' asked the barkeep. 'I'll close the pub for the evening.'

'Absolutely,' said Jim, raising his tankard.

Big Bob sauntered in. 'All filled,' said he, 'and the pump man refused my offer to render unto Caesar – he said that he supporteth Brentford.'

'God is on our side,' said Jim.

'Same again?' said the barkeep. 'And one for yourself, driver?'

'Adam's ale for me,' said Big Bob, ever the professional.

The barkeep drew John and Jim two more pints, waved the potboy to replenish the team's drinks and served up a glass of mineral water (drawn from a healthy Northern spring) for Big Bob.

'I could not but notice that you favour the biblical idiom,' he said to the big one.

'Thou speaketh truly.'

'I myself have an interest in the New Testament. In fact, I am presently writing a book on the subject.'

'Art thou?' said Big Bob, tasting the water of life and finding it wholesome.

'Yes indeed. Might I beg that you indulge me for a moment?'

Big Bob inclined his head. John Omally rolled his eyes, but tasted further ale and found it wholesome.

'Yes,' said the barkeep. 'You see, I've always had a problem with the accuracy of the New Testament. The trial of Jesus, for instance. You see, nothing that is written in the New Testament explains why he was crucified. Crucifixion was a punishment reserved for only the most heinous crimes. Jesus might have been considered a bit of a trouble-maker, but he wasn't a revolutionary proper and so he shouldn't have been crucified.'

'He had to fulfil prophecy,' said Big Bob, 'that the Son of Man would come and that man would put him to death. And then he would rise again, of course.'

'Of course, but I have this theory that it happened differently. My book is fiction, of course, because I can't be certain, but in my version of events, Jesus gets off. He has this clever lawyer, see, Saint Matthew.'

'The tax collector?' said Big Bob.

'He was a learned fellow, well educated – he could write. He got Jesus off and Jesus then went on to have other adventures. Have you ever seen that film *The Seven Samurai*?'

'It was remade as *The Magnificent Seven*,' said Jim.

'Exactly,' said the barkeep. 'So think about this: *The Magnificent Thirteen*, Jesus and his apostles going out, righting wrongs, getting into battles.'

'Battles?' said Jim. 'They were fishermen, not Samurai.'

'They had swords,' said the barkeep.

'Of course they didn't,' said Jim.

'They did,' said Omally. 'They drew them to defend Jesus in the Garden of Gethsemane when Judas kissed him. Well, at least one of them did. But I expect they were all tooled-up – they were dangerous days back then in Palestine.'

'They never were.' said Jim. 'Swords?'

'Big 'uns,' said Big Bob.

'That's not very apostley,' said Jim, 'swords.'

'It's in the Bible,' said the barkeep. 'So after Jesus gets off, he and his apostles go and have these adventures with swords. They save villages, things like that.'

'Do you have a title for this book?' Big Bob asked.

'I do,' said the barkeep. 'Remember the A Team?'

'I have the duvet cover,' said Jim.

'You do?' said John.

'Christmas present from my mum,' said Jim.

'Oh,' said John.

'Well,' said the barkeep, 'forget the A Team. My book is called *The J Team*. After Jesus. Good, eh?'

'Put me down for a copy,' said Jim. 'Where is the toilet, by the way? The Old Dog-Gobbler is beginning to take its toll on my bladder.'

'In the yard,' said the barkeep. 'Out of the door and turn left.'

'Thank you,' said Jim and he left the bar counter and made his way unsteadily to the door.

'One more all round,' the barkeep called to the potboy.

Jim took himself outside, leaned upon the doorpost and lit up a Dadarillo. He blew smoke towards the full moon that now swam proudly amongst the scudding clouds, for most of the fog had lifted.

'Nice fella, that barkeep,' said Jim to himself. '*The J Team*, though, what nonsense. A Brentford supporter, though – the barkeep, I mean, not Jesus,' and Jim giggled foolishly.

It was very cold out now, but Jim felt warm inside. Old Dog-Gobbler was exceptional ale. He'd only had a couple of pints, well, three at most, and he felt, what was the word? Merry.

'Good word, merry,' said Jim. But the word was not 'merry'. The word Jim was looking for was 'drunk'. Actually, it was two words – 'very drunk'.

'Now which way was the bog? Right or left? Right, I think.' And Jim staggered very drunkenly off towards the right.

A door presented itself to him and he turned the handle and pushed the door open and came upon a cosy kitchen room. Jim peered in, leaning on a new doorpost for support. He really did feel very drunk now.

Two folk stared at Jim from a kitchen table – a big, fat woman and a scrawny child. They were taking their tea. The scrawny child wore a football shirt. Jim grinned foolishly.

'I'm terribly sorry,' said he. 'I was looking for the toilet.'

'It doesn't matter, my dear,' said the big, fat woman. 'It often happens to folk who have foolishly imbibed more than a half-pint of Dog.'

'Ah,' said Jim. 'Yes.'

'Back out and to the left,' said the big, fat woman.

'Thank you,' said Jim, struggling to turn himself around. 'Aha,' said Jim, espying the scrawny child's football shirt. 'You're the young football supporter, I see.'

'Like my dad,' said the child.

'His dad's the barkeep,' said the woman. 'My husband.'

'Nice chap,' said Jim. 'But that shirt, it's not the Brentford strip.'

'Brentford?' said the child and he spat on to the floor. 'We gob upon Brentford here. We're Burnley Town supporters. Burnley Town for the Cup.' And he began a chant that Jim did not like the sound of at all.

'Burnley shupporters?' slurred Jim. 'But the barkeep shaid . . .'

And then that light came unto Jim, that light which folk sometimes see – that illuminating light that St John got, which lit up the Road to Damascus.[*]

Jim suddenly got it now.

'Treachery!' cried Jim. 'Duplicity! Sabotage!'

And Jim lurched from the cosy kitchen and staggered back to the bar.

---

[*]Bob and Bing were not in that one, either.

33

Big Bob Charker loaded the last of the unconscious bodies on to his great big bus.

'All present and incorrect,' said he, thrusting out his barrel chest and throwing back his head. 'And now I return unto The Slaughtered Lamb and there will slay all with the jawbone of an ass, which I keep in my toolbox for such eventualities.'

'No, Bob.' Jim Pooley clung perilously to that platform pole which bus conductors love so dearly to swing from (when they aren't doing crosswords, or putting the world to rights). 'No, Bob, please don't do that.'

Bob lifted Jim bodily and laid him on to one of the long bench seats. 'Whyfore not?' he enquired.

'It would reflect poorly on the team,' said Jim, blearily. 'A mass murder could put us out of the FA Cup.'

'But look unto the evil that they have wrought upon us.' Big Bob flourished a great big hand.

Jim's blurry vision took in the devastation that was Brentford United. The lads were seated, sort of, and draped across one another. Those that were actually upright, although not actually conscious, had the look of the now legendary James Gang in their post-mortem photographs.

'Look unto them,' commanded Bob the Big.

'It's not easy,' mumbled Jim, 'but please, please don't slay anyone.'

'Jim's probably right.' Omally was on his hands and knees, crawling on to the platform. 'Get us to the football ground. We'll try to sober them up.'

'We?' Jim Pooley's vision clouded. He was all but going under.

'To the football ground,' said John Omally, clawing his way towards Jim.

Big Bob Charker made growling sounds but took himself off to his cab.

As luck would have it, or chance, or both, or neither, Burnley really was but two miles up the road.

The country lane became a road, and this road a high street. The glories of Burnley rose to either side: gothic architectural splendours wrought from bricks of terracotta and black basalt and grandeefudge and snurgwassell.

Or so it seemed to Jim.

The bus passed a branch of Waterstones where, by luck, or chance, or both, or neither, the resident staff were playing host to the famous Brentford author P.P. Penrose, who was giving a reading of his latest Lazlo Woodbine thriller, *Baboon in a Body Bag*. Big Bob glanced over his big, broad shoulder. The team were not in the land of the living. Although, in truth, they were not actually dead, either.

'Woe unto the house of Brentford,' muttered the big one, changing down and tootling the horn.

For the streets of Burnley were full of folk, many folk, many football-loving folk, all bound for the match and all decked out in distinctive reproduction club shirts of a colour that has no name and a pattern that may not be described. Big Bob looked down upon them from his cab and the temptation was oh-so-big just to put his foot down hard upon the pedal and watch them scatter before him.

'Are we nearly there yet?' Pooley's drunken face peered into Bob's cab.

'Shortly,' said Big Bob. 'Yonder lies the ground.' And he pointed with his oversized mitt towards an oversized structure.

There was much of the Colosseum about it, much too of the Parthenon, and much of the Palace of Knossos and much of the hat that the Delphic Oracle used to wear on a Saturday night when she went out on the pull.

It was all very much of a muchness, really.

And all very daunting to Jim.

'We're doomed,' he wailed into Big Bob's ear. 'Oh misery, it is all my fault.'

'Give it a rest, before you even start.' Omally's hand was on Jim's shoulder. It was not a steady hand, but it still had steady ways.

'We are doomed,' said Jim. 'What are we going to do?'

'We'll do something, sober them up somehow. Never say die 'til you're dead, my friend.'

'But *I* can hardly stand. The whole world's going in and out of focus. Mostly *out*, as it happens.'

'Curious,' said John to Jim, 'because to me it's going around and around.'

A beer can suddenly bounced off Big Bob's windscreen.

'Wherefore art *this*?' Big Bob ducked, which wasn't easy, considering the size of him.

'We're under attack!' cried Jim, which had more than a word of truth to it.

The Burnley supporters had spotted the Brentford team and were not giving the Brentford team the kind of welcome that the plain folk of Brentford usually gave them upon their triumphant returns. Cans and bottles, sticks and stones and pickled whippets' tails (a Northern delicacy that many had brought with them to gnaw upon during the match) rained a deafening assault upon the great big bus. Big Bob made the face of fury and put his big foot down.

Folk before the bus scattered and those to the sides and those behind flung further projectiles and made loud their disapproval.

'They hate us,' cried Jim, assuming a foetal position. 'We're all gonna die.'

'A pestilence upon the tribes of the North.' Before Big Bob the stadium rose and gates were being opened. The big bus swept into the ground and these gates slammed shut upon its passing.

'Up, Jim,' John commanded. 'We're not nearly there anymore. We're here.'

Jim struggled into the vertical plane and clung to a seat for support.

'Hello in there, everybody, heigh-de-ho?'

'Heigh-de-ho?' said John. And he turned to view a small fat chap of the Pickwickian persuasion, who wore a most remarkable suit. It was remarkable in so much that it closely resembled that worn by Jim – other than for the fact that it was of a colour that had no name and a pattern that may not be described.

'Merridew Fairweather,' said the portly Pickwickian, making his way up the bus towards Jim and John. 'I'm the manager of Burnley Town. And oh my and skiddly-de.'

'Skiddly-de?' said John, doing his best to get a good look at the arrival, who just kept going around and around.

'Skiddly-de, skiddly-do,' said Merridew Fairweather. 'Your team taking a pre-match nap, is it?'

'Conserving their strength,' said Jim, trying to put his hand out for a shake, but failing dismally. 'I am Jim Pooley, manager of Brentford, and this is my PA, Mr Tom O'Shanter.'

'*John Omally*,' said John.

'Have you been drinking?' asked Merridew Fairweather.

'We're just a bit travel-sick,' said John.

'Then I have just the thing to pick you up in the club bar: a pint or two of Old Dog-Gobbler.'

And then Jim Pooley *was* sick.

It took a while for Big Bob to unload the team. The Scottish groundskeeper showed him to the 'visitors' changing room,' which looked for all the world to Big Bob to be the gents' excuse-me.

'Just lay them out wherever ya wish,' said the Scotsman, 'but don't go blocking my urinals.'

Jim and John now leaned in the doorway, sometimes on the doorposts and sometimes on each other. Jim viewed, as best he could, the dismal scene before him. It reminded him of a dismal scene in one of those disaster movies where the victims of a terrible train crash are laid out in the nearest building, usually a school or a church because it adds to the pathos. Jim sniffed the air.

'This *is* a gents' excuse-me,' he said.

'Start splashing water on them,' said John.

'You don't mean—'

'*No*, I don't mean that. Water from the basins. Start splashing.'

'Righty right.' Jim stumbled across the bog, trying not to step on members of the team. They snored away beneath him, with blissful looks upon their faces. Jim gave Barry Bustard a kick in his bloated pants.

'It won't do.' Jim splashed water on to himself. 'We're doomed. We're really doomed this time.'

'The show's not over 'til the fat lady does the trick with the champagne bottle,' said John, who was splashing at himself but mostly missing.

'We can't play.' Jim splashed a bit more. 'We'll have to call it off. There's probably some rule about that.'

'There is,' said John. 'We forfeit the match.'

'But this is so unfair. We were sabotaged.' Jim got his head down into the basin and ran cold water down his neck.

'I'll think of something,' said John. 'I'll think of something, or die in the process. I just wish that the world would stop spinning.'

'That's a bit drastic, John. Surely everyone would die if the world were to stop spinning. Don't wish that.'

John Omally looked over at Jim and managed the smallest of smiles. 'You buffoon,' he said.

'Hello in there, once again. Everybody heigh-de-ho?' Merridew Fairweather thrust his smiling spherical head into the visitors' changing room. 'Still having a bit of shut-eye, is it? Best to wake them up now, I'm thinking. It's only five minutes to the match.'

'*Five minutes!*' Jim Pooley began to flap his hands and turn in small circles. It was hardly a wise manoeuvre, considering his condition.

John Omally smacked him to a standstill.

'You hit me!' Jim's jaw dropped at the enormity of this.

'And I'll hit you again if you don't get a grip of yourself. We've got to get them on to the pitch. Somehow.'

'I can probably carry them two at a time,' said Big Bob, who had been looking on but keeping his own counsel. 'But I'll need a hand with the fat bloke and the Siamese twins.'

Burnley Town Stadium, or the Palace of Earthly Delights as it is more commonly known, seats twenty thousand and stands for twice as many stamping feet when the team are playing at home. On this particular night, it was full.

There were some Brentford supporters there who had actually taken the train up to Burnley to watch Brentford doing the business. Reproduction club kaftans were *not* in evidence, however. The Brentford fans were keeping the lowest of all low profiles.

It was either that, or risk being beaten to death.

Which was a shame, really, because they had brought a big banner, which they'd hoped to wave about and be caught on camera, because this game was being televised on something called Sky TV. What Sky TV was, the plucky Brentonians had no idea. They didn't have it on their television sets. They had BBC1 and BBC2 and the one with the adverts and *Coronation Street*. Perhaps Sky TV was an aeroplane channel, watched by toffs as they flew to their holidays down in the Costa del Sol.

Mighty floodlights lit the pitch. High up in the commentary box the Sky TV commentator, an ex-*Blue Peter* presenter who had run into a spot of bother involving restricted substances and a 'lady of the night', shared his match commentary with an ex-Page Three girl who constantly ran into all kinds of bother, but whose career appeared to thrive on it.

'So, John,[*]' said she, 'here we are at the Palace of Turkish Delight and it's a bit chilly here in the box.'

John smiled with his expensive caps. 'I can see that,' he

---

[*] As John is a generic name for *Blue Peter* presenters, no conclusions can be drawn as to his actual identity (thankfully).

said, 'but at least it means I've a choice of two places to hang my jacket.'

The ex-Page Three girl, whose name was Sam,[*] did professional gigglings and gave John's bottom a tweak.

'We're up for a big one tonight,' said John. 'Brentford, unbeaten in four matches and defying the predictions of all the football pundits, and Northern favourites Burnley Town, who will tonight be favouring, I'm sure, their famous four-two-four formation.'

'Would that be the famous four-two-four formation that was originally formulated by John Rider Hartley, manager of Huddersfield in nineteen thirty-seven, after he had a dream in which dancing fairies explained it to him? The four-two-four formation that took his team on to win the FA Cup on two successive seasons?'

'Er, um, maybe,' said John. 'But look now, they're coming out on to the pitch.'

'They're not,' said Sam. 'It's just my reflection in the commentary box window.'

'The *teams* are coming out.'

'So they are,' said Sam, 'and there's the Burnley team captain Leonard Nimoy, not to be confused with the other Leonard Nimoy, of course – the one in *Star Wars*. Leonard has scored six goals this season, three at home and two away.'

'Is your Teleprompter working properly?' John asked.

'It's broken,' said Sam. 'I'm styling it out.'

'Well, the Burnley team is on the pitch now, chipping the ball around, and the crowd is on its feet. They'll give their team every ounce of support. Listen to that applause. Did you ever see such a standing ovation?'

'More than once,' said Sam. 'And here come the Brentford team.'

'So they do,' said John. 'But what exactly is going on here? The Brentford team are apparently being carried on to the pitch. I don't think I've ever seen anything quite like

[*] But it wasn't *that* one. Because *that* one has a really litigious solicitor.

this before, but we've come to expect the unexpected from this team. The dancing formations, the running backwards, the mysterious weaving about – there's just no telling what these guys will come up with next.'

'And there's their manager,' said Sam, 'that Bertie boy. Don't you just love his suit, John? I've got his picture on my bedroom wall. I cut it out from the cover of *New Scientist*.'

'He's being helped on to the bench, Sam. He looks a bit the worse for wear.'

'Probably been out clubbing all night. They say he has to have two women every evening.'

'I think you'll find that's me, Sam.'

'Well, the whole team is out on the pitch now – flat out. I can't imagine what they're up to. We'll just have to wait and see.'

'Oh, the ref's going over to Bertie,' said John.

'Mr Pooley,' shouted the ref, trying to make himself heard above the roar of the crowd. 'What exactly is going on here?'

Jim Pooley downed a pint glass of water. 'What do you mean?' he shouted back.

'Your team would appear to be unconscious.'

'Appearances *can* be deceptive,' John shouted.

'Not, I feel, upon *this* occasion,' the ref countered.

'They'll soon be on their feet,' bawled Jim. 'No one could sleep through this.'

'Sleep?' yelled the ref. 'They *are* asleep. You'll have to get them up for the kickoff.'

'Is there any specific rule to that effect?' Jim's eyes were glazed. He wasn't sobering up at all – if anything, he was feeling more drunk.

'Right,' said the ref. 'I'll toss the coin and if your centre forward doesn't get up and call, then win or lose I'll give Burnley the kickoff.'

'Do your worst,' shouted Omally. 'We're not afraid.'

'We're not?' Jim couldn't manage another shout.

The ref stalked away to the centre of the pitch and flung

his coin into the air. The crowd momentarily stilled as the dazzling disc spiralled up and spiralled down again to fall upon the snoring face of Ernest Muffler. The ref looked down at the snoring face, shrugged his shoulders and awarded the toss to Burnley.

The Burnley supporters screamed their approval. The Burnley centre forward took the kickoff.

High up in the commentary box, John the ex-*Blue Peter* boy spoke into his mic. 'And it's Burne-Jones to Morris and Morris has chipped it to Rossetti and Rossetti has passed it back to Burne-Jones and the Brentford team are just lying there, there's no defence, no attack, no nothing at all. It's Burne-Jones over on the wing to Holman Hunt and Millais is inside the box and he *scores*! Oh, yes. *He scores!* And the crowd are on their feet once more. One-nil to Burnley.'

The ref blew his whistle. 'Offside,' he said.

'There,' said Omally. 'Cunning tactics, eh?'

Pooley squinted. 'You mean they can't score?' he said.

'Yeah, well, they can – they won't go so far into the box next time.'

And they didn't.

'One-nil!' announced the ref.

Jim Pooley buried his head in his hands. 'We're doomed,' he blubbered. 'Doomed.'

'Three-nil,' said John (the John in the commentary box). 'And this is really absurd. Burnley are just walking the ball around now. They're having a laugh. Oh look, they're heading it backwards and forwards now. The crowd are loving it.'

'It's not fair,' said Sam. 'The ref should stop it. Look at poor Bertie, he's all downcast.'

'Give me a pistol, John,' Jim shouted into John Omally's ear, 'or a sword that I might fall upon. I have had enough of life. This is all too much.'

'I have to confess,' John shouted back, 'that things look rather discouraging. I'm afraid, my friend, that only a miracle can save us now.'

'Four-nil,' shouted the John in the commentary box.

'A miracle,' said Jim. 'It's going to take more than a miracle.'

'*More* than a miracle?' John took out his mobile phone.

'Of course, that's it,' said Jim. 'Zap them with microwaves.'

'Give me a moment.' John tapped out digits and put his free hand over his phone-free ear. And then John began to shout into his mobile phone.

'What is the score, Jim?'

'It's six-nil, Professor. We're doomed.'

'Never say die, Jim.'

Jim's eyes did sudden startings from their sockets. His mouth did droppings open and his voice did stumbled speakings.

'*Professor?*' said Jim, turning on the bench towards the ancient scholar. 'Professor, you're *here.*'

'I'm sorry I'm a little late. I got a bit held up.' The professor spoke softly, but his words were clear to Jim even above the howlings of the crowd.

'They're killing us, Professor. This fiend of a barkeep got the team drunk. Look at them out on the pitch.'

Professor Slocombe scratched at his ancient chin. 'A difficult situation, I agree,' said he. 'And oh dear me, they are approaching the Brentford goal once again.'

And they were. And they were laughing with it. Burne-Jones passed the ball to Ford Maddox Brown (the Burnley striker and five-times winner of the Freshest Whippet on the Block Competition (Northern Chapter)). Ford Maddox Brown took a lazy kick at the goal.

And up from the turf rose Loup-Gary Thompson,

professional wolf-boy (and eater of whippets), up from the turf and into furious action. He stopped the ball dead and then took a monumental kick.

The ball soared high into the air. Incredibly high. Fantastically high. It soared and it soared and then it fell downwards, downwards, onward and onward. And straight into the Burnley goal.

Which was undefended, as the goalie was reading a newspaper.

The crowd did not erupt into applause. The crowd became silent and still.

'That was a goal, wasn't it?' said Professor Slocombe. 'Would you care to join me, Jim, in a Mexican wave?'

'Well *this is* new,' said the John in the commentary box. 'I've never seen anything like this before. There never seems to be more than one Brentford player standing at any one time. One jumps up, kicks the ball, then flops back to the turf. And then another one jumps up, passes the ball then *he* slumps back down. And, oh my lord, it's another one for Brentford. That's—'

'It's six-all,' said Sam. 'Impossible comeback and the ref is blowing his whistle for half-time.'

The Burnley team sat in their top-notch changing room, sucking their oranges and playing their mandolins. Merridew Fairweather waddled up and down before them.

'You clowns,' he shouted, 'we could have been thirty goals ahead by now, fiddle-de, fiddle-dum, but you took them for granted. You can't take these Southern nutters for granted.'

'But the fix was in, Boss,' said John Roddam Spencer Stanhope, the goalie and three-times winner of the Flattest Flat Cap Competition (Northern Chapter). 'I thought your brother at The Slaughtered Lamb had taken care of them, as he has done with all the other teams we've thrashed at home this season.'

'Hush your loquacity,' counselled Merridew. 'We need

this win. You go out there and do whatever you have to do – if you get my meaning.'

'What about the ref?'

'He is our referee in residence,' said Merridew. 'And he *is* my other brother.'

The Brentford team did not repair to the changing room come half-time. They apparently chose to remain resting on the pitch.

Jim Pooley downed another pint of water. Some degree of sobriety was returning to him.

'I don't know how you're doing it, Professor,' said Jim, 'but please just keep on doing whatever you're doing.'

'I don't know what you're implying, Jim.' The professor made the face of mock-wounding. 'The team are trying their best and playing their hearts out.'

'I particularly liked the way that the English twins managed to kick in that last goal without having any of their feet actually touching the turf,' said John. 'The way they just sort of hovered above the ground.'

'Skilful players,' said the professor. 'Very light on their feet.'

The folk who watch Sky TV – those toffs in aeroplanes, perhaps – no doubt enjoyed the second half of the match.

Assuming, of course, that they were *not* Burnley Town supporters.

Those toffs probably enjoyed all the news that followed also. It was *Sky News* and it was very thorough. The reporter 'on the ground' who covered the carnage was an ex-BBC topical news quiz presenter who had just lost his job at the BBC after getting into a spot of bother involving cocaine and hookers. His name was Angus[*] and he had to wear his special *Sky News* protective helmet and flak jacket. The mass rioting that followed the Brentford victory and culminated in the burning down of, amongst other things,

[*] It *was* that one. Allegedly.

the Stadium of Earthly Delights (which happily resulted in no actual loss of life, although many were hospitalised) made for excellent television.

At three a.m., martial law was declared and a squadron of Challenger tanks escorted the Brentford big bus to a safe point well beyond the city limits.

The moon shone down upon John and Jim, who lazed upon the open upper deck, gazing over their shoulders towards the orange glow in the sky that had up until so recently been the town of Burnley.

'I think we can chalk that one up as another success,' said John.

'Do you want to wake the team and tell them?' Pooley asked.

'Nah, let them sleep. It will be a nice surprise for them in the morning.'

'Where did the professor vanish away to?' Jim asked.

Omally tapped at his nose.

'And what does *that* mean?'

Omally grinned and his mobile phone began to ring. Words were exchanged and Omally tucked the thing away into his pocket.

'Who was *that*?' Jim now asked.

'Sky TV,' said John. 'They're offering sponsorship. They want to put their logo on our kaftans.'

34

Norman numbered-up the Monday morning *Mercury*s.

He ogled the front page and read the headline aloud:

'BERTIE'S BEES BURN BURNLEY –
10-6 VICTORY SPARKS RIOTS.'

Norman shook his head and straightened his wig. Another victory for the team. That put them through to the quarterfinals. Three more wins and they would have the cup.

And on Cup-Final Day, *he* would have his millions.

Norman gnawed upon a knuckle blackened by newsprint. *He* would have his millions, but what had he done? He had claimed those patents for his own and sold them to this William Starling, who was the King of Darkness, and who sought to rule the world. And, what was it? Ah, yes, hasten the Apocalypse.

Hasten the Apocalypse?

That was 'bring on the bad stuff'.

And if the bad stuff was going to be brought on, it was all Norman's fault for being so greedy.

But was it *really* his fault? Norman cogitated once more upon this, as he had been cogitating so frequently of late. Had it really been *his* fault? Was it not more that he had been put in the frame, as it were?

It had all started with Norman wanting to find The Big Figure. But that *had* been his idea.

Or had it?

Norman added rackings of the brain to his cogitations.

How had he come up with that idea in the first place? Had he actually come up with it himself? A dark thought entered Norman's head, along with a sudden flash of remembrance. Wavy, wavy lines seemed to move across Norman's mind and the sounds of harp music accompanied these wavy lines.

And Norman had a flashback.

He was standing in his shop, numbering-up the morning's papers and thinking about improvements he could make to the better mousetrap he was building – the one that he felt certain would have the whole world beating a path to his door.

And then the shop bell had rung-in a customer.

Except that it *wasn't* a customer. It was a pasty-faced young man in dark specs and a suit of lacklustre grey. This young man carried a bulging suitcase. He bid Norman good day and proffered his card:

LUKE SHAW
Sales representative for Dadarillo Cigarettes
A subsidiary of the Consortium

The card was rather grey also and Norman peered up from it and into the matching face of the sales representative.

'I don't want any,' said Norman. 'Goodbye.'

'I think you'll *FIND* that you do,' said the young man, with exaggerated politeness. 'I think you'll *FIND* that you do.'

'I won't,' said Norman, 'whatever you have to offer.'

The young man gave Norman's shop a good looking over. Well, Norman assumed that he did so, because although his eyes were hidden, his head moved around and about.

'What are you looking for?' Norman asked, following the direction of the moving head.

'Mr Hartnel?' said the sales representative. 'Mr Norman Hartnel, not to be confused with the other Norman Hartnel?'

'I'm rarely confused,' said Norman, 'although sometimes I get puzzled.'

'But only about *THE BIG* problems in life, I'm thinking.'

'Actually, yes,' said Norman, 'although I've found that even the biggest problems have simple solutions, generally involving a Meccano set somewhere down the line. Feather by feather the goose gets plucked, you know.'

'You are a most interesting man, Mr Hartnel. An interesting *FIGURE*.'

'Why do you talk like that?' Norman asked.

'Like what, Mr Hartnel?'

'Putting very heavy emphasis upon certain words that do not need heavy emphasis putting upon them.'

'I'm from Penge,' said Mr Luke Shaw.

'Ah,' said Norman. 'That explains it. I understand that Penge is a very nice place, although I've never been there myself.'

'Very nice.'

'Home is where the heart is,' Norman said. 'And a boy's best friend is his mother.'

'Quite so,' said Mr Luke Shaw. 'How many packets will you take?'

'I won't take any,' Norman said. 'I can't sell new brands of cigarettes to the locals. They won't wear it. They're very stuck in their ways.'

'I think you'll *FIND* that *THE* offer I'm making you will reap *BIG* profits. The *FIGURE* I'm selling them for is most competitive.'

The ringing of the shop doorbell brought a sudden end to Norman's reverie.

'*FIND THE BIG FIGURE*,' mouthed Norman.

'What are you saying?' asked Mr H.G. Wells.

Norman stared into the face of the Victorian time-traveller. 'Oh,' said Norman, 'Mr Wells. Good morning. What are you doing here?'

'I have come,' said Mr Wells, 'to enquire as to your

progress. I have been here for months now and although Madame Loretta Rune provides basic amenities and I have made many acquaintanceships in The Flying Swan and The Stripes Bar and have become an active supporter of Brentford United Football Club.' Mr H.G. Wells raised a fist and cried, '*Brentford for the Cup!*' before regaining his composure and his gravity and concluding, 'I wish to return to my own time and the comfort of my own house in Wimpole Street, W. One.'

'It's still there, you know,' said Norman. 'There's a blue plaque outside with your name on it.'

'I have pressing business.' Mr Wells raised his voice once more.

Norman shushed him into silence. 'Peg is in the kitchen,' he said. 'She's still rather upset about the back wall. I've been meaning to fix it, but I'm spending all my spare time trying to fix your machine.'

'Pressing business,' Mr Wells said once more. 'Time is of the essence.'

'I've been thinking about that.' Norman distractedly numbered-up several papers. 'I mean to say that it doesn't really matter how long you stay in this time, does it? Because you can always return to the very minute you left your own, if you want to.'

Mr Wells leaned forward over the counter top and glared hard at Norman. Norman smiled back at Mr Wells.

And Norman did a little sniffing, too.

The smell of Mr Wells fascinated Norman. He smelled like, well, a Victorian – the smell of the macassar oil that he put upon his hair, and the moustache wax, and the fabric of his clothing. Although . . .

Mr Wells wasn't smelling all that savoury now. He'd been wearing the same set of clothes since his arrival.

'My problem regarding time does not concern the past,' said Mr Wells, whose breath was none too savoury either. 'My problem with time concerns the present.'

'I don't understand,' Norman said. 'Do you think you could lean a little further back?'

'The present,' said Mr Wells, 'and what might occur in the very near future if I have somehow erred in my sacred mission. If the destruction of the computer you acquired and the program that was running on it has not forestalled the rise to power of the King of Darkness.'

'Let's not be pessimistic,' Norman said. 'I'm sure it has.'

'But if it *hasn't*?' Mr Wells made fists with both his hands. 'I do not wish to be here when the Apocalypse occurs. I must be back in the past, preparing to make another assault. I do not wish to be here to watch humanity crushed and millions die, for I might well become one of those millions.'

A terrible shiver ran up Norman's spine. 'There's something I think I ought to tell you,' said Norman.

'What?' asked Mr Wells.

'Well—'

'Norman!' boomed the voice of Peg, putting the wind up Norman and also up Mr Wells. 'Norman, come in here. My toenails need a cut.'

'I'll speak to you later,' said Norman. 'How about lunchtime, up the road in The Flying Swan?'

'The Flying Swan,' said Mr Wells. 'My favourite drinking house.'

'Mine, too,' Norman said. But he said no more, as Peg boomed his name again with greatly renewed vigour.

'And what is your name, lad?' asked Old Pete.

The elder sat upon Jim Pooley's favourite bench before the Memorial Library. He leaned upon his stick and looked up at the ragged youth that stood before him.

'Winston, gov'nor,' said the lad, chewing upon one of Norman's gobstoppers.

Old Pete smiled wanly at the lad – his younger self. It was a most uncanny sensation.

'And why are you not at school?' the ancient asked.

'Never been to school, gov'nor. Schools is for toffs, Gawd dance upon me dangler if they ain't.'

Old Pete gazed with rheumy eyes at the face of his younger self and he scratched at his antiquated head, for herein lay a mystery. Old Pete could remember well when, as young Winston, he had broken into Mr Wells' house and hitched a ride upon his Time Machine into the future.

The future that was now the here and now. And he remembered his arrival in Norman's kitchen and Norman shipping the Time Machine to his allotment lock-up. There was no doubt he'd remembered that, which was why he'd gone as Old Pete to the allotment to witness it, to prove to himself that it had been true.

But he had no recollection of this – he did not recall that as a young lad he had met this old man in a park in the future. Why couldn't he remember that?

'Can you spare us a penny?' asked Young Pete/Winston. 'Me mum's dying of consumption and I need it to buy 'er a new 'ot water bottle.'

'That isn't the truth,' said Old Pete, 'and you know it.'

'Nah,' said Young Pete/Winston. 'It's for meself, to pay for a poultice to put on me bum. It's covered in workhouse sores.'

'How old are you?' asked Old Pete.

'I'm as old as me nose, and a little older than me teeth, two of which need pulling – could you make it a three-penny bit to pay the quack?'

Old Pete dug into his waistcoat pocket, and then he hesitated. He recalled a video he'd rented from Norman. *Time Cop*, it was called. He hadn't actually meant to rent *Time Cop*. He'd meant to rent *Strap-On Sally's Sex Salon*, but Norman had put the wrong video in the case.

But regarding *Time Cop*, it had starred this fellow that *wasn't* David Warner but looked a bit like him. And this fellow had travelled through time and met himself. And the two had touched, with disastrous consequences. Something to do with the same self being being unable to occupy the same place in two separate time periods. Something to do with the transperambulation of pseudo-cosmic anti-matter, or something.

Old Pete did not wish to touch his younger self.

Just in case.

'I'll tell you what,' said Old Pete, 'I won't give you a threepenny bit, but I will give you something much, much more valuable. Have you ever heard of the Ford Motor Company?'

Young Pete/Winston shrugged his shoulders, sucked upon his gobstopper and gave his ill-washed head a shake.

'Get yourself a job and invest in shares,' said Old Pete, 'the moment the company sets up. Do you think you can remember that? Try very, very hard to remember that.'

His younger self shrugged once more. 'The Ford Motor Company,' he said.

'And hang on to all your shares when the Wall Street Crash comes in nineteen twenty-nine. And buy land in Florida then, too.'

His younger self eyed his older self queerly. 'Nineteen twenty-nine?' he said. 'What's your game, gov'nor?'

'I'm thinking of my future, *your* future, I mean. You must try to remember what I've told you. It will make you rich.'

'Big oak trees from little acorns grow,' said Young Pete/Winston.

Bloody Norman, thought Old Pete. 'But you will try to remember?'

'I remember asking you for a threepenny bit.'

Old Pete drew same from his waistcoat pocket and flipped it towards his younger self. 'I didn't think it would work,' he said dismally.

'What's *that*, gov'nor?'

'The Ford Motor Company! *The Ford Motor Company!*'

'Yeah, yeah, I remember that. Invest what I earn.'

'Exactly,' said Old Pete.

'Yeah, well, thanks for the threepenny bit, gov'nor. And good day to you.'

'Good day,' said Old Pete. 'And good luck with your life.'

Winston turned away and ambled off down the road. *Silly old duffer*, thought he.

'I think the books will balance for a while,' said John

Omally. 'I thought they wouldn't, but with the sponsorship money from Sky TV coming in, I think I might treat myself to a new suit, just like your lucky one.'

Jim Pooley sat at his desk in his office and puffed upon a Dadarillo Super-Dooper King. 'And what about buying new players to replace our rapidly diminishing stock?' he suggested.

'Do you think really it matters?' John Omally asked.

'*Matters?*' said Jim. 'We have the FA Cup to win.'

'Yes, I know that, but we have the substitutes. And let's face it, Jim, the team are only winning through the professor's intervention. You saw what happened on Saturday.'

'I was going to ask you all about that.'

'Oh no, you were not. The professor used some kind of magic to animate the team – you know it and I know it. So it doesn't really matter who plays as long as he is there pulling the magical strings.'

'And if he isn't?'

'Then we're stuffed,' said John. 'The ground is lost and the Apocalypse and the End Times begin. Personally, I do not find that prospect appealing. Hence I have faith in the professor's magical skills and favour the Brentford-winning-the-cup scenario, along with the attendant prosperity that it will bring to our good selves.'

'Should Bob the Bookie pay up on the bet. Which, frankly, I think he will not do.'

'Oh, he'll pay up, Jim, or we'll drag him through the courts. That man has taken many pennies from you in the past. It's only just that you get a few back in return. And even if he doesn't pay up, *you will* be the manager of an FA Cup-winning side. There's a fortune in that. Trust me—'

'I know,' said Jim, 'you are a PA.'

John sat down upon Jim's desk and helped himself to Jim's mug of tea. 'So who are we up against next?' he asked. 'We're in the quarterfinals. Three more games and we're there.'

'A team called Arsenal,' said Jim. 'Ever heard of them?'

Omally shook his head. 'They're not Up North, I hope.'

'London team,' said Jim. 'Quite popular, it seems. They're amongst the favourites to take the cup. Top-division side.' Jim grinned foolishly at John. 'Apparently,' he said, 'Arsenal have a manager whose name is Arse.'

'I'll give them a call on my mobile,' said John. 'Perhaps after we've given the team a sound thrashing they might care to purchase space on our kaftans to advertise for a new manager.'

'I can manage,' said Neville as the brewery drayman rolled an eighty-eight-pint cask of Large down the chute between the open pavement doors and into The Flying Swan's cellar.

Neville caught the weighty cask, lifted it with ease and stacked it on top of the rest.

The drayman peered down from the sun-bright street above into the shadowy regions below. 'Are you all right down there?' he called.

'Fine,' called Neville. 'You can drop them in two at a time, if you want.'

The sweating drayman shook his head. He was wearing an Arsenal T-shirt. 'I don't know what you're on, mate, but if it's on the National Health, I want some, too.'

Neville did not reply, but awaited further incomings of ale.

He *was* on something and he knew it. Something that added a string to his bow, put lead in his pencil and even hairs on his chest. And he was loving every minute of it. He'd never felt so alive before, so full of vim and vigour. He was fit as a fiddle and bright as a butcher's bull terrier.

But his stocks of Mandragora were running dangerously low and Old Pete's prices were now running dangerously high. That old villain had Neville by the short and curlies (which were now rather *long* and curly) and Neville knew it.

But he *was* having the time of his life and he really didn't want it to stop.

'Neville,' a voice called down to him, but not from the pavement doors. 'Neville, Pippa and I are getting lonely up here in the bar.'

'I'll be with you in just a moment,' Neville called back. And to the drayman, '*Three* at a time now, if you will, I've business upstairs that will not wait.'

'Down to the business at hand,' said Professor Slocombe. 'You know why I have summoned you here, gentlemen.'

Three men sat in the professor's sunlit study, tasting whisky. One of these men was not a man, but something else entirely. His name was Mahatma Campbell and what he was was well known to the professor.

The other two were men indeed, young men and as full, in their ways, of vigour as was Neville.

'We are *your men*,' said Terrence Jehovah Smithers, raising his glass.

'Your acolytes,' said the Second Sponge Boy, raising his in a likewise fashion.

Professor Slocombe toasted his guests. 'I hope that I have taught you well,' said he.

'You have, Master.' Terrence drained his glass. 'You have schooled us in astral projection and the reading of men's auras through the opening of our third eyes.'

'Positively Rampa,' said the Second Sponge Boy.

'And you will need all these skills when we meet our adversary.' Professor Slocombe lowered his fragile frame into the chair behind his desk. 'The time grows closer. We must be well prepared.'

'Can we not just smash them now?' asked the Campbell. 'Put a torch to the Consortium building and burn the blighters out?'

'I have tested their defences.' The scholar moved a pencil about. Without the aid of his hands. 'They will not be caught off-guard again.'

'Then when, sir?' The Campbell took possession of the Scotch decanter and poured himself another.

'The day of the Cup Final, that is when.'

'But that is *the* day,' the Campbell said. 'The Day of the Apocalypse – if we do not succeed.'

'We *will* succeed.' The professor's pencil rose into the air and spelled out the word 'SUCCEED'.

'Regarding the *business at hand*,' said Terrence, wrestling, with difficulty, the Scotch decanter from the Campbell's fingers. 'What *exactly* would this business be?'

'It is my understanding,' said Professor Slocombe, 'that the tentacles of the Dread Cthulhu and the influence of the being that has raised him from R'leah, our enemy William Starling, are spreading slowly and inexorably across the borough of Brentford. You must be vigilant and watchful – there is no telling who might become consumed and overtaken by the evil.'

'And *that* is the business in hand?' asked Terrence.

'It is part of it.'

'And the other part?'

'Have you ever heard of a team called Arsenal?' Professor Slocombe enquired.

'All enquiries must be put through the switchboard,' said Ms Yola Bennett, 'which is currently engaged. Please call back tomorrow.' She slammed the telephone receiver down and returned to doing her nails.

'Ms Bennett.' The voice of Mr Richard Gray came through the intercom. Ms Yola Bennett ignored it.

She was in a bad mood, was Yola Bennett. She hadn't seen Norman for ages. He didn't e-mail and he didn't phone. And she was certain that he had recently ducked into a doorway when he'd seen her coming down the Ealing Road. Things were not going quite the way that she had planned.

'*Ms Bennett!*' The voice was somewhat louder now. Yola Bennett flipped the switch with an undone nail and said, 'What do you want?'

'And don't adopt that tone of voice with me, young lady.'

'What do you want, *sir*?' said Ms Bennett.

'A moment of your time in my office, if you please.'

Yola Bennett slouched from her seat and slouched into

the office of Mr Gray. 'Yes?' she said, a-lounging at the doorpost.

'Come in, please, and close the door.'

Yola Bennett did so.

'And sit down.'

She did that also.

'I will not beat about the bush,' said Mr Gray, viewing Ms Bennett across the expanse of his expansive desk and noting well the shortness of her skirt. 'I feel a change of attitude is called for from yourself.'

'Oh yes?' Yola blew upon those nails that were mostly done.

'Your attitude will not do, young lady. You have been ignoring telephone calls, leaving correspondence unanswered and taking overlong lunch hours. Not to mention your record of attendance.'

'My record of attendance?'

'I told you not to mention that.[*] I feel that I may be forced to let you go.'

'Let me go?' Yola made a sudden face of horror. And outrage, also. And effrontery. It was a complex face. It quite bewildered Mr Richard Gray.

'Let you go,' said he. 'If you don't buck up your ideas, you're out.'

'Stuff your job,' said Yola Bennett. 'And stuff you, too, as it happens. All men are quite the same. And all of you are bastards.'

Mr Gray smiled, thinly. 'Things not going too well for you with Mr Hartnel, then?' he said.

'What?' said Yola.

'Please don't mess around with me. I know what you've been up to.'

'You know nothing and whatever you know is none of your business anyway.'

'I know what I know. And I know what you want. I want these things, too.'

[*] The very last time. I promise you.

344

'Pervert,' said Ms Yola Bennett.

'I don't mean *those things*. I mean the money he has coming to him.'

'I don't know what you're talking about.'

Mr Gray sighed. 'Oh, well,' said he, 'then I must be mistaken. It is a pity, because I think you'd make the perfect couple. And I feel absolutely certain that when Mr Hartnel receives the *many millions* that he will so shortly be receiving, you would be capable of enjoying your share of this wealth. Assuming, of course, that you were actually able to marry Mr Hartnel.'

'Piss off,' said Yola.

'Oh well, then.' Mr Gray leaned back in his overstuffed chair. 'Forget it. Join the dole queue if that is your wish. There are plenty of other fish in the sea, as they say. Or in the fridge, as Mr Hartnel would probably say. I will take on another secretary and put my proposition to her.'

'Proposition?' said Yola.

'Proposition,' said Mr Gray. 'I have been thinking long and hard about this ever since Mr Hartnel callously spurned my offer to act on his behalf.'

'That would be when you threw yourself out of the window and into the dustbins.' Yola tittered.

'You are dismissed,' said Mr Gray. 'Please go and clear your desk.'

'About this proposition?' said Yola.

Mr Gray leaned forward once more. 'Together,' said he, 'we are going to take that wig-wearing schmuck for every penny he has.'

'Does this involve Arsenal?' asked Ms Yola Bennett.

'No,' said Mr Gray. 'Why did you ask me that?'

'I've no idea,' said Yola. 'So tell me all about this proposition.'

Mr Richard Gray smiled upon Ms Yola Bennett and he swung slowly about in his chair and gazed out through the window. And the eyes of him turned blacker than night. And the skin of him did also. And a voice murmured low in the throat of Mr Gray, in a language that was of no human tongue.

But Yola Bennett did not see or hear this fearful transformation. 'Tell me what you have in mind,' she said, raising her skirt a little higher and giving her legs a cross.

35

Arsenal?
  Schmarsenal!

36

Chelsea?
Schmelsea!*

*Or is that now Chelski? Schmelski!?

37

Jim Pooley sat in the saloon bar of The Flying Swan.

It was a Friday lunchtime in May.

Jim had a certain face on.

Neville passed a pint of Large across the highly polished bar counter and accepted Jim's small change.

'Two questions,' Neville said, as he rang up 'no sale' on the publican's piano. 'Firstly, why are you here? And secondly, why do you have that certain face on?'

Jim swallowed ale and Jim shrugged his shoulders. 'In answer to your first question, Neville,' said he, 'why are any of us here? And in answer to your second question, it's the speed.'

'The speed?' said Neville, addressing himself to the latter of Jim's answers. 'What do you mean by "the speed"?'

'The speed of all *this*.' Jim made an expansive gesture with his pint-free hand. 'Bang, bang, bang, Brentford United, four, Arsenal, nil. Bang, bang, bang, Brentford United, three, Chelsea, one.'

Neville managed a chuckle at this. 'The Chelsea striker hammered that one right past the circus giant you now have as a goalie,' said he.

'But the speed of it all,' Jim said with a sigh. 'It's all just happened so fast. One minute it's November and now it's May.'

'And the FA Cup Final is tomorrow,' Neville said. 'And the team is up against Man U. Should I venture a fiver on them, do you think?'

Jim did a bit more sighing. 'Is it real to you?' he asked. 'For it certainly is not to me.'

'Hm.' Neville took up a dazzling pint pot and took to the polishing of same. 'I don't really know what's real any more.' And he rolled his good eye towards Pippa and Loz, who stood, topless as ever, chatting away at the other end of the bar.

'But *you're* doing all right for yourself,' said Jim, as he followed the direction of Neville's eye-rolling. 'You're having the time of your life.'

'And you too, surely,' said Neville. 'You could never have dreamed that it would come to this.'

'I never volunteered for this job, Neville, and in truth I don't enjoy it. The responsibility is too much for me. I wish things were just as they used to be.'

'Well, it will all be over tomorrow – one way or the other.'

'Your words offer little comfort to me.'

'I'm sorry,' said Neville, 'but what can I say?'

'Nothing,' said Jim Pooley. 'Nothing.'

Norman Hartnel now entered the bar. And if Pooley had a face on him, so, too, did Mr Hartnel.

The shopkeeper slouched up to the bar counter and slumped himself on to a stool.

'Norman,' said Jim.

'Jim,' said Norman.

'Drink?' Neville asked.

'Large whisky,' said Norman.

'Large whisky?' Jim asked, as Neville did the business. 'Isn't that a little strong for this time of day?'

'I am a man sorely vexed,' said Norman. 'I am a man consumed with sorrow.'

Neville proffered Scotch and the shopkeeper drained it away in one.

'But surely,' said Neville, 'your ship comes in tomorrow. Don't I recall you telling me that tomorrow you will receive the many millions for your patents?'

'Oh yes,' said Jim. 'I'd quite forgotten about that.'

'It's true,' said Norman with gloom in his voice. 'But money can't buy you happiness.'

'To quote Jon Bon Jovi,' said Neville, ' "anyone who says that money can't buy you happiness is shopping in the wrong store." '

'Jon Bon who?' said Norman.

'Jovi,' said Neville. 'Pippa is a fan of his music. She likes to have it playing when we . . .' Neville's voice trailed away and his good eye glazed over.

'Well, I'm not happy,' said Norman. 'It never rains but it damn well buckets down.'

'Would you care to share it with me?' Jim asked. 'A trouble shared being a trouble halved, as they say. As *you* say, actually.'

'Another Scotch, please,' said Norman to Neville.

'On me,' said Jim, fishing out further small change.

'The fruit machine at The Stripes Bar still raking it in?' asked Neville.

'Perk of the job,' said Jim, and to Norman he said, 'Go on.'

Norman accepted his second Scotch and turned the glass between fingers that were in need of a wash. 'I have done a bad thing,' he said. 'I didn't really know that it was a bad thing when I did it. Well, I knew it was a *bit* bad, but not as bad as it may well prove to be.'

'Go on,' said Jim once more.

'But I don't want to talk about *that*,' said Norman. 'It's women that are causing me grief.'

Jim held his counsel and Norman continued, 'I think Peg's putting it about.' And Jim and Neville raised eyebrows to this. 'She is,' said Norman. 'I followed her in my van. She's having it away with Scoop Molloy from the *Brentford Mercury*.'

'The cad,' said Neville. 'I'll bar him the next time he comes in.'

'I don't really blame her,' said Norman, 'because I've been—'

'Banging the bird from the solicitor's,' said Old Pete, who'd been listening in.

'And that's the real problem,' said Norman. 'Apparently she's pregnant.'

'Unfortunate,' said Neville.

'And she wants me to meet her tonight. I think she's going to blackmail me, or something.'

'*Is* that really a problem?' Jim asked. 'If you're really going to become so rich and everything.'

'I don't want the money,' said Norman. 'I wish I'd never got involved in that patents business in the first place, but I just don't know what to do.'

'Are you sure it's your baby?' Jim asked.

'No,' said Norman. 'Of course I'm not.'

'Call her bluff,' said Old Pete. 'If she's thinking to black-mail you, hold your nerve.'

Norman's shoulders slumped some more. 'I don't know what to do for the best,' said he.

'Maybe she doesn't want to blackmail you,' Pooley said. 'Maybe she just wants to talk – she's probably very upset, too. Perhaps everything can be done in a civilised manner, no matter what it is.'

'Do you really think so, Jim?' said Norman.

'Certainly,' said Jim, in the most convincing tone that he could muster.

'Jim,' said Norman, 'would you come with me? Tonight, when I meet her. I'd feel a lot happier if I had a friend with me.'

'I can't do *that*,' said Jim. 'It's between you and her. She wouldn't appreciate my presence.'

'You wouldn't have to sit *with* us, just be nearby, for moral support, as it were. I'd feel a lot happier.'

'I'd like to help you, Norman, but I'm rather busy at present. The team I manage *is* playing for the FA Cup tomorrow afternoon.'

Norman sighed. 'Never mind,' he said. 'You have troubles of your own. And I have to leave. I have a pressing appointment, a loose end that must now be firmly tied up once and for all.' Norman drained his Scotch and rose from his stool to take his leave.

'Hold on,' said Jim. 'Where and when are you meeting her?'

'In The Beelzepub,' said Norman. 'At ten this evening.'

'I'll do my best to be there,' said Jim, 'but I won't make any promises.'

Norman shook Jim by the hand. 'I'll be forever in your debt,' said he.

'Debts?' said John Omally. 'What debts are these?'

John had been sitting at Jim Pooley's office desk when the man with the suit had entered without knocking. He was a very large man, broad at the shoulders and at the hips also. He carried a metal executive case and this he placed upon the desk, having first swept papers to right and left to make a spot of room.

'Steady on,' said John.

'Many debts,' said the big, broad man, flipping the catches on the case. 'Many court costs and damages.'

'Many *what*?' John asked.

The big, broad man lifted the lid of his case and brought out many papers. 'You are John Vincent Omally,' he said.

'Well—' said John.

'It wasn't a question,' said the man. 'You *are* John Vincent Omally, personal assistant to James Arbuthnot Pooley, manager of Brentford United Football Club.'

John made a face not dissimilar to that which Jim had recently been making.

'The court summonses were all addressed to you,' said the man, 'but you failed to attend any of the proceedings.'

'I'm a very busy man,' said John, who vaguely recalled a lot of official-looking correspondence arriving for him, all of which he had consigned to the bin without opening it.

'Perhaps you believe yourself to be above the law,' said the big, broad man.

John made a so-so face towards this.

The big, broad man affected a smirk. 'The court found in favour of the following,' said he, and he read out a list of names.

Omally did groanings. These were the names of the town

353

councillors who had fallen through the floor of the executive box during the Brentford-Orton Goldhay game.

'They all sued, and they all won, as their cases went undefended. I'm surprised you didn't read about it in the *Brentford Mercury* more than a month ago.'

'I only ever read the sports page,' said John, 'and the front page when it's about one of the Brentford team's wins.'

'This was on the *court* page. But no matter, I have all the information here. Perhaps you'd care to write me out a cheque – assuming that you have a lot of ink in your Biro.'

The big man laughed. The humour was lost upon John.

'So,' said the big man, suddenly grave, 'cheque, is it, or repossession?'

'Repossession?' John asked.

'I represent a firm of bailiffs,' said the big man, now proffering his card. 'We have taken over the debts. I must demand payment at once or I will be forced to take possession of the premises and all property within them – which would include the team's strip, boots, oranges for half-time, et cetera.'

'Oh no,' said John, 'you can't do that. We're playing for the FA Cup tomorrow.'

The big, broad man replaced his papers and closed his executive case. And then he lunged forward over the desk, snatched John up by his lapels and hoisted him into the air.

'I trust,' said he, as he did so, 'that you are not intending to obstruct a bailiff in the course of his duties.'

'I . . .' gurgled John, lining up to swing a punch that would in all probability prove to be his last. 'I . . .'

'Put Mr Omally down, if you will.'

John peeped over the big, broad shoulder. The Campbell stood in the doorway. 'Put him down, says I.'

The big, broad man let John slip from his fingers. He turned upon the figure in the doorway. 'And who might you be?' he asked.

'Mahatma Campbell,' said the Campbell. 'Take your leave now, if you will.'

The big, broad man stared at the Campbell. 'On your way,' said he.

'I'll stand my ground,' said the Campbell. 'And I'll stand this ground. Take your case and begone.'

The big, broad man lifted his metal case from the desk and then, before John's horrified eyes, he flung it with terrific force straight at the Campbell's head.

And John looked on as, with unthinkable speed, the Campbell drew his claymore and swung it at the oncoming case. There was a crash and a flurry of sparks as the claymore cleaved the case into two neat halves, which crashed to the floor amidst a flutter of neatly sliced court summonses.

The Campbell tucked away his claymore. 'Away upon your toes,' said he.

The big man glared at the Campbell, and the big man's eyes darkened, darkened to black. And a blackness fell all about the office and John Omally took to the ducking of his head.

'There's no ducking out of this one,' said Sir Alex Ferguson, manager of Manchester United Football Club. 'Tomorrow is the big match and we are going to win it.'

His team sat before him in the well–posh executive boardroom of the world's most successful football club.

'I don't want to have to be chucking any more football boots at players' heads, if you know what I mean, and I'm sure that you do.'

His team shifted upon their well-posh executive board-room chairs. The chairs were Bauhaus classics; the bums that sat upon them were separated from them by Armani suit trousers and Calvin Klein boxer shorts.

'This is a game that we *must* win,' continued Sir Alex. 'A game that we are *going* to win.'

Team heads nodded enthusiastically.

'We'll win, Boss,' said a player whose name had a trade-mark stamp upon it.

'We will,' said another whose face adorned a million bedroom walls.

'You will,' said Sir Alex. 'But that is not why I have assembled you all here. I have done so because I want to introduce you to someone. You will not be aware of this, but the club has recently become involved in certain financial negotiations. In fact, the club has changed hands for a more than lucrative sum – one that will assure that when you *win* tomorrow, and you *will win*, you will each receive a cash bonus to the tune of half a million pounds.'

The team did *oohings* and *aahings*. Even with all the money they made every week, half a million smackers in cash was not something to be sneezed at.

'Allow me to introduce to you the new owner of Manchester United.' The big well-posh executive board-room doors swung open to reveal a tall, slim man with a dark suit and a head of blondy hair.

'Mr William Starling,' said Sir Alex Ferguson.

'Mr Omally,' said the Campbell, 'you can come out now.'

John raised his head from the devastation that had so recently been Jim Pooley's office.

'Has he gone?' John asked.

'For ever,' said the Campbell, wiping something black from his claymore on to the hem of his kilt.

'He was one of—'

'Lord Cthulhu's dark and scaly minions, aye. I'm think-ing that you should accompany Mr Pooley to a place of safety for the night. I would advise the professor's.'

John rose to his feet and did dustings down of himself. 'Starling took a magical oath not to harm Jim or me.'

'Best to be safe,' said the Campbell. 'Unless you think otherwise.'

'No,' said John. 'And thank you.'

'Thank you, gentlemen, for coming here once again,' said Professor Slocombe. Terrence Jehovah Smithers and the Second Sponge Boy grinned at him from the fireside chairs in the professor's study.

'We came at your calling,' said Terrence.

'Positively trotlike,' said Sponge Boy.

'And I appreciate this.' The professor seated himself at his desk and toyed with a nail from the true cross. 'Tomorrow it must be – are you both prepared?'

'We are, Master,' said Terrence. 'But why did we have to wait for so long?'

'Many reasons,' said the professor, 'but now the time has come. You are to destroy the Consortium building. The streets of Chiswick will be deserted during the big match. This is when it must be done. Also, this is the period during which our adversary will be at his weakest regarding the defence of these premises. He will be concentrating his efforts upon the defeat of Brentford United.'

'You know that he bought out Man United?' said Sponge Boy.

'I am aware of this,' said the professor. 'I shall be attending the match in person. I am prepared for a battle of wills, as it were.'

'And magic,' said Sponge Boy. 'Positively Dr Strange and Baron Mordo.'

'I do not expect things to be easy, but in the popular parlance of the football manager, I am "quietly confident".'

'Will we have the Campbell with us?' asked Terrence.

'You will,' said the professor, 'and he will fight to the death, if needs be, and beyond that, I should imagine.'

Sponge Boy said, 'Professor, might I be permitted to ask you a question?'

Professor Slocombe nodded his aged head.

'What *is* the Campbell?' Sponge Boy asked.

'A familiar,' said Professor Slocombe. 'A witch's familiar. A lost soul conjured from the regions of Hell to aid one who had sold their own soul to the King of Darkness.'

'And he is in *your* employ?'

'I liberated him,' said the professor, 'many years ago. I freed his soul.'

'Positively Faustian,' said Sponge Boy. 'And he *can* be trusted?'

'Absolutely. Have no fear for that. I would say to you that

he is my man, but the Campbell was never a man. He may appear to be a man, but he is not. The Campbell was once a Skye terrier.'

'A dog?' said Terrence. 'He's really a dog?'

'A sprout?' said Mr H.G. Wells. 'Do you mean to tell me that the motive power behind my Time Machine is a Brussels sprout?'

'You built the thing,' said Norman, whose pressing appointment had been with Mr Wells and young Winston at Norman's allotment lock-up. 'Surely you know what powers it.'

'Hm,' said Mr Wells. 'Perhaps it slipped my mind.'

'Well, it's definitely the sprout,' said Norman. 'I have had this thing to pieces time and time again over the last four months.'

'Long months,' said Mr Wells, 'in this dire time.'

'And at my expense,' Norman said. 'You've run up enormous bills with Madame Loretta Rune, not to mention at The Flying Swan and The Stripes Bar.'

Mr Wells did *not* mention The Flying Swan or The Stripes Bar. 'Merely keeping body and soul together,' he said.

'Well, be that as it may, I have reinstalled the sprout, rebuilt its broken mountings with Meccano and I truly believe that your Time Machine is now fully operational once more.'

Mr Wells patted Norman on the shoulder. 'Then thank you,' said he. 'Winston and I will now return to the Victorian era. Our prolonged stay here has at least assured me that the King of Darkness has not acquired any of the Victorian supertechnology I thought existed upon the computer system that you reconstructed. And so my work here is done.'

Mr Wells climbed into his Time Machine and young Winston climbed in beside him. 'I am returning now to the Victorian era,' said Mr Wells, 'to change my clothes and drop off young Winston here. But I will be popping back to

this time briefly tomorrow. I wouldn't wish to miss Brentford United winning the FA Cup.'

'Pleasure knowing ya, gov'nor,' said the ill-washed
youth. 'Gawd scupper me scrote if it weren't.'

Mr Wells fastened his safety belt and prepared for takeoff.

Norman dithered.

And then Norman blurted.

'Mr Wells,' he blurted, 'before you go, there's something
I have to tell you – something I should have told you
before, but I just couldn't pluck up the courage.'

'Yes?' said Mr Wells. 'What do you have to say?'

'You're really not going to like this,' said Norman. 'And
I'm really, really sorry.'

38

John Omally went in search of Jim.

But Jim, it seemed, was nowhere to be found.

John called at Jim's rooms, The Plume Café and the bench before the Memorial Library. He returned to Griffin Park and The Stripes Bar and eventually to Jim's office, where he found the Campbell sitting cross-legged on Jim's desk, his claymore cradled in his ample arms.

'I can't find Jim,' said John, and he glanced at his wristlet watch. 'And it's almost ten of the evening clock now.'

'Did you try The Flying Swan?' asked the Campbell.

'I didn't,' said John. 'But I have no idea why not.'

The Campbell raised an eyebrow towards his turban. 'Best guard your thoughts,' said he. 'The evil is truly amongst us now. It will distract you.'

'You mean—' said John.

'I do,' said the Campbell. 'Try The Flying Swan.'

Omally set out towards The Flying Swan. There was a chill wind whipping up and thunder in the heavens. John turned up the collar of his jacket and pressed on down the Ealing Road.

The Swan's saloon bar was crowded. Brentford fans in reproduction kaftans sang club anthems, drained their glasses and raised them once refreshed towards the team's success on the morrow. Neville stood at the end of the bar, ready to serve all comers. But the all comers directed their requests exclusively to Neville's topless bar staff.

'Neville,' said Omally, elbowing his way through the crush.

'At last,' said Neville. 'How might I help you, sir? We have eight hand-drawn ales upon tap – two more than at Jack Lane's and *five more* than at The Stripes Bar. If I might recommend—'

'Has Jim been in?' Omally asked.

'A pint of Large, would it be?'

'I have to find Jim, it's very important.'

'A half then, although you won't feel the benefit.'

'Neville, have you seen Jim?'

'Oh,' said Neville, raising himself as if from a trance. 'Jim, you say?'

'Have you seen him? Has he been in here?'

'He was in earlier, but now he's gone.'

'Do you know where he might be now?'

Neville shrugged. Omally turned to take his leave.

'Hold on there, Omally.' Old Pete laid a wrinkled palm upon the Irishman's shoulder. 'You're looking for Jim,' said Old Pete.

'I am,' said John. 'Do you know where he'd be?'

'He's with Norman.'

'At his shop?'

'No,' said Old Pete, 'at another pub. Norman's meeting his lady friend there and he wanted Jim to go along.'

'For a *threesome*?' said Omally.

'No, for moral support. Although Pooley couldn't offer support to a pair of trousers if he had both belt and braces.'

'Which pub have they gone to?' John Omally asked.

'The Beelzepub,' said Old Pete.

John made haste through the gathering storm. The night had a horrible feel to it now. Omally's ears popped as if from pressure and his footsteps echoed hollowly, as if he marched upon the skin of a drum. Brentford seemed suddenly alien and Omally felt most ill at ease.

Lights glowed a hideous red from the mullioned gothic windows of the deconsecrated Spiritualist church that was now Brentford's satanic theme bar, The Beelzepub.

Omally paused, breathing heavily, before the portal.

Upon the arched brickwork above the door, words were printed in gothic script:

ABANDON HOPE, ALL YE THAT ENTER HERE.

Omally shuddered. 'Get a grip on yourself, John,' said he.

Taking a deep yet unsteadying breath, he pushed upon the heavy door and entered The Beelzepub, to face the indecorous décor.

The walls and vaulted ceiling were painted the blackest of black. So black, it appeared that they were hardly surfaces at all, more dark voids of space. Many of the chapel's original fixtures and fittings remained. The pews had been drawn about to flank long medieval tables and the altar now housed the obligatory inverted cross and a naked woman, who sat darning socks.* From the rafters hung realistic facsimiles of human corpses in various degrees of decomposition. Deicide's greatest hits blared from an unseen jukebox. The air was rank with the smell of brimstone and redly bulbed iron *torchères* lit each and everything to imperfection.

Omally squinted about the bar. In a far corner he spied Norman. Omally made off in Norman's direction.

'Oi, you,' a harsh voice called out to him. 'If you're not buying, then you're out.'

Omally turned to the source of this voice and recognised it to be that of Mr Gwynplaine Dhark, the landlord. Gwynplaine stood behind a bar counter distastefully composed of human skulls. He wore a black undertaker's suit that highlighted the paleness of his gaunt facial features. Omally approached the bar counter.

'What will it be?' asked Mr Gwynplaine Dhark.

'Anything,' said John. 'It doesn't matter.'

'As you please.' Mr Gwynplaine Dhark drew off a pint of

---

* Possibly something to do with that movie *The Exorcist* and the now legendary line, 'Your mother darns socks in Hell!'

Ssenniug — a pint of white ale with a jet-black head. He presented this to John, who viewed it with suspicion.

'Ssenniug,' explained Mr Gwynplaine Dhark, 'is satanically back-masked Guinness.'.

'Most amusing,' said Omally, parting with a pound note and receiving from it no change.

'You're Mr Omally, aren't you?' said Mr Dhark as Omally was about to make off towards Norman. 'I'm very pleased to meet you.'

The landlord extended his hand for a shake and Omally grudgingly shook it. The landlord's hand was cold and cadaverous. Omally shook the thing with haste. 'I must be on my way.'

'Oh, please stay a while and talk. We don't get many celebrities such as yourself in here, as you can see.'

Omally cast an eye across what clientele there was, which wasn't much, mostly underage youths in black T-shirts and Gothy girls with nose studs.

'I have an appointment,' said John Omally. 'My friend is waiting over there.'

'Waiting for his girlfriend,' said Mr Dhark, 'and for your employer, I understand.'

'You do?' said John.

'Such is what he told me. He was very talkative. Said he'd got something really big off his chest this afternoon and was now prepared to take on the world and all it had to throw at him.'

'Really?' said John, peering once more in Norman's direction. 'And my employer, that would be Mr Pooley you're talking about?'

'Such I believe to be his name — the manager of Brentford United. Do you think you could get me his autograph? I'd ask myself, but I'd be embarrassed — you know how it is.'

Omally, a man who was not wholly averse to employing the occasional untruth should the situation so require, could almost smell the lies that issued from the landlord's mouth.

'I must warn you,' said John, 'that if you have done

anything to harm Mr Pooley, you will have me to reckon with.'

'I have no idea what you're talking about. How's your Ssenniug, by the way?'

Omally took a sip. 'Foul,' said he, replacing his glass upon the counter.

'Thank you, sir,' said Mr Gwynplaine Dhark. 'If it tastes like shit and smells like a rotten corpse, then it's all right with us.'

'Don't forget what I said,' said John. And he stalked across the black-tiled floor to where Norman was sitting in a corner.

'Where is Jim?' John asked.

Norman looked up at John. 'Hello, John,' said he.

'Jim,' said John, 'have you seen him, Norman?'

Norman shook his head. Norman looked rather drunk.

'Have you been drinking?' John asked.

'Silly question, John. I'm sitting in a pub. Wine wears no britches and where there's life there's hope. And if it's a "Road" film, there'll probably be Crosby, too.' Norman tittered foolishly.

'Where is Jim?'

Norman shrugged. 'He hasn't turned up. He was going to give me some moral support, but I don't think I really need it now.'

'So you haven't seen him?'

'I haven't.' Norman shook his head. 'And I'll have to ask you to leave me now, John – Yola is coming over. I have to speak to her in private.'

Omally turned to watch the approach of Yola Bennett. She looked particularly stunning tonight, with heels of the highest persuasion on her thigh-high patent-leather boots. Her leather skirt was scarcely a waistband and her bodice, a black latex corset, gave her the breasts of a Manga babe. Her long blonde hair flowed every which way and she walked with a wiggle and a wowser!

Her handbag was by Vivienne Westwood.

Shampoo by L'Oréal.

Because she was worth it.

John Omally caught his breath. Now that *was* a sight to be seen. Especially the handbag.

'Good evening, John,' said Yola, rolling her tongue about her full red lips. 'We must get together sometime soon.'

'We must,' Omally agreed.

'But for now, piss off, why don't you? I need to speak to Norman.'

'Right,' said John. And he turned back to Norman. 'You really don't know where Jim is?' he asked.

Norman turned up the palms of his hands. 'I haven't seen Jim,' he said.

Omally felt his stomach knotting. 'Where are you, Jim?' said he.

Jim Pooley sat before the bar counter at The Four Horsemen.

Jim was well within his cups and feeling all right with the world.

'I don't know what I've been worrying about,' he told Jack Lane, the octogenarian landlord. 'Everything will be all right, I just know it will.'

'You'll have to speak up,' said the ancient. 'I've misplaced my hearing aid.'

Jim spoke up. 'What was it like?' he asked.

'A pink thing made out of Bakelite.'

'Not your hearing aid. I mean what was it like for you when you captained the Brentford team and led them to victory in nineteen twenty-eight?'

'Ah,' said Jack Lane, 'that. That was real man's soccer back in those days. None of those leaping nancy boys you have now, with their girlie haircuts and earrings. You went out on the pitch and you fought, hammer and tongs. Kicked the bejesus from their shin pads and whacked the bastard ball into the net.'

'You reckon your lot could have taken on a present-day side, then?'

'We'd have made mincemeat of them.'

Pooley chuckled.

'But what about your lot?' said Jack Lane. 'It's bloody Billy Smart's now, your lot.'

'We'll succeed,' said Jim. 'And when we bring the FA Cup back to Brentford, you can put it up on the shelf behind your bar.'

'Do you promise?' asked Jack.

'You have my word,' said Jim.

'Then the next drink is on the house. A half of shandy, wasn't it?'

'It was a *pint*,' said Jim, 'of Large.'

Old Jack Lane squinted up at his clock. 'I thought you told me, when you came in here four hours ago for *a quick one*, that you had a pressing engagement, offering some chum of yours a bit of moral support.'

Jim now squinted up at the clock. 'Norman,' he said. 'Oh dear, I'd quite forgotten about Norman.'

'Norman,' said Yola, seating herself beside Norman on his pew and crossing her legs in a manner so provocative that words are insufficient to describe the erotic effect. 'Norman, aren't you going to buy me a drink?'

'A drink?' said Norman. 'Not in your condition, surely?'

'My condition?'

'Our baby,' said Norman. 'Does it move yet, can I feel it?'

'What?' said Yola.

'It's wonderful news,' said Norman. 'Peg and I are really thrilled.'

'Peg?' said Yola. 'You've told Peg?'

'Of course,' said Norman. 'I tell her everything.'

Yola narrowed her eyes towards Norman. 'Everything?' said she.

'Absolutely,' said Norman. 'A boy's best friend is his mother, but a wife can do things a mother cannot. She's very thrilled. You see, she and I could never have any kiddies. She's got something amiss with her internal workings caused by an overintake of pies, possibly. But she's keen to adopt. And if you're not keen on that, then you're welcome to come and live with us at the shop. You'll enjoy working there, it will be a bit like working for Mr Gray, except you won't have your own desk.'

Yola made a disgruntled face. 'Work in your shop?' said she. 'Are you mad?'

'Mad?' said Norman. 'Why do you say that?'

'Because you have twenty-three million pounds coming to you tomorrow. You surely weren't thinking of keeping your shop. Or, indeed, your wife.'

'It's really Peg's shop,' said Norman. 'She made me sign one of those prenuptial agreements.'

'But the twenty-three million is yours?'

'Seemingly not,' said Norman. 'What's mine is hers and what's hers is her own, apparently.'

Yola looked deeply into the eyes of Norman. 'Ah,' she said. 'Nice try, Norman, you almost had me believing you.'

'Excuse me?' said Norman.

'I said "nice try". Who put you up to this? Was it John Omally?' Yola glanced about the bar, but John Omally had gone.

'No one put me up to anything,' said Norman.

'You're a very sad little man.'

'Excuse me once more,' said Norman.

Outside thunder crashed and lightning flashed and the rain fell down in torrents. Jim Pooley peered out from the porch of Jack Lane's pub. 'It will lift in a minute,' said Jim to himself, 'and then I'll be on my way to offer my moral support to Norman.'

'Norman,' said Yola, 'there's someone here to see you.'

'Who?' said Norman. 'I don't understand.'

Mr Richard Gray smiled down upon Norman. 'Good evening to you,' he said.

'Oh,' said Norman, looking up to take stock of the man

in the long, dark coat with the astrakhan collar. 'Mr Gray, I didn't see you coming.'

'Really?' said Mr Gray, seating himself opposite Norman and placing a pint of Ssenniug before him on the table. 'Mr Omally left this at the bar upon his departure. A shame to let it go to waste.'

'What is going on here?' Norman asked.

'Business,' said Mr Richard Gray. 'Strictly business. You should have taken the deal I offered you when you came into my office and showed me the contract for your patents.'

'Oh that,' said Norman. 'Well, *that* doesn't matter anymore.'

'It matters,' said Mr Richard Gray. 'Believe you me, it matters.'

'It doesn't,' said Norman, 'because after the match tomorrow there won't be any patents any more, nor will there be any money.'

'He's lying,' said Yola. 'He just told me a pack of lies and now he's telling more.'

'I'm not,' said Norman. 'Well, perhaps I was a bit before, but I'm not now. I did a very bad thing. Those weren't really my patents – I discovered the technology on an antique computer system. This friend of mine thought they'd been destroyed when he destroyed my computer, but they hadn't because I'd already patented them in my own name and sold the rights – to a very, very bad man, it seems, who will do terrible things if he has them.'

'Mr William Starling,' said Mr Richard Gray. And the whites of his eyes turned horribly black and these black eyes gazed upon Norman.

'But it's all going to be sorted,' said Norman, 'after my friend and I have been to the match at Wembley tomorrow. Apparently he's booked seats in the executive box. At my expense, apparently, but that doesn't matter. But what does matter is that after the match he is going to go, er, *back* and sort out all the business with the patents. Everything is going to work out fine.'

'Mad,' said Yola. 'He's as mad as a drawerful of jewellery.'

'A drawerful of jewellery?' said Norman. 'I've never heard that one before.'

Mr Richard Gray pulled an envelope from the pocket of his long, dark coat with the astrakhan collar and pushed it across the table towards Norman.

'What's this?' Norman asked.

'Open it,' said Mr Richard Gray.

Norman opened the envelope and read its contents. 'It's a Last Will and Testament,' said Norman. 'It's a Last Will and Testament made out in my name.'

'Read it aloud,' said Mr Richard Gray.

Norman read it aloud. ' "This is to testify that I, Norman Hartnel, not to be confused with the other Norman Hartnel, being of sound mind, do hereby bequeath my worldly goods as follows:

"To Yola Sarah Hopkins Bennett of Thirteen Willow Cottages, Kew, the sum of £12,500,000. And to Mr Richard Gray of Eighty-two The Butts Estate, Brentford, the sum of £12,500,000 and all further income deriving from the rights upon any patents that exist in my name.

"Signed . . ." '

Norman looked up at Mr Richard Gray.

'You want me to sign *this*?' he said.

Mr Richard Gray took out his fountain pen and handed it to Norman. 'Now, if you will,' said he.

'But I've told you,' said Norman, 'there won't *be* any money.'

'Then where's the harm in signing it?'

Norman looked into the eyes of Mr Richard Gray and saw there only darkness.

'I don't feel comfortable with this,' said Norman. 'And wills have to be witnessed.'

'The landlord will witness it,' said Mr Gray.

'I'll have to think about it,' said Norman.

'But I insist that you sign it now.'

'I'm leaving,' said Norman, and he made to rise, but to his horror found that he could not.

'I'm incapacitated,' said Norman. 'My knees won't work at all.'

'Sign the will,' said Mr Richard Gray.

'It will soon lift,' said Pooley, sheltering still beneath the porch. 'It's a goodly storm, but it *will* lift.'

'Lift the pen and sign your name,' said Mr Richard Gray.

'But there won't *be* any money,' repeated Norman, 'I told you. What have you done to my legs? You've done something terrible to them.'

'They'll lift you up once you've signed.'

'All right,' said Norman. 'I'll sign.' And he did so without a flourish. 'Happy now? And can I please go home?'

'Home?' said Mr Richard Gray. 'Home?'

'Home,' said Norman. 'I do have a home to go to. Home is where the heart is and there's no place like home.'

Mr Richard Gray laughed hideously and, to Norman's further horror as he looked upon the solicitor's teeth, he saw that they were now as dead dark black as Mr Gray's coal-like peepers.

'There's no going home for you,' said Mr Richard Gray. 'A will is nothing more than a piece of paper until the man who signed it is dead. And tonight, Mr Hartnel, you are going to die.'

'Yola.' Norman turned to the woman beside him. 'Yola, do something – this man is a monster. Yola, you can't let this happen.'

But Yola's eyes were now also black. And so, too, were her breasts.

'Time, gentlemen, please,' called Jack Lane. 'And Pooley, I can still see your shadow on the glass of my door. Get off into the rain and offer your friend your moral support.'

'Time, gentlemen, please,' called Mr Gwynplaine Dhark

and, approaching Norman's table, he added, 'Where would you like me to put my signature, Mr Gray?'

'Time, gentlemen, please.' Omally heard the words called out by the barman of The Shrunken Head. Jim wasn't in there either, and John set out once more into the storm.

'Let me go,' begged Norman. 'I've signed the will. You never know, I might die a natural death in my sleep tonight. It could happen. Death keeps no calendar, you know.'

'Up,' said Mr Richard Gray. 'Your knees will work for you now. Up, we have places to go.'

'What places?' Norman asked.

'The canal,' said Mr Richard Gray. 'We'll take a walk to the canal. You're going to have a tragic accident.'

'No,' begged Norman. 'No. Won't somebody help me, please?' And he shouted out 'Help!' at the top of his voice. But The Beelzepub was now empty.

Empty, that is, but for Norman, Yola, Richard Gray and Gwynplaine Dhark, the landlord.

'Take him out,' said Gwynplaine Dhark, 'and do what must be done.'

'No,' begged Norman. 'No!'

But Yola dragged him from his seat with a most unnatural strength and propelled Norman in the direction of the door.

'Help me!' wailed Norman. 'Won't somebody help me? Somebody help me, please!'

'There's no help for you,' said Gwynplaine Dhark, pulling open the door and holding it so.

Rain lashed down beyond, exploding all over the street. Thunder groaned above in a sky that the lightning tore apart.

Jim Pooley's face peered in from the maelstrom. 'Is Norman still here?' he asked.

39

Gwynplaine Dhark tried to slam shut the door, but Jim put his shoulder to it. There was something of a struggle, but presently Pooley prevailed.

The landlord stood back, breathing heavily. Jim stood in the doorway, viewing the tableau before him. Norman stood trembling, held in the grip, it seemed, of a woman who had surely stepped out from the glossy pages of one of the racier publications that filled Norman's uppermost shop shelves. And to the other side of Norman stood a man in a long, dark coat whose face was all over black.

Jim Pooley blinked at this tableau. The word 'out-numbered' entered his thoughts.

'Norman,' said Jim. 'Norman, are you all right?'

'I'm not,' said Norman, struggling to no avail. 'These lunatics are going to drown me in the canal.'

'That's not very nice,' said Jim. 'I think you'd better come with me.'

'I think *not*.' Gwynplaine Dhark did gesturings.

The door of The Beelzepub slammed shut behind Jim with a death-cell finality.

'Now, let's not do anything silly,' said Jim.

'Luck indeed.' Mr Gwynplaine Dhark rubbed his clammy palms together. 'Two birds with one stone, as it were – the moneyman and the manager of Brentford United. My master was forced to take a magical oath not to harm you.'

'*Your* master?' said Jim.

'William Starling,' said Mr Gwynplaine Dhark. 'I have been his man from the start. If your friend Neville had not put his spoke in at the council meeting, the football ground and what lies beneath it would already be in the hands of my master.'

'This is new,' said Norman. 'What is this all about?'

'Unfinished business,' said Mr Dhark, 'but it will be finished tonight.'

'Your master took the oath,' said Jim. 'You cannot harm me.'

'But this man is your friend,' said Mr Dhark, pointing a pale finger towards Norman. 'What would you do to protect your friend from certain death?'

'Whatever I could,' said Jim. 'And whatever I can.'

'Even if it were to cost you your own life?'

'Oh, I don't think it will come to that.'

Rain lashed in once more through the once-more-open doorway. An open doorway in which now stood John Omally.

'You!' said Gwynplaine Dhark.

'Me,' said John Omally. 'I came back. I knew Jim would not let down a friend, even though he might be a bit late. Jim is a good man, you see, although you'd know nothing of that.'

'Pleased to see you, John,' said Jim. 'Norman and I were just leaving.'

'No,' said Gwynplaine Dhark. 'Nobody leaves. Alive, that is.'

'Remember your magical oath,' said John. 'It must not be broken.'

'I just mentioned that,' said Jim.

Lightning struck home near to The Beelzepub and the bar's windows rattled in their mullions and the brightness cast shadows that were blacker than the walls.

'A dilemma,' said Mr Dhark. 'But you all must surely die.'

'We're leaving,' said Jim. 'Come, Norman.'

'You will find,' said Mr Dhark, 'that the door will not open. In fact, you will find that there's no door there at all.'

Norman looked and John looked and Jim Pooley, he

looked, too. And where the door to the street had just been, there was now but an empty wall.

'It all ends here,' said Gwynplaine Dhark.

'The oath,' said Jim. 'The oath.'

'The oath,' said Mr Dhark. 'And the threefold law of return, wherein a magical calling misdirected returns against the sender with thrice the power to destroy him.'

'Such is the power of the oath,' said Omally. 'The professor explained it to me. Your master dare not break it, or threefold will the power return to destroy him.'

'Under normal conditions, yes,' said Mr Dhark.

'*Normal* conditions?' said John. 'Nothing is particularly Norman about magic.'

'Did you mean to say "Norman"?' said Norman. 'No, *I'm* confused now.'

'What night is this?' asked Mr Dhark.

'Friday night,' said Omally. 'Friday the thirteenth of May.'

'The night before the FA Cup Final, and the very Eve of the Apocalypse. And a significant night in the magical calendar. It is the feast of *Corpus Negrum*, the night of the Black Sabbat, second only to Walpurgis night, but more powerful in that it is the night of the magical reversal, when those normal conditions I mentioned earlier no longer apply.'

'What?' said John.

'I don't like this,' said Jim.

'I'm sorry,' said Mr Gray, 'but I regret to inform you that you have walked into a trap. A carefully laid trap, one that relied upon friendship. That Norman here would turn to a friend – you, Mr Pooley – and that you in turn would have a friend who cared deeply for you and would follow you into this trap. Tonight the three of you die and the winner, my master, takes all.'

Beyond the walls, the storm seemed infernal.

Within the walls, matters seemed none too hopeful.

'Kill them all,' said Mr Gwynplaine Dhark. 'And leave me only their skulls for my counter.'

'No!' cried Norman. 'Have mercy, don't kill us.'

John Omally raised his fists.

Jim Pooley flapped his hands about and began to turn in small circles.

And then the red lights dimmed to black and horrible slaughter began.

40

Professor Slocombe clapped his hands. 'Let there be light!' he commanded.

Light flooded The Beelzepub, dazzling radiant light. The would-be murderers of John, Jim and Norman fell back before it.

The professor stood in the doorway. The Campbell stood at his side.

'Slay them,' said Professor Slocombe. 'The two men and the woman also.'

'The woman also?' said the Campbell.

'The evil inhabits her now. There is nothing I can do.'

The Campbell raised his claymore high.

More horrible slaughter began.

41

Jim Pooley awoke from a nightmare that involved horrible slaughter. Jim yawned and stretched and did easings into consciousness. And then Jim felt knottings in his stomach regions and lay, staring up at his bedroom ceiling.

He had just dreamed all that, hadn't he?

All that hideous stuff?

Jim issued forth from beneath his duvet*, swung his legs down to the floor and cradled his face in his hands.

What *had* happened last night? His memory failed him.

How much *had* he drunk?

Memories came drifting back to Jim. Well, not so much drifting as elbowing brutishly in. Jim shook his head fiercely, torn between trying to remember and hoping that he never would.

'John,' said Jim, and, 'Norman.'

But he recalled that his two friends had also survived unhurt. 'I'm really fed up with all this,' grumbled Jim. 'I wish it was all over.'

In the not-too-far distance, the bells of St Joan's Church clock struck nine and Jim took deep and steadying breaths and sought to prepare himself mentally for the big day that lay ahead.

The big FA Cup Final day when Brentford would meet Manchester United upon the hallowed turf of Wembley.

Jim Pooley's hands began to shake. He couldn't do this, he really couldn't. The responsibility was all too much. Best to do a runner now, slip away, come back when it was all

---

* The one with the A Team-patterned cover.

377

over with a tale about losing his memory. That would be for the best. No one would hate him for that.

'I know what you're thinking,' said John Omally, 'so please stop thinking it right now.'

Jim turned in considerable surprise. 'John,' he said, 'what are *you* doing here?'

'I slept the night upon that instrument of torture which passes for a sofa in your sitting room cum dining room cum why-do-you-never-dust-it!'

'Oh,' said Jim. 'I don't remember. My thoughts are all confused.'

'Well,' said John, flexing and clicking his shoulders and doing stretchings of the neck. 'On with your lucky suit, Bertie, we have a match to win.'

Jim surveyed the lucky suit that hung from the mantel-shelf on its hanger. 'I really don't want to do this,' he said.

'I know you don't, and who can blame you? But it's all going to come to an end today, one way or the other. And if it goes our way, which I have every confidence that it will, you and I will be wealthy men. You still have the betting slip, I trust?'

Jim's hand slipped under his pillow and found the betting slip. 'He'll never pay up,' he said.

'He'll pay,' said John. 'The professor will see to that.'

'And if any harm comes to the professor?'

'No harm will come to him. Now pack it in, Jim, tog up in your tweeds and I'll treat you to breakfast at The Plume.'

Norman took breakfast at Madame Loretta Rune's in the company of Mr H.G. Wells and an ill-washed youth named Winston.

Crockery tinkled with the tune of the knife and the fork. Polite conversation was to be heard between Japanese tourists come to view the wonders of Brentford, a salesman travelling in tobaccos and ready-rolled cigarettes, a heavy-metal rock band, Stub'n, whose tour bus had broken down on the flyover, and a pair of teenage runaways who were making their way to Gretna Green. All in all, your usual group of b. & b. clients, with the possible exception of those at Norman's table.

'So they nearly topped ya, gov'nor,' said young Winston, tucking into bacon, eggs, fried bread and tomatoes, all at the very same time. 'The Dark One's 'enchmen. Nearly 'ad your liver and lights.'

'It was close,' said Norman, 'and very scary indeed.'

Mr Wells made *tut-tut-tuttings*. 'You have no one to blame but yourself,' said he.

'I know,' said Norman. 'I know. But you will be able to sort it all out, won't you?'

Mr Wells did noddings of the head.

'And you will stay to watch the match before you travel off through time? We can drive there in my van, take the Time Machine with us in the back. I have seats in the executive box – bought them from Omally, cost me a fortune – but I'd love you to be there. My treat. My way of saying thanks for everything.'

'It will be a pleasure,' said Mr Wells. 'I've become quite a – what is the word? – fan of Brentford United over the last few months. Do you really think they are going to win?'

'I'm quietly confident,' said Norman. 'Fate leads the willing, but drives the stubborn.'

'You're a rare 'n, gov'nor,' said Winston. 'Gawd pulp me pud if you ain't.'

'It ain't rocket science,' said Pippa, fluttering her eyelashes and trying to pay attention.

'It's very important,' Neville told her. 'Changing a barrel correctly, it's an art.'

Neville stood with Pippa and Loz in the cellar of The Flying Swan. 'I don't want anything to go wrong, it's very important to me,' said the part-time barman.

'Nothing will go wrong, Nevvy.' Loz stroked Neville's cheek. 'And you'll only be away for a few hours and most of Brentford will be at the match with you. There won't be much custom anyway.'

'But I've never done anything like this before,' said Neville.

'What, been to a football match?'

'Actually, no. But I mean I've never missed a lunchtime session.'

'You go and enjoy yourself,' said Loz. 'Cheer the team on.'

'It's something I just don't want to miss,' said Neville. 'Brentford haven't played at Wembley since nineteen twenty-eight, when Jack Lane, who now runs The Four Horsemen, led them to victory. I doubt it will ever happen again.'

'You go,' said Pippa. 'Have a good time. Bring us back some candyfloss or something.'

'Thank you,' said Neville, and he put his arms about the shoulders of Pippa and Loz and kissed each one in turn upon the cheek. 'Keep the champagne on ice,' he said. 'I think this is going to be a day that all of us will remember.'

'Now remember, Jim,' said Omally as he and Pooley munched their breakfast in The Plume Café, 'you must show no sign of your nerves to the team. They'll be nervous enough as it is. You must display supreme confidence, spur them on to victory.'

'I'll do my best,' said Jim, forking a sausage into his gob.

'Oh, and this is for you. I picked it up from your doormat when we left your place.' Omally delved into his pocket and brought out an envelope, which he handed to Jim.

Jim looked the envelope over. 'The professor's handwriting,' he said. ' "For the attention of James Pooley. Not to be opened until five minutes before the match." It will be the tactics for the game. Should I open it now, do you think?'

'Go on, then,' said John. 'Let's have a look.'

Pooley dug his thumbs into the corner of the envelope's flap and sought to tear it open, but the envelope remained intact. 'That's odd,' said Jim, applying further force. Jim wrestled with the envelope, but only succeeded in nearly taking a thumbnail off.

'Use your knife,' said John.

'But it's all eggy.'

'Use your knife.'

Jim now dug at the envelope with his eggy knife and attempted to slit it, but the knife merely skidded away and nearly took off his other thumbnail.

'Give it here,' said Omally. 'You're like an old woman, you.'

Jim sucked upon his wounded thumbs. 'It won't be opened,' said he.

'Of course it will.' John took the envelope between both hands, put it across his knee and tried to tear it in half, after the manner of those fellows who do the trick with telephone directories (although not so much these days, as the practice seems to have gone out of fashion. Like the Yo-Yo, or the Scooby Doo. Not to mention the Rubic's Cube.)

Nobody mentioned the Rubic's Cube.

'It's giving,' said John. But it wasn't.

'I almost have it,' said John, the veins on his neck standing out.

But he didn't.

John Omally took off his jacket, rolled up his sleeves and made an all-out assault on the envelope. He bit at it and ripped at it, he went down on his knees and he wrestled with it. But the envelope remained adamant. The envelope wouldn't open.

Lil leaned over her counter top. 'Is he having an epileptic fit?' she asked.

'Trying to open the mail,' said Jim.

'Shrink-wrapped, is it?' said Lil. 'I have certain lady's things that arrive in the post, shrink-wrapped. I generally give them a little toasting over the hob to soften them up. Not that I want them soft, if you know what I mean.'

Jim didn't.

Omally was now jumping up and down on the envelope.

Jim Pooley watched him at it and Jim began to laugh.

'It's no laughing matter,' said John. 'I won't be defeated by a damned envelope.'

'You will,' said Jim. 'You will, don't you see?'

John turned a sweaty face towards Jim. 'See what?' he asked.

'The professor,' said Jim. 'He knew we'd try to open it, and he knew what frame of mind *I'd* be in. It's his magic, John. It won't be possible to open the envelope until five minutes before the match. He did this to show us his power, John, and, in turn, to boost our confidence.'

'And you came to this conclusion all on your own?'

'I suppose I did,' said Jim. 'I suggest that we finish our breakfasts and head off to Griffin Park.'

John picked up the envelope from the floor. For all of his stompings, it wasn't even besmutted.

John handed the envelope to Jim. 'Ready for the challenge, then?' he asked.

'Brentford for the Cup,' said Jim. 'Brentford for the Cup.'

And Brentford looked festive upon this May morn. Bunting hung between lampposts all the way up the high street, union flags fluttered from upper storeys and colour photographs of Jim's grinning face, taken from the centrefold of the day's *Brentford Mercury Special FA Cup Final Edition*, were displayed in many shop windows. The sun beamed its blessings down upon the borough and it was as if the storm and the horrible doings of the night before had never occurred at all. A crowd had already gathered outside Griffin Park, and this crowd, which seemed for the most part composed of fellows wearing reproduction team kaftans and young girlies wearing fetching versions of Jim's lucky suit, cheered loudly as John and Jim approached.

'Big warm welcome,' whispered John. 'Smiles all round and lots of confidence.'

Jim Pooley beamed smiles all around, had his picture taken and signed autographs.

'Can you tell us anything about the tactics you mean to employ?' asked Scoop Molloy.

'No,' said Jim. 'Strictly confidential, but I'll tell you this.' And Jim whispered words into Scoop's small-and-shell-like: 'Stay away from Norman's wife,' whispered Jim, 'or I'll have the whole team come around to your house and use you for a practice ball.'

'Thank you very much, Mr Pooley,' said Scoop. 'And very good luck today.'

The crowd cheered on. Jim signed more autographs and then he and John entered the ground. The Campbell locked the gates behind them.

'Are the both of ye well?' he asked.

'We are,' said Omally.

Jim Pooley nodded. 'About last night,' said he.

'Speak no more about it,' said the Campbell. 'Press on with what must be done.'

'Are the players all here?' Omally asked.

'Players?' said the Campbell. 'I suppose so, if you care to call them that.'

John and Jim entered The Stripes Bar and beheld the players, who were starting the day with a swift pint to get themselves going.

'Now, now,' said Jim, 'you shouldn't be drinking. Remember The Slaughtered Lamb?' Those who had been there remembered, those who hadn't did not. 'Just the one, then,' said Jim. 'And plenty of crisps for protein. Where is Ernest Muffler?'

Barry Bustard puffed in Jim's direction. 'He's not here and nor is Dave Quimsby.'

'So where are they?'

'No one knows. Big Bob called to pick them up, but they'd gone.'

'Bottle job,' said Omally. 'Just like the rest of them.'

Jim Pooley made the face of alarm. 'We don't have a full team, then,' said Jim.

'We do,' said Barry. 'Meet Bobo and Zippy.'

Bobo and Zippy presented themselves.

Jim shook hands with Bobo and Zippy. 'A clown,' said Jim, 'and a pinhead. We're d—'

'*Delighted*,' said John. 'Delighted to make your acquaintance. Thank you for stepping into the breach at the last moment.'

Jim took John aside. 'This is a disaster,' he said. 'We now have a team composed entirely of circus performers. Not a single member of the original team remains. We have a clown as centre forward. This is a mockery of the beautiful game.'

'It's unorthodox, I agree,' said John. 'Do you have any other suggestions?'

'I seem to recall going on and on at you over the last few months about buying in new players.'

'With what? We're broke. And with all those damages claims against us and—'

'What damages claims?'

'Nothing,' said John. 'Shall we have a pint before we set off?'

'Ludicrous,' said Jim, throwing up his hands. 'This is all totally ludicrous. A team of circus performers taking on the most famous football club in the world. I can't see how even the professor's magic is going to get us through this.'

'Jim,' said John. 'Jim, you are my bestest friend and I love you dearly, but if I hear one more pessimistic word come out of your mouth, I swear that I will remodel your beak with my fist.'

'I'm quietly confident,' said Jim.

'Boss,' said Jon Bon Julie, the half-man, half-woman and centre mid-fielder to boot since Alf Snatcher had gone missing before the Arsenal game. 'Sorry to interrupt you, but Bobo wanted me to ask – is it okay if he sits upstairs on the bus above the driver and stomps his big boots until the driver comes up and threatens to chuck him off?'

Big Bob Charker sat in his driving seat, *brrming* the engine of the great big bus. The great big bus looked splendid. It had been resprayed in the team's colours at Big Bob's own expense. Bunting hung along its sides and Big Bob himself had put aside his normal cap in favour of a woolly bobble hat knitted in the team colours by the mother who loved him. As Jim led the team towards the big bus, the crowd beyond the gates cheered wildly. Big Bob smiled to himself.

Professor Slocombe wasn't smiling. The professor's face was grave. Before him in his study, to either side of the fireplace, sat Terrence Jehovah Smithers and the Second Sponge Boy.

'The time is upon us,' the professor said. 'Today what must be done, must be done. After the events of last night, I implore you to be on your guard.'

'You will be attending the match?' said Terrence.

'I must,' said the professor. 'Our adversary will be there, that is for certain. If I fail to make an appearance, he might suspect my plans.'

'I wish I was going,' said Sponge Boy. 'Seeing Man U getting its arse kicked is always a joy to us Southern boys.'

'I've set the video,' said Terrence. 'We'll watch it this evening. Assuming—'

'That you survive?' asked the professor.

'Something like that, yes.'

'But you trust me?'

'Of course we trust you, Master,' said Terrence.

'Then follow the plan to the letter and all will be well. The team bus will arrive shortly to pick me up. When I have gone, go at once to Griffin Park. The Campbell will be waiting for you. He will arm you as necessary and at the time agreed you will proceed to the Consortium building and lay waste to it and the evil that dwells within. There should be no loss of innocent life, as all the streets will be deserted. All eyes on the match, as it were.'

'You said that the Campbell will *arm* us,' said Sponge Boy. 'Will we be having big guns?'

'You will,' said the professor. 'I have arranged for certain munitions to be made available to you.'

'Uzis?' said Terrence, miming the use of an Uzi. 'Will we have Uzis?'

'Kalashnikovs,' said Sponge Boy. 'Kalashnikovs are better than Uzis.'

'No,' said the professor. 'You will have neither Uzis nor kalashnikovs.'

'Aw,' went Terrence.

'Shame,' said Sponge Boy.

'No,' said the professor. 'I have ordered for each of you a 7.62mm M134 General Clockwork mini-gun.'

'A 7.62mm M134 General Clockwork mini-gun,' said Dave Quimsby.

'A what?' asked Jim Pooley.

'It's a rotary machine gun,' Dave explained. 'I just over-heard someone talking about it. Perhaps it's a link, or a continuity thing, or something.'

'It would be very poor continuity, then,' said Jim, 'because you're not even on the bus with us.'

'Oh yes,' said Dave. 'You're right.' And he vanished away.

Omally nudged Jim's elbow. 'You look like you're in a trance,' said he. 'What are you thinking about?'

Jim stirred from his reverie. 'Guns, for some reason,' said he. 'I hope that's not a bad omen.'

The big bus stopped outside Professor Slocombe's home and Big Bob left his cab to help the ancient aboard.

'Morning, sir,' called Omally.

'Going upstairs?' asked Jim.

'I've my best boots on, John. I thought I'd get in some stomping over Big Bob's head.' Professor Slocombe went upstairs and evicted Bobo from his seat.

The great big bus set off towards Wembley.

'Something very bad happened last night,' said Jim. 'I think I should go upstairs and talk to the professor about it.'

'Let it be, Jim,' said John. 'Just concentrate upon victory. We're on the road to Wembley.'

Now, Bob and Bing never starred in *The Road to Wembley*. And it had been a good many decades since a Brentford team had. But the sun shone down on Big Bob's bus and at length the great stadium appeared on the skyline in all its Art Deco splendour.

'Would you look at *that*,' said Omally.

'Now *that is big*,' said Jim.

'And I understand that there are plans to pull it down, too. So Heaven knows what biblical nasties might lie beneath that one.'

'You're supposed to be cheering me up,' said Jim.

'True,' said John. And he called out to the team, 'Let's sing the team song, lads.'

'Team song?' said Jim.

'Team song,' said John. 'It's an oldey but goody.'

And the team sang 'Knees Up, Mother Earth'.

42

Neville had purchased a reproduction Brentford United team kaftan, and he did not look out of place as he sat in one of the many coaches that had been chartered to ferry plucky Brentonians to the match. Neville sat down next to Small Dave, the postman, and waved a greeting to Archroy, Soap Distant, Old Pete, Councillor Doveston, Jack Lane and Bob the Bookie (who had come along hoping to watch a crushing defeat of the local team).

All and sundry set off upon the Road to Wembley, leaving most of Brentford and Chiswick deserted.

Wembley was far from deserted. Thousands streamed towards the stadium, vast legions in the colours of Manchester United, but many also in those of Brentford. For say what you will and say it how you'll say it, this glorious nation of ours loves an underdog.

John and Jim were on the top deck of the big bus now, up at the front with the professor. The entire team was up there also, waving to the crowds. Below, Big Bob clung on to the steering wheel. 'Maketh Barry Bustard and Long John Watson sit down!' he shouted up to Jim. 'Or they'll have the bus over. Verily and so.'

The crowds before the stadium parted before the big bus and Wembley's Scottish groundskeeper waved it into the special enclosure reserved exclusively for big team buses. And from there he led Jim, John, Big Bob, the professor and the team towards and to the changing rooms.

'Cocktails will be served shortly,' said he, in an accent of the Glaswegian persuasion. 'Then the *chef de cuisine* will call in with the menu for lunch. Might I recommend the salmon *en croûte* and the filet mignon *Americus*. They go down a treat with a chilled Chablis.'

'How swank is *this*?' said Omally, gazing all around and about at the swankness of the changing rooms. They had recently been done out by a Mr Laurence Llewelyn-Bowen in the style of one of the *Titanic*'s upper decks, with steamer chairs and portholes, quoits and lifebelts and the ceiling painted all sky-blue, with cotton-wool clouds stuck to it. Rod Stewart's voice sang 'We Are Sailing' through hidden speakers and stuffed seagulls hung on nylon cords from the sky-blue ceiling above.

'A jungle theme,' said Jim. 'Nice.'

'And if you and your entourage will follow me, Mr Pooley,' the groundskeeper continued, 'I'll lead you to where all the big knobs hang out.'

'The toilets?' said Jim.

The Scottish groundskeeper shook his tam-o'-shantered head. Indulgently. 'Most amusing, Mr Pooley. I refer, of course, to the executive suite.'

'Of course you do,' said Jim. 'Lead on.'

It was a bit like a film première. Not that Jim had ever been to a film première, but he had never seen so many famous people all together in one room at the same time. In fact, Jim had hardly ever seen any famous people at all, aside from some that he hadn't recognised who had been pointed out to him during his visit to Stringfellow's.

'Hello again, Jim,' said Peter Stringfellow, admiring Jim's suit and shaking its owner by the hand. 'Looking forward to the match?'

'Certainly am,' said Jim.

'Is that Irishman with you?' Peter asked. 'That one who went off with two of my pole-dancers?'

'He's over there,' said Jim, 'chatting with Catherine Zeta-Jones.'

'I'll go and warn Michael Douglas, then.' Peter left Jim to shake other hands.

And the first of these was a royal one.

'Mr Pooley,' said Prince Charles, 'what an honour to meet you.'

Jim blinked his eyes. 'You're wearing—'

'A suit like your own,' said the prince. 'Had my chap in Savile Row run it up for me. Have you met my sons?'

Jim shook further royal hands. And admired the matching suits.

'Could I have your autograph?' asked Prince Harry.

Jim made his way to the bar, where he ordered a large, stiff drink. A hand fell on his shoulder and Jim turned to find himself looking up into the face of a tall, slim, well-dressed fellow with a head of blondy hair.

'You have come a long way, Mr Pooley,' said this fellow.

'We haven't been introduced,' said Jim.

'No, we haven't, but I know you well.' The fellow put out his hand for a shake and Jim Pooley shook it. And then Jim Pooley shivered. 'Your hand . . .' said Jim.

'A tad cold,' said the fellow. 'Poor circulation. Would you care to step outside with me for a moment? There are certain pressing matters that I must discuss with you.'

Jim blew warmth on to his fingers and rubbed them on his tweedy plus-foured trouser leg. There was something very wrong about this tall, slim, blondy-haired fellow, something decidedly—

Jim shivered once again—

Decidedly evil.

'Well . . .' Jim said.

'I don't think that would be a good idea.' Professor Slocombe smiled towards Jim. 'In case you haven't been introduced, this is Mr William Starling.'

Jim drew back – drew back, in fact, to a point that was somewhat to the rear of the professor.

'Fear not, Jim,' said Professor Slocombe. 'He will not harm you. His moment has passed.'

'My *moment* has yet to come.' William Starling glared at the professor. His eyes shone glossy black and darkness appeared to form all about him.

Prince Charles said to Harry, 'Your granny used to do that.'

'Rather public for this kind of thing, don't you think?' The professor smiled on, placidly. Starling didn't smile back.

'I now own the opposing team,' said Starling. 'This is one game that you will *not* win.'

'We shall see,' said the professor.

Starling leaned close to Professor Slocombe. 'You have caused me a considerable amount of inconvenience,' he snarled, his voice a harsh and rasping whisper, 'but today comes the reckoning. When the final whistle blows, Griffin Park will be mine and, by tomorrow, all the world.'

The professor smiled on. 'We shall see,' was all he had to say.

Starling glared, turned and stalked away. Upon reaching the doorway, he slipped upon a banana skin that appeared to have simply materialised and fell heavily to the plushly carpeted floor.

Jim looked at the professor.

'Whoops,' said that man.

'Hoops,' said Barry Bustard to the waiter in the sharp black suit. 'I ordered spaghetti hoops.'

The team were tucking into their lunches in a swanky luncheon area. They sat at a long luncheon table; the Manchester United team sat nearby at another. The Manchester United team's luncheon, however, kept being interrupted by members of the Brentford team asking them for autographs.

And it did have to be said that the Man U lads were finding it rather hard to keep straight faces, because for all of Brentford's wondrous rising through the Cup qualifiers, the thought of playing the FA Cup Final against a team composed entirely of circus performers – well!

'Well,' said Professor Slocombe. 'Doesn't time fly. It's half-past two already.'

Jim had just returned from the toilet, where he had made the latest of many trips.

'All right now?' the professor asked.

'I can't keep my lunch down,' said Jim. 'The quails' knees in Canaletto sauce have done for me.'

'Courage, Jim,' said the elder. 'We will prevail. Now best you go down to the changing rooms and give the team one of your inspirational pep talks.'

'But I can't think of anything to say.'

'You will.' Professor Slocombe patted Jim's shoulder. 'Believe me, you will.'

The team sat in the changing rooms and the team looked most uncomfortable.

'What's up?' Jim asked. 'You all look a bit down. You didn't eat the quails' knees, did you?'

Long John Watson raised a mighty hand. 'Boss,' he said, 'Boss, they laughed at us.'

'Who laughed?' Jim asked.

'The Man U team, they mocked us.'

'Ah,' said Jim. 'Take no notice of that. That is what they call a psychological tactic – psyching out the other team. I've read about that.'

'But they're right,' said Barry Bustard, tucking into a bargain bucket of something highly calorific. 'We can't play against *them*. They're a *real* team.'

'All the other teams you've played against have been real teams, and we've won every match.'

'But this is Wembley, Boss. Wembley is, well, sacred. We won by luck, by flukes, or by something,' said Barry.

'And we'll win this.'

'No we won't, Boss. This is *real*.'

Jim sighed. He knew exactly what Barry meant. This was well and truly real. 'No, wait,' said Jim. 'I have this,' and he pulled out the professor's envelope. 'Today's tactics.'

'What?' said Loup-Gary Thompson. '*Now? Nooooooooo-oooooow?*'

'Easy on the wolf calls,' said Barry. 'But do you mean now, Boss? With no practising?'

'Trust me.' Jim put his thumbnail to the envelope. It shredded like rice paper. Jim unfolded the missive and read aloud from it.

' "The show must go on," ' he read.

Jim paused and reread this, silently and to himself, then turned over the parchment sheet. The other side was empty of words. Jim turned the sheet back over and read it silently once more.

'The show must go on,' said Admiral Theodore Peanut, the thirty-inch-high right mid-fielder.

'The show must go on,' said Clarence Henry, frog-boy and mid-fielder.

And the words were passed from fellow to fellow. And 'Ah,' said Jon Bon Julie, the half-man, half-woman centre-half. 'The show must go on, I see.'

'You do?' asked Jim.

'Of course,' said Long John Watson, whose head was on high amongst the stuffed seagulls. 'You know what he means, lads, don't you?'

Blank faces slowly became those of the enlightened.

'The show must go on,' said Bobo, juggling three half-time oranges. 'It's a masterstroke. It's inspired.'

'Ah yes. Ah yes.' Heads began to nod. And voices turned into cheers.

Jim did gawpings all around. 'The show must go on,' he said. Blankly.

'You're a genius, Boss,' said the human half of Humphrey Hampton. 'That is the one thing that every performer understands – the sacred code of the performer. We won't let you down.'

'I'm so pleased,' said Jim.

'And the modesty of the man,' said Don to Phil. 'Coming up with something like that and not even wanting to take the credit.'

'The man's a saint,' said Phil. 'The show must go on.'

And Don and Phil cheered heartily, and so did the rest of the team.

Pooley shook his head and all manner of hands. 'Good, because you're on in two minutes. I just have to use the toilet.'

Professor Slocombe awaited Jim outside, in the corridor.

'How went the pep talk?' he asked.

'The show must go on,' said Jim.

'Then all will be well. And Jim?'

'Yes, Professor?'

'We *will* succeed.'

Jim Pooley went off to the toilet.

John Omally sat upon the turf-side bench, in the dugout (as it is oft-times called) that was reserved for the Brentford team. Beside him sat Big Bob.

'Verily I say unto you,' said the big one, 'this is one hell of a stadium.'

Big Bob had to raise his big voice above the chantings of rival supporters and the brass outpourings of the Iain Banks Big Band that marched up and down on the pitch. The atmosphere was, as they say, electric. Because there is truly no place like Wembley.

Truly electric it was.

'Electric, you see,' said Terrence Jehovah Smithers. 'The barrels spin and six thousand rounds per minute come out of them.'

'They've very heavy guns,' said the Second Sponge Boy, 'and this is a very cramped little van.'

'It's not a van,' said the driver, one Mahatma Campbell. 'It's a Morris Traveller – a half-timbered classic piece of automotive history famous for its light petrol consumption and its top speed of sixty-five miles per hour.'

'And running like a dream through these empty streets of Chiswick,' said Sponge Boy. 'Positively downstream.'

'I will park around the back of the Consortium building. We can then storm the premises from there.'

'Storm the premises,' said Terrence. 'I like that.'

'And you have the explosives?' Sponge Boy asked the Campbell.

'I have enough Semtex here to blow the Dread Cthulhu's tentacles so far up his unholy arse that—'

'The building's ahead,' said Terrence, pointing. 'And my sweet Lord, look at the size of it.'

'Size isn't everything, Terry,' said Sponge Boy. 'It's what you do with it that counts.'

'And we're counting down to the big match,' shouted world-famous, soon to be knighted for his services to commentating, five times voted bestest BBC commentator at the FA Cup and lovely fellow who spends most weekends with his family and to whom no taint of a scandal would ever attach itself, Mr Mickie Merkin. He sat in the commentary box, holding one of those special microphones that look like an oxygen mask over his face, probably in an attempt to stifle out the roaring of the crowd and the other commentators who shared the box and shouted into theirs. 'And what a match this is going to be. Giant-slayers Brentford United up against the other United, Manchester, fielding today a team unsurpassed in its history in terms of finance. Multimillionaire William Starling, who purchased the club this week, has spared no expense bringing in the very cream of the world's talent.

'A quick run-down on that line-up. We have Ronaldo, Rivaldo, Ricardo, Riviera, Rivaleno, Risotto, Rikkitikki-tavio, Riboflavino, Ridleyscotto, Rizlapapero and Sir David Beckham. This is possibly the most formidable side ever fielded in footballing history.

'And their opponents, what can you say about their opponents? As extraordinary as it might seem, not a single member of the original Brentford United team who began this sensational season will be playing today. This team is composed entirely of performers from Count Otto Black's *Circus Fantastique*. Today they are fielding:

'Clarence Henry, frog-boy.

'Bobo the clown.

'Zippy the pinhead.

'Don and Phil English, conjoined twins.

'Loup-Gary Thompson, wolf-boy.

'Barry Bustard, fattest man south of the Wash.

'Admiral Theodore Peanut, smallest man who ever lived.

'Humphrey Hampton, half-man, half-hamburger.

'Jon Bon Julie, half-man, half-woman (no hamburgers, bacon sandwich, hair pie).

'Harry the Human Holdall.

'And Long John Watson, their giant goalkeeper, nine feet tall and with a reach of over ten feet.

'The FA Cup Final has certainly never seen a team like this before, and frankly, the mind boggles. I tried to catch a word with their manager earlier, the now legendary James "Mr Bertie Wooster" Pooley, fashion icon and team's inspiration, but he had to rush off to the toilet. I spoke instead to his personal assistant, John Omally.'

'Run VT,' said the director, who lurked unseen, somewhere or other.

'Mr Omally,' said Mr Merkin to John, in the executive suite. John had his arm around the shoulder of a certain blonde female Swedish TV presenter. 'Mr Omally, this has been a remarkable season for Brentford United.'

'It's been a very special season for us,' said John. 'The last time Brentford won the FA Cup was in nineteen twenty-eight, when Jack Lane captained the team to its second successive victory.'

'And you really think that Brentford can do it again?'

John grinned broadly towards the camera. 'Are we not men?' he said. 'We are Brentonians.'

'Would you care, then, to make a prediction?'

John's hand tweaked a buttock of the blonde female Swedish TV presenter. 'We're going to score,' said he.

'We're going to score,' said Mickie Merkin. 'And who is going to doubt them? And yes, the teams are coming on to the pitch. The crowd is in uproar. This is the time and this is the place and history might well be made once again here for underdogs Brentford.

'And yes, they are lining up for the national anthem. And yes . . .

'Oh dear.

'Bobo the clown has just custard pied Sir David Beckham.'

43

Jim Pooley buried his face in his hands. 'He pied David Beckham,' he said. 'The game hasn't even started and . . .' Jim looked up. 'Oh no, the ref's showing Bobo the yellow card.'

'And what's Bobo showing the ref?' Professor Slocombe asked.

'Oh no,' burbled Jim and he buried his face in his hands once again.

'It will be all right.' The professor soothed the distraught manager. 'Look, Mr Beckham's personal hairstylist has come on to the pitch, and his manicurist, and his fashion consultant is bringing him a new pair of Ray Bans to replace the ones that got custard pie on them.'

'That's a relief,' said Jim.

'The Manchester United fans don't* seem best pleased.' The professor ducked a flying starfish* that had been hurled in Jim's direction. 'They're pelting the pitch.'

'We've known worse,' said Jim. 'Remember Burnley?'

'I'm trying to forget it. Ah, Mr Beckham's entourage have left the pitch. The ref is tossing the coin.'

And the ref tossed the coin into the air.

And the eyes of Professor Slocombe focused on that coin (for, like Old Pete, his eyesight was acute). And the eyes of William Starling also focused on that coin (though Starling's eyes were black as death and glowed a little, too). And the coin rose and rose and reached its apogee.

And there it stayed.

---

*Probably thrown by the chef who had prepared luncheon.

The ref gawped up at the hovering coin, and the teams looked up, and those in the crowd with acute eyesight did also.

Then the coin twisted one way and then the other.

The professor's eyes narrowed. Starling's bulged from his head.

And, curling and twisting, the coin descended.

To land upon its edge.

Although only the ref could see this, for it lay at his feet in the grass.

The ref waved his hand towards the Man U team.

'Hm,' said Professor Slocombe.

Now, one of the many interesting facts about football – and there are so *many* interesting facts. Facts, figures, things you didn't know, there's books and books and books about them. Far too many, in fact! – but *one* of those facts is that playing the game is very different from watching it.

Watching it on television or from the stands, the watcher receives an overview, seeing everything from above, spread out beneath. You get as near to the whole picture of what is going on as it really is possible to get.

Which is very unlike being there on the pitch, on the horizontal plane. There's so much that the players and the ref can't see[*]. And Wembley has such a BIG pitch.

And of course, being down on the bench, level with the pitch, the manager cannot see everything either.

'What happened there?' Jim asked. 'Who took the kick-off?'

'Ricardo,' said Professor Slocombe. 'And he's passed to Rivaldo, who's tapped it across the wing to Ronaldo. And Ronaldo to Rikkitikkitavio to Ravioli, back to Ricardo, who's passed it to Ravishankar, to Beckham, to—'

'That's not the way I see it,' said Jim. 'It's Bobo to Bustard, Bustard to Bon Julie, Bon Julie nice little chip to Clarence Henry who's hopping with the ball, and he's

---

[*] This is *not* one of the many interesting facts about football.

passed it to Zippy who's sitting down on it as if he's laying an egg. And Hampton's kicked to Henry, carrying the ball to Admiral Peanut, who in turn is carried with it . . . oh, and Beckham's got the ball again.'

'You're both getting it wrong,' said Omally, who had his mobile phone to his ear. 'I'm tuned to Five Live commentary – would you like to listen?'

'No thanks,' said Pooley, lighting a Dadarillo. 'That thing will ruin your health.'

'And it's Riviera . . .' said Omally.

'It's Riviera,' bawled Mr Merkin, 'to Riboflavino, brought down by Bustard who passes to the English twins, who seem to be arguing over whose legs should kick it, and it's tackled away from them by Rikkilake, no it's Ridleyscotto, who has his number-seven shirt on upside down, which made me think it was a number-ten shirt, to Rizlapapero to Risotto to Rivaleno to Rio Grande to Rip Van Winkle, across to Ringwormo, who passes it to Rocky Three (the one with Mr T out of the A Team in it).'

'Hang about,' said Jim. 'How many players have Man U got on the pitch? I'm sure I can count about twenty.'

'Oh dear,' said Professor Slocombe. 'Let me deal with this.'

'Robroyo,' bawled Mr Merkin, 'to Robocopo – no, he's lost the pass, it's Loup-Gary Thompson now to Dopey, Dopey down the wing to Sneezy, who blows it across to Doc, across to Happy, over to Sleepy, who slowly dribbles it down the right wing to Bashful.'

'That's more like it,' said Jim. 'But that was only six of the seven dwarfs.'

'Nobody knows all seven,' said Professor Slocombe. 'It's like knowing all Ten Commandments or the Seven Wonders of the World. No one knows the name of the seventh dwarf.'

'It's Baldy,' said Jim.

'It's Horny,' said John.

'Tommy?' said Jim.

'Timmy?' said John.

'Jonny?' said Tim.

'Jimmy,' said Tom.

'I'm getting all confused now,' said Jim. 'I don't want to do any more dwarfs.'

'That will please Snow White,' said John. 'And who's *that*?'

'That's Grumpy,' said Professor Slocombe. 'And *yes*! He's scored for Brentford!'

And the Brentford portion of the crowd went mad.

But the ref shook his head.

'He's disallowing it,' said John.

'Why?' asked Jim.

'Probably due to something in the law book that says you can only have eleven men in your team.'

'*They* started it,' said Jim

'I don't think that matters,' said John.

'These things matter,' bawled Mr Merkin. 'Laws are laws. And it's coming up on my monitor screen now: "Eleven men only shalt thou have, nor aided shall they be by familiars, divers demons, succubae or Walt Disney ™ characters." Dates back to medieval times, that rule, apart from the last bit, which means nothing to me, oh Vienna.'

'Man U seem to be back to their original eleven players again,' said Jim.

Professor Slocombe rubbed his wrinkled palms together. 'I'm really quite enjoying this,' he said.

'I could do with a beer,' said Jim.

'Me, too,' said John. 'I'm far too sober for this kind of excitement.'

'I shalt geteth them in,' said Big Bob Charker. 'Beers all round?'

'Why not?' said Professor Slocombe.

'Right then, I shall not be a moment.'

Big Bob returned with a tray of beers. 'Didst I miss anything?' he asked.

'One-all,' said Jim.

'*One-all?*' said Big Bob. 'How happeneth that so fast?'

'Only kidding,' said Jim.

'Thank the Lord for that.'

'It's *two*-one – we're winning.'

'*Now* thou art talking.' Big Bob raised his glass in toast.

William Starling glared with his black eyes at the field of play. It was true – the Brentford side were literally running rings around his own players. And he just couldn't see how they were doing it.

'Exactly how *are* you doing it?' Jim asked Professor Slocombe.

The old man tapped at his sinewy nose. 'I have to concentrate,' said he.

Jim turned to John. 'It's not right, all this,' he said. 'This is Wembley, the very cathedral of the beautiful game. This should be sport. This is all wrong.'

John nodded thoughtfully. 'You *do* have a point,' said he. 'So shall we suggest to the professor that he stops doing whatever it is that he's doing? And we'll let Starling's team win the FA Cup and Starling demolish Griffin Park, release the Serpent of Eden and bring damnation to all the world as we know it?'

Jim gave the matter some thought.

'Come on, you Bees!' he cheered.

William Starling put on his sunglasses.

They were very *special* sunglasses.

They filtered the incoming light through a process involving the transperambulation of pseudo-cosmic anti-matter. And they'd cost him an arm and a leg, although not *his*.

William Starling peered through these special sunglasses and observed that each Brentford player on the pitch appeared to be enclosed within a glittering transparent dome known in occult circles as a *cone of protection*, and in SF circles as a *force field*.

'So,' said Starling, and he spoke in the words of a language older than time.

Barry Bustard swung his foot to boot the ball Man-U-goalward, then suddenly stumbled and all but vanished into a hole in the ground.

'Starling,' said Professor Slocombe, 'has us, as our American cousins care in their fashion to put it, "rumbled". '

'Barry Bustard's fallen into a hole,' said Jim.

'And there goes Zippy,' said John.

'And Don and Phil and Jon Bon Julie.'

Professor Slocombe raised his hands and spoke many words of his own. The Brentford players, who were sinking like golf balls on a par-one pitch-and-putt, rose once more to set their studded boots upon terra firma.

But it was all too late and Beckham passed to Rivaldo and Rivaldo hammered in the equalising goal.

And then the ref blew his whistle.

And it was half-time in the match.

44

Jim Pooley entered the Brentford United changing room.

'Two-all,' said Jim. 'Not at all bad, considering. But we are going to have to put in that extra bit of effort if we're going to win. And we *are* going to win.'

Jim cast an eye over the players. They were *not* sucking their oranges.

They were changing out of their heavily logoed team kaftans and putting on their circus clothes.

'What are you doing?' Jim asked. 'You have to play in your strips.'

'Sorry, Boss,' said Barry Bustard in a sheepish tone, 'but we're leaving.'

'Leaving?' Jim staggered in the doorway. 'What do you mean, *leaving*?' You can't leave at half-time.'

'No choice, Boss. Sorry,' said Barry.

'No,' said Jim, stepping forwards and gripping the fat man's ample lapels. 'You can't just walk out. We have a match to win. Have you all gone mad?'

'No choice,' said Barry Bustard.

'What do you mean, "no choice"?' Jim's hands began to flap.

'It's the circus,' said Barry. 'The circus is leaving town, now, and we have to leave with it.'

'You can't do that. The circus can wait. This is far more important.' Jim tried to control his flapping hands and found that most of himself was now flapping. 'Football is more important. Winning this match is more important.'

'*It's not!*' Barry Bustard glared into Jim's eyes. 'The circus is leaving *now* and our families with it.'

'You can catch up with them later.'

'You don't understand.' Barry Bustard turned away and drew off his tentlike kaftan.

'I certainly do *not* understand.' Jim stood, quaking and flapping.

'I do,' said John Omally, entering the changing room.

'You *do*, John? Make them see sense, please.' Jim wrung his quaking shaking flapping hands. Which wasn't as easy as it might sound.

'I've just been having a word with Jon Bon Julie, the half-man, half-woman (no hamburgers, bacon sandwich, hair pie). He/she was dithering over which toilet to use. Apparently Count Otto Black's *Circus Fantastique* was bought out this very morning by a certain William Starling. The circus has upped sticks from Ealing Common and been moved away to an undisclosed location. The team have just received word that if they play the second half, they will never see their loved ones again.'

'*No!*' said Jim, turning to the team. 'Is this true?'

Heads nodded sombrely.

'The bastard,' said Jim. 'The evil bastard.'

'We'd like to stay,' piped Admiral Theodore Peanut. 'We'd really like to win the match for you, Boss, but . . .'

Jim Pooley sighed. 'It's not your fault,' said he, reaching down to pat the midget's tiny shoulder. 'I should have known. This Starling made attempts upon the lives of John and me. He was thwarted and forced to swear that he would never do so again. But it all makes sense now, why we lost Brentford players before each match. He swore not to harm John and me, but—'

'He snuffed out the team,' said John in an appalled tone.

'The circus folk substituted and so he bought out the circus,' said Jim.

'So they're dead.' John Omally, although made of sterling stuff, found his knees now trembling. 'Alf and Dave and Ernest and all of them.' John's voice trailed off.

'Or maybe he just put pressure upon them,' said Jim, 'like he has here. Told them to get out of town, *or else*.'

'Let's hope so,' said John.

Jim slumped down upon a bench. 'It's all over,' he said. 'Starling has won.'

'We really would like to help,' said Admiral Theodore Peanut.

Jim waved a hand. 'You've all done your best,' said he. 'You have all done wonderfully, every last one of you, and I thank you for it. I can hold nothing against you. You must put your loved ones first. Go now. Go to your loved ones and go with my blessings.'

'Thank you, Boss,' said Admiral Theodore Peanut.

And with that, the circus folk left the changing room, each in his or his/her own special way.

Leaving Jim alone with John.

'We're doomed,' said Jim. 'This time we're *really* doomed.'

John slumped down on to the bench and gave Jim's shoulder a pat.

'We're finished,' said Jim, and there was a tear in his eye.

John put an arm around his best friend's shoulders. 'You did your best,' he told him. 'You really did, Jim. It's not your fault. Everybody tried their hardest – you, the professor, the circus performers – but Starling outsmarted us. Big business, Jim. Big business and big, big money. An undefeatable combination.'

'But there must be something we can do, John. It can't just end like this.'

'We can't play without a team, Jim. I'm afraid there's nothing we can do.'

Jim's head slumped further and then it jerked up. 'We could,' he said. 'We could do something.'

'What?' Omally asked.

'Get the lads together, all the lads from The Flying Swan, and you and me – we could make up a team.'

John looked hard into the eyes of Jim and then John shook his head. 'Can't be done,' said he. 'It's against the laws of the game. You can't field an entirely new team in the second half.'

'Perhaps if I asked the referee nicely,' Jim suggested.

John squeezed Jim's shoulder. 'Sorry,' he said, 'but it was a nice try. I'm afraid that nothing short of a miracle is going to help us. We'd need God himself to walk into this dressing room right now.'

The dressing room door swung slowly open.

John looked at Jim.

And Jim looked at John.

And then the both of them looked . . .

At Norman.

Norman stuck his head around the dressing-room door. He had dyed his wig the team colours. 'Hello, lads,' said he. 'How's it going? Two-all, eh? Pretty good going. But I just saw the Brentford team getting on to the bus.'

'A miracle?' said Jim. 'We're doomed.'

45

Jim Pooley returned, in the company of John, to the pitch-side Brentford bunker bench/dugout jobbie. Jim would dearly have preferred to run far, far away. And then some more. But he knew that he could not. He owed a duty to the Brentford supporters, the thousands of them who had grown from the few when the season began.

The atmosphere in the great stadium had changed somewhat since the end of the first half. Word had clearly got around regarding the Brentford team's departure – spread, no doubt, by William Starling. The Manchester supporters were thrusting their down-pointing thumbs in the direction of the Brentford fans and chanting, 'Lo-sers, Lo-sers, Los-ers.' The Brentford fans appeared to be practising Primal Scream Therapy. Jim put his hands over his ears. This had to be the very worst day of his life.

Professor Slocombe joined Jim and John. Jim looked up hopefully into the old man's face, but it was a face that was drained and grey. Professor Slocombe shook his head.

Across the pitch, upon the bench of the opposing team, William Starling raised a champagne flute in mocking toast to the men he had defeated.

Upon the field, the Manchester United players made victory signs, did walking-that-line swankings and turned the occasional somersault. With no Brentford team to play the second half, they would clearly win by default.

Up on high in the commentator's box, Mr Merkin hollered into his oxygen-mask microphone. 'Well, I told you that this was likely to be an FA Cup Final unlike any other,' he bawled, 'and given that most remarkable first half, I think you'll agree that so far it has been. But now there have been even more remarkable developments. Word has reached me that the entire Brentford team has quit the match and left the ground. The referee is on the pitch now, and yes, he's signalling. He's giving the Brentford team one minute to come on to the pitch or they will forfeit the game.'

'Professor!' shouted Jim, trying to make himself heard above the mad cacophony. And hunching his shoulders, too, as beer cans and toilet rolls began to rain down upon him. 'What can we do?'

'Nothing, Jim. I'm sorry.'

'Should I go and speak to the ref?'

'If you think it might help.'

'I'll do anything,' shouted Jim. 'All these supporters – everything we've been through – we can't just let everybody down now.'

Jim rose from the bench. The Brentford supporters cat-called and hurled abuse and the Man U fans did likewise. Amidst a hailstorm of empty beer cans, small change and the occasional seat-back, Jim made the walk of shame across to the centre of the pitch.

The referee addressed him sternly. 'Are your team returning to the field of play?' he asked. 'They have thirty seconds left to do so.'

'They've been taken sick,' said Jim. 'The lunch. Food poisoning. We suspect that it was deliberate. I request a rematch at a later date.'

The referee glared at Jim and Jim saw the darkness, the terrible darkness filling the whites of his eyes. 'Twenty seconds,' he said. 'No team, you forfeit the match. That is final. That is that.'

'But,' said Jim, 'please. I beg you. Please.'

'Ten seconds,' said the ref. 'Nine . . . eight . . . seven . . . six . . . five . . . four . . . three . . . two . . .'

A mighty cheer suddenly went up – a mighty cheer that

came from the throats of the Brentford supporters. So mighty was this cheer that it nearly had Jim off his feet.

Jim looked towards the dark, dark eyes of the referee. They were gazing widely beyond Jim towards the players' tunnel beneath the south stand.

Jim turned and stared and Jim's mouth fell hugely open.

Footballers were jogging on to the pitch. But they weren't the circus performers. They were complete strangers to Jim. They were short and stocky, with short-back-and-sides haircuts and old-fashioned Brentford United strips, the shirts tucked into shorts that all but reached their ankles. They jogged forward with military precision.

Jim gawped at these footballers. 'What is going on here?' he asked.

Mr Merkin bawled further words into his oxygen-mask mic. 'Now this *is* beyond belief,' he bawled. 'Brentford are apparently attempting to field an entirely new team for the second half, which is in absolute defiance of all the FA rules.

'The referee is in consultation with Mr Pooley. Officials are on the pitch. The crowd is in absolute uproar.

'Now wait, wait. Something is coming up on my monitor. I have a list of the team members and I certainly don't recognise any of these names. Cottingham, Christie, Haigh, Gein, Denke, De Rais, Beane, Fish, Landru, Holmes and the team captain and centre forward, Jack Lane.

'And there's more. Well, I never knew this. Apparently the FA lawbook was supplemented in nineteen twenty-eight after the last Brentford victory. It states that "in the unlikely situation that a team in the FA Cup Final is composed entirely of circus performers, and these performers are unable to continue into the second half, the team may be replaced by a reserve team of the manager's choosing". Well, that *is* news to me. I thought I knew all the laws of soccer, but I never knew that. And yes, there's a footnote. Apparently the law was added by the temporary FA Cup committee chairman – chairman for one day only, apparently – a Mr Norman Hartnel, not to be confused with the other Norman Hartnel.'

There was much confusion on the pitch. William Starling was on the pitch, shouting at the ref. The ref was shouting at Jim Pooley. Jim Pooley was shouting back at all and sundry. Certain officials with copies of the FA Cup Rulebook were doing shoutings of their own.

The only folk not actually shouting were the players. The Man U fellows stared at the mysterious Brentford team. The Brentford team stood about, hands in pockets, nonchalantly smoking Wild Woodbine cigarettes.

The ref's shouting diminished as the officials with the rulebooks demanded that he begin the second half. William Starling stalked from the pitch. Jim shrugged and returned to the bench where Professor Slocombe sat.

Norman sat with the professor and John Omally and a portly fellow that Jim knew to be Norman's Uncle Herbert.

Jim Pooley viewed Norman and Jim Pooley blinked. Norman, it seemed, had grown a moustache. Surely you couldn't do that in just ten minutes.

Norman put his thumbs up to Jim, who slowly sat down beside him.

'Sorted,' said Norman.

Jim Pooley shook his befuddled head. '*You* had something to do with this? How?'

'Don't ask,' said Norman. 'But it took a great deal of effort and a great deal of *time*.'

'But who are they?' Jim pointed towards the Brentford side, who were now doing knee-bends and arm-stretch exercises whilst still sucking on their Wild Woodbines.

'Surely you recognise them,' said Norman. 'You've seen their photos in The Four Horsemen often enough. Back by popular demand, you might say. It's the nineteen twenty-eight Brentford FA Cup-winning team.'

Jim shook his head once more.

'Actually,' said Norman, 'you really have my Uncle

Herbert here to thank. He let me borrow his, er, conveyance. Jim Pooley, allow me to introduce to you Mr H.G. Wells.

'You see, he's not really my Uncle Herbert,' Norman continued. 'He's really Mr H.G. Wells, inventor of the Time Machine.'

The referee blew his whistle and the second half was on.

The Second Sponge Boy pulled a ski-mask down over his face.

'What is *that*?' asked Terrence Jehovah Smithers.

'Disguise,' said Sponge Boy. 'CCTV cameras and all. Here, I've brought one for you.'

'Thank you, Sponge.' Terrence donned the ski-mask.

'Positively Eddie "the Eagle" Edwards.'

'How about one for the Campbell?'

Sponge Boy viewed the Highlander, who sat in the front seat of the Morris Traveller sharpening his claymore on an oilstone. 'I don't think a mask will help,' said Sponge Boy.

An alarm clock suddenly rang, putting the wind up Terrence and Sponge Boy. The Campbell plucked it from his sporran and beat it to silence with his oilstone.

'It's time,' said he. 'Let us go into action.'

It was all action at Wembley stadium. Mr Merkin was jumping about in his seat. 'And it's Lane, Lane to Haigh, a long chip to the outside, intercepted by Rivaldo, and Rivaldo brought down by Gein. The ref's blown his whistle, he's showing Gein the yellow card. Gein is bowing to the ref, he's shaking the ref's hand. Lane is shaking the ref's hand also. Oh, and the ref didn't see that, that was on his blind side – Holmes has kicked Ronaldo in what I can only describe as the testicles. Ronaldo is down, he's complaining, but the ref hasn't seen him, he's calling for the free kick. And Rivaldo has taken it, to Beckham, Beckham to Rivaldo – a lovely cross there, and he's inside the box and he's *scored*! Oh yes. A *beautiful goal*. A *magnificent goal*. Three-two to Manchester United.'

Jim looked towards the professor. 'They scored,' he cried. 'You let them score.'

'I'll take no part in this, if Starling does not,' said the professor.

'What are you saying?'

'Let's allow a little bit of sportsmanship here, Jim. Holmes clearly fouled Ronaldo behind the ref's back.'

'But he's on our side, Professor.'

'Yes, but this *is* Wembley.'

'But we have all the world to play for.'

'The game's not over yet, Jim. Football *is* a game of two halves, you know.'

Jim shook his head towards John. Who shrugged.

Jim lit up a cigarette. 'I could do with a beer,' said he.

'I'll go and get a round in,' said Norman. 'Any particular decade you favour? I'll be back before you even know I'm gone.'

'Go! Go! Go!' shouted the Campbell. Sponge Boy kicked the Traveller's rear doors open and he and Terrence hefted their awesome weaponry into the Consortium building's car park. The Campbell flung himself from the vehicle, wielding his sacred claymore.

The two men and the man who was no man at all advanced in haste across the car park. Terrence aimed and fired his minigun, and the rear doors of the building exploded into shattered fragments.

'Into the building,' ordered the Campbell.

Alarm bells started to ring.

'Some alarm here from the Brentford supporters,' Mr Merkin bawled into his mask-mic. 'An easy goal there for Manchester United, the Brentford offensive formation showing its weakness there. I see Mr Pooley, in his distinctive attire, shouting out to his team and they're changing

413

positions. He's put De Rais on the right wing, and has moved Beane to centre half. But having never seen this particular side play, I can't say whether that's a good move or not. But the ref's blown his whistle and Lane is taking the kickoff. And it's Lane to Holmes to Denke, a neat little pass there, Denke dribbles the ball, and in a fashion we don't see any more. The Brentford team's tactics seem positively pre-war.'

'Positively ripping,' said Sponge Boy as he, Terrence and the Campbell burst into the Consortium building.

Professor Slocombe cast his ancient eye across the pitch towards William Starling. Starling had a mobile phone against his ear and he was shouting into it. As the professor looked on, Starling rose from the bench and took his leave.

'He's going,' said Jim. 'Why is he leaving?'

'I believe he has received an alarm call from the Consortium building,' said the professor.

'But he's going to leave the match? Knowing that you—'

'Knowing that I must follow him, Jim. He is confident that his team will beat ours. After all, didn't his boys just score that easy goal?'

'Ah,' said Jim, 'I see. But about the team . . . ?'

'Have confidence, Jim. I must go.'

'Then I must go with you.'

'No, Jim, you stay here, advise the team on tactics. You're better at it than you think.'

'But I should be with you.'

'I'll be fine, Jim. All will be well.'

Professor Slocombe rose from the bench and he, too, took his leave.

Jim looked towards John. John shrugged once again.

Norman appeared with a trayload of beers. '*Circa* nineteen-thirty,' he said, 'from the first-class bar of the *Mauritania*.'

★

'First-class shooting, Sponge,' said Terrence as the Second Sponge Boy strafed the foyer of the Consortium building, bringing down fixtures and fittings that spoke, sang and in some cases chanted of distant classical folderol.

And also the elfish receptionist, who was watching the match on a portable TV.

'A bit harsh on the dwarf,' said Terrence.

'But he was a baddie,' said Sponge Boy.

'Point taken. Shame you shot the TV, too. On to the next level then, is it?'

'The next level, Terrence. Positively *Street Fighter Two*.'

'A level playing field,' bawled Mr Merkin, 'and everything to play for now. Landru across to Denke. Intercepted by Rivaldo, and nicely, too. Down the left wing, and at a most remarkable speed, to Ricardo, across to Beckham. And they're making another run towards the Brentford goal. But Gein is there – nicely acquired, across to Fish, up that left wing again. And across to Lane and no one's defending. And *yes*! Beautiful goal. Brentford equalise, it's three-all.'

'I'm going after the professor,' said Jim.

John looked towards the field of play. 'I'm coming with you,' he said.

'But lads,' Norman cried, 'I thought we'd go medieval next round. Mugs of mead and all that.'

'And all to play for,' bawled Mr Merkin. 'This is the big one. Just listen to the crowd.'

William Starling heard the crowd. 'Another goal for Man U,' he said, as he stalked across the posh-persons' exclusive car park towards the night-black limo that stood awaiting, his chauffeur at the wheel. An electronically operated rear door opened before him and William stepped into the car.

'To the Consortium building?' asked the chauffeur.

'In just a moment.'

Professor Slocombe issued, panting, into the car park.

'Now?' the chauffeur enquired.

'Give him just a moment. His cohorts will join him.'

A moment passed.

John and Jim did issuings.

'Now,' said William and the limousine slid away.

'Go back,' the professor told Pooley and Omally. 'I can deal with this.'

'I don't believe that you have a car,' said John. 'Do you number levitation and swift flight amongst your remarkable achievements?'

'I'll hail a cab.'

'Not necessary,' said John, spying Norman's van. 'We'll take this one.'

'Second level secured,' called Sponge Boy. 'Let's take the third.'

Up the stairs they went. And down the stairs came Hellish things to greet them. Hellish dark things, darker than dark, of a blackness that had no specific name: the dark and scaly minions of the dread Lord Cthulhu. Sponge Boy and Terrence blazed away, and bullets blessed by the professor and coated with Old Pete's sacred herbs issued from their weapons at six thousand rounds per minute. Dark things melted into light and were gone.

'Get a move on, John,' shouted Jim. 'He's gone. We've lost him.' John, Jim and the professor were squeezed into the front seat of Norman's van. John was frantically attempting to hot-wire this van.

'It won't start,' cried John. 'I don't know what's wrong with it. *Bloody van!*'

Norman's van burst into life and did its *brrrm, brrrm, brrrmming.*

Unnoticed by John, Jim or the professor, a mysterious figure with a large carrier bag scuttled across the car park, opened a rear door of Norman's van and slipped inside, closing the door soundlessly behind him.

John Omally put his foot down. 'Go on, you beauty,' he cried.

The engine of Norman's van spluttered and died.

'*Bastard!*' cried Omally.

Norman's van burst into action once again.

'I recall Norman telling me about this,' said Jim. 'You have to shout at the van. It works on road rage, or something.'

'Move on, you ★★★★★,' and John Omally's language took a turn for the deepest blue.

And Norman's van got a hurry up and hurtled in hot pursuit of William Starling's limousine.

William Starling was on his mobile phone. 'Building compromised?' he was saying. 'Intruders now on level ten? Speak up, damn you. I can't hear your voice above the alarms.'

Alarm bells were ringing in the Brentford Nick. Lights were flashing also upon a sort of hi-tech emergency board that had been installed there by a sort of hi-tech emergency technician who worked for the Consortium.

'Turn that damn thing off,' Constable Meek told Constable Mild. 'I'm trying to watch the FA Cup Final here.'

'I'm trying to watch it, too,' replied Constable Mild. 'You go and turn it off.'

Inspectre Sherringford Hovis looked up from his viewing of the match. 'Which lights are flashing?' he asked.

Constable Mild said, 'Emergency ones – it's the Consortium building in Chiswick High Road. There's a pink light flashing, too. It has the words "TERRORIST ATTACK" printed beneath it.'

Inspectre Hovis yawned. 'Tricky,' said he.

'So what should we do, sir?' asked Constable Mild. 'Press the panic button? Alert the lads from Scotland Yard?'

'Well . . .' Inspectre Hovis suddenly leapt from his seat. 'Goal!' he cried.

Jim Pooley fiddled with Norman's car radio. 'Did you hear the word "goal"?' he asked. Static fizzings dissolved into the voice of Mr Merkin, live on Five Live.

'Four-three,' he bawled. 'Incredible.'

'Four-three to who?' Jim asked. The radio fizzed into static once again.

'Bloody useless radio!' swore Jim.

Norman's van leapt forward with renewed vigour.

There was a great deal of vigorous gunwork going on at the Consortium building. Black and ugly shapes bulged from black marble walls, minigun barrels rotated and spat bullets by the bucketload. The Campbell hacked down incoming darksters, the going was hideous and fire was beginning to take hold of the building.

Inspectre Hovis took hold of the telephone receiver. 'Scotland Yard?' he said. 'Sherringford Hovis, Brentford Constabulary, here. We have a Code One at the Consortium building in Chiswick High Road.'

'A code ten?' said the telephonist at Scotland Yard. 'That would be a price request, would it?'*

'Terrorist attack!' bawled Hovis. 'Cross it to Lane, don't hog the ball.'

'What?' asked the receptionist.

'Don't let him do that. Foul, referee. That was a foul. What is the matter with you?' said Inspectre Hovis.

'I'm going to put the receiver down now,' said the telephonist.

'No,' said Hovis, 'terrorist attack, Consortium building, Chiswick High Road. Send everything you have. Send ZZ9. *My God, ref, are you blind?*'

'Who is this, again?' asked the telephonist.

---

* The telephonist had recently worked in Budgens.

A Code 10 *is* a price check at the checkout.

A Code 14 is a man exposing himself in the customer car park.

'Where is he?' asked the professor.

'Up ahead,' replied John. 'I can see him heading on the road to Brentford.'

Now, *The Road to Brentford*, Bob and Bing never made that one. Which is a shame, because—

'Catch up and run him off the road,' said the professor.

'Professor,' said John, 'this is a weedy A40 van. They have a limousine. It's probably bulletproof.'

Jim Pooley tinkered further with the radio, then took to thumping it. 'Stupid piece of rubbish!' he shouted.

Norman's van accelerated.

'Oh and this is fast!' Mr Merkin was out of his seat once more and straining his voice into the mask-mic. 'Landru to Lane and back to Landru again. Intercepted by Ricardo, no, it's Rivaleno. Oh no, it was Ricardo. But to no good.

'Landru back to Lane. And Lane is on course, but no, Lane is down, brought down by Beckham. The crowd are on their feet. The ref is showing Beckham the yellow card. It's a free kick for Brentford just outside Manchester's penalty area.'

'Nice area,' observed Jim. 'Is this Penge again?'

'It's Southall,' said John, 'but there are many similarities. Hold on tight, everyone. And get a move on, you useless piece of ★★★★!'

The A40 van drew level with the limo. On the wrong side of the road, though, to the great consternation of oncoming traffic. Cars swerved and mounted the pavements, ploughing into kerbside displays of exotic fruit and electrical goods and saris and socks and Blu-Tack.

John slammed the van into the side of the limo.

A blackly tinted window swished down. The chauffeur's hand appeared and offered John a finger gesture that in America is known as 'flipping the bird'.

'*Bastard!*' shouted John.

Norman's van gained speed.

'Have at you!' roared John, swerving in front of the limo and applying the brakes. The rear of the van struck home, upending its mysterious hidden occupant. Headlights shattered on the limo, but it accelerated, thrusting Norman's van forward at alarming speed.

Ahead were red lights. Van and limo rushed through them. Vehicles with the right of way swerved and applied their brakes and mashed into one another.

'Exciting this, isn't it?' said Professor Slocombe.

Jim Pooley cowered and ducked his head, still twiddling the radio's dials as he did so.

John clung on to the steering wheel. 'He's going to have us off the road.'

They were approaching a junction, one of those T-junctions where you can turn either left or right, but there is nowhere to go straight ahead. Except directly into a building. A Gas Showroom, upon this occasion.

One of *those* junctions.

'Turn left here, I think,' said the professor.

'I can't,' shouted Omally. 'We're going too fast. We're going to crash.'

Behind them and grinding into the van's rear bumper, the limo pressed onward, gathering speed. The driver's eyes shone that blackest of blacks. His teeth ground together, teeth that were blacker than the blackest of blacks. His foot (in a green driving shoe, because he had verrucae) pressed further down upon the accelerator pedal.

'Left, please,' said the professor. 'Left, please – *now*, I think.'

Omally, both feet on the brake and telling Norman's van what a lovely van it was, heaved the steering wheel portside.

The van hit the junction, swerved and then rolled.

The limo rushed on towards the Gas Showroom building before it.

'Ooooo!' went John and Jim and the professor and the mysterious stowaway in the back as Norman's van rolled over and over, scattering pedestrians and cyclists and oncoming cars and cats and dogs and a casual observer.

The limousine struck the Gas Showroom building before it.

A mighty explosion occurred.

46

Jim Pooley raised his head from a tangle of twisted limbs and body parts that were not his own.

'Am I dead?' Jim asked.

'Not dead,' came the voice of Omally. 'Get your damned foot off my head.'

'Professor?'

'Fine, Jim – somewhat battered, but fine. The van seems to have landed the right way up, which is a blessing.'

'Untangle me,' said Jim. 'There's a hand in my trouser parts that is not my own.'

The Gordian knot that was John, Jim and the professor was finally cut with the aid of oncoming onlookers, or good Samaritans as they are sometimes called.

'Now, in my opinion,' began a casual observer. But he said no more, for Pooley swung open the passenger-side door and knocked him from his feet.

'Has anyone been listening to the match?' Jim asked the onlookers. 'Anybody know what the score is?'

Professor Slocombe crawled from the van. 'Your assistance would be appreciated,' he told Jim.

Jim Pooley hastened to oblige the scholar.

'The limousine,' said the professor. 'Starling. Is he dead?'

Jim viewed the devastation fifty yards behind them. 'Are you okay, John?' he asked.

Omally heaved himself from the van. 'Battered but all in one piece.'

'We have to see if Starling survived,' said Jim.

'I'll finish him off if he has.'

As the onlookers onlooked and the casual observer

observed small stars and sailing ships and sausages and sprouts, the three front-seat survivors made their way towards the now open-fronted building from which projected the rear of the limousine. Smoke was rising freely and flames crackled around and about the wrecked automobile.

'Careful,' said the professor. 'If he is alive, he won't be pleased to see us.'

Jim Pooley took hold of a rear doorhandle. 'It's hot,' he said, blowing on to his fingers.

'Open it, Jim, but be careful.'

Pooley dragged open the door and peered into the rear compartment. It was very much of a mess, thoroughly mangled, and shards of twisted metal had ripped through the seats. But of William Starling there was nothing to be seen.

'He's not in here,' said Jim. 'He's gone.'

A sudden cry of pain was to be heard.

The three men turned. Along the road, beside Norman's somewhat dented van, they saw Starling. His clothes were torn, but *he* was still in one piece. The cry of pain had come from a motorcyclist whom Starling had unseated. As the three men looked on, William Starling climbed astride the motorcycle and swerved away at speed.

'Back to the van,' the professor cried. 'And after him.'

'It's all go nowadays, isn't it?' said Omally.

'Maybe the crash will have got the radio working again,' said Jim.

Sponge Boy, Terrence and the Campbell were working their way steadily up the many floors of the Consortium building. Flames now roared beneath them in the stairwell.

The Campbell had a sweat on, but his claymore arm was still more than sound. He hacked away with a vim and vigour, cleaving darksters before him.

In his claymore-free hand, the Campbell carried a tartan holdall. Within this holdall lurked many pounds of Semtex.

'The crash and the explosion should have killed him,' said

Jim, as John swore at Norman's van and Norman's van set off once more at speed.

'We are dealing with no ordinary man,' said Professor Slocombe.

'Who – or what – is he?' Jim asked.

'A man from another time,' said Professor Slocombe. 'Another period of time – the late-Victorian age. He sold himself to the Dark Side, if I might put it so, and he should have died when the clock struck twelve midnight on the thirty-first day of December in the year eighteen ninety-nine.'

'Time travel,' said Jim. 'Is that what all this has been about? Norman there bringing Brentford's nineteen twenty-eight team to Wembley with the help of Mr H.G. Wells? This really is beyond belief.'

'I think I'm probably able to believe absolutely anything at all now,' said Omally, 'no matter how absurd it may appear. And thus I think I'll give up being a Catholic and become a Wiccan instead. Get on, you worthless ★★★★.'

Norman's van got on at the hurry-up.

'Another world existed in Victorian times,' Professor Slocombe continued, 'a world of supertechnology, but it vanished from the pages of history. It was erased at the stroke of midnight, with the coming of the twentieth century.'

'This supertechnology,' said Jim, 'is this the stuff that you mentioned to us? The stuff you said Starling needed to free the serpent from beneath Griffin Park?'

'The very same, Jim. William Starling should have died when the holocaust occurred at the turn of the twentieth century and all the supertechnology was destroyed. I do not know all of the details. It all has to do with alternative histories and alternative futures. Such things cause the mind to spin. Somehow some remnants of the supertechnology survived, and Norman acquired them.'

'His patents?' said Jim.

'They were not *his*. Starling had accumulated his wealth because for a period he had been able to travel freely from his present into our present. Consequently he knew what to invest in, and he knew what would happen before it did so. But then, I am not without knowledge and I was able to predict what would occur – including the arrival of my old friend Mr H.G. Wells, with whom I have had the pleasure of spending many delightful chess-playing evenings over the last few months whilst Norman worked on repairing his Time Machine. The one in the back of the van here. I hope it didn't take too much of a knock in the crash.'

Jim shook his head, but it didn't help to ease his confusion. 'Are we nearly there yet?' he asked.

'Nearly,' said John.

'Can't you catch up with Starling?'

'He's riding a Harley Davidson,' said John. 'And I do not know swearwords of sufficient obscenity to make this knackered old van keep up with a Harley.'

'I do,' said Professor Slocombe. 'Press on.'

And Professor Slocombe spoke Babylonian cusswords.

And Norman's van went even faster.

And William Starling's purloined Harley soared into the car park of the Consortium building. Smoke issued freely from the shattered windows on many levels. Starling stepped from the motorcycle and gazed up at the conflagration. And words issued from his mouth. Words of no language spoken by man. Words of the language of the Great Old Ones.

The language of the Lord Cthulhu.

Starling reached into an inner pocket of his ruined jacket, drew out a pistol, tore the jacket from his shoulders and flung it aside. And then he stalked across the car park and entered the unholy building.

'Unholy bastards.' Terrence blasted away at darksters that rose up before him. And then gun barrels continued to spin, but nothing issued from them. 'Sponge Boy,' shouted Terrence, 'I'm out of ammunition.'

They were on the topmost floor, advancing along the black marble corridor that led to the terrible room.

'Hate to be the bringer of bad tidings,' said Sponge Boy, dropping his own mighty weapon to the floor, 'but I'm also out.'

'Never fear.' The Campbell hewed and slashed, and dark shapes shredded before him. 'We have reached our object-ive. I will set the charges.'

'Then do it speedily,' said Terrence, 'and we might get back in time to see the end of the match.'

'You're videoing it,' said Sponge Boy.

'Yeah, but it's not the same as seeing it live.'

Something alive that wasn't alive, that lived, yet did not live, stirred behind doors that were adorned with scenes of abominable horror. Great eyes rolled evilly, batlike wings rustled, tentacles curled and twisted. A fearsome inhuman intelligence sensed danger. Tentacles rolled, forced open the doors and spread hideously about the Eye of Utu, between the cabinets of fossils, towards the outer doors.

The Campbell unzipped his tartan holdall and took from it explosives. Affixed these to the doors. Did primings and pressing of buttons. Little red liquid-display figures began their countings down.

'How fast can you laddies run?' asked the Campbell.

'Quite fast,' said Terrence.

'Well, you have three minutes to flee from the building.'

'*Very* fast,' said Sponge Boy. 'Let's do it.'

'Do it,' said the Campbell. 'Do it now.'

'Come on, then,' said Terrence.

The Campbell shook his head. 'Not I,' said he. 'I tire. I am done with being a man. It never suited me well.'

'Come on,' said Terrence. 'Don't mess about now. Come with us.'

'Two minutes and forty seconds,' said the Campbell. 'Run fast, wee laddies, run fast.'

Terrence looked at Sponge Boy.

Sponge Boy looked at Terrence.

And then they both turned tail and ran.

Very fast.

Mahatma Campbell raised his claymore and faced the doors behind which lurked the horror.

'Come at me, if you will,' cried he. 'I am ready for thee.'

'Come on,' said the professor.

'We're there,' said John, swinging into the car park. 'And there's the motorcycle.'

'There is little time left, John. What must be done must be done, and Starling must not stop it.'

John and Jim aided the ancient scholar through the shattered rear exit door, along a corridor and into the ruined foyer. Smoke swirled. The lads fanned at their faces.

'This place really has gone downhill since the last time we were here,' said Jim.

'Needs a bit of a face-lift,' said John. 'They should call in that Robert Llewellyn Jones.'

'Isn't he the bloke out of *Red Dwarf*?' asked Jim.

'No, that's Craig David.'

'Charles,' said Jim.

'Charles Atlas?' said John. 'I thought he was a body-builder.'

'No, that's—'

'Stop,' said Professor Slocombe. 'This is neither the time nor the place.'

'Sorry,' said Jim. 'Just trying to keep our spirits up, what with impending death seeming so high upon the agenda at present.'

'I understand that.' Professor Slocombe peered into the swirling smoke. 'Light,' he commanded.

The swirling smoke parted.

'Impressive, that,' said John.

The swirling smoke parted to reveal . . .

Mr William Starling.

'Take not another step,' said he.

Professor Slocombe took another step.

'No,' said Starling and he raised his pistol.

'Put that aside,' said the professor. 'Face me as a magician, one magician to another.'

'I think not, Professor. You cannot be trusted. You have wrought great harm upon my premises. Hardly playing by the rules, was it?'

'That you would relinquish your financial hold on the football ground if the team won the Cup. I feel, Starling, that you might have reneged upon that particular deal.'

'Which is why you waited until this hour to attack my master. Cunning, Professor. Very cunning.'

'The game is up for you, Starling. You have lost. Even now, above—'

'Your Scottish creature seeks to wreak destruction. He will be gone in but a moment. But you first.'

William Starling cocked his pistol.

Behind him, coming down the stairs, were Terrence Jehovah Smithers and the Second Sponge Boy. They put fingers to their lips and did furtive creepings.

'Gentlemen,' called Starling without turning his head, 'please don't even think about trying to take me from behind. Walk slowly around, please, or I will shoot the professor in the face.'

Terrence and Sponge Boy slowly walked around. 'Sorry, Professor,' said Terrence.

'Starling,' said Professor Slocombe, 'there are only moments remaining. Deliver yourself now, willingly, into my hands and I will deliver you from the evil that lurks within you.'

William Starling laughed. 'Oh no,' said he. 'I have plans, great plans. All this world will be mine. I have been into the future, seen it for myself. And I will go there again. All is preordained – that you should be here, at this time, that you should deliver Mr Wells' Time Machine to me. It is in the van in the car park, is it not? You cannot kill my master. That which does not live cannot die. Your time has been wasted. You have come here only to die, that I should be rid of further annoyance from you.'

From above there came a mighty rumble. But it was not that of an explosion, rather of a titanic force that splintered walls and tore doors from their hinges. The Campbell fell back as tentacles engulfed him. He fought with ferocity.

With the ferocity of a Skye terrier.

The floor of the foyer shivered.

'My master stirs from his dreamings,' crowed Starling, 'and now all of you will die.'

Tentacles whirled and whipped, penetrated walls, swept down staircases and lift shafts, curled through offices, down and down and down.

'But you die *now*.' Starling aimed his pistol at Professor Slocombe's head and pulled the trigger.

'No!' John Omally leapt in front of the professor.

A single shot rang out and John Omally fell to the shaking floor of the foyer.

John Vincent Omally.

Entrepreneur and Ladies' Man of the Borough of Brentford.

Was dead.

47

Pooley looked down in icy horror at the body of his bestest friend.

'No,' cried Jim. 'No.' But the bullet hole in Omally's forehead left no room whatever for doubt.

'Murdering bastard.' Jim Pooley's gaze rose. 'You will die for this.'

Pooley took a step forward, but Starling raised his hand and Pooley could no longer move. 'You are *my* man,' said Starling. 'You were mine from the moment that you first put a Dadarillo cigarette into your mouth and sucked upon it. The darkness is inside you. You will do as *I* command you now.'

Pooley fought to move, but strange things seemed to be happening. He wanted to kill Starling, he wanted that more than anything else in the world, but somehow he seemed detached from himself, as if he was looking down from above.

'Kill the professor,' ordered Starling. 'Kill him now!'

Jim turned upon wooden legs, arms outstretched, fingers crooked into claws.

'Jim,' cried the professor. 'Jim, try to concentrate. This isn't you.'

The whites of Jim's eyes were black now. Jim's hands closed about the professor's throat.

'What now?' crowed Starling, waving his pistol. 'Will you employ your magic, Professor, kill your good friend before *he* kills *you*? And back, you two!' Starling's gun swung towards Terrence and Sponge Boy.

From somewhere above, Jim looked down upon himself,

at the puppet that was himself being pulled by strings that were not of his pulling. The puppet that was draining the life from Professor Slocombe.

And a hand seemed to touch Jim Pooley and he saw a face. It was the face of a ginger-haired boy.

Jim stared into this face. 'I know you,' he said.

'We met long ago,' said the ginger-haired boy. 'You left your body – astral projection. We met on top of the floodlights at the football ground.'

'Yes, I remember,' said Jim. 'You said you'd fly with me to Tibet. But I could never do the astral projection thing again.'

'Such a very long time ago,' said the boy. 'I thought I'd never see you again. But you shouldn't be doing that, you know – what you are doing to that old man. You're killing him and he is your friend. It is the other one you should be killing, the one who murdered your dearest friend. Go back now, return to your body, and do what must be done.'

Professor Slocombe's face was a deathly white. Fire roared on all sides now. Starling stood, crowing with laughter. Pooley's eyes, glazed and black, began to focus, fading slowly to white. Pooley turned to confront William Starling.

'You two,' shouted Jim to Terrence and Sponge Boy, 'help the professor. Take him outside. And also the body of John.'

'What is this?' Starling's pistol swung towards Jim. Jim lunged forward and swept it aside. 'Now you die,' said he.

And, high above, the Semtex exploded, ripping the top from the Consortium building, bursting upwards, outwards, downwards, pulverising, smashing, evaporating the Dark Lord Cthulhu, raining fire and devastation.

A ball of flame roared down the stairwell.

'Out!' Professor Slocombe coughed and gagged. 'Everybody get out.'

'Not me!' Pooley was upon Starling now, the murderer of his bestest friend. As Terrence and Sponge Boy and the professor dragged John's lifeless body from the holocaust, Jim Pooley's fingers found the throat of William Starling.

And the darkness formed, spreading all around and about Pooley, engulfing and choking him. But driven by terrible revenge and with no care whatsoever for the loss of his own life, Jim kept his hold upon the slender throat and squeezed and squeezed and squeezed.

And fire rained down, and falling masonry and black glass. And floors subsided and collapsed and flames roared up and the Consortium building fell in upon itself and collapsed into ruination.

And Professor Slocombe and Terrence Jehovah Smithers and the Second Sponge Boy looked on.

'Positively Apocalyptic,' said Sponge Boy.

'And good God, he's survived somehow,' said Terrence.

'Starling?' Professor Slocombe turned fearfully, prepared to hurl magic.

But from the devastation, dust and chaos, it was Jim Pooley who stepped.

Stepped and walked and staggered and fell beside the body of John.

And Jim Pooley wept bitter tears and Professor Slocombe put his ancient hand upon Jim's shoulder.

'Why?' Jim's tear-streaked face looked up at the ancient.

'I'm sorry, Jim,' said the professor. 'He was a good man. A brave man.'

'He was my friend,' said Jim. 'And now he's dead.'

'I am so very sorry. If there was anything I could have done . . . could do.'

'Work your magic, Professor. Do something.'

'*I* cannot.'

Pooley pressed his face against John's and wept.

'Starling is dead,' said Jim. 'All this is ended. But the price has been too high, Professor.'

'I think I might be able to help you, old chap.' The rear doors of Norman's van opened and the mysterious figure stepped into the car park.

Pooley looked up.

'Archroy,' he said.

'Archroy,' said Professor Slocombe. 'For one terrible moment, I thought that you had not survived the crash.'

Pooley looked towards the professor. 'What is going on?' he asked.

Archroy stepped forward, took from his carrier bag the Golden Fleece and placed it carefully across the body of John.

The Fleece glowed. Rainbow patterns ran over and about it.

Pooley looked on in awe as the bullet hole in John Omally's forehead healed over and was gone.

And John Omally stirred.

And looked up.

'Jim,' said he. 'What happened? Why are you crying? Don't tell me the team lost.'

48

But the team didn't lose.
   The team won.
   Five-four.
   It was tight.
   But they won.

Which just goes to prove . . .
   Well, whatever you like.
   But the team won, all the same.

49

And yes it was tight, that drive back to Wembley.

Omally had to shout very loudly at Norman's van.

It was rather crowded, what with Terrence and Sponge Boy also crammed into it.

But they did arrive there in time . . .

To see that final winning goal . . .

With but one minute of time left to go.

And Jim was there to applaud Jack Lane as, for the third time, he lifted the FA Cup aloft to the deafening cheers of the Brentford fans.

And puffed upon his Wild Woodbine.

50

To say there was celebrating in the streets of Brentford would be to underegg the pudding of proverb. The borough had never known such celebrations.

Well, at least not since the last time that Brentford had won the FA Cup, way back in 1928.

Big Bob Charker, having listened to the second half of the match upon his cab radio, returned to Wembley with haste after dropping off the desolate circus performers. And now he proudly drove his big bus through the bunting-hung and all-gone-mad streets of Brentford, with Brentford's winning team waving from the open top deck.

And Jim Pooley clinging to the cup.

'They did it,' called Jim to John. 'They did it. Without magic and with little help from me.'

'You played your part, Jim. You did your bit.'

'But Brentford won the cup, John. Brentford won the cup.'

The Flying Swan was packed beyond capacity, but Neville served each and all with speed and professional pride. Omally elbowed his way to the counter.

'Where are your lovely ladies tonight?' John asked.

'Gone,' said Neville, smiling hugely. 'Happily gone.'

'Happily gone?' said Omally.

'Young Master Robert came by an hour ago and took them away. Apparently he found out that they and I were, well, *you know*.'

'And you're not sorry to see them go?'

'Somewhat relieved,' said Neville. 'It wasn't really me,

that kind of behaviour. It was all the work of Old Pete's Mandragora. I'm done with that. I liked things the way they were, as they were and as they should be now and hopefully will be ever to come – do you know what I mean, John?'

'I do,' said Omally. 'You're a good man, Neville. Three pints of Large, if you will.'

Norman was squeezed into a corner with Mr H.G. Wells. 'Thank you very much for the loan of your Time Machine,' said Norman. 'And it is still in working condition. Do you want me to take the nineteen twenty-eight team back to their own year now, before you depart yourself?'

'I think they should be allowed to enjoy their latest victory,' said Mr Wells. 'Tomorrow will do. There's always plenty of *time*.'

'Ho, Norman,' said Jim Pooley, detaching himself from the loving arms of young and female fans. 'I owe you a very big thank you. We all do. All of Brentford. All the world. You have no idea what you have done.'

'I think I do,' said Norman.

'And your millions?' Pooley asked. 'The professor told me you won't be getting them now. I'm sorry.'

'Doesn't matter,' said Norman. 'There's always tomorrow. I'll come up with something. All's well that ends well and tomorrow is another day, you know.'

'I do indeed,' said Jim.

'But surely you're a rich man yourself now, Jim. Your bet with Bob the Bookie, it's no secret. Bob's been whinging about it for months.'

Jim proffered a bundle of money notes. 'He emptied his cash register for me,' he said. 'Said he would owe me the rest. I shall be calling by at his establishment as regularly as ever I did. However, I shall be making withdrawals rather than investments in the future.'

'Here's to you, then,' said Norman, raising his glass.

'And to you,' said Jim, raising his. 'And to you, sir, Mr Wells.'

The Victorian scientist raised his glass. 'I really enjoyed

the match,' said he. 'And I'll know who to bet on in nineteen twenty-seven and twenty-eight.'

Jim turned away to find Professor Slocombe smiling at him. 'Cheers, Jim,' said the professor.

'Cheers to you,' said Jim.

'Are you feeling all right, in yourself?' asked the professor.

'Never better. This has been a remarkable adventure. Very scary, but remarkable. And everything worked out in the end, although it's terrible what happened to the Campbell.'

'He is free,' said Professor Slocombe. 'He played his part and he is free now. But what of you, Jim? What does the future hold?'

'I am a man of means now,' said Jim. 'Well, for a while. I don't know how much more money I can squeeze out of Bob the Bookie, but it will be fun trying for as long as it lasts.'

'You don't think you will continue as Brentford United's manager, then?'

'Brentford United no longer has a team,' said Jim. 'Exactly what will happen next season is anyone's guess. We'd need a millionaire to step in and put up the money. You're not friends with that Liberace chap by any chance, are you?'

Professor Slocombe shook his head. 'You might think of having a word or two with Old Pete,' he suggested. 'He's just received a telegram. It seems that certain investments that he made in the past, in the Ford Motor Company and land in Florida, investments that he had somehow forgotten that he'd made, have been building up in his bank account. He's a very wealthy man now. Very wealthy.'

'Good for Old Pete,' said Jim. 'But I am done with football now.'

'What a pity, Jim. I would truly have liked to have seen . . .'

'Seen what, Professor?'

'Well, Jim, do you remember me telling you about the

research that I have been doing for my book *The Complete and Absolute History of Brentford*?'

'Vaguely,' said Jim. 'But that seems a long time ago now.'

'Something about the possibility that Brentford was indeed an independent state – indeed, an independent country.'

'Ah yes,' said Jim. 'I remember that.'

'Well, it *is*, Jim. Brentford is an independent country.'

'Good old Brentford,' said Jim.

'Good old Brentford,' said Professor Slocombe. 'Which makes it such a shame that you no longer wish to be the team's manager.'

'Why?'

'Because the World Cup Qualifiers will be coming up this year. Don't you think it might be a challenge to lead Brentford on to win not only the FA Cup, but the World Cup also?'

Jim Pooley looked warily towards the professor. 'Would there be monsters involved?' Jim asked.

'No monsters,' said the old man. 'Merely sport. With a team put together and paid for by Old Pete's many millions. I am certain that if I spoke nicely with him he would be eager to oblige.'

'Only sport?' said Jim.

'Only sport,' said the professor. 'A challenge for an entrepreneur and a man who likes a bet.'

Jim Pooley smiled at Professor Slocombe and called across the overcrowded bar to his best friend, John Omally.

'John,' called Jim, 'come over here. I've something that might just interest you.'

And the May moon shone down upon Brentford.

And the celebrations lasted long into the night.

It was a regular knees-up, Mother Earth!

THE END